MW00650312

THE VANISHING BRIDGE

THE VANISHING BRIDGE

ELENA GRAF

PURPLE HAND PRESS

Purple Hand Press
www.purplehandpress.com
© 2023 by Elena Graf

This is a work of fiction. Names, characters, places and incidents are the product of the author's imagination or used fictitiously, and any resemblance to actual persons, living or dead, businesses, institutions, companies, events, or locales is entirely coincidental.

Trade Paperback Edition
ISBN-13 978-1-953195-19-7
ePub Edition
ISBN-13 978-1-953195-20-3

Cover photo © www.123rf.com/profile_linux87, used by permission.

04.21.2023

To Sheila

1

"Sue, can you help this customer?" asked the manager. His tone was polite, but it was not a request.

"It's Susan," she muttered under her breath. "My name is *Susan*." If she'd told him once, she'd told him a dozen times, but he never seemed to hear because he was always turned away, his hands busy, his eyes watching the associates. Maybe it was good that he took his job seriously. Nowadays, so few people did. She just wished he would remember her name. She hated to be called Sue.

Her shift was over, but she couldn't leave until her replacement appeared. She knew she should have taken the day off, but she wasn't the kind to call in sick when she wasn't and never asked for personal time. After months of flipping burgers, she still hadn't earned any vacation days.

Since the invitation to orientation for new teachers had landed in her inbox, she'd been planning how to get there on time. Her shift was scheduled to end thirty minutes before the meeting. She didn't want to show up at the elementary school in a McDonald's uniform, reeking of hamburger grease. That morning, she'd stuffed a change of clothes and dress shoes into her tiny locker. She had intended to duck into the staff bathroom and change right after clocking out. Now, her careful strategy was unraveling.

When she entered the keycode to open the register, her fingers trembled. To divert attention, she enthusiastically greeted the customer, an older mother with three young children. The woman glanced nervously at the long line of impatient people behind her. It was well past lunchtime, but the place was packed—the beach crowd coming in with the tide. The children couldn't make up their minds. Frustrated, the mother finally ordered Happy Meals for each of them. The youngest whined, joined by a chorus of complaints from her older siblings. Too late now. The order had been entered.

Susan rushed to the fries table to fill four small bags. At this point, she could barely stand the sight of French fries, never mind eat them. The smell alone could make her nauseous.

She assembled the colorful boxes and quickly filled them with the required items. The dessert was apple slices treated with citric acid to keep them from darkening. When her hand reached into the bin for a plastic action figure for boys, she found it empty. It was someone else's job to keep it filled, but like every business in town, they were shorthanded. The other associates were either helping other customers or working in the kitchen, so there was no one to ask for help.

In the storeroom, Susan opened the cartons until she found the right one. She scooped up a generous armful of plastic dragons—a promotion for the *Game of Thrones* spinoff. When she returned, the Happy Meals boxes she'd been filling had been pushed aside. One had fallen off the counter. According to regulations, anything that hit the floor had to be discarded. She'd have to rebuild that meal from scratch. When she looked up at the wall clock, she saw the second hand greedily devouring the time left before the meeting.

"Sorry I'm late," said a sullen male voice.

Susan looked up into a young, tanned face. The boy's hair was wild and matted in the back, proof that he'd just crawled out of bed. An abundant crop of acne pimples scattered in the sparse stubble on his chin always made him look unappetizing. Susan hated to watch him handle food. Not following the hygiene procedure had stiff penalties, but the place was so understaffed that no one ever checked.

"I've got it," said Susan, rising to her feet. She disposed of the mess, assembled another box, and replaced the items. The youngest child was still whining when Susan brought the order to the counter.

"I'm leaving," she told her shift replacement with the force of a threat. She banged the keys of the register to log out and rushed to the back to enter her hours into the break-room computer. Her shift replacement was always late, and the overtime had been adding up. This week, she'd get at least three hours more pay. Every little bit helped. She'd been short for groceries last week. Now that it was July, her landlord had raised her rent to the summer rate.

She couldn't get the combination for her locker right. On the third try, it opened. She snatched her purse, shoes, and the dress out of the cramped space. The door to the staff bathroom often locked accidentally and wouldn't open, so she joined the long line for the customer bathroom.

When a stall finally became free, she yanked the McDonald's polo shirt over her head and kicked off her sneakers, not bothering to untie the laces. She shook out the dress. The purposely crinkled fabric didn't show wrinkles and she'd rolled it to prevent hard creases. She stepped into her pumps and gathered up her work clothes.

She had to wait for a place at the sink and quickly ran a brush through her hair, hoping it didn't smell of grease. The odor of spent cooking oil stuck in her throat long after her shift ended and clung to everything. Since she'd been working at McDonald's, she'd started washing her hair every day.

The traffic on Route 1 was bumper to bumper in both directions. She despaired of ever getting out of the parking lot. Then a car stopped. Maine tags, of course. She waved her thanks. As she inched forward to the light, she tapped the steering wheel impatiently. Finally, she made the left turn into the elementary school driveway.

The school halls were dark. Sunblind, Susan tried to remember the location of the faculty room while her eyes adjusted. Her memory nudged her to the left.

Courtney Barnes, the acting principal, was speaking when Susan found the right door. "Susan! Come in!" the pretty blonde called with a longtime educator's enthusiasm. "We were just getting started."

"I'm sorry to be late. The traffic…"

"Oh, we all know how that is!" Courtney said, nodding. The other heads at the table bobbed in agreement. The principal gestured to an empty chair at the table. "Before you get too comfortable, there's iced tea in the fridge." After a long shift with barely a sip of water, Susan could practically taste the cold tea, but she decided to pass because she was late.

"Now that we're all here," Courtney began again and asked the attendees to introduce themselves. The new teachers were all women, two right out of college. To Susan, they looked like high school girls. The new ones looked younger every year. The others were seasoned veterans like herself.

The principal turned on a projector. "Today, I'm going to show you how to navigate the intranet we use for internal communications. It's where the state curriculum is posted for your reference. You'll also find forms, and information about our policies. We'll be reviewing these documents this afternoon."

Susan took a pad out of her bag to jot down some notes. She noticed the younger teachers were using their tablets.

"Don't worry," said Courtney with a gentle smile directed at Susan. "This is a Power Point. I'll send everyone the slides."

At the end of the meeting, Courtney gave out the classroom assignments. Before everyone left, she took the new teachers on a tour of the school, ending in the large atrium at the entrance. The others headed out. Susan hung back to apologize for being late.

"I have another job," she explained, her eyes modestly focused on the floor, a holdover from her convent training. "That's why I couldn't get here in time."

"It's okay," said Courtney, touching Susan's shoulder, which made her look up. "A lot of teachers need to work during the summer to make ends meet. You're not the only one." Her warm tone made Susan relax for the first time that afternoon. They'd met at a dinner party the summer before Susan had to return to South Dakota.

"I was so glad to get this position even though I applied late. I'm looking forward to getting a regular paycheck."

"Unfortunately, that won't be until September. After you start, you can set up a schedule to spread out your salary payments over the entire year. You've been teaching a long time, so you probably already know that."

Susan nodded. Of course, she knew.

"We feel lucky to get experienced teachers like you. Because of the shutdowns, the new ones had to do their classroom training virtually, and since the pandemic, there's such a shortage of teachers."

"My old district in South Dakota is asking veterans, who could have retired, to stay on."

"I'm not surprised. I got a letter the other day from the Connecticut teachers' union begging me to come back. Apparently, they didn't look at my records to see that I'd moved out of the state and gone into administration. Not that it matters."

"I belonged to teachers' unions in other states. They're all terrible at record keeping."

"I was surprised to see that you once taught in Catholic schools. I can't imagine surviving on the tiny salary they pay." In fact, Susan couldn't support herself working in Catholic schools, so she'd found a public school job in one of New York's worst neighborhoods. Between teaching and the scholarship from Union Theological Seminary, she'd scraped together enough to get her divinity degree.

Courtney seemed kind, so Susan decided to tell her. "Most of the time I was teaching in Catholic schools, I was a nun. The order took care of my housing and other expenses."

The principal's brown eyes grew wide. "Oh," was all she could say.

Susan smiled to show she wasn't offended by her surprise. "Some people have funny ideas about religion. I don't tell everyone that I'm a priest either, but now that I'm working at St. Margaret's, I'm sure I'll run into parents and students at church."

"Hobbs Elementary isn't a gossipy school compared to some, but it's hard to keep secrets in a small town." Courtney reached out her hand. "Glad to have you on board, Susan. We like teachers with Catholic school backgrounds. Good classroom management." Susan heard the backhanded compliment. Teaching nuns' reputation for corporal punishment had never left the popular imagination. "If you wait a moment," said Courtney, "I'll walk out with you. Let me just get my things from the office."

The principal was showing her favor, and Susan had nowhere special to go. While she waited in the cool atrium, she closed her eyes to center herself after the rushed afternoon. She said a prayer of thanksgiving for getting to the meeting almost on time.

"I see my ride is out there," said Courtney, returning with her bags. Susan looked through bulletproof, reinforced glass entrance doors. After Sandy Hook, every school had become a fortress. A Subaru, much newer than Susan's, was waiting at the curb with a familiar driver at the wheel.

"Gas is so expensive, we've been carpooling when we can," Courtney explained. "You remember Melissa. Come out and say hello."

Courtney opened the passenger door. Susan bent to look across the front seat. The intelligent face of the driver broke into a smile. She was a pretty woman in her forties with compelling blue eyes. A mass of curly hair flowed over the shoulders of her sundress.

They briefly caught up on how things had changed since they'd last seen one another. Melissa was carrying on about how much they loved living at the beach, when Courtney gently interrupted. "Honey, we have to pick up Kaylee from soccer practice." She turned to Susan. "She's trying out for the traveling team," she explained proudly.

"I guess we won't have time to check the water at Liz's place. I'll do it later," said Melissa, starting the engine. "We promised to keep an eye on the garden while they're in Europe."

"I can check the water," Susan said, "I don't mind going that way."

She regretted her spontaneous generosity as soon as she she hit the traffic on the Post Road. Liz Stolz's house was north of town, which meant making a turn against traffic. Susan patiently waited for some kind motorist to take pity on her and let her merge. The only driver to stop had Maine tags.

Approaching the three-story house hidden from the road, Susan hoped Lucy wouldn't suspect an ulterior motive if she found out she'd been in her yard. But unless Susan told her, how would she ever know?

✻✻✻

Lucy slowly opened her eyes and looked across the aisle to where her daughter slept soundly, curled into her companion's body like a sleek red cat. Their heads touched; their fingers intertwined tenderly. Gently nudging her wife, Lucy pointed in their direction.

Liz took out one earbud as if it would enable her to speak better. "I guess they're sleeping together again. Ain't young love grand?" She sighed theatrically.

"Liz! Don't be such a cynic! You're in love too."

"Really?" Liz's pretense of ignorance earned her a jab. She raised her arm to block another blow. "We should put down the armrest. We'll be landing soon."

"You just want to get away from me," said Lucy with an accusing stare.

"After being cooped up with you for hours, sure I do. Plus, your elbows are sharp."

Lucy pressed the button to raise the seat back. While she'd been asleep, the blower nozzle blasting cold air on her face had numbed her cheek. One foot was pins and needles. She flexed it to restore the sensation and felt around with her toes. To pull on her shoe, she had to insert a finger in the heel because her feet had swelled during the flight.

The multiple discomforts reminded her why she'd come to hate air travel. For an opera singer, it was an occupational requirement. In the early days, when she'd needed the exposure, she'd jammed her calendar with engagements. But she shouldn't complain. After thinking her career was over, she should be grateful for the opportunity to sing again, but she was glad she could be choosey about when and where. At her age, she couldn't expect her body to tolerate the constant long-distance travel. Fortunately, the Festival of Lyric Arts at Aix-en-Provence paid its featured singers well. On this flight from Paris to Boston, they were traveling first class.

Lucy pulled herself up into a more comfortable position. She'd read that the airlines had been reducing the seating space. If she felt crowded, she couldn't imagine how her much taller wife felt, but Liz, who'd replaced her earphones, looked content, if not comfortable.

"What are you listening to?" Lucy asked, nudging her to get her attention.

Liz pulled out an earbud. "Some of Denise's early recordings. I can hear how much her voice has changed. You've done a great job with her."

"While we were in Europe, she lined up three more performances on her own. That's in addition to those Roger already booked for her."

"That's great." Finally getting the idea that Lucy wanted to talk, Liz removed the earbuds and stowed them in their case. "Is Roger officially her agent now?"

"As a favor to me."

"He doesn't strike me as someone who does things for charity. He must see potential in her."

"We all know she has potential. This is just the beginning. I bet she's fully booked by the end of the year."

"Congrats, Lucy, you made this happen."

"I helped, but Denise made it happen. She worked hard, and having Roger on her side will ensure she gets the opportunity to prove herself."

"He's certainly persistent," Liz said, making it clear it wasn't a compliment. She frequently complained that Lucy's agent was too pushy. Lucy didn't enjoy being pressured by him either.

"He's dragging his feet with Denise's record company. They haven't removed her dead name or her photos as a man from their album liners. I kind of get it. A countertenor who's transitioned is a phenomenon. A talented female alto is just one of thousands."

"What's the record company's excuse?"

"They claim it would be too expensive to recall all the CDs, reprint the liner notes, and reissue the albums."

Lucy watched Liz adding up the expenses in her mind. "But how much could that cost? A few hundred dollars, at most."

"I know, but the margin on classical music is low, and they say they can't afford it. Roger says he's working on it."

"Glad he's good for something."

Lucy studied her wife, trying to determine the reason for her irritability. "What's going on with you?"

Liz shifted in her seat and tried to sit up straight. She glowered at the low-hanging baggage compartment overhead. "I get stiff from sitting for a long time. I'm not as young as you are." Lucy scrutinized her wife. Liz was one of those fit, active seniors who could be a model in an AARP ad. She almost never complained about getting older or mentioned the nine-year age gap between them, but she had a birthday coming up. "I never learned to sleep on planes. If I had a long-distance medical conference, I always booked a day ahead, especially if I was giving a paper."

"I had to arrive a few days in advance for rehearsals, which took care of the jet lag. Plus, the recirculated air on planes isn't great for the voice." Additional explanation to a rabid opera fan who also happened to be a doctor was unnecessary.

Liz lowered the armrest separating their seats and checked her watch. "Half an hour till we land," she said, answering Lucy's unspoken question. They'd only been married a month, but already Liz could read her mind.

"I can't wait to get home," said Lucy, although the time away had been like a mini vacation. The performance of Mahler's *Second Symphony* at the Aix Festival had been their reason for going to France, but they'd found time to take in the local sights and share intimate dinners while Emily and Denise went off on their own.

"Too bad we missed Fourth of July while we were away," said Liz. "I love watching the fireworks from the boat. I was thinking about taking The Wet Lady up to Bar Harbor for a few days."

"Then you'll have to go by yourself. When I get home, I need to work. Reshma and Tom have been holding down the fort, and he needs time off to finalize plans for his wedding."

"What about Susan?" Liz eyed Lucy with a little frown. "You're still not sold on her working at St. Margaret's."

"Do you trust people who lie to you?"

"Lucy, she was desperate. She only lied because she was afraid you wouldn't help her."

Lucy wondered why Liz was defending Susan, especially after she'd tried to come between them. "A lie of omission is still a lie."

"Susan just wants a chance to prove herself, and you should give it to her. People can earn back my trust if I see they're sincere and don't fuck up again. Sounds like you're expecting she will."

"You know that recidivism in newly recovering alcoholics is high. I won't have her wrecking my parish after I worked so hard to rebuild it."

"Lucy, you're not really worried about that, are you?"

"Well, no." Liz leaned forward to look into Lucy's eyes. "All right, I'll be honest. That lie really hurt. If Susan had told me she was running from the police in South Dakota, I still would have helped her."

"You did help her. We all did. Me. Brenda. You. But Susan also did her part. She faced the charges in South Dakota, did her rehab, and she's in AA. Count it as a success." Lucy could feel Liz intensely studying the side of her face. "You know, Lucy, for someone who makes a living counseling people, you certainly have high expectations of human nature."

"I have high expectations of people I love and thought I could trust."

The expression in Liz's blue eyes softened. "You're angry with yourself because you didn't see the warning signs."

"And with the Church for sweeping her problems under the rug."

Liz chuckled. "For Catholic priests, alcoholism is practically a job requirement."

"If they'd let them marry, they wouldn't have so many problems. And look at the benefits they would get from the unpaid spouses of clergy."

"Like me?" Liz rolled her eyes. "I hate being a church lady!"

"I know, sweetie," said Lucy, stroking Liz's thigh, "but you make such a good one." That drew another eyeroll, so Lucy decided to change the subject. "How about spending the weekend at the beach house instead of boating up to Bar Harbor?"

"Oh, Lucy, you know how crowded Hobbs will be. I'd rather stay home."

"We can bring in food instead of fighting the summer people in the restaurants, and it would give Emily and Denise privacy. I'm not sure I like the idea of them spending the night in the rectory. That's how rumors get started."

Lucy glanced across the aisle. Gazing into her daughter's sleeping face was like seeing herself in a distant mirror, except her daughter's red hair was still bright. Lucy decided to wake Emily so she'd have some time to get her bearings before they landed. It was a long way from their arrival gate to the baggage claim. With all the clothes they'd needed for the performance and side trips, they'd be claiming a fleet of bags in Boston.

"Emily, sweetie, time to wake up," Lucy called softly.

Her daughter pulled back her unruly mane of red hair and sat up. "Are we there yet?" she asked, arching her back like a cat.

"Almost. You should wake Denise."

"I kept her up late last night," Emily explained shyly. "I'm sure she's tired."

So, they were sleeping together. Lucy wondered what Denise had done to help Emily overcome her aversion to sex, but that wasn't something she could ask. Maybe when Denise needed advice, she'd confide in her again.

"Mom, do you have any mints?" asked Emily. "My mouth tastes disgusting." The young woman's scrunched face was a slightly defective representation of disgust, but for someone on the spectrum, she had come a long way.

Lucy rummaged in her bag for the mints she always carried. Emily woke the sleeping woman beside her and offered her the open tin. Denise, still groggy from sleep, looked across the aisle and mouthed the word, 'thanks.'

"We'll be landing soon," Lucy said. The words were barely out of her mouth when the booming voice of the pilot announced their imminent arrival in Boston.

✳✳✳

The cartons piled in the small room made it seem even more stifling. Susan wished she could turn on the air conditioner or even the window fan, but the electric bill would come after she moved out, and she already knew she couldn't afford it.

September couldn't come quickly enough with its promise of a regular paycheck. By then she would be living in the rectory, so she could save the money currently allotted to rent. She knew how lucky she was that the vestry had allowed this arrangement. She was only part time. Many parishes could no longer afford to provide housing even for full-time clergy.

With Tom Simmons moving out, Susan could take the largest apartment. She wondered why Lucy or Tom never seemed worried about scandal. Everyone knew the associate rector was living with his boyfriend. Now that they were engaged, Tom apparently felt free to move in with him officially. Not that anyone in the parish seemed to care. Hobbs bordered on Webhanet, the unofficial gay capital of Maine. If the conservative parishioners had objections, they kept them to themselves.

Susan drew the shades for privacy. The houses on the barrier islands had been built on top of one another to make use of every inch of space. July was the busiest month for tourists. People were always passing right outside her window. Even when they kept their voices low out of courtesy, the sound echoed in the little apartment. The walls of the building were paper-thin. Susan could hear her next-door neighbors and the tenant above talking as clearly as if they were in the same room. She often switched on the TV, not to watch—she hated TV, except for British series and the news— but because the white noise disguised the specific words of conversations.

A drop of sweat broke away and ran down between her breasts. If she continued to sit in the sweltering room with the windows closed, she might pass out in this heat, or even die. She imagined the police finding her aging body slumped on the stained sofa, eyes staring lifelessly at the ceiling, her mouth gaping wide. Since her sister had died, Susan had no family. They might notify Lucy because of her job at the church. Her death would be reported in the police blotter weeks after it happened, but maybe not. The bad publicity of a forgotten woman dying alone might hurt the tourist business.

Susan dismissed the melodramatic fantasy as self-indulgent. Instead of being shut up in the heat, she could do something about it. She could have both privacy and air if she sat in the dark. After turning off the lights, she went into the bedroom and opened all the windows.

The alarm clock, which had come with the rental, clicked down a red numeral. It was much too early for bed, so she decided to listen to music. A boy at her last school had given her an obsolete iPod. Even if she weren't useless at technology, she could no longer update the operating system or add music. The student had shown her how to fill it with classical music, mostly Lucille Bartlett recordings. Tonight, Susan chose the Fauré *Pavane* over opera arias because the sound of Lucy's voice was too stimulating.

Another red numeral clicked down. Some of the pixels had burned out. Susan remembered how foolish she'd felt using a pen and paper to take notes at the orientation meeting. Compared to the young teachers, she was as outmoded and derelict as the old clock. The things she'd learned to teach—cursive handwriting, diagramming sentences, grammar, punctuation, and spelling rules since superseded—were anachronisms now. But schools suddenly wanted them taught because what they'd been doing wasn't working. No surprise to Susan. Children needed structure and discipline along with knowledge. Not that anyone would dare to say such things aloud.

The red numerals now read 9:00. On her break, Susan had checked the schedule from Charles De Gaulle into Logan. The last flight would have landed that afternoon around four. Even with customs and rush hour traffic, and maybe a stop for dinner, Lucy should be home by now. Jet lagged and tired from travel, they might already be in bed. Susan imagined Lucy in one of those delicate lace nightgowns that made each of her lovely breasts look like a blushing bride.

The first time Susan had stayed the night in Lucy's Manhattan apartment, she'd felt shabby in a simple nightgown like they'd worn in the convent. Lucy explained that she wore feminine things to feel attractive after the rape had left her torn and ugly. Pretty nightgowns and underwear were her secret weapon against the man who'd tried to steal from her what she didn't want to give.

That night, they'd done nothing except spoon each other in Lucy's double bed. It took several such visits before Lucy finally let her kiss her and fondle those creamy breasts. In the convent, Susan had only "touched above the waist," which was considered less sinful. That was as far as she'd dared to go with a woman until Lucy showed her there was more to making love.

Lucy had sat naked on the bed with that intense look of concentration in her green eyes. Her unbound red hair cascaded in waves over her elegant shoulders. She'd taken off her makeup, and all her freckles showed, so many they could never be counted.

"Do you know how to make yourself come?" she'd asked gently. Susan did know, but she was ashamed to tell Lucy, never mind meet her eyes. The confessional was the only place she'd admit her personal sin, and then in whispers. The convent chaplain often gave her the entire rosary to say as penance. The other nuns probably wondered which mortal sin she'd committed.

Lucy had opened her arms and gathered her in. "Come here. I'll show you." There had been so much fumbling that night, but in the moment of release, Susan had wept fierce tears of gratitude.

In Liz Stolz's garden that afternoon, Susan had studied the house, wondering which of the many windows belonged to the master bedroom. She'd never been upstairs. From what she'd seen of the house and Liz's decorating style, she guessed the place where they slept would be large, airy, and minimally adorned. It was probably on the third floor for the view of the ocean.

Were they making love now? Susan wondered. Was Lucy lying with her legs spread wide to welcome her lover? Susan knew she especially liked that. Liz, with her cocksure attitude and rakish smile, seemed like the type who could be forceful. After all Lucy had suffered, Susan hoped she would never hurt her. But now that Lucy had gotten past the rape, maybe she enjoyed self-assured confidence more than timid caresses.

Thinking of Lucy making love left Susan throbbing. When she shifted her weight in her seat, she felt how damp it was between her legs and knew it wasn't from the heat.

Coveting someone's wife was forbidden, explicitly called out in the commandments as sinful, and she should beg forgiveness. While she was praying, her phone began to play loud music. She silenced the ringer before the merry Mozart theme disturbed the neighbors. The screen showed the name of her caller: Roberta Lantry.

"I hope it's not too late," Bobbie said apologetically.

"No, between the noise from the street and the heat, I'm still awake." The statement of fact sounded like a complaint, which Susan hadn't intended. She forced a smile to change her tone. "I'm sitting in the dark, listening to music."

"I bet you'll be glad to get out of there."

"For the quiet alone, yes, but also to stop living out of boxes. When I got the job at the elementary school, I knew I'd be in Hobbs for a while, so I cleaned out the locker where they stored my sister's things. Everything has been piled up in boxes in the living room."

"When you get the green light to move into the rectory, I'll help you move the boxes."

"You'd do that? That's so kind, but first, I need to get in there and do some cleaning. You know how men are, even the tidy ones."

"When do you plan to clean?"

"Saturday morning. First thing."

"I'll help. Let's meet for breakfast, and we can go together."

"Thanks, but you don't need to help me clean."

"That's what friends are for."

Susan smiled. She had a friend. It had been such a long time since she'd applied that word to anyone, even Lucy.

❊❊❊

Since they'd crossed the state line, Liz had been counting down the mile markers. The six-hour time difference from Europe made driving the long, monotonous highway even harder. During her training, she'd learned some tricks to stay alert. Getting enough oxygen was key, which was why she'd turned off the air conditioner and opened her window. On break from long shifts on surgical duty, she used to stand on the hospital balcony to get fresh air. In those days, the New Haven sky was often thick with smog, so the term was relative.

The reflective white paint of the green highway sign warned that the Hobbs exit was two miles ahead—Liz's signal to wake her sleeping passengers. She reached over to touch Lucy's thigh, feeling her warmth through the thin knit of her summer dress. She felt Lucy's hand cover hers. "Are we home?" she whispered and sat up.

"Almost. Want to wake up the crew in the back seat? I can take you and Emily home first and then drop off Denise."

"That's backtracking. Let's head to the rectory first."

The soft voices had gotten Emily's attention. Her head popped up in the back seat. "Mom, I'm staying with Denise tonight."

Liz could feel Lucy's expectant gaze on her cheek. Emily sharing a curate's studio with St. Margaret's music director would not be a good look for anyone. Lucy cleared her throat, urging Liz to say something.

Liz engaged Emily's eyes in the rear-view mirror. "It's late, Emily. Why don't you invite Denise to stay with us?" In the dark, Liz could feel Lucy's smile of approval.

"Would you like to stay?" Emily asked Denise, who'd been sitting beside her silently, waiting to see how the family dynamic played out.

"Really, Denise. It's no trouble," Liz assured her. "You can stay downstairs. It's completely private." The first-floor bedroom was set off by its own hallway. It was where Liz put her sexually active guests.

"That's very kind, Liz. I accept."

In the rear-view mirror, Liz could see how much the invitation had pleased Emily, despite her limited ability to express emotion. As a bonus, Liz could avoid the tourist traffic in downtown Hobbs. On a Friday, it would be brutal.

Liz felt good about the decision. For tonight, she'd made two young people happy, but she and Lucy would need to discuss how to handle such situations in the future. Although Lucy had encouraged the invitation, Liz knew she had misgivings about the on-again, off-again relationship between Emily and Denise. There was the age gap, amplified by Emily's strict religious upbringing in the home of her adoptive family. Her Asperger's didn't help.

"I hope Melissa remembered to check the water," Liz said as her headlights flashed on the front windows.

"You paid all that money for your fancy watering system, but you don't trust it?" Lucy said.

"When I lived in Connecticut, I twice came home to an empty well. If you're going to drag me around the world for your performances, we need an irrigation system that works."

"Don't make me your excuse to buy expensive tech toys." Lucy unbuckled her seat belt and opened the car door. Liz stared at her wife, wondering what she'd done wrong. The answer was, nothing. After traveling for the entire day, they were all exhausted.

Liz opened the cargo area and lined up the bags on the driveway. Ordinarily, she'd carry in the luggage for guests, but Emily and Denise were a fraction of her age and certainly not helpless.

"Come on, Denise," said Emily. "I'll show you where your room is."

Liz rolled the enormous suitcases up the side ramp.

"Let's unpack tomorrow," Lucy said, unloading her hand luggage in the front hall.

"Good idea, but I'll bring the bags upstairs in case we need something." Liz piled as much as she could on the suitcases. Dragging the load through the hall, she thanked Sam for suggesting an elevator to the third floor. She parked their luggage in the small room Maggie had used as an office. It was still bare, although her ex-wife had been gone for over a year.

"Thank you for inviting Denise to stay," Lucy said, unbuttoning her blouse. She sighed as she unhooked her bra and released her breasts.

Liz forced herself to look at something else to avoid wanting to caress them. She guessed that Lucy was probably too tired for sex tonight.

"Looks like Denise and Emily are sleeping together again," Liz said. "I guess this trip made her relaxed enough to like sex."

Lucy gave her a sharp look. "Liz, keep your voice down. Don't make me sorry for sharing that with you."

"They can't hear us up here. Sam soundproofed the entire house."

"Even so, keep it down," said Lucy, walking naked into the bathroom. "I'm going to take a quick shower."

"While you do that, I'm going to purge the security footage and reset the cameras. Want anything from downstairs? A glass of wine?"

"No, thanks. I just want to sleep."

Liz decided to skip the elevator this time. Her knees, stiff from sitting on the long flight, followed by the drive, complained as she walked down the stairs. The house smelled stale and shut up, so she stopped on the second floor to open a few windows. Emily's bedroom was empty, which she expected. Liz smiled, imagining what was going on downstairs.

Checking the door to the garage gave her an idea. She went in and looked up the stairs to the door of the apartment she'd built for her mother. Monica Stolz had blamed Maine for taking her daughter far from her childhood home and declared that she hated the entire state. The old woman had died without once staying in the apartment.

Now that Melissa and Courtney were renting Lucy's beach house, the roomy studio was empty. Emily could use it as a permanent place to store her stuff. The separate entrance would give her privacy to entertain guests, but the second-floor bridge would give her access to the main house—a perfect situation for a young woman trying to find her way into adult life. Liz decided to suggest the idea to Lucy when she went upstairs.

She locked up the garage and headed to the media room. In the room behind the stage was the video studio Maggie's daughter had set up during the lockdown. Alina had used it to edit her news stories and broadcast live entertainment provided by her mother's talented friends. Now that

Maggie was spending more time in Hobbs, and the frost was beginning to thaw, maybe they could do it again. Tony Roselli and the gang from the Webhanet Playhouse would jump on the idea.

Liz sat down at the security console and checked in with all the security cameras. One caught Emily and Denise sneaking into the kitchen to look for alcohol. Liz smiled as the file ran back to the beginning at high speed. She did a spot check at random intervals. The garden camera showed Melissa coming into and leaving the garden around the same time every day. When Liz had asked the young attorney to monitor the water, she knew she would be reliable.

Then she saw the unexpected image of Susan Gedney and slammed down the pause button. She went back to the frame where Susan had appeared and replayed it at normal speed. She watched Susan approach the house and study it intently, unaware that she was looking right into the camera. After going into the alcove where the water valve was located, she left through the garden gate.

Unnerved by seeing Susan's pale face staring back at her, Liz played the scene again. She looked at the timestamp. It was close to when Melissa usually came to check the water. Maybe she'd delegated the task to Susan. Before deleting the file, Liz saved the segment to cloud storage.

Lucy had declined a glass of wine, but Liz poured two anyway. Balancing them as she walked up the stairs, she debated whether to tell her wife about seeing Susan on the video. She decided it would only upset Lucy, especially right before bed.

Lucy was wearing one of her casual nightgowns. Liz took it as a message to manage her expectations.

"Oh, what a dear you are!" Lucy exclaimed when Liz handed her the glass of wine. "How did you know when I saw yours, I'd change my mind?"

"I just did," said Liz with shrug.

"The water is probably still hot, if you want to take a shower."

"Is that a suggestion?" Liz sniffed her armpit.

Lucy smiled. "You smell fine, but I always feel grungy after being on a plane. Don't you?" She moved over and patted the place next to her. Sitting cross-legged, Liz settled beside her. "All quiet below?" Lucy asked.

"I caught the kids sneaking into the kitchen on the security camera."

Lucy glanced at the door as if she expected someone to be outside. "Good idea to keep them downstairs. Gives us privacy too."

"Agreed." Liz took a sip of wine and set down the glass. "Luce, I have an idea. What do you think about offering Emily the garage apartment? It's a place to store her stuff. She could join us for meals or ignore us. Her choice."

"That's generous Liz, but you'll have to heat the place and keep the power on while she's at Yale."

"That's easy to manage."

Lucy leaned back against the pillow. "I like that idea. It will give her a feeling of independence."

"Good. We'll tell her tomorrow after Denise leaves."

Lucy petted Liz's thigh. "Sweetie, why don't you jump in the shower, so we can go to bed?" She gave Liz a sexy side-eye to indicate she had more in mind than sleep.

"You're not too tired?"

"I'm overstimulated from all the travel. Sex always relaxes me."

"Mother Lucy," Liz said, dramatically feigning shock, "in your book, you say that sex is *only* for expressing love."

"Liz, you know I love you to the moon and back, but relaxation is not a bad reason to have sex."

Liz finished her wine in two gulps. "I'll be right back."

2

When Bobbie came out to the porch to say goodbye, a glance at the checkerboard told her it was not a good day. Natalie, the social work graduate student who usually stayed with Joyce on Saturdays, was clearly winning the game. Her opponent stared listlessly at the board.

"She got off to a good start," Natalie said in an encouraging tone. She was specializing in geriatrics, which was why Bobbie had chosen her from among the many applicants for the empty bedroom. Natalie's expert knowledge of Joyce's disease gave her useful insights into her behavior. "I think we might give the game a break and listen to music for a while."

"Sounds like a good idea."

"I'll bring her into the family room." Natalie helped Joyce get to her feet. "It's getting warm out here already. I hear it's going to be a hot one today."

"We got off easy this summer," said Bobbie, helping to steady Joyce. "We're lucky the heat held off till now. Would you shut the windows out here if it rains? Thunder showers in the forecast."

"Of course," said the young woman. "Go help your friend. We'll be fine."

"I made salmon salad for lunch. It's in the fridge."

Natalie grinned. "I saw it when I got Joyce her protein drink. Thank you! Salmon salad is my favorite."

Bobbie knew. That's why she'd made it. "There's iced tea and lemonade too. Not homemade. Didn't have time this morning."

"Doesn't matter. I know you have a busy job."

Bobbie bent to give Joyce a kiss. Lately, she'd been in a sweet, affectionate phase and turned up her face expectantly. Bobbie pressed her lips to the pale forehead. All those years as a corporate executive had left it lined, but since dementia had freed her of those worries, her brow no longer puckered. The only good thing about this disease—if one could call it such—was that things that once seemed so important no longer mattered.

"Come back…soon?" Joyce asked, her eyes bright with anxiety.

"Don't worry. I'll be back this afternoon."

Bobbie had stopped specifying a time for her return. For one thing, she didn't want to be bound by it, especially with her work schedule. Her appointments often ran long, which was mostly her own fault because she liked to be thorough. Also, she wasn't sure that Joyce still had a clear sense of time. She could read a clock, but sometimes she couldn't tell if it was day or night, although her confusion and agitation always grew worse after dark.

Bobbie grabbed her purse from the hook inside the hall closet. The pattern of light streaming through the front door made her eager to step out into the sunshine. Any reason to get out of the house. Things other people dreaded, like going to work or grocery shopping, she saw as an escape. Even going to the dump with the trash was a welcome reprieve.

She opened the back of her SUV and checked the cleaning supplies she'd packed before Joyce had awakened. Bobbie had tried to include everything she thought they'd need. After hearing that a man had been living in the apartment, she'd expected the worst. She'd found that men tended to be bad housekeepers, especially where bathrooms were concerned. She'd often speculated that they ignored toilets because they didn't have to sit on them as often. It was a wonder they didn't notice the filth when they aimed into the bowl. Sometimes, the dark stains got so bad, the only way to remove them was to scour them out. Joyce, who'd been the CEO of one of the world's largest plumbing fixture manufacturers, always warned that pumice stones damaged the porcelain. At this point, Joyce had forgotten more about toilets than most people ever knew.

Housekeeping wasn't Bobbie's favorite thing. Usually, she paid a local woman to clean the house, but she didn't mind helping a friend, especially Susan. She was Bobbie's first friend in Hobbs outside the practice.

They'd met when Bobbie had signed up for beach cleanup, part of Hobbs' annual Earth Day celebration. The event had been canceled two years in a row by the pandemic, so there was plenty of debris to collect. While the volunteers snacked on treats donated by Hobbs' famous donut restaurant, the organizers explained their plan for the day. Bobbie had been standing next to Susan, so they ended up in the same group. They were dispatched to one of the town's four beaches. Hobbs, as the chamber of commerce advertised, had more miles of sandy shore than any town in Maine, one reason that Joyce had chosen it over trendy, overtly gay Webhanet.

Susan and Bobbie had chatted while they picked up the beach trash, everything from condoms to spent shotgun shells. After the event, Bobbie had invited Susan to lunch. Since then, they'd been meeting every Thursday after work for coffee.

Bobbie gauged the congestion on the Post Road against the time on the dashboard clock. She'd left early, knowing the weekend traffic would be heavy. She wondered if Susan was a stickler for punctuality like Joyce. It was hard to guess. Susan was friendly but guarded. The priest thing had thrown Bobbie at first. Mostly they avoided sharing things about the past and focused on their common passion—historical fiction. Bobbie often sacrificed sleep to consume enormous books that transported her to long-ago times. Her guilty pleasure was lesbian fiction, but she hadn't shared that with Susan.

They'd agreed to meet at Awakened Brews because it would be easier to get a table. After work, they usually went to the Hobbs Diner for the blueberry pie. Susan tried to avoid Awakened Brews because it was her boss's favorite café. Bobbie understood. She wouldn't want to run into Liz Stolz on a Saturday morning either.

The line to get into the café was out the door. Susan's old Subaru was already parked in the back lot, indicating she might be one of those chronically early people.

After Bobbie pushed past the waiting people, she was pleased to see Susan at one of the booths near the front. Bobbie waved, but Susan was busy watching the other patrons. Sometimes, when Susan thought she wasn't being watched, she had a strange deer-in-the-headlights look that saddened Bobbie but also made her cautious. As someone who made a living in a caring profession, she had a soft heart. When she got close to someone, it was hard to avoid being sucked into their problems. That's why she always tried to keep their conversations light.

Susan finally turned her blue eyes on Bobbie and smiled. Her face always seemed to glow from within. The only word Bobbie had come up with to describe that other-worldly look was 'saintly.'

"Good morning," Susan said in a cheerful voice. "Thank you so much for coming."

"I said I'd be here, didn't I?" said Bobbie, sliding into the booth, which was a little snug because of her girth.

"Not many people look forward to cleaning."

"Actually, we have someone clean our house." Bobbie glanced at Susan for signs of judgment but saw none. "But no matter how good they are, they never clean like you do. I order all the cleaning supplies, and we have plenty, so I brought everything I thought we'd need."

"That's so kind. Thank you. I brought some too."

The waitress came to pour their coffee. "Have you decided yet?" she asked, hands on hips, understandably impatient because of the crowd at the door.

"I was just going to have an English muffin with jelly," said Susan, pointing to the pods of grape jelly neatly stacked beside her plate.

"I'm hungry, so I'm going to have a real breakfast," declared Bobbie. "Eggs over easy, homefries, bacon. The blueberry pancakes sound good too." Susan's breakfast was a better choice, but Bobbie wanted company, so she dismissed the guilt. "Susan, you need energy if you're going to clean. And don't worry. I'm paying."

***

Susan made the expected protests, but she accepted Bobbie's generosity because the twenty in her wallet had to last until payday. If she could avoid breaking the bill beforehand, even better.

Her mother had drilled into her that living beyond one's means was the road to disaster. Left with debts from her husband's failed business ventures, the young widow was forced to return to her parents' house with her two young daughters. Susan's grandfather, an angry, rigid man, had never approved of his daughter's choices and constantly reminded her of her "big mistake," namely getting pregnant before marriage. Susan's grandmother had tried to protect her daughter and grandchildren from the constant abuse but couldn't. Once, she got between them and her husband and ended up with a black eye.

Susan's mother had finally escaped her father's moralizing and violence by saving every penny she'd earned from her secretarial job. One day, she walked out of her parents' big house on Main Street and moved into a tiny, cheap apartment on the wrong side of town. Susan missed her grandmother, a gentle, intelligent woman, but she never saw her again.

Susan was eleven when they'd moved out, old enough to understand and make some resolutions. The first was finding a more reliable safety net than marriage. She figured out that education was her ticket to security, but given her station, her options were limited. She considered the navy, which offered educational benefits, but the Vietnam War had recently ended, and like many young people, she was suspicious of military service. The convent was better than being part of an immoral war machine, and there was nothing wrong with trying to save the world. Before she entered, she convinced herself that her vocation was sincere, that God had chosen her for a reason. Over four decades later, she was still trying to discern what it might be.

Bobbie gave their order to the waitress. Susan liked her self-assurance, how she smoothly took control of the situation. Once Susan had been confident too, but the setbacks of the last few years had left her shaky. Now, she took time to assess where things stood before asserting herself.

After the waitress left, Bobbie asked, "Have you seen the place we're going to clean today?"

"No, but Lucy said it only needs a freshening. In the past, a housekeeper would clean for the rector and cook his meals. It would have been her job to prepare the room for a new curate. These days, parishes can barely support a priest, never mind staff. I was lucky to get a part-time position at St. Margaret's, especially now that we have a deacon."

"You mean the young black woman you were telling me about?"

"Yes, Reshma John. She came as a refugee from Africa as a child. Lucy says she's smart as a whip and has been a big help to her."

Bobbie shook her head. "I still find it strange that a woman runs your church. When I was growing up, only men could be ministers."

"Same for me. If I hadn't switched to the Episcopal Church, I still wouldn't be a priest. The Catholic Church moves at glacial speed."

"Maybe there's hope. With global warming, glaciers are moving faster." Bobbie laughed at her own joke, then frowned and shook her head. "Those damned men will never give up their privilege. They'll cling to it until the whole damn thing goes down in flames. How dare they tell other people what to do? They ripped Native American children away from their families. Treat women like dirt, molest children. Anyone who hurts a child should be shot!"

Listening to the rant, Susan wondered if Bobbie lumped her in with the hateful people she condemned.

"I don't know much about your denomination," admitted Bobbie, "but it seems more enlightened than the rest. My boss is married to your pastor. She seems like a nice woman."

"Lucy? Oh yes, she's wonderful."

"I was invited to their wedding like the rest of the office staff, but I had a previous commitment, so I couldn't go."

Susan's first instinct had been to decline the invitation. After her humiliating departure from Hobbs, she expected Lucy's friends to have negative attitudes toward her. Finally, she decided it would look worse if a newly hired priest didn't show up at her rector's wedding.

As she'd feared, some of the guests snubbed her. With all the alcohol flowing, it was difficult to resist taking a drink. But just when she thought she'd be sitting alone all night, Cherie Harrison, who probably knew the whole story from her wife, came to sit with her. Then the police chief, who'd escorted Susan to the airport to face charges in South Dakota, sat down beside her wife. Tom Simmons came by and chatted for a while. Even Liz Stolz spent a few minutes at Susan's table. Maybe Hobbs wasn't such a bad place after all.

"You missed a beautiful wedding," said Susan, "and the food Ms. Enright and Ms. Fitzgerald prepared was delicious."

"That reception was a miracle after the fire at Cliff Manor. We're still treating the victims as outpatients. Dr. Stolz volunteered in a burn unit when she was in medical school. Sometimes, I'm amazed at how much that woman knows."

"They say she's going to retire soon," said Susan, probing to see if Bobbie had any inside information.

"Doesn't look like it to me. If anything, she's even more involved. It's like her marriage reinvigorated her. Maybe it's the sex." Bobbie wiggled her eyebrows suggestively. Susan really wished Bobbie hadn't shared that thought.

After the generous breakfast, Susan felt satisfied for the first time in days. Her limited food budget had helped take off the extra pounds that alcohol had added to her midriff. She tried to resist junk food and prepared meals, even though they were often cheaper.

When the waitress brought the check, Bobbie grabbed it before Susan could even reach out her hand.

"Thank you," Susan murmured. "Once I start teaching in September, I'll return the favor."

"Never mind. Paying for your breakfast isn't going to break me. You eat like a bird." Bobbie turned around to look at the line still extending out the door. "I suppose we should let them clear the table and give other people a chance to sit down." Susan liked that Bobbie always thought of others.

They elbowed their way through the crowd gathered in the waiting room outside the door.

"Looks like we came at just the right time," Bobbie observed, tapping a young man on the shoulder who'd ignored her "excuse me." He gave her a filthy look but moved aside. The heat wave had caused people's tempers to rise along with the thermometer.

While they'd been inside, the traffic had backed up on Route 1, but Susan knew an alternate route to the rectory. "Follow me. It seems like the long way, but it's really faster." She watched in the rear-view mirror to make sure Bobbie was behind her as she drove through a maze of local roads leading to the church parking lot.

"Thanks for showing me that short cut," Bobbie said, getting out of her car. "There are so many hidden streets on this side of town." She opened the hatch of her SUV to reveal a complete collection of cleaning supplies from buckets, mops, and rags to old-fashioned powder cleanser.

"Looks like you thought of everything," Susan said, reaching for a double bucket filled with an assortment of spray bottles.

"I wanted to make sure we had what we need. Getting into the super-market on a Saturday morning during the season is impossible. I'll leave this stuff here after we finish. Cleaning supplies have gotten expensive, like everything else."

"You don't need to. You've already been so…" Susan started to say, but Bobbie gave her a firm look that stopped the protest.

After standing in the blazing sun to unload the cleaning supplies, the interior of the rectory was dark, but the cool air inside was welcome.

"Lead the way," said Bobbie, looking around curiously.

"The apartments are upstairs. Once this entire second floor was the rector's residence. Now, there are two studios for curates and visiting clergy. The music director and our deacon live in them."

While Susan was struggling with the recalcitrant lock, one of the doors down the hall opened. An exceptionally tall woman wearing a floral sun-dress strolled in their direction. She carried a sling chair in a bag over her shoulder and a straw beach tote that matched her broad-brimmed hat. She raised her sunglasses and peered at them.

"Hello, Mother Gedney," said Denise. "Moving in today?"

"Tomorrow after services. Just doing a little tidying."

"If you need help moving in, just let me know."

"Thank you, Denise. Are you heading to the beach?"

"If I can get parking. Usually, the lot is full by this time of the morning. But it's high tide, so maybe I'll get lucky." She smiled at Bobbie. "Hi, I'm Denise Chantal. You look familiar."

"Bobbie Lantry, Hobbs Family Practice."

"That's right. Now, I remember. Nice to see you. Thanks for helping Mother Gedney."

"Please, Denise. Call me Susan."

"How's *Reverend* Susan? Will that do?" asked Denise.

Usually, young people were all for informality, so Susan didn't understand the resistance. "Better, but I hope you'll change your mind once we get to know one another. Just don't call me Sue."

"Never!" Denise agreed theatrically. She patted Susan's arm. "I need to go. I'm meeting someone at the beach." Susan noted the perfect sway of Denise's hips. Did it come naturally, or had she practiced it while she was transitioning?

"Your neighbor seems nice," Bobbie said.

"She's a very talented singer." Susan saw Bobbie's eyes follow Denise down the hall and wondered what she was thinking.

The lock still refused to budge. Susan applied more pressure and hoped the key wouldn't break. Finally, the barrels engaged, but the door wouldn't open until she rammed it with her shoulder. Everything was sticky from the heat. As a precaution, Susan propped the door open with a chair. The interior smelled stale and needed a good airing. Otherwise, the place looked clean and neat.

"It's a nice little apartment," Bobbie said, sounding surprised as she looked around. "I wonder if it has air conditioning. Not many people had it in Maine before the climate began to change."

"I think there's a window unit in the bedroom. It's an old building. Turn of the century, I think."

They carried the cleaning supplies into the kitchen. "We should probably start here," said Susan. "I'll clean the stove."

"I'll tackle the refrigerator. I brought some boxes of baking soda to leave behind."

"You really did think of everything."

"Nurses are good at details."

"I hear that doctors couldn't survive without you."

"Probably true, but we don't tell them that, of course. We let them think they do everything."

The humidity caused the rubber gloves to snag as Susan tried to pull them on. She opened the oven, relieved to see it wasn't as bad as she'd expected. Because of the heat, she'd pass on using the self-cleaning feature.

Bobbie pulled out the refrigerator drawers. "The fridge looks spotless. This guy isn't the slob we expected."

"He's gay. Maybe that makes a difference."

Bobbie looked at Susan strangely. Maybe she shouldn't have outed Tom. She had no idea how Bobbie felt about LGBT people, but Susan didn't give her a chance to voice an opinion. She stuck her head into the oven and began to wipe it out.

They'd mostly finished the kitchen when Susan heard a familiar voice calling hello. When Lucy leaned into the room, her pretty sundress revealed her gorgeous décolletage. Susan stared at the floor to avoid admiring it.

"I hope I'm not intruding," said Lucy with one of those brilliant smiles that could melt Susan into a puddle of adoration. "I saw your car outside. Reny's was having a big sale, so I picked up a few things I thought you might need. They're in the car. Okay if I bring them up?"

"I'll help you," said Susan, washing her filthy hands in the sink. By the time she got to the parking lot, she found Lucy pulling shopping bags out of the back of her SUV.

"What's all this?" Susan asked, reaching in to help.

"I thought you could use a new mattress pad and some sheets."

"I didn't know the church provided linens."

"It doesn't. I paid for them. A little housewarming gift."

"I appreciate it. I only have twin-sized sheets. I see the bed here is queen-sized."

"The mattress is nearly new. I bought it when I lived here." Lucy frowned slightly. "A lot has happened since, but it wasn't that long ago."

They carried the bags up to the sitting room, where Lucy displayed their contents—new pillows, extra blankets, sheets with a coordinating comforter, and a complete set of fluffy bath towels. "And I couldn't resist these." Lucy held out dish towels embroidered in a shore motif. "In case you miss your place by the ocean."

"The beach isn't far away. I can walk from here. But thank you for all these gifts. I don't know what to say." Lucy's generosity was especially surprising because she'd frankly admitted her doubts about hiring her. What had changed?

Lucy seemed to understand the question in Susan's eyes. "I'm always telling people that kindness goes a long way. I figured I should practice what I preach. Besides, I can never resist a sale. I love to shop." She look around the apartment. "Now, what can I do to help?"

❖❖❖

"You want people to think you're tough, when you're so kind," said Lucy in an obviously flattering tone. "And you know so much about plumbing." Liz was glad Lucy couldn't see the scowl on her face through the phone.

"All right, Lucy, but I'm doing it for *you*, not her."

"I know, but no matter who you're doing it for, it's still a good deed."

Liz growled, which only made Lucy laugh.

Despite Lucy's protests that she was mechanically incompetent, her descriptions were accurate enough for Liz to figure out what she'd need. She mentally scanned the storage bins in her workshop, arranged by type of work: electrical, plumbing, masonry, drywall, and painting. The portable power tools and hand tools were in their own section, carefully labeled.

Sam called Liz's devotion to organization an illness, but she didn't care because she always knew where to find what she needed.

The list of problems Lucy had described was long: the lavatory stopper was seized, the toilet tank kept filling, the faucet leaked, blocked drains in the bathroom and the kitchen, a dead light switch, and multiple lights needing replacement bulbs.

Working on Susan's apartment was not how Liz had intended to spend her day. The weather was perfect for boating, and she'd planned to take out The Wet Lady for an afternoon of fishing, the first since they'd returned from France. Before the gas prices fell, filling the tank of her boat could easily cost what for some people would be a week's salary. Although Liz could afford it, she couldn't justify the expense.

She found almost everything she needed in her shop. The one thing missing was the stopper rod for the sink. There was a remote chance the hardware store might have one, so she decided to avoid the crowd at the home center and stop in town first.

As Liz pulled into the hardware store parking lot, she saw a tall woman loading a pickup truck. She swung into the adjacent parking space.

"Hey, Sam," said Liz, sliding out of the driver's seat. "Need help with those?"

"Sure. Thanks." Sam threw a forty-pound bag of water-conditioner salt into the bed. "Can't believe how much the price has gone up. Shit, it's just salt!"

"Transportation costs. Labor costs. No one can get help. It all contributes to rising prices."

"I know the reasons, Liz, but it's doubled in price since I moved up here. And now that Maggie's staying with me more often, I'm going through it faster."

Liz forced herself not to grimace at the mention of her ex-wife. The little twinge of jealousy proved she still didn't like Sam being with Maggie. Liz didn't begrudge her ex companionship, but why did she have to choose her best friend?

Liz threw a bag of salt into the truck bed and grabbed another. "Why didn't you ask one of the guys to help you with these?"

"Only women in there today," said Sam.

"What? You too gallant to ask another woman to help you? You accepted my help."

"That's different," Sam said.

"Why?"

"I know you."

"Sam, that's completely illogical."

"So what?"

Working together, they got Sam's order loaded in no time. She slammed closed the tail gate. "Liz, can I buy you a cup of coffee?"

"Thanks, but I've been summoned to the rectory by my wife. Tom's apartment needs some work. He never said anything and probably didn't care because he was living with Jeff. Like he thought people didn't notice."

"Everyone knows everything in Hobbs. We just don't talk about it." Sam gave Liz a playful slap on the shoulder. "Try to behave yourself around Susan. I know she's not your favorite person. And say hi to Lucy for me."

"Will do," Liz said and grudgingly added, "Say hi to Maggie for me."

When Liz spotted the stopper rod on the plumbing replacement parts display, it was better than winning a lottery scratch off. Hoping to cut down on return trips, she scanned the pegboard for anything else she might need. The price ticket on the washer assortment she'd found in her shop was from a long-defunct home-center chain. When the rubber hardened with age, washers were useless. Liz tossed a new assortment into her shopping basket.

When Liz arrived at the rectory, she carried her tool bag and supplies upstairs. The door to the rector's apartment was wide open, so she didn't bother to knock. She followed the voices into the kitchen, where she found herself face-to-face with her nurse practitioner.

"Hello, Bobbie," said Liz, leaning down to peer into her eyes. "What are you doing here?" Susan was a patient in the practice, but that didn't necessarily explain the connection.

"Helping Susan clean before she moves in."

"I can see that." Liz put down her bags and continued her inquisitive stare. Socializing with patients was quietly discouraged, but in a small town like Hobbs, it was nearly impossible. In fact, Liz was the worst offender because she knew just about everybody.

Bobbie just smiled, evidently unimpressed by Liz's intimidating stare. "If you're looking for Lucy, she's in the bedroom, dusting."

With a grunt, Liz shoved her tool bag out of the path of traffic and went to find her wife.

"Liz!" said Lucy, meeting her in the doorway. She stood on her toes to kiss her. "Thank you so much for coming!" They were married now, so there was nothing to hide, but Liz glanced anxiously at their audience. Bobbie smiled in approval. Susan's expression was hard to read.

"Thank me after I fix everything. That is…if I can." Liz always believed in managing expectations.

"The bathroom is the biggest problem. Start there," said Lucy, escorting her by the arm, even though Liz knew the way. "The sink leaks and the toilet runs. That's not only wasteful, but it's driving up our water bill."

"Well, we certainly can't have that," said Liz sarcastically. "Let me get my tools, and I'll see what I can do."

When Liz returned from the kitchen, she passed the bedroom, where she found Lucy making the bed. "Aren't these gorgeous? I found them on sale, and I couldn't resist. I got a set for the bed downstairs too." Liz found the floral pattern unbearably bright and busy, certainly not anything she'd ever choose.

"Sleeping on all those flowers would kick up my hay fever."

Lucy pouted. "Liz, they're pretty. This room needs something cheerful. It doesn't get much light."

Liz looked around the room. The building was solid, but the original woodwork, authentic Arts-and-Crafts, made the room seem dark and smaller than it was. "I can't believe you lived in this dreary place."

"When I lived here, I was so busy learning to do my new job as rector

I didn't have time to think about how the place looked. I came home, ate whatever I found in the refrigerator, and collapsed."

"Not much of a life."

Lucy shrugged. "It's what I signed up for."

At this point, Liz would usually insert a snarky remark about Lucy's priesthood. That was before Lucy had confessed her doubts about her faith. Now, Liz tread more lightly. Her issues with religion and the Church hadn't gone away. She just never discussed them with Lucy.

"This shouldn't take long," she said, "Maybe we can finish up here and take the boat out."

"Oh, wouldn't that be lovely!" Although Lucy didn't share Liz's obsession with fishing, she loved being on the water. "Well? What are you waiting for? Get to work!"

Liz opened the tub drain and started fishing out the trapped hair with a long tweezer.

"Now there's a messy job." Liz looked up to see Bobbie standing in the doorway.

"Not as bad as unblocking toilets. When Tom was living here, I had to replace the seal on that one. Damn thing leaked into Lucy's office, but I fixed the leak, and we cleaned up the mess before she found out."

"I didn't know you were a plumber on the side," said Bobbie. "I have a few leaky fixtures at my house that could use attention."

"I know a real plumber if you need one." Liz said, setting the alarm on her gold chronometer to time the action of the drain cleaner. "I didn't know I'd see you here today," she said casually. "Did you meet Susan at the practice?" She'd tried to say it in a way that didn't sound critical but let Bobbie know she was paying attention.

"No, we were on the same team for spring beach cleanup. She was new in town, and so was I, so we started meeting for coffee."

That sounded harmless enough.

"How about you?" Bobbie asked. "How do you know Susan?"

Ordinarily, Liz would be evasive when staff asked personal questions, but she liked Bobbie. She nodded in the direction of the bedroom. "Lucy and Susan went to seminary together." Liz's watch alarm went off with a trill. She opened the hot water spigot all the way to flush the drain. The sound of crashing water also cut off further conversation.

"I'll let you get to work," called Bobbie over the noise. "You look busy."

Liz liked to work on old plumbing because it was so simple. That is, if she could get it apart. After Bobbie left, Liz drained the toilet. She threaded out the old flushometer so the tank could drain into a bucket.

"I appreciate your doing this more than you know," said Susan, leaning into the doorway.

Liz glanced over her shoulder. "Not a big deal. Shouldn't take long."

Susan stepped into the room. "Lucy told me you did the plumbing when you donated the washer and dryer in the laundry room. It's not often that you find a doctor who fixes toilets and stops leaks."

"Surgery isn't that different from plumbing," Liz said in a philosophical tone. "Except pipes don't heal like body parts."

"You're trained to observe strict hygiene. Don't you find working in toilets disgusting?" asked Susan, watching Liz inspect the slimy flushometer.

"People always ask me that. In fact, the human gut is a mucky place." Liz finished mopping out the toilet tank with a sponge. "Did you enjoy your visit to my garden the other day?" She looked up to see Susan's reaction. Her face was bright red.

"How did you know?" she stammered.

"My security camera caught you."

"I didn't know you had a security camera."

"Well, you do now."

"I thought Maine was such a safe place."

"I live out in the woods. People know I'm a doctor. They may think I keep drugs in the house, which I don't." Liz took a razor knife off her belt and slit open the plastic bubble holding the new toilet parts.

"I was only trying to help. Melissa Morgenstern came to pick up the principal after a teacher's meeting. They were rushing to get her daughter from soccer practice. I volunteered to check the water."

Liz scrutinized Susan's face and decided that she was telling the truth. "I thought there might be a reasonable explanation."

"Does Lucy know I was there?" asked Susan, glancing anxiously toward the bedroom.

Liz shook her head. "I wanted to talk to you before I said anything."

"Will you tell her?"

"Lucy and I both have sensitive jobs. We need to keep professional confidences. But outside of that, I don't keep secrets from my wife."

"Does she really need to know? I mean, I wasn't trespassing. You need to believe I had a legitimate reason to be there." Despite the completely plausible explanation, Susan *looked* guilty.

"Susan, Lucy is trying really hard to trust you. Going out of my way to tell her something that will only frighten her isn't going to help."

"So, what are you going to do?"

Liz gave her a long, measuring look. "I won't tell her this time, but for your own good, stay off my property unless you're invited."

"You can be sure it won't happen again."

"Good. Glad we understand each other," said Liz, positioning the new flushometer. When she looked up, she saw Susan hugging herself. "By the way, thanks for checking on the water. I do appreciate it."

Susan nodded and disappeared. Liz shook her head as she crouched to tighten the nut under the toilet tank.

3

"L u-u-u-cy!" crooned a small voice. Lucy waved to the little girl standing in the doorway.

Every other Wednesday, Lucy put on her collar and worked in the rectory office. Most parishioners knew it was her day to write her sermon, but she always expected drop-ins. People often stopped in for social reasons, but a casual visit could turn into an opportunity to help someone in need.

The girl raced into the room and climbed into Lucy's lap.

"Megan! You get down!" her mother ordered, finally catching up with the girl. "You think Mother Lucy wants bruised thighs from your bony backside? Bad enough you make me all black and blue!"

"It's all right, Cherie," said Lucy, giving Megan the hug she wanted.

Cherie sighed in exasperation. "I'm sorry, Mother Lucy. We're trying to teach them some discipline, but it isn't easy." Cherie's stern look made her adopted daughter tense, so Lucy held her closer. "Megan, I know you love Mother Lucy, but she is the rector here. We need to be respectful. Get down from there. Now!" The scolding only caused Megan to shrink deeper into Lucy's body.

Lucy heard the frustration in Cherie's voice, but after the trauma her children had experienced, they were needy. Their father had shot his wife and then himself. When the police arrived, they'd found Megan and her brother cowering in a bedroom closet. Cherie's wife, the police chief, had taken the children home, and the couple had decided to adopt them.

Lucy wondered what to say. Cherie, with her training in therapy, should know the kids needed extra reassurance and affection. Unfortunately, professional knowledge was often useless when it came to your own children. Dealing with Emily often frustrated Lucy.

"Megan just wants to say hello," said Lucy, kissing the top of the girl's head. She waved to Keith, who ran into Lucy's outstretched arm. "Hi Keith, I missed you too!" She said, hugging him. "How are you?"

"Good," he murmured before wiggling out of Lucy's arms. He took a step away and shyly shuffled his feet.

"Sweetie, Mama C wants you to get down," Lucy whispered into Megan's ear. "Give me another hug and then let me go. Okay?"

Megan threw her arms around Lucy's neck, squeezing with all her might. "I love you!" she declared.

"I love you too, Megan."

The girl finally slid off Lucy's lap and ran back to her mother.

Cherie shook her head. "Kids adore you, Mother Lucy. I don't know what you have."

"I don't either," Lucy admitted, brushing Keith's hair out of his eyes, "but as long as it works, I'll use it."

"Brenda keeps saying that the kids need a firm hand."

"That's how she was raised, and I'm sure her police training reinforced it, but you know one size doesn't fit all. Kids need affection to balance the discipline."

Cherie stared guiltily at her feet. "I'm trying, Mother Lucy. I'm really trying."

"Of course, you are." Lucy rose to give Cherie a little hug. "You're doing great. Becoming a mother when you're fifty isn't easy."

"As you well know."

"At least mine was nearly grown when she came back." Lucy studied Cherie's discouraged face. "Why don't you come talk to me when Brenda gets home? Stop in before your therapy sessions."

"Another day. I know Wednesday is your day to write your sermon. I don't want to take up your time."

"Cherie, you know better. I'm happy to give you my time. And don't worry about my sermon. Reshma is preaching at my services this week."

"But I won't stay long. We saw your car outside and hoped you might be free. Someone wanted to say hello."

A familiar figure stepped into the doorway. Cherie's Aunt Simone had finally arrived, and not a moment too soon. Hopefully, the retired school principal could give her niece some pointers on dealing with young children.

Lucy reached out both hands to the tall, elegantly dressed woman. "Simone! Welcome back."

"Oh, Mother Lucy. It's so good to see you. I'm so looking forward to being part of your parish again." When Simone embraced Lucy, she could smell her old-fashioned eau de cologne and a hint of Cajun cooking spices.

"Aunt Simone is talking about joining the choir," volunteered Cherie.

Lucy checked with Simone, who just smiled. "I hear you've gone back to singing, Mother Lucy. Good for you. You shouldn't waste the talent that God gave you. It's something special, all right."

"That's what everyone keeps telling me, but I'm not giving up my day job."

"Good thing too," said Cherie. "We don't want to lose our priest."

Lucy gestured to the visitors' chairs, but her guests declined to sit, so Lucy continued to stand. "How are you settling in, Simone?"

"Oh, there's still a mountain of boxes to unpack, but I sold most of what I had in my house in Louisiana. There is only so much room in my apartment in that senior residence. It's been years since I gave a big dinner party, so why would I need place settings for twelve? I gave some things away to family, but I donated most of it to the church thrift shop. I darn near died when I saw the prices they were asking. They're practically giving my things away!"

Lucy knew that charity thrift shops priced items to sell and keep the inventory moving. The real monetary worth of donations was only casually considered. No one ever thought about the item's sentimental value.

"It's my own fault," Simone continued. "I shouldn't have looked at the prices, but my friend wanted to shop, and I went along. It reminds me of what the Lord says, 'Sell your possessions, and give alms. Make purses for yourselves that do not wear out, an unfailing treasure in heaven, where no thief comes near, and no moth destroys.'" Amazed by Simone's ability to quote scripture, Lucy wondered if she could so easily pluck an apt passage from memory.

Simone gave Lucy's shoulder an appreciative caress. "My, my, don't you look all pretty in that pink clerical blouse? Cord is so nice and cool in the summer."

"My wife insisted I buy some pastel blouses for hot weather."

"That Dr. Stolz is one smart woman."

"Actually, it was my first wife," said Lucy, still smiling, even though her voice had thickened at the mention of Erika, and the last note sank.

Simone's face crinkled with sympathy. "Oh, Mother Lucy, I'd forgotten you were married before. I'm so sorry, dear. It's so hard to lose a spouse."

Lucy swallowed hard. Hearing condolences for Erika's death still made her emotional. The easiest way to deal with the sympathy was to turn it around. "Simone, how long ago did you lose your husband?"

"Oh, almost eight years now, but time doesn't heal all wounds like they say. The intensity of the pain eases. You get used to it, but it never completely goes away."

"No, it doesn't, and we wouldn't want it to. That's the space that love left in our hearts." Lucy tapped her chest.

"That's a sweet way to look at it."

Cherie touched Simone's shoulder. "*Ma tante*, we should let Mother Lucy get back to work. I'm sure she's busy."

"Thanks so much for stopping in. Welcome back." Lucy gave Simone another hug. "I look forward to seeing you around. Maybe your niece will bring you to choir practice. We always welcome new voices." Over Simone's shoulder, Lucy saw Cherie's nod of approval.

Megan skipped over to Lucy for another kiss. Keith hung back, waiting until Lucy bent down and opened her arms. He smelled like a boy, a little musky around the ears, although Cherie kept both children scrupulously clean.

"Please give my best to Brenda," Lucy called after them.

After they left, Lucy sat down at her laptop to pull up the edited copy of Reshma's sermon. The first time the deacon was scheduled to preach, Lucy had reveled in the fact she wouldn't have to write a homily...until she discovered it was harder to help someone else write one than to do it herself. Lucy's coaching was finally paying off. The draft that Reshma had submitted was solid. It only needed a few tweaks to make it compelling.

Lucy printed out the file with her edits. The time at the top of her computer screen showed six minutes past the hour. It wasn't like Reshma to be late. If anything, she usually arrived early. As the last page ejected from the printer, Lucy heard rapid footsteps in the hall. A young, dark-skinned woman skidded into the doorway, like a ballplayer sliding into home.

"I'm sorry, Mother Lucy, but I was out on a home visit, and I almost forgot our date," stammered Reshma.

"Pastoral care always comes first," Lucy reminded her. "Come on in."

Reshma seated herself in the closest visitors' chair. Sitting beside her, Lucy handed her the printout with her notes and edits.

"Wow. Looks clean for a change. You hardly made any changes," said Reshma, scanning the pages.

"You're getting better at this, which is what we want. After you're ordained, you won't have someone looking over your shoulder."

Reshma gave Lucy a sheepish side eye. "You know I asked for my ordination to be delayed." It was part statement, part question—a test to see how much Lucy knew.

"I heard something to that effect," replied Lucy with an innocent smile.

"Did the bishop tell you why I'm hesitant?"

"No, he only told me you'd had an experience that was holding you back. He said he wasn't sure you knew yourself."

Reshma looked thoughtful. "That's perceptive and probably true."

"Do you want to tell me about it?" asked Lucy.

"Actually, I would." Reshma stared at the floor, her dark eyes stubbornly refusing to meet Lucy's. Whatever the young woman was struggling to share was deeply personal and hard to admit.

"You don't have to tell me unless you want to," Lucy said gently.

"Mother Lucy, have you been following the Lambeth Conference?"

Surprised by this unexpected diversion, Lucy sat up straight. She had been following the controversy at Lambeth. The world's Anglican bishops were meeting for the first time in sixteen years. An earlier conference had been postponed because the Communion was so divided over the role of LGBT people in the Church. Many provinces, including the Church of England, still prohibited same-sex marriage and insisted that LGBT people remain celibate. Now, a group of conservative bishops from Africa and Asia was trying to force a vote to affirm a 1998 resolution condemning homosexuality.

"I've been reading about the conference," said Lucy. "Did you see the article about Bishop Greene in the Portland paper this morning?"

Reshma nodded. The Episcopal bishop of Maine, a married gay man, had provided the local press with an irresistible news angle. Lucy didn't always agree with Bishop Greene, especially when he'd insisted that she hire Susan. Now that the poor man had become a poster boy for the potential schism in the Anglican Communion, she felt more sympathetic toward him, even if he seemed to be enjoying the publicity a little too much.

"That was the first time I've seen a photo of the bishop's husband," said Reshma. "It's horrible that he's being excluded from events because he's gay. What is *that* supposed to accomplish?"

"Archbishop Welby is trying to thread a needle by inviting the gay bishops but banning their spouses from official events. Last time, the LGBT bishops weren't even invited, so this is progress."

"Really? Will those African bishops be able to force a vote to ban same-sex marriage?"

"I hope not, but this is a hot-button issue in countries where homosexuality is not just frowned upon, but illegal."

"I know. I've been studying up on my African background," said Reshma. "It was kind of erased when I went off to that Episcopalian boarding school. Not deliberately, of course, just routine cultural dominance. Those churches that paid my tuition thought they were doing good, and they did. I got an excellent education."

"And, smart person that you are, you took advantage of it."

"I read that the animus against gay people in Africa is a vestige of colonialism. Europeans brought their anti-homosexual laws from their home countries."

Lucy wondered how to steer the conversation back from the global to the personal. She studied Reshma's intelligent face, trying to figure out the connection between Lambeth and her doubts about being ordained. "Is the erasure of your culture by the Church why you're questioning your vocation?"

"No, it's closer to home. You know that Denise and I have become friends?"

"Yes, and I'm glad because it hasn't been easy for her as a trans woman."

"Mother Lucy, I support trans rights on principle, and I look for Christ in everyone I meet, but…"

Lucy waited patiently for her to continue, but the pause extended until it became unnatural. "…but?" Lucy prodded.

Reshma shook her head and threw up her hands. "I'm so confused! Most of my life has been focused on getting an education, first in college, then in the seminary. My convictions were never road-tested in real life."

"Reshma, what are you trying to say?"

"I've been hesitant to talk to you about this because Denise is dating your daughter."

Again, Reshma found the floor extremely interesting. Her loud swallow was audible, and Lucy realized she was fighting back tears. She reached over and touched her arm, which finally made the young woman look up.

"It's okay. You don't have to tell me until you're ready…or ever unless you want to."

"But I want to tell you because I need your advice." Reshma took a deep breath. "While Emily and Denise were trying to figure out what to do about their relationship…"

Despite her intense curiosity, Lucy assumed her most patient face.

"I had no idea I could be attracted to a woman. All I knew was I didn't have any interest in men. For a long time, I thought I might be asexual. Now, I don't know what I am."

"You slept with Denise," ventured Lucy cautiously. "Now, you're confused because she's trans?"

"I know she's chosen to be a woman, but what does that mean? Is she a man with the body of a woman? Does changing her body and taking hormones make her a woman? Am I attracted to her because she was once a man?"

"Okay. Now, I understand why you're confused. A lot of people are confused about that. But when we're attracted to someone, we don't usually ask them for their genetic profile. We're drawn to how they present. You have to look very closely to see that Denise wasn't born female."

"Exactly! She's more feminine than many cis-gender women I know. The way she dresses, her perfume. If she hadn't told me she was trans, I might never have caught on, but she was up front about it. It was one of the first things she told me. I was like, 'okay, that's cool.' Until…"

"Until you became sexually involved."

"Yes."

Lucy knew she couldn't ask if the physical experience had made Reshma more aware that Denise was trans. That would mean asking for intimate details that might make her uncomfortable. Later, she'd ask Liz for a clinical perspective.

"The Church of England won't allow trans people to marry any more than they'll allow same-sex marriage," said Reshma.

Lucy sighed because they were back to the global issue instead of Reshma's personal dilemma.

"We're Episcopalians, Reshma. It matters what other branches of the Communion do, but we need to listen to our own bishops. You also need to determine your own truth. What *you* believe." Lucy gave Reshma's arm a gentle pat to get her attention. "As far as I'm concerned, what Emily does in bed is her own business. Don't worry about offending me because you may have gotten between her and Denise. They seem to be back together now, or am I misreading it?"

"No, they're back together," said Reshma. "You've got that right."

"How does that make you feel?"

"Happy for them, but even more confused. I pushed Denise away after we slept together. We didn't speak for weeks."

"That must have been hard since you're living right next door."

"We nodded in the hallway, but we stopped cooking together. I missed our family dinners. We're talking again and sharing meals, but it's not the same."

"Having sex with someone crosses a line. Physical intimacy changes a relationship forever. Sometimes, it strengthens the bond. Other times, it pushes people apart. That's why it's important to consider the outcome before having sex."

"I *did* think about it. I prayed over it. It seemed a natural extension of our friendship, a way to deepen it. But now, I think I made a mistake."

Lucy sat back in her chair while she considered what to say. "Don't rush to judge yourself for exploring your feelings. You're young and still learning. Sexuality is complicated. Religions have tried to enforce strict rules around it, but human reality doesn't always agree."

"I don't think sex is sinful. If I've sinned, it was in using Denise as an experiment or simply for my own pleasure… It was very pleasurable, which scared me even more."

Lucy imagined she could see Reshma blushing beneath her dark skin. "Reshma, did you hear what I just said about not judging yourself?"

"I heard."

"Which of these issues, all of which are complicated, is making you doubt your vocation?"

"All of them. The experience with Denise was a wake-up call. Once I decided to become a priest, I went straight to seminary, finished early, and got ordained a deacon. Maybe I'm rushing too much. If I don't know myself, how can I minister to other people? And if I reject Denise, how can I say I'm meeting Christ in everyone?"

Lucy leaned forward so that she was at eye-level with Reshma whose gaze was fixed on her shoes. "Don't be so hard on yourself. Life is a process of discovery, and the Spirit works in strange ways. We think we know our own mind, and then something happens to change it. That's how we learn and grow." Reshma had looked up and was clearly listening, so Lucy continued. "While I was recovering from the rape, it was very important for me to embrace my faith. When I decided to write a book about sex, my first wife encouraged me to go back to school. My doctoral studies opened my eyes to facets of our faith that I had never considered before. For a time, I had so many doubts, I wondered if I could continue as a priest."

Reshma's dark eyes had grown wider as Lucy told her story. "You?"

"Yes, me."

"But you chose to stay in the priesthood."

"Yes, because I believe in Jesus' message of love and feel called to spread it to anyone who will listen."

"So you think I should request ordination?"

"Reshma, I think you are called to ministry, but it's not for me to decide. I will say this. Don't let an experience that you embraced out of love keep you from your vocation."

Reshma nodded thoughtfully. "And I thought I was coming for a critique of my sermon, but I got a whole lot more."

Lucy smiled. "It was a great sermon before I got my hands on it. And it's always a privilege to listen to you. Reshma, never hesitate to come to me because my family may be involved. We're all in this together, and we owe each other transparency."

Reshma looked enormously relieved. "Mother Lucy, may I give you a hug?"

Lucy smiled. "Of course." When she got up, Reshma leaned down and scooped her up in her long arms.

"Thank you," she whispered into Lucy's ear. "Now I'm sorry I waited so long to talk to you."

"You waited until the time was right. That's okay."

Misty-eyed, Reshma nodded.

Lucy sighed as she watched the young woman head for the door.

***

"That was absolutely delicious," said Bobbie, pushing back from the table and rubbing her ample belly. "I hope I haven't made a pig of myself!"

"Not at all." Susan swelled with pride over the success of her meal. She'd been anxious for days over this dinner with Bobbie. She'd had the ingredients for a week, double-checking to make sure she had everything she needed except the ground beef which she'd purchased fresh that afternoon.

Bobbie pointed to the casserole dish. "Promise you'll give me this recipe."

"With pleasure. It's my mother's. It was her go-to meal when money was tight, we liked it so much it became a family favorite. After we moved out of my grandparents' house, Mom had to figure out how to stretch our food budget. That woman could feed us for a week on a pound of hamburger." Susan's smile faded as she remembered those difficult days. She could brag about her mother's ingenuity, but she could also remember days when her young stomach growled with hunger.

"Clearly, your mother was an inventive cook."

"She was great at using pantry items like pasta and canned tomatoes. She'd stock up and even buy dented cans when they went on sale." In response to Bobbie's worried look, Susan added, "She taught us to watch for bulges and other signs of contamination, but she was rescuing food from the dumpster long before it was fashionable." Susan scrutinized her guest for signs that her tale of her childhood poverty had diminished her in her guest's eyes. If anything, Bobbie seemed to look at her with new respect.

"This recipe is so good you could even make this for company," Bobbie said.

"I just did."

Bobbie laughed merrily "Yes, you did." The smile on Bobbie's face faded. "But I feel a little guilty, eating here, especially knowing how pressed you are for money."

In fact, Susan's finances had greatly improved since she'd moved into the rectory. There was no rent to pay and the church paid for all the utilities.

The electric bill from her beach rental hadn't been as bad as she'd expected, so she'd even saved a few dollars. They'd already been earmarked to freshen her wardrobe now that she was starting a new job in a fashion-conscious resort town. Fortunately, the thrift shops along the Post Road offered hardly worn dresses, slacks, and tops, some with the tags still attached.

"I told you I would cook you a dinner to thank you for helping get the place ready, so don't feel guilty," said Susan, collecting their plates.

Susan tried to interpret Bobbie's thoughtful frown. "I wish I could return the favor, but I'd really have to plan it."

"I thought you had your own apartment."

"I do. It's a mother-daughter house. Joyce has the main house. She has two students living upstairs. They help in exchange for lodging."

So far, this was the most Bobbie had said about her living situation. Susan assumed the look of open interest she'd found useful in pastoral work. It nearly guaranteed that someone would keep talking.

Bobbie leaned her elbows on the table. "It's an ideal situation from my point of view. One of the lodgers is working on a Doctor of Social Work. The other is getting her D.O. at the Osteopathy school. Chloe likes having me around because I help her study for exams. We share meals sometimes. I enjoy the company."

All those women living together cooperatively sounded like a secular convent. Susan had loved living communally with other women. The only reason she'd left the order was the ordination fever she'd caught from her feminist sisters.

Bobbie was staring at her, probably wondering why she hadn't responded to her comments about her housemates. "I'm sure you're a big help to that medical student," Susan said. "You're as knowledgeable as any doctor I've met."

"Some doctors are brilliant, like my boss. She knows so much about everything."

"Sounds like you admire Dr. Stolz. How do you like working with her?" asked Susan, adjusting her expression so she wouldn't look too curious.

"I do. She's always fair to the staff. She made sure I got health insurance even though I'm only part time. That was unexpected but generous."

"Yes, it is."

"Like most surgeons, she doesn't have the best bedside manner," said Bobbie, settling back in her chair. "She's an old-fashioned doc. She still does physical exams. The connection is important. Plus, it forces her to slow down and engage with the patient. She's brilliant and can diagnose a patient on the spot. It's hard for her to let the patient go on about their symptoms. Sometimes, she cuts them off before they're ready to stop talking. Sounds crazy, but listening is treatment too."

"No, I completely understand," said Susan, "That's what pastoral counseling is all about. People want someone to listen, to be present. I bet you're good at that."

"Nurses are trained to listen and be observant. Surgeons are too, but their focus is on solving problems. Their goal is to get in, fix it, and get out. Even follow-ups can be a burden for them. I was an OR nurse for years. I've seen surgeons patiently root around in someone's guts for hours and then find it hard to touch the patient again. They send the junior docs or their PAs to handle the post-op." Bobbie gave Susan a quick, guilty look. "Sorry to talk about guts after we've just finished eating."

"I have a strong stomach."

Bobbie frowned. "I've said too much. You're friends with Liz's wife. I wouldn't want anything negative getting back to her."

"Don't worry. Priests are good at keeping confidences."

Bobbie's eyes scanned her face. "I never think of you as a minister."

Susan was about to explain that in the Episcopal Church, she was called a priest. But that fine point could wait for another time. "You just ate dinner in a rectory," she replied dryly.

"I wasn't raised with religion, so I don't have any context. It doesn't mean anything to me."

"Come to one of my services and see me in action. Maybe that will make it real for you."

Bobbie looked skeptical. "I try to stay away from churches. I don't like the way they treat women and gay people."

"Christians have gotten a bad reputation for intolerance. Episcopalians are better than most, although we have our dark side. No pressure. I usually do the nine o'clock service in the summer chapel."

"That little stone church right on the ocean? It's beautiful there. Maybe you'll see me. No promises."

"That's fine too."

Bobbie studied her empty plate. "Sundays are hard. I like to give the girls the weekend off. They're not girls, of course, although they seem like that to me. I don't know what I'd do without them. They cover for me while I'm at work or out shopping or just need to get out for some fresh air."

"Are you Joyce's primary caregiver?" Susan asked gently, hoping it didn't sound like she was prying.

"Yes."

"It takes a special person to do something like that. How long have you been doing it?"

"I've done private duty nursing since I went back to school to get my CNP and needed money to pay my tuition."

Susan glanced around the table at the empty dishes and half-eaten casserole. "Would you like more to eat, or can I clear the table?"

Bobbie patted her midriff. "I'd love more, but I'm trying to be good. Dr. Pelletier says I need to lose a few pounds."

"Lead us not into temptation," said Susan, getting up to cover the casserole with plastic wrap. She slid it into the refrigerator. "Would you like dessert now? It's nothing fancy, just a parfait made of wild blueberries, vanilla yogurt, and home-made granola. I learned that one from my mother too."

"Did you pick the blueberries?"

"I did."

"Then I will definitely have some, but can we wait a few minutes for our dinner to digest?"

"Sure," said Susan with a smile, hoping that meant Bobbie would stay longer.

❋❋❋

Liz listened to Lucy coming into the kitchen. The legs of the stool scraped softly as it was pulled from the island. Lucy usually dumped her laptop bag on the seat. The refrigerator opened. Liz had left a wine glass on the counter. Bare feet padded across the wood floor in the hall leading to the screen porch. Liz moved over on the wicker settee, but Lucy ignored the space and sat down on her lap.

"Lucy, do I look like a chair?"

"You didn't get up to hug me, so I'll get one any way I can." Lucy took a sip of wine and set down the glass. "I need hugs!"

Liz gathered Lucy in her arms and pulled her close. "Bad day?"

"Not especially bad, just busy. Very busy." Lucy curled up, making herself small. Being slight, she weighed very little. "I know it's really hot, but I just need you to hold me."

"Okay, but it is hot."

"Don't worry. I won't stay long."

Liz's fingertips unconsciously counted the vertebrae in Lucy's spine. "Tell me why your day was so busy."

"So many fires to put out and meetings! Denise got her singing engagement calendar set up, so we met with Maggie about filling in while she's away. Now, I have to figure out how to make it okay with the vestry. Maggie doesn't want any money, so that helps. But if this goes on, Denise will have to make some decisions...and you'll have to deal with seeing your ex more regularly."

"I think I can manage. I'm an adult."

"Sometimes."

Liz made a face even though Lucy couldn't see it.

"If Maggie's around, we'll probably see Sam more often, which I'm sure you'll like."

"I will. I miss Sam. She's been so busy between her museum project and her new lover. Can't spare time for her old fishing buddy."

"I'm sure people say that about us. We've been keeping to ourselves." Lucy sat up and moved off Liz's lap, leaving the high-performance fabric of Liz's shorts damp from their shared perspiration. The sultry evening was too hot for such close contact. Lucy picked up her wine glass. "I found out today why Reshma delayed her ordination."

"Why?" Liz asked because she was supposed to, although church business really didn't interest her.

"You know I can't tell you," Lucy teased with a little smile.

"Oh, shit, Lucy. Then why bring it up?"

"Because you asked why my day was busy, and I'm telling you. How was your day?"

Liz shrugged. "Uneventful. The usual summer complaints: tick bites, pulled muscles from hiking or cycling, allergies, UTIs, cuts and bruises. Nothing exciting. Cherie stopped by on her day off. Her Aunt Simone is back."

"I know. I saw her. They stopped in at my office too. Sounds like she likes that new senior residence. I'm glad they found room for her."

"Me too." Liz drained her beer bottle. "Did you solve Reshma's problem?"

"No, but I gave her some context to explore it. She's upset with all the homophobia the Lambeth Conference has stirred up. Like we all are."

"I saw the article in the paper about the bishop in the *Press Herald*. Almost made me feel sorry for the little prick. His husband is so tall, he looks like a midget standing next to him."

"Liz. Be nice. People probably say the same about us."

"It's different for women. I'm tall. You're petite. Short men have a reputation for having something to prove, and your bishop fits the bill."

"Admit it, Liz. You just don't like him."

"He's a pompous asshole. Likes all the attention focused on *him*."

"Can't argue that point." Lucy glanced in the direction of the kitchen. "I'm getting hungry. I smell something good cooking."

"The garden is giving us so many eggplants, peppers, and zucchini I don't know what to do with them. It's too hot to run the stove, so I threw them in the slow cooker with some tomatoes and made ratatouille. I'll make couscous and grill some lamb chops."

"Now, I'm even hungrier."

Liz got up. "I'll get you a snack to hold you over. Cucumber slices with hummus sound good?"

"Perfect." Lucy gave Liz a hug around the hips. "You are the best. I love you."

"You love me because I feed you."

"No, I love you for you. Not what you do for me."

"Uh huh," said Liz and headed to the kitchen. She took out the lamb chops to take off the chill and dusted them with za'atar. Then she prepared Lucy's snack.

"That should keep you for a few minutes while I finish making dinner," she said, setting the plate on the table next to Lucy. "I'm going out to light the grill."

"One thing before you leave." Lucy beckoned with a crooked finger. Her green eyes smiled in a way that told Liz exactly what she wanted. When she bent to kiss her, Lucy's hand snared the back of her neck to keep their faces close.

"I know you're hungry," said Liz when Lucy finally let her go, "but that hummus will be more satisfying."

"I don't know about that. Give me another kiss and we'll see." Lucy smiled seductively.

The kiss stirred some heat, so Liz gently pushed Lucy back in her seat. "Let me make dinner. We can get into mischief later."

While Liz waited for the grill to come up to temperature, she watched Lucy through the porch window. The sexy overture had taken effort. Now that Lucy thought she was unobserved, she had that frazzled, worn-out look that came from being "on" all day. Liz came back in to get the chops. "Lucy, you look deep in thought. What else is going on?"

"My publisher sent out advance review copies of my book. Some of the biggest journals refused them because of the subject."

"You knew that might happen. Are they especially conservative?"

"Yes, but some of the mainstream journals refused it too."

"Don't read too much into it. Others will pick it up. Sometimes, it depends on their publication schedule. You can resubmit it. Besides, academics put too much emphasis on journals that no one cares about anymore."

"I bet you didn't say that when you were at Yale," Lucy challenged indignantly.

"Peer review is essential in medicine. It's about the validation and dissemination of data, not tenure."

"I didn't go back to school to be a professor. I did it so people would take my book seriously."

"And did they?" Liz picked up a cucumber slice and raked it through the hummus.

"Hey, that's mine," Lucy protested, but Liz held it out of reach. "Liz, I'm hungry. Stop eating my snack. Go cook."

Liz bowed theatrically. "As you wish, Madam Bartlett."

She returned from the kitchen with the lamb chops. Lucy followed her out to the deck and parked herself on a lounge chair.

"What can I do to cheer you up?" asked Liz. "You look so discouraged."

"Well, I am. Even my publisher is surprised by the rejections."

"Don't worry. I'm sure you'll end up with tons of reviews. Sex is one topic no one can resist. And people are getting heated up about sex because of the election—abortion, birth control, gender identity, gay rights. That will get you publicity. Maybe not what you were hoping for, of course."

"Why is sex the Right's favorite culture war issue? And the Catholic Church!" Lucy raised her eyes toward the sky. "Forbidding politicians Communion because they support abortion rights? Come on!"

"Men want to control women. Simple as that. One step forward. Three steps back. Erika and I often talked about how the cycle of progress and regression constantly repeats."

Lucy gazed into the distance with a thoughtful expression. "I wonder what she'd say about all the rejections."

"Probably the same thing I said. I know Erika's not here but consider me her agent." Liz held her hand over her heart.

"Except that Erika expressed her thoughts more tactfully, without all the tough love."

"Sorry, but I flunked tact."

Lucy raised an auburn brow. "You can be tactful when you need to be. You just enjoy 'telling it like it is'...for shock value."

"No, because I learned that ripping off the Band-Aid hurts less...just like they say."

Lucy looked skeptical.

"Luce, have another glass of wine. Enjoy your dinner. Then we'll go to bed. After I give you multiple orgasms, you won't even remember you wrote a book."

Lucy shook her head, but at least, she was smiling.

4

Liz looked up to see the outline of a stocky woman in the doorway. She had gently counseled Bobbie about the recent weight gain, but she knew the cause of her stress eating, so she didn't push it.

When she'd come in for the interview, Bobbie was candid about her situation. She'd explained that she was the caregiver of a family member but wanted to work part-time to keep her nursing license active and fund her Social Security. "I really need the social interaction," Bobbie confessed. "I feel so isolated."

Making the decision to hire Bobbie was easy. Her quick laugh and affable manner were infectious. Liz, who liked to deadpan during interviews, found herself smiling at her dry wit. Bobbie was hands down the most qualified of the applicants. She'd had extensive experience in physicians' offices and her training in geriatrics would come in handy in a town where the median age was over fifty.

Although it was obvious, Liz asked, "You looking for me?"

"Only if you have time. I don't want to interrupt anything."

"You're not." Liz closed her laptop. "I was reading the medical news while I wait for my wife. We're taking The Wet Lady out for a run tonight. The tenants in the beach house are coming along."

"Oh, that sounds lovely. I envy you."

"Maybe you can join us sometime. It would be fun."

Bobbie's smile gradually faded. Liz could guess what she was thinking. As much as Bobbie would like to accept the invitation, she knew she couldn't. Liz couldn't imagine being trapped in a situation like hers, but she knew many people were. Yet Bobbie was always pleasant and cheerful, except when she thought no one was looking. Then the stress pinched her pretty face.

Liz pointed to the visitors' chair and leaned back. "Tell me what's on your mind, Bobbie." She uncrossed her arms, hearing Lucy in her head, scolding her for the closed body language.

"None of my business really, but I was just wondering how much your wife knows about my situation."

The question surprised Liz, but she could honestly say, "Nothing."

"But you're married. Surely you—"

Liz showed her palms. "No, we don't. Lucy is very fussy about keeping professional confidences, and being a therapist and a priest, she's doubly bound." She sat up straight. "Bobbie, what's your concern?"

"Lucy and Susan went to seminary together. Susan told me they were once very close."

Liz debated how to address this statement without revealing too much. Finally, she decided to be frank. "They were close in school and when they worked together in Boston, but that was a long time ago. Before Susan came to Hobbs last summer, Lucy hadn't heard from her for years."

"Oh, I just assumed because Lucy was so kind, bringing her sheets, calling you to fix the plumbing…"

"That's just how Lucy is." For obvious reasons, Liz didn't add that she thought Lucy was overdoing the kindness out of guilt.

"Don't you share information about your mutual patients?" Bobbie asked, looking skeptical. Most couples discussed everything, so Liz could understand why Bobbie found it hard to believe.

"We do sometimes ask each other for advice. In that case, we might discuss a person's situation in theory, names omitted to protect the guilty. It makes for some interesting conversations."

"I bet."

"But we don't gossip about our coworkers, if that's what you're asking. When you started at the practice, I didn't run home and say, 'Guess what? My new nurse practitioner is living with a woman who has Alzheimer's!'"

Bobbie laughed. "No, Liz, I can't imagine you doing that. But I haven't told Susan much about my home life. I like her, and I don't want to scare her off. I'm still figuring out how to explain the situation."

Liz sat forward in her chair, torn between wanting to warn Bobbie and minding her own business. "Bobbie, I'm glad you've made a friend. Susan is a kind person and very supportive. She helped Lucy through a tough time, but be careful. There are things you don't know about…"

Neither of them had noticed the woman standing in the doorway.

"Oh, you're busy," Lucy said, looking apologetic. "I'll wait outside."

"No, it's okay, Luce. Come in. We're just wrapping up."

"Let me get out of here," said Bobbie, rising, "so you can go on with your evening plans. Nice to see you again, Dr. Bartlett."

"Please, I don't answer to Dr. Bartlett. It's still so new. Just call me Lucy."

Liz watched Bobbie melt under Lucy's radiant smile. Everyone did. "Her parishioners call her Mother Lucy."

"It's an old practice to call priests 'father,'" Lucy explained. "Some female clergy don't like being called 'mother,' but it's never bothered me."

"It fits you," said Bobbie after a long evaluation. She hurried to add, "I'm not saying you look motherly, Lucy. You just have such a kind face and the most beautiful smile."

Lucy nodded graciously, accustomed to people complimenting her smile. "Thanks, Bobbie."

"Well, I'll let you go. I need to get home. Enjoy your boat ride."

After Bobbie left, Lucy turned to Liz. "You should invite her to join us on the boat sometime. I bet she'd enjoy it."

"I did invite her, but it's hard for her to work it into her schedule." Liz knew from the instant change in Lucy's eyes that she'd read the subtext.

"There's a story there," she said with a shrewd look.

"Always is."

✱✱✱

From the door to the waiting room, Bobbie watched Liz and Lucy walk hand in hand to the truck, a charming reminder that they were still newlyweds.

"Lucky them," said Ginny, standing beside Bobbie. "They get to go for an evening cruise with their friends. I have to get home to make dinner for my husband."

"I know what you mean." Bobbie hadn't meant to sound bitter, but she had to rush home to relieve Chloe and feed Joyce. Staying late to talk to Liz had been pure procrastination.

Ginny gave Bobbie a sympathetic look. She knew Joyce's condition from her records and office visits. Bobbie forced a smile. She didn't want pity for her situation. She'd chosen it.

"I read in the paper this morning that since the pandemic, we've all forgotten how to have fun," Ginny said. "We need to rediscover how to relax and have a good time." She took a ring of keys out of her pocket. "Are you almost ready to go, so I can lock up?"

"Sure. Let me get my things from my locker. I won't be a minute."

"Don't rush. I'll wait for you."

Bobbie silently thanked the woman for her kindness. From the doctors to the medical assistants, everyone in this practice had gone out of their way for her. Liz set the tone. Although she could be gruff when she had something on her mind, she was basically kind. What a difference from the aloof, defensive attitude of Bobbie's Westchester practice. Dr. Amy Hsu, another recent transplant from the New York suburbs, often commiserated with Bobbie over their previous employers. Everything was different in Maine, even the staff in the grocery store. Instead of grunting and avoiding eye contact, they smiled and wished you a nice day.

Ginny locked up the main door and waved on her way to her car. Bobbie had been tempted to confide in the friendly woman who seemed able to listen to the most pitiful complaints with perfect equanimity. She was the one who calmed anxious patients and found a place in the schedule for the desperate. She had an impressive layman's knowledge of medicine. According to Liz, Ginny had come with the practice when it changed hands.

"We have to keep her until she retires because she knows where all the bodies are buried." Liz liked to say things like that to shock people, but everyone was on to her.

When Bobbie got home, Joyce was in the family room watching TV. She'd always been obsessed with the weather, but now the Weather Channel played constantly. If Bobbie asked about the forecast, Joyce could never remember. Early on, it had been one of the first signs that her memory was going.

Chloe looked up from her textbook and smiled. "Hey, Bobbie. How was your day?"

"Thank you, it was quiet for this time of year. How is Joyce doing?"

"Mostly a good day. She's enjoying this special on famous hurricanes." Bobbie glanced at Joyce, disappointed that being talked about hadn't gotten her attention.

"Would you like to join us for dinner?" she asked Chloe.

"No, thanks. I'm meeting with my study group for pizza tonight."

"Sounds like fun."

"Believe me. The pizza will be the only fun part." Chloe collected her books and tablet from the sofa.

"Chloe, before you go, I wanted to ask you a favor." The young woman stopped and looked attentive. "A friend invited me to a concert in Portland on Sunday afternoon. Would you be willing to stay with Joyce for a couple of hours?"

"Let me check." Chloe scrolled through her phone. "Looks like I'm free this Sunday."

"I'll pay you for the time."

"You don't have to. I live here for nothing. You're always feeding me."

"I know, but I'll pay you anyway. Joyce put aside money for her care."

"If you insist. I can always use the money. My student loans keep me poor."

"The concert starts at two. If I could count on you to be here from about one-thirty to five, that would be great."

"No problem," replied the young woman, tossing her long, blond hair over her shoulder. "Makes me feel less guilty for all you do for me."

After she left, Bobbie reached over and took Joyce's hand. She waited until Joyce gave her eye contact before asking, "How are you? Did you have a good day?"

"Big storms!" said Joyce, gesturing to the television. "Storms...called..."

"Hurricanes," supplied Bobbie, knowing what she was struggling to say. Bobbie always tried to maintain an even tone because Joyce was sensitive to sounds. She complained that the TV was too loud when Bobbie could barely hear it. She interpreted any change of volume as irritation and could become aggressive.

Joyce gave her a measuring look. "That color…good…on you." Bobbie was surprised because Joyce had always hated pink. Her mother had made her wear it to distinguish her from her fraternal twin. She'd said she hated it even more after her brother died in a waterskiing accident in his twenties. Knowing Joyce's aversion, Bobbie seldom wore any shade of pink, but that morning she'd put on the first scrubs she'd found in the drawer.

"Are you ready for some dinner?" Bobbie asked, rousing faux enthusiasm despite her fatigue. Being a nurse for years had made it second nature to sound cheerful even when she wasn't.

"What's for dinner?"

"One of your favorites—stuffed haddock."

Joyce made a face. "Fish. Again?"

Bobbie managed to keep smiling. "I'm sorry. You always liked fish. I can make something else."

"No. You tell people…I'm fussy." Lately, Joyce seemed more worried about what other people thought.

"Let me go cook," said Bobbie. "Are you all right in here? Should I leave on the TV?"

"Yes."

"I'll bring you a protein drink."

"No, don't want one."

"Okay," said Bobbie with a sigh and headed to the kitchen.

❋❋❋

Lucy's therapy training had taught her to notice every gesture, so her eyes instantly caught Courtney's hand covertly reaching for Melissa's. Their fingers tenderly entwined, and Melissa moved closer. Sensing that Lucy was aware, Courtney looked up. Her cheeks flushed pink. Lucy smiled to indicate her approval, but Courtney dropped Melissa's hand.

Lucy hoped the charged political climate surrounding LGBT topics in the classroom hadn't driven Courtney back into the closet. She'd come such a long way in accepting her sexuality. When she'd first come to Hobbs, she tried to hide the fact that she was dating Melissa. When they were in public, Courtney pretended she didn't even know her.

Lucy understood that the position of elementary school principal in a small town was sensitive, especially now that every school board meeting had become a battlefield. Even in tolerant Maine, the culture wars were heating up again. The popular female governor was up for reelection. A well-intended, deliberately vague video, created by a kindergarten teacher to explain trans, was running day and night as part of an attack ad. Its ominous message: the radical, liberal governor supports grooming youth.

In such a hostile environment, Courtney was understandably worried about her sexuality becoming public, but on a boat far from shore, there were no disapproving parents to point fingers or wagging tongues to carry the tale. With her friends, Courtney should feel relaxed enough to express affection for her partner. Lucy put her hand on Liz's thigh to set a positive example. Predictably, Liz turned and planted a soft kiss on Lucy's lips. Out of the corner of her eye, Lucy saw Melissa subtly nod in approval.

"Where's Kaylee today?" Liz asked, putting her arm around Lucy. "Is she with her father?"

That seemed to make Courtney relax. Lucy knew she looked up to Liz and often went to her for advice.

"Doug took her to Boston for the weekend."

"Lots for kids to do there. I used to take Maggie's grandkids and my nieces' kids to the Boston Museum of Science."

"I think it's on the agenda. Of course, the main event is the Sox game. If they have time, they plan to walk the Freedom Trail. Phys-Ed teachers aren't known for their intellects, but Doug loves history."

"Lots of guys are into history," Liz said. "At least, the Revolutionary War is one subject most Americans can agree on."

"Don't be surprised if they find a way to polarize that too," said Courtney bitterly, which saddened Lucy.

She took back her hand because Liz shifted, sitting with her ankle on the opposite knee. The position was one of Liz's favorites, despite, or perhaps because, it was considered a "masculine" pose.

"The Right doesn't own patriotism," she said. "I'm sorry the Aix Festival made us miss Fourth of July this year. Lucy and I are thinking of having a party. We can't provide fireworks, but we could have a picnic on the water like we always do."

"Fireworks are fun, but it's the company that makes it special," said Melissa. "And the food! When are you planning to do this?"

Liz shrugged. "Maybe the weekend after Lucy's concert at the cathedral. Hopefully, Brenda is off. I'd like to invite them and their kids. I'll invite Sam and Maggie and the grandkids. Can you get Kaylee that day?"

"If I talk to Doug early enough, I can probably arrange it."

Liz nudged Lucy. "You should invite your daughter and Denise."

"I will. And you should invite Susan," said Lucy, which drew a stare from Courtney. "I know it's awkward because you're her boss, but so am I. She knows hardly anyone in Hobbs. She needs opportunities to meet people."

"I'm hoping she makes some friends among the staff. We love having experienced teachers like her. People who've taught in urban schools have special skills. She's great with the kids, but she seems shy."

"I think she's trying to figure out how to fit in here," said Lucy. "We have a tight-knit community, but one that's not always kind to strangers."

"What brought her back to Hobbs?" Courtney glanced at her empty wine glass. Liz got up to refill it.

"She's a New Englander by birth," Lucy said. "South Dakota was too desolate for her."

"I'm not sure I could ever live in such a rural place," said Melissa.

"You think Maine is too rural," scoffed Courtney, "and Boston is a small town compared to New York."

"Well, it is," Melissa insisted. "There's no place like New York."

"I have to agree," Liz flatly stated in a voice so full of authority that no one would dare question it. Lucy wasn't fond of that trick, despite understanding that it was a vestige of a time when female surgeons were scarce, and Liz always had to assert her position. No matter how hard she tried to overcome her conditioning, it still poked through like sharp twigs.

"Lucy, how well do you know Susan?" asked Courtney. "I was surprised she didn't list you as a reference."

Liz inappropriately chuckled. Lucy gently elbowed her. "I know her very well. As in the Biblical sense."

Melissa's mouth formed a perfectly round circle.

"I know…the tangled webs we weave," Lucy said. "Susan and I went to seminary together. She helped me get through a particularly difficult time. And…" Lucy decided to let the explanation trail off there. Her young tenants didn't have to know everything about her. "Liz, maybe you should invite Bobbie, so Susan has company at the party." Liz turned and gave her a sharp look. Lucy ignored it and continued making suggestions for the guest list. "And don't forget to invite Amy Hsu. You know that Olivia will be furious if she's not invited. She's very sensitive to being an outsider."

"Well, if she weren't so overbearing, people would find her more approachable," Courtney said to Lucy's surprise. Usually, Courtney avoided political comments because of her position. "I know she's generous and saved your wedding reception, but she always has this take-no-prisoners attitude."

"Which is exactly why we need to include her," said Lucy. "We need to show her that she's accepted in the community."

By this point, Liz was glowering. Lucy knew she had taken her spousal privilege too far. "I'm sorry, sweetie," she said, gently stroking Liz's thigh to mollify her. "It's your party and you invite anyone you want."

"It sounds like a great party, Lucy, but The Wet Lady will sink under the weight of all those passengers." Despite her obvious annoyance, Liz got up to refill Lucy's wine glass.

"So why do we have to have it on the boat? Why not on the deck? It will be like our Thirsty Thursday parties. We can invite Tom and Jeff to join us…

and Tony and Fred. With Maggie here, we'll have great entertainment. You know what they say, 'build a longer table, not a higher fence.' We should be glad that our community is growing." Lucy nudged her wife for a reaction. Liz's grimace, pretending to be a smile, showed her clenched teeth.

Liz turned to Melissa and Courtney for sympathy. "See what happens when you marry a priest? Every situation becomes an opportunity for a sermon."

Melissa shook her head. "Lucy's right about maintaining good will in our little community. Olivia has been a big help to you professionally. You want to stay on her good side."

Lucy could see that Liz was warming to the idea. Her ankle returned to the opposite knee.

"I think Olivia's granddaughters are coming up soon," said Melissa.

"I like the idea of having more kids at the party," Courtney said. "Kaylee will love it."

Everyone turned to Liz expectantly. "I guess I'm outnumbered. Let's look at the calendar and plan something at the house."

❊❊❊

Dusk was Liz's signal to return to the harbor. She never liked to navigate the open ocean after dark. When they docked, Melissa and Courtney offered to stay behind to help shut down the boat. Usually, Liz would be grateful for the help, but she wasn't ready to leave.

"Thanks, but I think we'll stay and watch evening come on. You're welcome to join us." She secretly hoped they would decline. She wanted some time alone with Lucy after a busy week. When the young women decided to go home, she silently rejoiced. They took their cooler and headed down the dock.

"Nice kids," Liz murmured for Lucy's ears only.

"They're not kids, Liz. They're in their forties."

"Young enough to be my daughters. Emily could be my granddaughter."

"Mine too. I was nearly forty when I gave birth to her."

"That's a stretch, Lucy, but there are forty-year-old grandmothers." Liz pulled her sling chair closer and reached for Lucy's hand. "Thank you for agreeing to stay a while. At least here, we can sit outside without being eaten alive by mosquitoes."

"I love the way the waves rock us. I especially like being alone with you." Lucy hand stroked the inside of Liz's thigh, going tantalizingly close to her crotch.

"You're off tomorrow, and so am I. We could be lazy and sleep on the boat."

"Hmm," intoned Lucy, "sounds sexy. It's good to switch things up to keep sex fresh."

"Not much headroom in the sleeping berth. Won't that cramp your style?"

Lucy smiled slyly. "I'm not as tall as you, so I have more options. And I left some of our toys in the night table the last time we slept on the boat." Liz mimed alarm, which made Lucy laugh. "We'll have time for that later. Let's just sit here and look at the stars."

Liz looked up. The moonless sky was beautiful. Not a cloud in the sky. The light breeze was refreshing.

"Liz, I want to commend you for being open to a bigger party. I know it's more work for us, but it will make so many people happy. You should be proud of your role in creating our community of friends. You came up here, formed a bond with Tony and the Webhanet Playhouse, took over a failing family practice. You held Maggie hostage until she agreed to live with you. You encouraged Erika to buy the beach house. You talked Sam into renovating the house on Jimson Pond. You kept us together during the pandemic, and you grow our community by inviting new people."

"It's not something I planned. It just happened." Liz felt Lucy studying her face. "Don't tell me it's God working in strange ways."

"I wasn't, but why did you look so strange when I suggested inviting Bobbie Lantry? I know you like her. I do too."

"I don't want to encourage her friendship with Susan."

Lucy contorted her face into exaggerated disapproval. "Liz, I know you're not a Susan fan, but she's not a bad person."

"Neither is Bobbie."

Lucy tugged on Liz's arm to encourage her to look at her. "Sweetie, what aren't you telling me?"

Liz reached for her wine glass and shrugged. "Nothing."

"Liz! What's going on?"

"Lucy, it's privileged."

Once Liz used their code word, Lucy instantly backed off. The interrogation might have ended, but Lucy had that sly look. She'd get it out of Liz one way or the other.

5

"Dr. Bartlett, we'd like to set up your microphone."

Liz, who'd been scrolling through her phone because she was bored, looked up to see what Lucy would say.

"Thank you, Michael, but I don't usually sing with amplification unless I'm outdoors or in an enormous setting like a sports arena." The technician looked skeptical, but Liz knew Lucy wasn't bragging. She'd heard her sing from the stage of the Metropolitan Opera. Not only would her powerful voice carry in Portland's small cathedral, it would shake the roof timbers. At the thought, Liz rubbed her hands together in gleeful anticipation.

"A mic for you, Ms. Chantal?" the technician asked, turning to Denise.

"No, thanks." Denise had a strong voice too, but unlike Lucy's simple statement of fact, hers was full of bravado.

The young man was stowing the mic headsets in their case when Lucy touched his shoulder. "On second thought, when I sing the duet with Maggie Fitzgerald, I should have a mic. On Broadway, amplification is the style now." Liz slid down in the pew and made a face. She could remember when singers were expected to project in a theater. Her Broadway experience went back to hearing the original cast perform *The Sound of Music*.

The technician outfitted Lucy and Maggie with their mics. Liz watched curiously as he tested the sound from various locations in the cathedral. AV technology had changed so much since she'd sat in the production booth of her prep school auditorium and managed stage for college plays. The theater work had cut into Liz's study time, but she would have done anything to spend time with Maggie. *Fifty years ago*, Liz realized after a mental calculation, awed by the idea of that much time passing.

She watched Maggie work with the technician. Her ex-wife was theatrical even when she wasn't on stage. Theater work had trained her to stand and move in a considered way. Combined with her carefully applied makeup and her long, white hair, styled in a dramatic braid, her theatricality evoked the old-fashioned glamour of a golden-age movie star. At seventy, she could still compel the eye. Liz turned her attention to Lucy. In a casual setting like this dress rehearsal, she looked relaxed in jeans and a loose-fitting T-shirt that tended to fall fetchingly off one shoulder. She had no need to put on a show. Her natural beauty ensured that everyone looked at her, no matter what she wore or how she stood, although her opera training had given her a regal bearing and perfect posture.

Liz tried not to compare them, but it was impossible, especially when she saw them together. Personality-wise, the women she'd married couldn't be more different. Maggie always worried what other people thought; Lucy seemed to know their thoughts as if she could read their minds. Liz knew that Lucy wasn't an actual mind reader. She just listened intently and carefully observed people's behavior.

After some fiddling with the microphones, Lucy and Maggie launched into their signature duet from *Wicked*. The lyrics, describing how two bitter enemies become friends, had new meaning since the divorce and Lucy's marriage to Liz. She could see a subtle shift in their stage gestures and hear it in the phrasing when they sang. Things were different now.

After they'd run through all the Broadway numbers, the technician made one last sound check. Liz listened with a critical ear while Lucy sang her opera arias to the orchestra's accompaniment. Her voice had changed since she was on the roster of principal sopranos at the Metropolitan Opera. Compared to her recordings, her voice had grown deeper and more richly textured. Her interpretations were more nuanced, a gift of age and experience. Ironically, this second act of her career could be more significant than the first. Already, conductors were lining up to cast her for concerts and recordings.

At the end of the rehearsal, the orchestra members called their goodbyes as they packed up their instruments. Liz waited until Lucy finished her conversation with the conductor before approaching.

"How did I do?" Lucy asked.

"Superb, as always."

Lucy looked skeptical. "I hope you're not just saying that."

"You know I'm a compulsive truth teller."

"I'm not sure about that."

Liz searched for a way to express her thoughts tactfully. "Your voice isn't as bright as on your recordings, but it's gained so much depth."

"That's fairly typical of sopranos," said Lucy with a sigh. "Thanks for being honest. I trust your opinion. You've heard a lot of great singers in your day."

"You're still a great singer, Lucy. Don't sell yourself short."

"But I know this second chance is only a reprieve. Kiri Te Kanawa stopped singing because she couldn't stand to hear her own voice. That day will come for me too."

The sad look on Lucy's face made Liz want to scoop her up into her arms. She understood Lucy's fears. When she'd first noticed a slight loss of dexterity, she knew that her career as a surgeon would soon end. The arthritis that had afflicted her mother and grandmother had been creeping into her joints. Liz had spent a decade preparing to become a surgeon, and then suddenly, her time in the OR was over. "None of us is what we were. We're different, and in some ways, better." She put her arm around Lucy's shoulder to reassure her. "What do you say we go to the Eventide Oyster Company for dinner?"

Lucy glanced over to where Maggie and Denise were chatting. "We should invite the others to come along, don't you think?"

Liz saw her hopes for an impromptu date night dissolve, but she knew Lucy was right. They should include their friends, especially since they'd gone out of their way to appear in Lucy's concert. Tony Roselli had to leave early, but she would invite Maggie and Denise.

Maggie's hazel eyes studied her as she approached and narrowed for a moment. Almost instantly, she slipped into actress mode, and the wariness disappeared.

"Lucy and I are going for oysters. Would you ladies like to join us?"

"Thanks, Liz, but I can't," Denise replied instantly. "Reshma and I are cooking dinner for Emily tonight." She glanced at her phone. "Sorry, but I need to go...*this minute*." She reached out and patted Maggie's arm. "Thanks for pinch hitting for me while I'm on the road. I really appreciate it."

"You're very welcome. You've done a wonderful job with the choir. I look forward to working with them again," she called after Denise as she hurried out.

Liz tried to hide her impatience while Maggie considered her invitation. "Sure, Liz. I'll join you," she finally said. "I'm on my own tonight, and fresh oysters are better than heating up leftovers."

"I forgot that Sam is on the West Coast."

"Hopefully, this interview gets her the commission for that women's museum. She thinks she has a good chance."

"The other architects are amateurs compared to Sam, but they're trendy, so they have an edge." Liz's animosity towards Sam's much younger competitors went beyond loyalty to a friend. She resented the lack of objective standards applied to Sam's work and the fickleness of a culture driven by "influencers," people with no special expertise or talent except the ability to get likes on social media. Liz hated living in a world where all opinions, no matter how ignorant or biased, were equal. "I hope Sam enters more contests and gets her juju back."

"She told me she entered this one just for fun."

"Maybe. Between you and me, she's afraid to take it too seriously. Winning would make her want to go back to architecture, and she doesn't know how her work will be received."

Maggie studied her carefully. "That's an interesting observation. I've thought the same thing. But you've known Sam longer."

"After she won all those awards, she was under a lot of pressure. When people started saying she was only getting commissions because of affirmative action, she was crushed. Sam wasn't the most confident person to begin with. Her mother really did a number on her self-esteem." Liz stopped herself, worried that she had already said too much. Maggie was a saver. She held onto information to use later, but too late now. Any damage had already been done.

"Come on," said Liz. "Let's see if we can get into the restaurant before the dinner crowd arrives. I can drop you back here later. Parking is so hard to find in the Old Port."

"Maggie's joining us? That's great," said Lucy, smiling as they approached. Liz knew Lucy's smile was sincere, but she didn't trust Maggie's. After all this time, Liz still didn't know when she was acting. "Denise couldn't make it?" Lucy asked, looking around for her.

"She and Reshma are making dinner for Emily," Liz explained.

"Oh, that's nice," said Lucy, but her tone contradicted her words. Liz wondered why.

When they got to the Old Port, the nearest parking garages were full, and they had to walk a long distance to the restaurant. Fortunately, the wait to be seated was only twenty minutes. A temporary bar had been set up in the roped-in area on the sidewalk. Liz ordered a sudsy IPA for herself and a bottle of white wine for Lucy and Maggie. While Maggie occupied Lucy with her plans for the choir in Denise's absence, Liz watched the passersby.

After they were seated, Lucy excused herself to use the ladies' room. Finding herself alone with Maggie, Liz forced a smile. "Glad you could join us. You always liked this place."

"Thanks for the invitation. It's nice to catch up with Lucy."

"It was her idea to invite you."

"I know, but you went along with it. I bet she didn't have to twist your arm. You'll do anything for her." Liz silently counted to ten to avoid saying something she would regret. Maggie studied her face, and her expression softened. "You look good, Liz. Marriage to Lucy agrees with you."

Liz shifted uncomfortably, wondering where this was leading.

Maggie released her gaze and focused on the neighboring table. "Liz, I want things to be good between us because I'm going to be around more often. Sam asked me to move in with her."

Surprised, Liz sat up straight. "That doesn't sound like Sam. She likes her space. Did you push for it?"

"No, not at all. It was her idea."

Lucy returned and smiled at each of them, subtly taking the temperature of the conversation. "Did I miss the waitress?" she asked innocently.

"No, but you missed Maggie telling me that she's moving in with Sam."

"Really?" Lucy rarely showed surprise, but her lips parted slightly. "Wow."

Maggie unwrapped the cutlery and arranged it to align perfectly with the plate. "Lucy, it sounds like you don't approve."

"It's not that, Maggie. It just seems out of character for Sam to ask you or anyone to live with her. That doesn't mean I disapprove."

"I was surprised myself," Maggie admitted. "I was even more surprised when I told Alina, and she was happy about it. She's been seeing the news director at her station, and I think she'd like more privacy. The girls enjoy spending time after school with their friends, so I don't need to be there when they come home. Suddenly, I'm superfluous."

"I think you should see it as a positive," Lucy said in an encouraging tone. "Alina is finally moving on from her bad marriage. The kids are becoming established in the neighborhood, and you can have a life."

"But they don't need me anymore." Maggie's sadness was palpable.

"They still need you, Maggie, just not as constantly as before," Lucy said. "It's not a rejection. Be grateful you could be there when they really needed you."

"You understand, don't you, Liz?" asked Maggie, turning to her.

Liz hesitated to voice an opinion. Everything she said to Maggie became a bone of contention. "I'm glad Alina is finding her way. The girls are growing up. They're not babies anymore. They want to be with their friends. But honestly, I'm not sure moving in with Sam is a good idea."

"Why not?" Maggie challenged. "Don't tell me you're jealous!"

The accusation put Liz off balance because she was, in fact, jealous. She assumed the neutral expression she used with patients. "I'm just worried it's too soon."

"You should talk, Liz. The ink on our divorce papers was barely dry before you proposed to Lucy."

Lucy drew breath to intervene, but the waitress arrived to take their order. After she left, Lucy reached across the table and took Maggie's hand. "Why don't we just relax and enjoy our meal?"

Maggie gave Liz an overtly hostile look, but she remained silent. Obviously, time hadn't yet healed this wound.

***

When Bobbie opened the door to the common room, she heard Chloe calmly speaking to Joyce. The medical student already knew how the right tone could put a patient at ease. She would make an excellent doctor.

"Yes, it's a beautiful day. Would you like to spend some time outside?" she asked cheerfully as if she expected an answer. Joyce's communication in the last few days had been reduced to grunts. But that was how it was—good days and bad.

Bobbie knocked on the open door before coming into the room. The nod to privacy was directed toward Chloe rather than Joyce, but not completely. As she got older, Joyce had demanded more attention to social boundaries. In the beginning, they'd thought nothing of using the same bathroom or being naked while they'd dressed. Then Joyce decided she needed her own bathroom and took over the master bath. If she was naked when Bobbie came in, she anxiously covered her privates.

The withdrawal from intimacy was gradual, almost imperceptible. Even Bobbie, with special training in geriatric nursing, had failed to see it at first. Later she realized that she missed the signs because she didn't want to see them.

Other long-standing agreements began to shift. They used to divide the laundry by lights and darks. Bobbie had volunteered to do the light colors because they usually required less attention in the dryer. One day, Joyce declared she'd rather do her own laundry because she didn't like the way Bobbie handled it. With a shrug, Bobbie went along with the new system because it was easier than arguing.

They had innumerable arguments over things Bobbie told Joyce, but she couldn't remember. "You didn't tell me that," was a constant accusation.

Eventually, the denial softened into "I didn't know that," even though Bobbie knew that Joyce had once certainly known whatever it was. At least, the statement was less contentious, even if it was code for "I don't remember."

Chloe took in Bobbie's outfit and smiled. "You look really nice today," she said with obvious surprise. The young woman, who usually saw Bobbie in scrubs for work or the casual things she threw on to wear around the house, probably had no idea she owned other clothes. In the back of her closet, Bobbie had found a pantsuit she hadn't worn since her interview at Hobbs Family Practice. She'd made an effort with her appearance because of the concert. Instead of her usual dab of blush and dashed-on lipstick, she'd taken time with her makeup.

"I didn't know if this is a dress up occasion, but it's in a church." Bobbie assumed that people still dressed up for church, but she wouldn't know. Except for her mother's funeral, she hadn't been in one for years. She'd considered asking Liz what to wear, then decided she didn't want to seem ignorant.

"Joyce is talking about working in the garden today," said Chloe with an affectionate smile at her charge. Bobbie looked to Joyce for confirmation, but she didn't even stir at the mention of her name. That didn't necessarily mean things were getting worse. She'd been in and out for a while.

"Just make sure she's digging up the weeds and not the flowers," Bobbie said. She could remember a time when Joyce knew the name of every plant in the garden, even the Latin ones. She'd learned them from poring over the seed catalogs every winter in anticipation of spring. Now, Joyce would point to "the tall, yellow flower" or refer to "the pink things in the front." If Bobbie could remember the plant's name, she would supply it, otherwise she would simply say it was beautiful, and Joyce would agree.

After they'd bought the house, Joyce had planted all the borders and gardens. When she'd gone through a Victorian phase, she'd hauled heavy planters with tropical flowers out to the patio. The enormous, voluptuous leaves and obscenely bright flowers made their New England yard feel like a jungle. Unfortunately, the Maine summers were short, so the plants needed to be wheeled inside just a few months later. While they were still living in New York, the property management company watered them during the off-season. Bobbie finally got tired of picking up the yellowed leaves when they came up on weekends and asked the contractor to take the containers to the dump. By that point, Joyce didn't even notice.

Bobbie bent to kiss Joyce's forehead. "Enjoy your gardening. I'll be back soon."

A look of panic appeared on Joyce's face. "Be careful!" she warned ominously.

"I will. I promise."

The concern faded from Joyce's eyes. She'd already forgotten her worry.

"I promise to be back on time," Bobbie said, addressing Chloe this time.

"I'm not going anywhere. I have a big exam this week."

"Maybe I can help you study when I get back."

Chloe smiled. "That would be great."

Bobbie listed the snacks she'd prepared for them: raw vegetables, hummus, cut up fruit, each item carefully selected to keep Joyce healthy. When Bobbie began to explain where she'd put the snacks in the refrigerator, Chloe interrupted. "Bobbie, I know where everything is. Have a good time."

As Bobbie started her car, she was plagued by a nagging guilt that she was leaving Joyce with someone else while she went off to have a good time. She could easily justify leaving her when she went to work or shopped for groceries, but just to go to a concert with a friend? Liz kept encouraging her to make time for herself. "You know that exhausted caregivers put themselves at risk," she'd sternly warned. "You need to practice self-care too."

I know, Bobbie said, answering Liz in her mind.

The traffic was heavy on her way to St. Margaret's rectory. Even though the dashboard clock indicated there was plenty of time, she called Susan to say she might be late. "I haven't forgotten you," Bobbie said when Susan's warm alto greeted her. That's when Bobbie realized she'd only called to hear her voice.

"Don't rush. It's a concert, not a fire." Lately, sparks of subtle humor had been shooting up more often. Bobbie took it as a sign that Susan was warming up to her. She sometimes wondered how such a shy woman could be successful as a teacher and a priest. She guessed that something had put her off-balance. Maybe Susan would eventually tell her what it was.

Finally, Bobbie pulled into the rectory parking lot. The front door opened right away, and Susan came out, wearing a short-sleeved print sweater and black pants. She looked lovely, but Bobbie's eyes instantly went to the stiff, white band around her neck.

"Is this going to be a religious service?" she asked when Susan got into the car.

"No, but I usually wear my collar to church events to show that I'm clergy. The bishop will be there, and I'm new to the diocese."

The church protocol made little sense to Bobbie, but she understood needing to play by the rules when you're new. "Will Lucy Bartlett be wearing her collar too?"

Susan laughed. "No, she'll be wearing one of her gorgeous concert gowns. I bet you won't even recognize her."

"Hard not to…with that red hair. You can spot her a mile away!"

"Yes, she does draw the eye, doesn't she?" agreed Susan with a strange expression that made Bobbie curious. "Now that you're over the shock of seeing the collar, do I look okay?"

Bobbie could honestly say, "You look beautiful."

"So do you."

"Thanks. I didn't know what to wear."

"You look perfect," said Susan with a frankly admiring look.

Bobbie smiled as she headed to the highway. "Do you like classical music?"

"I do," said Susan enthusiastically. "That's how I met Lucy. I was always a fan of opera. When I was a girl, my mother used to listen to the live Met broadcasts on the radio. It was our special thing to do together. My sister hated it. She'd close our bedroom door to keep out the 'noise.' When I was in New York at seminary, I'd watch Met performances from the standing room section."

"Is that how you met Lucy?"

"No, I met her when she sang for an ordination at St. John the Divine."

"So, you go back a ways," Bobbie concluded. That was a good sign. Bobbie considered long friendships an indication of stability.

"But we lost touch for a while," Susan continued. "I went out to the Midwest. She stayed in Boston until she became rector here."

Bobbie revised her thinking, although she'd come in and out of people's lives too. During her mother's illness, around the same time Joyce was diagnosed, she couldn't spare any time for her friends, and most had drifted away. Now, she was too embarrassed to get in touch with them.

"Will this concert be religious music?"

"Not according to the diocesan newsletter. And not just classical music, although that's Lucy's background. There will be some Broadway too."

"I heard Lucy was once a big star. Why did she stop singing?"

"She mentioned it in her book, so it's no longer confidential. I'll give you the short version. A powerful man at the Met sexually assaulted her. When she went to management to complain, they sided with him, and he had her blacklisted."

"God! That's horrible, but there was so much of that in those days. No one believed women when they complained. I remember doing all that sexual harassment training back in the nineties, but where powerful men were concerned, it didn't matter."

"No, even when they were caught, no one believed their accusers, who were risking their careers. Things haven't really changed. It's still going on."

The first signs for their destination were appearing along the highway. Bobbie turned to Susan. "When we get there, I could use your help finding this place. I haven't been in Portland much."

"Don't worry," said Susan. "I know where we're going."

***

The turnpike was jammed with vacationers heading north to Maine's rugged shores and peaceful lake country. As they approached the split in the interstate, a caravan of campers, from brightly painted converted buses to humble popups, hemmed them in on both sides. Bobbie's watchful gaze noted a pickup truck changing lanes without a signal. On the other side, a huge tractor trailer barreled onto the highway without yielding to oncoming traffic. Bobbie smoothly switched lanes to give both vehicles wide berth. Susan checked off 'conscientious driver' on her list of desirable character traits. Until now, she hadn't realized she'd been keeping track.

While she navigated the heavy traffic, Bobbie effortlessly kept up a non-stop conversation. Her voice was easy to listen to—warm, calm, and full of the quiet authority that Susan would expect from a healthcare professional. Not that Susan needed reminding that Bobbie was a nurse. Whenever they met after hours for coffee, she wore brightly colored scrubs. Today, she'd dressed up. Her pantsuit was stylish, if a little warm for the August weather. Susan allowed her eyes to linger on Bobbie's full breasts, imagining their softness and warmth under the clingy cotton sweater. The sudden arousal at the thought took her completely by surprise.

At first, the few extra pounds Bobbie carried on her short frame had put Susan off. When she'd finally admitted that her own struggle with her weight had prejudiced her, she looked past the slight chubbiness and saw how pretty Bobbie was. She had a full head of sandy curls. Her skin was fresh and youthful with only a few faint lines around her brown eyes, which had fascinating gold flecks, like stars reflecting in one of Maine's deep lakes.

The GPS suddenly barked out instructions, rousing Susan from her thoughts.

"Remember. You promised to be my navigator," said Bobbie. "I've only been up here a couple of times. It's always so crowded in the summer."

"Turn left here," ordered Susan. A moment later, the female voice of the GPS confirmed the instruction. "At least, your lady-friend and I agree."

"She's been known to be wrong," Bobbie said cheerfully. "That's why I always look at the map before I leave."

So, Bobbie liked maps too. Susan loved them and took pride in having a good sense of direction. She'd only come to the diocesan headquarters a few times when she was interviewing for her priest's license, but she was sure she remembered the way.

They'd come early in the hopes of getting good seats and managed to get one of the last spaces in the cathedral parking lot. Despite the heat, Bobbie slipped on her suit jacket after getting out of the car. Susan realized she was wearing it as a form of respect, which touched her.

They went up the stairs and through the crowded chapter room. At the door to the sanctuary, a smiling, gray-haired woman took their tickets. "Welcome to St. Luke's Cathedral. I hope you enjoy the performance."

"Follow me," said Susan, proudly leading the way.

Bobbie looked around. "It's much smaller than I expected," she said, sounding disappointed. In fact, the parish church in Boston, where Susan was ordained, was bigger.

"Maine has a small population," she explained. "The entire diocese only has about ten thousand regular members."

"But I thought most WASPs were Episcopalians."

"Back in the day, yes, but the ordination of women and then gay marriage split the church. There were lawsuits over the property. Ironic because many congregations can barely afford to keep up the churches they own. Some churches in Maine are being repurposed as community and arts centers."

"I know people are turned off by evangelicals—churches siding with the right-wing politicians, clergy preying on children. I guess we lump you all together, which probably isn't fair. How does that make you feel?"

"I try to stay focused on my mission and ignore the haters."

"Do you identify more as a priest or a teacher?" asked Bobbie, looking intensely curious.

"Being a teacher is what I do for a living. Being a priest is my vocation."

Bobbie frowned at the collar.

"Does it really bother you?" Susan asked, covering it with her hand.

"No, I'm just seeing you in a new way."

Susan noticed Liz Stolz waving to them from the front of the church. She hooked her arm in Bobbie's. "Come on. I think we may have found the best seats in the house, that is, if you don't mind sitting with your boss."

Bobbie caught sight of Liz. "I don't care. She's good people."

Liz moved down the pew to make room for them.

"How did you know we were coming?" asked Susan.

"Lucy said she gave you the tickets. That's one way to get a friendly audience. Invite all your friends." Liz gestured to Emily and Reshma. Down the aisle Olivia Enright and Amy Hsu waved.

Susan was glad when Bobbie chose to sit next to Liz because she never knew what to say to her. She occupied herself with studying the program while Bobbie and Liz chatted.

"Reverend Gedney!" Susan looked up to see Bishop Greene standing at the end of the pew. He was wearing a tasteful, if somewhat flamboyant plaid suit with stripes that exactly matched his magenta bishop's stock. He offered a politician's smile as he extended his hand. "How nice that you've come up from Hobbs to support our star."

"I wouldn't miss it. I've been a Lucille Bartlett fan for decades." He gave her a strange, knowing look, which made Susan wonder if Lucy had told him about their involvement. She was grateful when he turned his attention to Liz, who'd gotten up to shake his hand. She was polite, but Susan could sense from her stiff posture that she loathed the man.

"Is that your boss?" Bobbie asked in a whisper after Bishop Greene walked away.

"Technically, Lucy is my boss. He's my grandboss." Susan mirrored Bobbie's smile at the quip. "We don't have a hard 'chain of command' like other denominations. It's more democratic."

The bishop ascended the steps to the pulpit and tapped the microphone. The murmur of the crowd died slowly, but he waited until there was absolute silence. "Good afternoon! Welcome to St. Luke's, the cathedral church of the Episcopal diocese of Maine. Ordinarily, the dean would welcome you, but I've asked for this privilege because our star performer has agreed to do this concert at my request. I'm an opera fan, but I never realized that we had a genuine star in our diocese. Before she was called to the priesthood, the rector of St. Margaret's, known to her parishioners as 'Mother Lucy,' sang for many years at the Metropolitan Opera. She's returning to the Met this season and will be singing with the New York Philharmonic in October. Please welcome our own Reverend Doctor Lucille Bartlett!" He gestured toward the sacristy and began to clap.

Enthusiastic applause accompanied Lucy as she came out and ascended the raised platform in front of the main altar. She was wearing a beautiful off-the-shoulders concert gown, green, her best color. Her necklace and dramatic drop earrings dazzled in the overhead spotlights. She curtsied graciously to the crowd's adulation and waited with a star's poise for the clapping to die down.

"Thank you all for coming. This concert is being sponsored by the cathedral, so I asked the bishop if I should sing religious music. He said that he loves opera for what it does best—celebrating passion. The first selection I'm going to sing is one of opera's most passionate: "La mamma morta" from Giordano's *Andrea Chénier*. It was Maria Callas' signature aria, and you may recognize it from the Academy Award winning film, *Philadelphia*. Opera is full of arias with religious themes. Even if you don't understand Italian, you can hear the sacred in this one."

Susan was surprised that Lucy would lead with such a big aria and wondered if the small orchestra could do the accompaniment justice. All her worries disappeared when Lucy's powerful soprano filled the church. The orchestra, despite its size, was remarkably good. The applause at the conclusion was wild. Lucy obviously had many fans in the audience.

Lucy's next selection was another powerhouse aria: "Ecco Respiro Appena" from *Adriana Lecouvreur*. The low notes were richly textured; the highs cut through the air with stunning clarity. This was the powerfully vibrant voice that Susan had only heard on recordings. By the time they'd met, Lucy had already built a shell around herself like an oyster enclosing a pearl. Her physical form remained luminous, but the ardor that had once made her a great singer was gone.

Susan had tried to open her up through selfless devotion and tender lovemaking. Susan would have given anything to help Lucy when her career was failing. She'd spent hours holding her while she cried. Reluctantly, she'd sent her off to singing engagements overseas. It had been so hard to let go for weeks at a time, and pointless. Despite Lucy's persistence and discipline, something was missing from her once-extraordinary voice. Over time, there were fewer singing engagements, until Lucy finally quit.

Looking down the pew, Susan saw the source of Lucy's renewed vocal prowess. Apparently, the gray-haired, plainspoken doctor had reignited the fire in Lucy's voice. Was it the sex? Susan blocked the image of the two of them in bed. She had told Lucy that she'd accepted her marriage, and she had meant it.

Perched on the edge of her seat, the way churchgoers sat when their knees were too bad to kneel, Liz hung on every note that flowed out of Lucy's throat. The cocky doctor had effortlessly given Lucy back something she'd lost—passion.

The magnificent aria came to an end. Liz's enthusiastic clapping and shouts of 'Brava' were nearly deafening. Lucy gave a deep, opera singer's curtsey. When the applause finally stopped, she addressed the audience. "Now, I'd like to introduce a brilliant young alto who's made a career in baroque music. At my instigation, she's been expanding her repertoire into *Verismo* opera. Please welcome the music director of St. Margaret's, Denise Chantal."

An exceptionally tall woman came out to polite applause. "Thank you," said Denise. "I've had the privilege of working with Madame Bartlett for the past year. As my vocal coach, advocate, and mentor, she's taught me so much. I'm going to sing a prayer, one of the many scenes in opera when a desperate woman begs for help from the Mother of God. This is one of the lesser-known settings of the "Ave Maria," from Mascagni's opera, *Cavalleria Rusticana.*

The applause for Denise was strong, but not as loud as it had been for Lucy. Denise bowed, as most younger singers of any gender did now. Susan was sad to the see the elegant traditions fading. Actresses were called actors. Differences were merging into oblivion. Looking at Denise's convincing presentation, Susan supposed that could be a good thing.

"And now, Mother Lucy will sing another 'Ave Maria,'" said Denise, introducing the next selection. "Desdemona in Verdi's opera, *Otello* is one of Lucille Bartlett's signature roles, and I love to hear her sing it. I'm sure you will too." Susan settled back to listen. This aria was one of her favorites.

After the enthusiastic applause for Lucy ended, Denise sang an aria from *Samson and Delilah* in a creamy voice rich with sensuality. At the conclusion, she left the improvised stage to loud applause and cheers. Through the noise, Bobbie tried to say, "They're doing an amazing job. Wow. I've gone to local concerts, but I never expected this."

Lucy sang other signature pieces from her repertoire, including a few Wagnerian arias. Then Maggie Fitzgerald came out, and there was a dramatic change of style. When the duet from *Wicked* concluded, Denise returned with a thin man with a goatee.

Lucy stepped forward to introduce him. "We asked our friend Tony Roselli, music director of the Webhanet Playhouse, to sing the baritone part in this trio from *The Witches of Eastwick*." She looked around the audience with a devilish smile. "First Wicked, and now another song sung by witches. You all knew we couldn't stay holy for long!" The crowd roared with laughter.

The number brought the concert to a spectacular Broadway finish. During the curtain calls, Liz leaned across Bobbie to say they were invited for refreshments in the chapter house. Bobbie glanced at her watch.

"Do we need to leave?" Susan asked anxiously.

"We have a few minutes. I'd like to tell Lucy how much I enjoyed the concert." They followed the crowd, but when they entered the chapter house, they found Lucy surrounded by a throng of people "Maybe we should leave," said Bobbie, her eyes anxiously gauging the length of the line. "We'll never get to talk to her."

"Sure, you will," said a confident voice behind them. "Let me show you how it's done." Liz gently nudged the well-wishers aside as she cut a path straight to her wife.

"Hey, Luce. These ladies would like to congratulate you on your performance, and so would I."

"Oh, Lucy, you sound even better than the old days!" Susan gushed, unashamed of sounding like such a fan.

Lucy touched her cheek to Susan's and whispered into her ear: "Liz is organizing a dinner party after the reception. Please join us and invite your friend."

Susan turned to Bobbie. "We're invited to dinner."

Bobbie's eyes widened with sudden apprehension. "I can't. I have to get home."

Lucy reached out sympathetically. "Bobbie, do you mind if Susan joins us? We can give her a ride home."

"Thanks, but—" Susan started to say.

"No, Susan. Go with your friends," Bobbie said, extending her hand to take Lucy's. "You were absolutely wonderful. What talent you have. I'm so glad I came."

Lucy nodded graciously. Bobbie quickly stepped aside, so the next person in line could move up.

"Bobbie, I should go back with you," said Susan.

"No, I wouldn't feel good about you missing out because I'm on a tight schedule. I really enjoyed the concert. See you on Thursday. Sorry I can't stay."

Watching the swirling crowd engulf Bobbie and drag her through the exit, Susan felt guilty. She wondered how Bobbie would find her way through downtown Portland, then reminded herself that her friend was exceptionally capable.

"Here, Susan, you look like you could use a drink," said Liz, holding a plastic glass filled with a fizzy, purple liquid. "Don't worry. It's just blueberry soda. Not bad."

"Thank you." Susan tasted it and found that Liz was right. The drink was quite pleasant. "You didn't have to include me in your dinner plans, but I appreciate the invitation."

Liz smiled at a passing woman who obviously knew her. "You're Lucy's friend. I get points for being nice to you. It never hurts to rack up points with your spouse." Liz winked rakishly, and Susan could see how her smooth confidence had charmed Lucy.

Susan leaned closer to speak privately. "Liz, do you know why Bobbie always has to hurry off?"

Liz shrugged, but her expression became suddenly guarded. "Why don't you just ask her?"

6

The diner was nearly empty at that time of afternoon. A few elderly couples were eating supper before the dinner crowd arrived. One of the specials was always reasonably priced and bland enough to suit their tastes. Despite its national reputation as a tourist destination, The Hobbs Diner drew the year-round residents in too. The blueberry pie was the best in town. The whoopie pies were unrivaled, even in a town known for its bakeries. The shabby interior was charming. An old-fashioned neon sign promised "breakfast anytime." A shadow box held intricate origami shapes from stars to paper cranes, all folded from crisp one-dollar bills.

While Susan was admiring the wall art, Bobbie finally arrived. Instead of heading straight to their table, she stopped to chat with an elderly man at the counter. Susan didn't begrudge the old man Bobbie's attention, but their coffee dates were always on such a tight schedule. Bobbie was often late and then had to rush home to relieve the caregiver going off duty. What kind of life was that—no time to relax with a friend, go for a walk on the beach, or sit down and read a book?

The waitress approached. "More coffee, Mother Gedney?" She was a member of the parish and especially attentive whenever Susan came into the diner.

"Yes, thanks. And will you pour a cup for my friend?" She nodded in the direction of the counter. The waitress filled the other cup. Susan hoped it wouldn't get cold. Then Bobbie ended the conversation with the old man and headed toward their table.

"Sorry," Bobbie said, sliding into the booth. She opened a creamer pack and dumped the contents into her cup. "Thanks for getting me coffee." She glanced back toward the counter, where the old man was waving goodbye. Bobbie returned the wave.

"One of your patients?" asked Susan.

"Poor man has no family. He hangs out at the diner for company."

"Don't you have an actual social worker in your practice?"

"Cherie Harrison is a licensed therapist, but when she's in our office, she's treating physical ailments. She helps Lucy Bartlett part time."

"Lucy is always talking about the shortage of mental health workers in Maine."

Bobbie helped herself to the half of the enormous whoopie pie Susan had left for her. "Maybe you can help them."

"Lucy's licensed to practice psychotherapy. I'm not."

"But don't you get training when you study to be a minister?"

"Priest," Susan corrected gently. "Yes, we take classes in pastoral counseling in divinity school."

Bobbie smiled with pleasure as she savored the devil's food patty filled with marshmallow cream. She covered her mouth to speak with her mouth full. "I bet you're really good at it."

Susan appreciated the vote of confidence, but for now, staying sober was challenging enough. "My day job as a teacher keeps me busy."

Bobbie studied her over the rim of her coffee cup. "I hope you don't mind me saying so, but it would be good for you to get more involved in the community. For your teaching job too. Visibility is important in a small town."

"Sounds like you speak from experience."

"I'm not actually. I'm giving myself the same advice."

"I've been meaning to say you need to get out more."

"It's just hard right now. I need to make some arrangements. Maybe bring in home healthcare. I really enjoyed the concert, even if I know nothing about classical music. And it was fun to see my boss in a different setting." Bobbie rescued a piece of whoopie pie that had fallen to her plate, dabbing up the crumbs with her fingertip. "I had no idea that her wife is so talented. She has an amazing voice."

Susan smiled proudly. "I told you so."

"You never took your eyes off her while she sang." An uncomfortable heat rose in Susan's cheeks.

Fortunately, Bobbie's attention had been diverted by a loud man at the cash register. She frowned in his direction and turned back to Susan. "Some people are so dammed rude. I can't wait until the tourists go home." A woman at the next table gave Bobbie a filthy look. She gave it right back, showing a hard side Susan hadn't seen before. "Usually, I don't mind them," Bobbie continued, "but sometimes these people forget they're guests in Hobbs, and we live here."

"They see themselves as paying customers," said Susan diplomatically.

"Fine. That doesn't mean they own the place." The woman at the next table gave Bobbie another hostile look. This time Bobbie ignored her, and Susan was glad. Overt confrontations made her uncomfortable. She hated to break up school yard fights, and she shrank when voices got loud in AA meetings.

"Sorry about that," said Bobbie, frowning at the woman at the next table. "Had some walk-ins today. Liz made sure the place is well- equipped, but some people expect services a small family practice just can't provide. They get annoyed when I send them to urgent care or down to Southern Med."

After working at McDonald's, Susan knew exactly what Bobbie meant. The tourists' entitled attitude could be infuriating—one reason she'd been so glad to quit. The manager had looked shocked when she had told him that she'd be teaching at Hobbs Elementary. He'd stared at her like he'd never really seen her before.

Bobbie exhaled a long sigh and smiled. "On a happier note, I want to have you over for dinner. I just need to figure out coverage for that night. I hope you don't mind eating late. I want to make sure Joyce and her care-giver have something to eat first."

"It's not necessary to invite me for dinner. I don't want to make your life any harder than it is," said Susan, but she was curious to see where Bobbie lived.

"How's next Friday?"

"Fine. I don't have to work the next day. But won't that put you under a lot of pressure?"

"No, I have some vacation time. I can't go anywhere, so I spread out my days off."

"Why can't you go anywhere?"

"It's a long story, but don't feel bad for me. I took time to see the world when I could. Every year I checked off another destination on my bucket list—Rome, Japan, Egypt, Alaska. Now, I live in 'Vacationland,' so why should I go anywhere?"

"Will I meet the woman you care for?"

Bobbie blinked, apparently startled by the question. "If you want, but don't be surprised if you don't get much response from her."

"That's so sad."

"Yes, it is," Bobbie agreed. "But you'll come for dinner?"

"Of course. What can I bring?"

"Maybe a bottle of wine?"

Susan tensed at the suggestion. She'd eventually have to confess her secret if the friendship with Bobbie went anywhere, but not today. "I'm not a big wine drinker. Can I bring something else?"

"Forget the wine. I have plenty. Bring whatever you like to drink."

Before they parted in the parking lot, Bobbie gave Susan a quick kiss on the cheek in addition to her usual full body hug. After she drove out, Susan waited a minute before starting the engine. She was afraid to hope the kiss was significant. Maybe Bobbie just wanted someone to talk to instead of listening to the silence of the four walls. When Susan shut her door at night, she often longed to hear another human voice. *Stop feeling sorry for yourself! Things are so much better now.* Those long, winter nights in South Dakota, with the wind whistling outside her window, had been some of the loneliest of her life.

When she came into the rectory, Susan saw a puddle of light outside Lucy's door and remembered Bobbie's suggestion about pastoral counseling. Helping Lucy would make her more valuable to the parish and relieve some of the burden when Tom left for Florida. She just didn't know if she was ready for that. Taking on someone else's problems was a big responsibility.

Lucy's open door seemed like an invitation. Susan hesitated for only a moment before heading down the hall.

Lucy's auburn brows were knit, but she looked up and smiled when Susan cleared her throat to get her attention. "Hi, Susan. How was your day?"

"Better than yours apparently."

"There are days when you wonder why you bother getting up."

Lucy was one of the sunniest people Susan ever met. If she looked so obviously discouraged, something serious had caused it.

"What's going on?" asked Susan. "May I sit down?"

Lucy gestured to a chair. "The early reviews of my book are coming in. Some are downright nasty."

Since Lucy had told her she was writing her doctoral dissertation on sex, Susan had worried about a negative response. "Sex is always a controversial issue in religious circles."

"Even though I went out of my way to stay within doctrine...mostly."

"Lucy, you openly support relationships outside of marriage. Your chapter on masturbation made me blush."

Lucy laughed. "Not really."

"Yes, really."

"But it's a natural part of human sexuality. And many people don't have partners."

"True, but some readers might be shocked by a priest speaking so openly about a private subject, including me."

"But we *need* to talk about it!"

Susan decided not to debate Lucy. She already looked so upset. "It's late. What are you still doing here?"

"I'm trying to center myself before I go home. Liz always listens to my work problems, but she hears plenty of complaints as a doctor. She doesn't need me unloading on her every night."

"You could talk to me. You used to trust me to give you good advice."

Lucy's eyes narrowed. "Things are different between us now, Susan."

"That's obvious. You're my boss now."

"That has nothing to do with it."

"I didn't think so. You were never into power."

"Before I found out about the mess in South Dakota, I so hoped we could be partners again like we were in Boston—not the physical part, I was already committed to Liz—but all the good we used to do together. Then you lied to me."

"Lucy, that was my addiction talking. I'm in recovery now."

Lucy studied her with those penetrating, catlike eyes. "I know you're a good person, Susan. You were there when I needed you, and I'll never forget it."

"Then let me be here for you now."

Lucy gazed out the window. Finally, she turned back and said, "The bad reviews hurt more than I expected," she admitted with a tremor in her voice.

"The bad reviews threaten something you doubt, namely your intellectual abilities. You feel like they're attacking you instead of your ideas."

"Some of the criticism sounds so personal, like I somehow offended the reviewer. People are leaving one-star reviews on Goodreads and Amazon. I know my book isn't that bad!"

"It's a great book. I might not agree with everything in it, but there's no way it deserves a one-star review. Who do you think is behind this?"

Lucy shrugged. "I have no idea. I don't recognize the names. It's like someone sent out a call to trash my book."

"Probably right-wing Christians who don't agree with your views or who've decided you're going to hell because you're a lesbian."

"Fine not to agree, but the cruelty and nastiness of the comments are so hurtful and unfair. Some of the journals are acting like the book doesn't even exist. I guess that's how it is now. You can't just have a difference of opinion. You have to destroy the other side or erase their existence."

"Maybe you shouldn't look at the reviews."

"That's what Liz says. It's probably the best strategy but hard to do. This is my first book. I want to know what people think."

"Lucy, most of those people leaving bad reviews or rude comments probably haven't read your book and never will. If they did, I doubt they'd understand it. I know you tried to make it accessible, but it's still a book written by a trained theologian filled with complex arguments most laymen couldn't ever understand."

"Liz understood. She helped me edit my dissertation."

"Your wife is not an ordinary layman. She's an educated woman. Didn't you say she studied theology at one time?"

Lucy nodded. "But it's not just the reviews. I had to shut off comments on my Facebook page. Maybe I'll have to leave social media, which will be a shame. It's been useful in my ministry, especially for reaching out during the pandemic."

Susan had no clue how to use social media, but she understood that Lucy was hurt, and that was all she needed to know.

"I think you should give your mind a rest. Turn off your computer and go home. I bet Liz is making you a nice dinner right now."

Lucy finally smiled. "I bet she is. Thanks, Susan…for listening. I feel better."

"Any time."

Elated, Susan headed up to her apartment. She'd gotten a dinner invitation from Bobbie, and Lucy had listened to her advice. In all, it had been a very good day.

❈❈❈

The conversation stayed with Lucy on the way home. She was grateful for Susan's sympathetic ear and relieved that she was settling into her job and parish life. Her sermons were well-received, no surprise because Susan had aced homiletics in divinity school. The church ladies loved her because she was unassuming and personable. In short, she made the perfect curate.

Lucy supposed she should be glad that Susan wasn't trying to get ahead, especially after competing with Tom when he'd first come to St. Margaret's to "retire." He was a man, so people automatically looked to him to lead. To his credit, Tom always deferred to Lucy because she was the rector. He'd turned out to be her biggest supporter, and he always offered excellent advice. She would miss him when he went off to Florida for the winter.

Unlike Tom, Susan's only ambition had been to become a priest. It had taken years for her to be ordained because of her own troubled conscience. Now, similar doubts afflicted another young woman of exceptional promise. Lucy wondered if Susan could help Reshma get perspective on her dilemma.

Lucy arrived home without remembering how she got there, unfortunately a frequent occurrence of late. As she drove in, she noticed Emily's car parked in front of the garage, but not Denise's. Hopefully, that meant her daughter was taking some time for herself before she returned to Yale.

Lucy wondered whether the young romance would survive the separation, which would be more frequent now that Denise was making a name for herself in Europe. When Lucy had traveled the world as an opera singer, she'd had no time for relationships. Sex, yes, in those days with men, brief affairs in strange cities, always unsatisfying, although at the time, she didn't know why.

Emily's car blocked the door to the garage. Lucy backed into the guest parking area and almost hit Sam's truck. The sight of the big Ford parked in the clearing took her by surprise. Now that Sam had Maggie waiting for her at home, she almost never stopped by after work.

Lucy collected her bags, which seemed heavier by the day. Liz always lectured her about dragging so much weight around and putting strain on her back and hips.

"Liz!" called Lucy, shutting the door with her shoulder as she came into the house.

A familiar voice greeted her, but it wasn't Liz's.

"Hello, Lucy," said Maggie, stepping into the hall. "They're in the basement replacing something in the hot water heater. Sam and I were down in Webhanet when Liz called, so I came along." Seeing Maggie emerge from what used to be her kitchen triggered an uncomfortable déjà vu.

"Oh," said Lucy. Liz hadn't mentioned any problem with the hot water. "Is it something serious?"

Maggie shrugged. "I have no idea. But if they don't get it fixed tonight you won't have hot water. You know how Liz likes her hot shower in the morning." Lucy didn't need the reminder that Maggie probably knew Liz's habits better than she did. "I said I'd cook dinner because they're so involved."

"Can I help you?" Lucy asked only to be polite. Although Olivia had tried to teach her to cook after Erika died, Lucy's culinary skills remained rudimentary.

"No, you get changed. Make yourself comfortable."

On such a hot, sticky day, Lucy couldn't wait to get out of her work clothes. She'd taken off her collar the minute she'd gotten into her car, but all her pastel clerical blouses were in the laundry, so she'd had to wear black.

"Go ahead," urged Maggie. "You look hot. Put on something cooler."

After changing into a T-shirt and capris, Lucy returned to the kitchen to find Maggie opening one cabinet door after another.

"I see Liz rearranged *everything*," she said in a tart voice.

"You know how she is. She likes things a certain way. I'm not a cook, so I don't know."

"Well, I am a cook, and I assure you THIS is NOT the way to organize a kitchen."

"Complaining about me again?" said Liz, coming up the basement stairs. "Maggie, you don't need to tell Lucy what a pain in the ass I am. She's already figured it out." She turned on the sink faucet and held her hand under the water until it steamed. "Works!" she shouted, apparently expecting Sam to hear her in the basement. "That's a relief." She opened the refrigerator and took two beers from the door.

"Hey, Lucy," Sam said, coming up from the basement. She bent to kiss Lucy on the cheek. "Good to see you."

"Sam, has Maggie rearranged your kitchen?" asked Liz.

"No, but she hasn't been there long. Should I be worried?" Frowning, Sam turned to look at Maggie.

"I have no problem with your kitchen, Sam. There's flow. Not like this." Maggie gestured to the cabinets.

Until now, the exchange had seemed good-natured, but Lucy sensed an argument brewing. "Maggie, why don't you tell me what I can do to help?"

"Why don't you all get out of my way?" Maggie aggressively suggested with a shooing motion. She went to the closet and took out an apron that had been hanging there since Lucy had moved in. No one ever wore it. Liz might have rearranged the kitchen, but swapping the location of a few pots and utensils hadn't removed Maggie's presence.

"Wine for you, Lucy?" Lucy awoke from her thoughts and realized Liz was looking at her expectantly. "Wine?" Liz prompted again. She poured a glass and set it on the counter for Maggie, not even asking if she wanted it. How easily they fell back into their familiar patterns. Lucy remembered being in this kitchen while Maggie and Liz had cooked together without needing to exchange a single word.

"Yes, I'll have a glass," said Lucy. "Thanks, Liz."

Liz poured another glass of pinot grigio. She unwrapped a block of cheese, stabbed it with a knife, and dumped some crackers into a bowl. "Okay, Maggie. We'll get out of your hair. The kitchen's all yours."

"Is Emily coming for dinner?" asked Lucy.

"I invited her," said Liz. "She's going to see Stefan about her dissertation and eating at the senior residence with the 'mummies.'" Lucy was disappointed she wouldn't see Emily at dinner but happy she was spending time with her honorary grandfather.

After Liz went out to the deck, Maggie began to select vegetables from the basket on the counter. Lucy stood by helplessly, feeling obligated to stay and offer her assistance.

"Go on, Lucy," said Maggie. "I've got this. You should go out and keep an eye on those two. Plus, you look exhausted." The kind words reminded Lucy of the days when they called one another best friend and she had often been a guest in this house.

"You will call me if I can help?" Lucy said.

"Of course," Maggie said, but her dismissive tone made it obvious that she wouldn't. Feeling like an alien in her own kitchen, Lucy picked up the wine Liz had poured for her and went out to the deck.

Liz and Sam were deep in a conversation that included words like "circuit breaker" and "heating element." Trying to calm herself, Lucy was glad her attention was not required.

Then Liz reached over and gave her arm a little squeeze. "Hey, babe. Thanks for being okay with having company for dinner tonight." Lucy was grateful for the acknowledgment, even though it wasn't unusual for Liz to invite people to dinner on the spur of the moment. "Sam came right away when I called her. The least I can do is give her a beer and feed her."

"Sorry to invade your space, Lucy," said Sam, leaning forward to see across Liz. "Thanks for having us."

Lucy raised her glass to Sam. "Thank you for rescuing us from cold showers." Sam grinned, getting the implication.

The window from the kitchen opened and Maggie called out. "Liz, you can turn on the grill."

Liz leaned on her knees to launch herself to her feet. "Leave it to Maggie to get dinner on the table in minutes." Lucy couldn't say why, but it really bothered her to hear her predecessor praised.

Maggie was a trained chef, so of course, the dinner was excellent. Liz and Sam monopolized the conversation with plumbing talk, which was just as well. What Lucy had to say needed privacy. Fortunately, their dinner guests didn't stay long.

As soon as Liz shut the front door, she pulled Lucy into a hug. "Sorry about the unexpected company. I'm sure you're tired."

"Liz, I love that you're so generous and invite people to join us for dinner, but next time, please warn me."

"I thought of texting you, but then I got sidetracked looking for the right heating element. The home center didn't have it, so I had to rush to the plumbing supply before it closed."

"We could have managed without hot water until tomorrow. There's plenty of hot water at the beach house or that fancy new bathroom Sam installed at your practice."

"I know, but I didn't want to inconvenience you. It's tight enough in the morning between your walk on the beach and your singing practice."

Being made the reason to fix the water heater sparked Lucy's temper, but she tried to speak calmly. "Liz, I just wanted to come home to some peace and quiet. That was more important than hot water or my convenience in the morning. Can you understand?"

"Why? What's going on?"

"Jodi made a mistake in the bulletin and had to reprint the entire run. A client melted down in my office. The critics are bashing my book, and people are posting filth on my Facebook page."

"Then change your privacy settings," responded Liz bluntly. "Suspend your account for a while."

"It's not that simple. I use it for work, and I made certain agreements with my publisher."

"I'm sure that doesn't include taking abuse on social media. Maybe it's a good thing most religious people are old farts. If they were millennials, you'd be canceled by now."

Lucy knew that Liz never meant to be tactless, but she often blurted out the obvious without thinking. In fact, her innocent brutality was one of the things Lucy loved about her. She never had to worry that Liz wasn't telling her the truth.

"Luce, why don't you go upstairs and watch the news? I've got the dishes tonight."

Lucy hardly ever had time to see the headlines during the day and liked to catch up by watching the evening news. With the midterm elections only a few months away, the commercials were mostly political attack ads. Lucy's nerves were too jangled to listen to such obvious lies. She switched off the TV and meditated on Gospel passages about loving your enemies.

Liz came in and glanced at the dark TV. "What? No news tonight?"

"I can't deal with bombings in Ukraine, the winter outlook for viruses, the political venom..."

"Everyone is sick of it. I can't wait for these stupid midterms to be over." Liz flopped down on the sofa and pulled Lucy close. "I'm sorry I didn't think before inviting them to dinner."

"Liz, I love that you always welcome everyone. Think of all the times I showed up on your doorstep and you invited me to dinner."

Liz's body tensed. "Maggie's probably not glad about that, considering how things turned out." That was an understatement. "I was so busy running around looking for parts, I didn't think twice when Maggie offered to get dinner ready. And I'm trying to be less hostile. Hobbs is too small to keep the animosity going."

Lucy ran her hand under Liz's T-shirt and rubbed the soft skin of her belly like she was petting a puppy. "Liz, I know you need Sam, especially now that Erika's gone. We all need someone to talk to. I'm blessed to have you to listen to me. What do people do who don't have anyone?" Lucy wondered aloud and thought of Susan.

7

Bobbie watched Joyce finish her meal of meatloaf and mashed potatoes at a painfully slow pace. When Bobbie had planned this date with Susan, she should have expected to be squeezed on time. Joyce had always been a slow eater, taking her time, savoring every bite. Bobbie, used to wolfing down meals since nursing school, always finished before her. She leaned on her hand, watching Joyce leisurely spoon the unappetizing mush of mashed potatoes and meatloaf into her mouth.

When they'd met, Joyce had impeccable table manners, one of the things that Bobbie, who came from a working-class family, had always admired about her. Joyce had taught Bobbie how to set a formal table, which forks went where, and which glasses to use for each kind of wine. Bobbie tried to remember when Joyce began cutting all the meat on her plate into tiny morsels like she was going to feed a child. Although Bobbie came from humbler circumstances, she knew to cut only a few pieces at a time.

An especially annoying change in Joyce's table manners was her sudden resistance to chewing. Every meat that presented more resistance than chicken was too tough. Joyce started hiding anything she didn't want to chew in her napkin. With the price of meat driven so high by the shortages after the pandemic, the waste infuriated Bobbie. She started cooking more meals with chopped meat. Tonight's meal was meatloaf partially because Chloe, who was on duty, liked it. She said it reminded her of her grandmother.

Bobbie slightly turned her wrist to check the time. She wondered if Joyce was dawdling with her meal because she sensed the time constraint. She felt guilty even thinking it because she'd soon enjoy lively conversation with Susan, while Joyce would be left staring at the TV while Chloe studied.

Food remained on Joyce's plate, but she announced, "I'm done."

Bobbie tried not to show how relieved she was. "Let me clear away your dishes. I'll put on one of your shows. You can watch until Chloe gets home."

"Where is she?" asked Joyce, glancing at the door with an angry look.

Bobbie shrugged. "I'm sure she'll be home soon. She promised. I told her I'd invited a friend for dinner."

"Where is she?" demanded Joyce again.

"I don't know."

"Your friend."

So, that part of Bobbie's statement had connected, and Joyce had zeroed in on it. Even at this late stage, Bobbie was still surprised by the things that Joyce understood or didn't.

Chloe flew into the dining room. "Oh, my God! I'm so sorry to be late. I had to talk to my clinical supervisor." The young woman looked not only rushed, but exhausted. Bobbie felt guilty for saddling her with Joyce for the evening, but it was too late now. Susan would arrive at any minute.

"I fixed you a plate," said Bobbie. "It's in the fridge. All you need to do is heat it up in the microwave. There's salad too."

"Thanks! I'm starving." Bobbie envied Chloe's youthful figure and the fact that she could eat incredible amounts of food and remain slim. Even at her age, Bobbie had struggled with her weight.

"Will you sit with me while I eat?" Chloe asked Joyce.

"Guess so. Bobbie's going." Joyce made a face. "She doesn't like to eat with us."

"You eat too early," Bobbie said, which was true—not that she would invite Susan to dine with Joyce and their housemates. At least, not yet. Maybe after they knew each other better and she'd explained the arrangement.

Chloe returned to the table with a plate heaping with food and began talking about her day. She'd just started her pediatrics rotation and loved working with children. Joyce stared politely but didn't say anything. Bobbie wondered how much of Chloe's bubbly chatter she understood. Out of courtesy, Bobbie remained a few minutes longer to listen.

"Just leave the dishes in the sink," Bobbie told Chloe. "I'll do them later."

"Don't worry. I've got it. Your meatloaf is delicious, by the way."

"There's more. Help yourself."

"You can be sure I will. It's outrageously good. Go on. Joyce and I will be fine."

Bobbie headed to her apartment. The space had been planned for Joyce's mother, Clare, who was still mostly lucid when they'd bought the house and liked the idea of having her own space.

Bobbie could certainly appreciate her need for privacy. She was "on duty" all the time—in the office all day and at home the minute she walked in the door. Even in sleep, she wasn't alone. Although the two young women slept there, it was Bobbie who kept an eye on the video feed from Joyce's bedroom. Knowing she was safe in a secured space, with electronics that responded to voice commands, Bobbie could usually get a good night's sleep.

She'd hoped to give the cheese more time to come to room temperature before her guest arrived, but since Joyce's illness, so few of her plans ever played out the way she intended. Bobbie had learned to have fail-safe options. Earlier, she'd set out crackers and nuts in the tiny sitting room, which she'd never used for guests. It was where she read and occasionally watched TV.

Exactly on time, the doorbell rang. Bobbie smiled at Susan's face peering curiously through the glass. She was carrying a bunch of miniature sunflowers. Bobbie tried to remember if she had told Susan that sunflowers were her favorite. Unlocking the deadbolt, Bobbie realized she'd left the key in all day. She could almost hear Joyce warning how an intruder could easily punch through the glass and let himself in. Hobbs had a low break-in rate, so it was an overblown worry. Bobbie had ignored that early sign of paranoia, which had only registered as a symptom when Joyce had insisted on locking her car in the locked garage.

"Hi, I hope I'm not too early," said Susan. "I didn't know exactly where the house was, so I gave myself extra time. What a great location!"

"It was a lucky find thirty years ago. Now, only the ultra-rich can afford property on Gull Island." Bobbie opened the door wider. "Come on in!"

Susan handed her the flowers and a large bottle of unsweetened iced tea. "You said to bring what I like to drink. I know it's not very exciting."

"I love iced tea. Thank you! But if you'd like a glass of wine, I have plenty."

Susan suddenly had that deer-in-the-headlights look. "Thanks, but I don't like to drink and drive."

Bobbie found a vase under the sink and trimmed the stems of the sunflowers to keep them fresh, a trick she'd learned from Joyce.

"What can I do to help?" asked Susan, looking curiously around the kitchen.

"Would you mind bringing out the veggie tray to the living room? It's through there." Bobbie indicated the direction with a side nod. "Just put it on the coffee table. I'm right behind you."

Susan looked hesitant, but she picked up the tray of cutup vegetables and the bowl of dip.

"Your place is beautiful," she called from the living room. "How long have you lived here?"

Bobbie wondered what to say. "It was just a summer place until last year."

Susan leaned in the doorway. "When you started working for Dr. Stolz?" she asked, inadvertently leaving Bobbie an out.

"That's right." Bobbie opened Susan's bottle of iced tea. "I don't have any lemon. I could go next door and get some."

"Don't bother. Plain is fine."

Bobbie poured herself a glass of wine. "Come out and sit down. Tell me about your day."

Being asked seemed to please Susan. "I'm getting my classroom ready for the first day of school. One of my favorite things since I started teaching."

"How long have you been a teacher?"

"If I tell you, you'll guess how old I am," Susan said with a coy smile.

"I already know from your medical records." Bobbie cut a piece of cheese and mounted it on a cracker. She presented it to Susan, who looked delighted to be served.

"I was in such a panic that day I showed up at the practice. If you hadn't gotten me in to see Liz, I don't know what I would have done."

Bobbie shook her head. "You didn't believe me when I told you your heart sounded okay. But I know, Liz is a doctor and I'm just a nurse practitioner."

"Really, I meant no disrespect. When I was growing up, there were doctors and there were nurses."

"Don't worry. I'm used to it." Bobbie sliced some cheese for herself. "You didn't answer my question about how long you've been teaching."

"Since I got out of college. Forty years ago...this year. And you? How long have you been a nurse?"

"Same. I'm only eight months younger than you. It's so nice to have a friend the same age. Most of my friends are older." Most of Bobbie's friends had been Joyce's, so of course they were older.

"Mine too. Some of them are dying off, especially those still left in the..." Susan blinked, apparently just catching herself.

"You're not allowed to do that," ordered Bobbie. "Finish what you were going to say."

The delicate skin of Susan's cheeks flushed pink. "I was in the convent for a while."

Bobbie allowed her eyebrows to rise. "You were a nun before you became a priest?"

"Yes. I wasn't going to tell you. Some people think nuns are weird."

"I don't have much experience with nuns. My Catholic friends tell me they were mean, but all I think of is Sally Fields in *The Flying Nun*."

"You're dating yourself," said Susan, accepting another cracker with cheese.

"I saw it in reruns, sitting in the nurses' room during breaks. We saw so much suffering on duty we always had inane shows playing in the background." Bobbie raked a carrot stick through the dip she'd prepared. "You need to eat some of this, or I'll eat it all myself. I've been stress eating way too much lately."

"It can't be easy being a caregiver."

Bobbie looked up to see Susan's blue eyes coolly watching her.

"It's not. It's one of the hardest things anyone can do."

"You promised to let me meet her…the woman you take care of."

"I will. Before you leave…if she's still awake. Why is it so important?"

"I'm just curious," Susan admitted.

Bobbie dunked a zucchini spear in the dip and offered it to Susan. "Did you decorate your classroom with pretty fall leaves? That's what my teachers always did."

Susan smiled. "As a matter of fact, I did."

When Bobbie had to cook, they relocated their conversation to the kitchen. It was an easy meal, one of Martha Stewart's skillet chicken recipes that cheats by using cream cheese to enrich the sauce. While they ate, they talked about the BBC series they followed.

"Ice cream for dessert," Bobbie offered, when Susan put down her fork. "Wild blueberry flavor from that wonderful place on the Post Road. I also have raspberry explosion and moose tracks."

"I can't just yet," said Susan, patting her tummy. "What a delicious meal. I want that recipe."

Bobbie's culinary repertoire had expanded by necessity. Unlike Joyce, who used to browse cookbooks as bedtime reading, Bobbie cooked to eat. When Joyce's memory first began to fail, Bobbie had tried to help her do something she'd once so enjoyed, but Joyce had forgotten her own recipes. She couldn't retain the cooking times and temperatures and asked Bobbie repeatedly to confirm them. Standing by to supervise the process, Bobbie felt like she was cooking with a child.

"Would you like to sit out on the deck until you find room for ice cream?" Bobbie asked Susan after she'd put away the food.

"Sounds wonderful."

Bobbie refilled their glasses, and they headed outside. After such a warm day, the wind off the ocean felt deliciously cool. The backyard was brown and dry from the drought. The landscapers had stopped watering the grass to save the gardens. Unless it rained soon, they'd need to resow the lawn in the spring. *Another thing to deal with*, thought Bobbie with a sigh.

"It's so peaceful here," said Susan. "Just the sound of the birds and the children playing next door. You can hear the traffic on the Post Road in the rectory." Her hands flew up, showing her palms. "But I'm not complaining. The church pays for my utilities. I even get free Wi-Fi."

"Sounds like a good deal. Where do I sign up?"

"Why? You have a nicer place here."

Before she could answer, Bobbie heard footsteps approaching from the side of the house. "I might trade you for the privacy," she said as Chloe stepped up on the deck.

"Thought I might find you out here. Joyce is getting restless. Is it all right to give her the sedative early?"

Bobbie heaved out a long sigh. "Let me take a look." She leaned heavily on the arms of the Adirondack chair to get up. "Well?" she said, glancing at Susan. "You wanted to meet her. Here's your chance."

They walked through the main house. Susan looked around curiously, taking in the expensive artwork on the walls and the designer furniture. The house didn't scream wealth, but even to an unsophisticated eye, it was obvious.

"I'll get her meds," volunteered Chloe. "...be right back."

Bobbie led Susan into the library. Joyce, obviously twitchy, was chattering to herself.

"About time!" she said irritably.

"Do you want something to calm you down?" Bobbie asked in a soothing voice.

"Not time yet."

Bobbie was surprised that Joyce was aware of that fact. As evening came on, her sense of time became unreliable, but the long summer days threw her off. "No, it's not time, but I think you can use it."

"Who's this?" she asked, carefully taking Susan's measure.

"This is my friend, Susan Gedney." Bobbie waved Susan forward. "She teaches at the elementary school, and she's a minister at the Episcopal Church."

"Priest…" Susan corrected softly.

Joyce looked Susan over from head to toe. "Your new girlfriend?" she asked in a venomous tone.

"Joyce!"

"Your new bitch?"

Bobbie's mouth opened in shock. She glanced at Susan, who clearly understood the insinuation. "She doesn't know what she's saying," Bobbie said rapidly.

"Oh, yes, I do!" Joyce insisted. "I have eyes. I can see!"

"I think I'd better go," Susan said, staring at the door. "I need my bag. How do I get back to your apartment?"

"I'll go with you as soon as Chloe gets back."

Chloe hurried into the room with a glass of water and the pills in a small plastic cup. "Sorry, it took so long. Natalie put the bottle in a different place." She leaned down to offer the pills to Joyce, but she slapped them out of her hand.

"Joyce! Stop!" ordered Bobbie.

"I need to go," said Susan. "Tell me how to get out of here."

"I'll take you," said Chloe, picking up the pills. After handing them to Bobbie, she grabbed Susan's arm to lead her away.

Once they left, Joyce became placid.

"That was really nasty," Bobbie said, scolding Joyce like a child. "Why did you do that to me? *Why*?"

Joyce only shook her head and stared at Bobbie's feet.

❊❊❊

Liz mixed the bean salad again, hearing her mother's voice remind her to taste it for salt before serving.

"That looks so pretty with those bright flecks of green and red," said Simone, arranging her deviled eggs, bright with a dusting of paprika, on an antique plate.

"My mother always put in parsley for color. I switched to cilantro and added diced peppers. Gives it a Mexican twist." Liz ended up adding a little salt.

"Every generation makes little improvements."

"So, we like to think."

"I make my Aunt Viola's fried chicken recipe, but I use less pepper."

"I love your fried chicken."

Simone stared at her. "Don't you doctors discourage fried foods?"

"An occasional treat is not a tragedy. When whole-belly clams are on the menu, I always order them."

"I'm glad you're not one of those doctors who thinks in absolutes."

Liz shrugged. "It's pointless. People do what they want anyway, and they resent the preaching."

"Who's preaching?" asked Lucy, coming into the kitchen. She opened the refrigerator and took out a bottle of chardonnay.

"I don't preach," said Liz, putting some muscle into mixing the bean salad. "That's your job."

"Reshma's giving the sermon at my nine o'clock, and Susan's got the summer chapel, so no preaching for me." Lucy's bright sundress revealed her abundant freckles. Just the sight of them made Liz want to cover Lucy's back and shoulders with kisses, but with company there, she had to restrain herself.

Lucy took the last bottle of red wine out of the carton and searched the counter for the corkscrew. "Do we have more wine in the basement? They're going through it quickly."

"Two cases," said Liz. "I'll bring some up while people are getting their food." She handed a stack of spoons to Simone. "Please taste the salads and see if they need anything." She brought over the pepper grinder from the stove and found the bottle of apple cider vinegar advertised as including "the mother." Liz wondered if the average grocery store customer knew it was a sign of active fermentation and not just some cloudiness and sludge on the bottom of the bottle. Liz hated hipster affectations, but she had no quarrel with minimally processed foods. She waited with her arms folded, watching Simone's face change as her palate made subtle judgments. She shook more salt into one bowl and added vinegar to another. After a quick mix, she tasted again and pronounced, "Good. Real good."

Cherie came in looking for her aunt. "That's nice of you to help Liz. I was just coming in to see what I can do."

"I'm just the taste-tester. She's got everything covered. Is Brenda watching the kids?"

"The older kids organized a kickball game in the backyard. Sam appointed herself umpire. There are plenty of responsible adults out there. I'm not worried."

"Dr. Liz, your salads are mighty tasty," said Simone. "They don't need another thing. Now, if you don't mind, I'm heading out to get myself a refreshing glass of something. Some sweet tea would be just right."

Cherie waited for her aunt to leave before saying, "Looks like she's settling in. What do you think?"

"Seems happy. I'm sure that old house was a burden. I read how elderly people are struggling to keep up their homes. They're too big now that their children are gone. In this market, they can't afford to buy something smaller. That is, if something's available."

"Too bad we can't figure out how to put that empty space to good use. Things are just crazy now. Rents going up. Mortgage rates too. Oil prices through the roof." Cherie looked around. "I was hoping to see Bobbie here. Did you invite her?"

"I did, but she couldn't make it."

Lucy looked curious as she opened the wine, but she popped the corks and brought the bottles out to the deck.

Even though they were alone now, Cherie leaned closer to speak privately. "Bobbie needs to get out more. She's been in a pissy mood lately. She needs to figure out how to get more help. Isn't there something we can do?"

Liz looked up from shredding the pulled pork. Cherie never complained, so she must really be concerned. "I've suggested a service, but she says she's got it covered."

"What does Lucy say about it?"

"I haven't told her."

"You sure do take professional confidence seriously," said Cherie with faint disapproval. "If I couldn't tell Brenda my troubles, I don't know what I'd do. I know I can trust her to keep what I say to herself."

"And you can. Brenda will never tell a soul. I used to use Erika as my sounding board. Now that she's gone, I split up my complaining between Brenda and Sam. I don't like to burden any one person too much."

"That's considerate of you," said Cherie with a quick laugh.

"Practical too. That way, I don't wear out my welcome."

"Mind if I taste my potato salad for seasoning?" asked Cherie, removing the plastic wrap from a bowl. "I know it's a different recipe, but I always feel like I'm competing with yours."

"People like variety," said Liz.

Maggie came into the kitchen. "Hi, Cherie. I see you're doing the same thing I'm coming in to do."

"You can always tell the serious cooks. They're the ones who end up in the kitchen." Cherie looked from Maggie to Liz. "How did you two stay out of each other's way when you lived together?"

Liz was glad when Maggie answered the question. "When I cooked, Liz was the sous-chef, and vice versa."

"It took a long time for us to get to that point," said Liz. "We both like to be the boss."

"As you know, Liz is *extremely* bossy," Maggie said, giving Liz the eye.

Cherie pursed her lips. She was too smart to touch that one. "Liz, it looks like you have plenty of help. I'm going to head outside where the fun is."

Maggie opened a drawer. "Nope, not there." She opened another drawer. "Not there either. Hell, Liz, did you move *everything*?"

"No, but if you're looking for the serving spoons, they're over there." Liz pointed to a drawer.

"Your kitchen organization makes no sense to me."

"It does to me, and you don't cook here anymore." As if Maggie needed the reminder. Liz wanted to bite her tongue. "I'm sorry. That was unnecessary." Liz turned around and saw Lucy standing in the doorway.

"I came in to see if you needed help, but it looks like there's plenty."

"I'm finished here," said Maggie coldly. "I was just leaving."

Lucy watched her leave. "Liz! When are you two going to stop fighting?"

"When she stops making little digs about everything I do. I'm sick of her petty resentments. It's my kitchen now, and I'll arrange it any fucking way I want."

"I thought it was *our* kitchen." Hands on hips, Lucy stared at her. "It's still not our house, no matter what the deed says."

"Oh, Lucy, please don't you start with me too. We have all those people waiting to come in and serve themselves."

"I'm sorry, but it's hard to see Maggie here. It reminds me of happier times when we were all friends."

"Do you want me to stop inviting her?"

"No, of course not."

"We should talk about this later." Liz put serving spoons in the salads.

"I'm done," said Lucy. "I said what I had to say."

"Then go out and ask our guests to come in and serve themselves," said Liz tersely. "And make sure Stefan gets something to eat."

✱✱✱

Lucy was glad that Olivia was finally closing her argument. Hopefully, that meant they would leave soon.

"But Liz, the town *needs* you," Olivia said in an exasperated tone. "You're a natural leader, not hyper partisan, well-established here, even though you're 'from away.' We don't know when we'll get another chance to fill a select board seat."

The idea of Liz running for town office had come up before. She'd always said she was too busy, but Lucy couldn't see Liz as a politician. She was too direct, and when people didn't agree, she asserted her authority rather than trying to persuade them.

When Olivia drew breath to continue the argument, Lucy stifled a sigh of impatience. The party was obviously over. Why wouldn't people just *go home*? Most of the guests had already left. Sam and Maggie were in the kitchen doing cleanup. Lucy felt guilty, but Maggie had even chased Liz out, so she was not about to go in there.

On the side table, Lucy's phone lit up with a message from Goodreads. She glanced around to see if anyone had noticed, but Olivia had everyone's attention. If Lucy picked up her phone, they would probably assume it was a church matter. A pastor, like a doctor, was always on call. She tapped open the notification. *Damn! Another two-star review! What is wrong with these people?*

Meanwhile, Olivia's blue eyes had become steely. She was used to getting her way, and Liz's intractable resistance was clearly annoying her. Fortunately, Liz was mellow now that the party had wound down and she'd imbibed a few celebratory drinks.

"Liz, I can appoint someone to fill the spot until the June elections, but I really would like to know if I can count on you," insisted Olivia.

Liz, slouching in her usual three-point position, ankle on the opposite knee, sat up. She was getting bored with this conversation. "No, promises, Liv. I'll think about it."

"That's what you always say."

Liz stubbornly returned Olivia's officious gaze. Lucy tensed, knowing how much Liz hated to be pressured. Olivia's expression became opaque. "We should probably go." It wasn't an admission of defeat. As a skilled Wall Street negotiator, Olivia knew when to pause a discussion.

Amy Hsu, Liz's senior partner in the practice, perked up. She'd been obviously patient while Olivia made her case to Liz. They'd driven to the party together. Amy had said it was for the sake of parking, and it was a valid reason. The cars were lined up along the driveway to the house.

No one really knew what was going on between Amy and Olivia, who never hesitated to get what she wanted. When she'd had her eye on Sam, she didn't waste any time getting her into bed. Maybe Olivia was still worried about her heart, and Amy, as her cardiologist, might be too. Lucy could only guess the status of the relationship. Olivia popped in and out of therapy, depending on how miserable she felt. Things must be going well because she hadn't shown up in Lucy's office for months.

Sam came out to the screen porch. "Hey, we're going. The kitchen is mostly cleaned up."

"You didn't have to do that," said Liz, rising.

"I know, but it was a big party, and you did most of the cooking. The least I can do is help clean up."

"Thanks, Sam," said Liz, giving Sam's shoulder an affectionate pat.

Lucy stood on her toes to kiss Sam on the cheek. "Where's Maggie?"

"Trying to put things away and still bitching about Liz's new kitchen arrangement."

"Oh, for fuck's sake!"

"Liz, leave it alone," advised Lucy gently. "Let's go in and say good night."

"We're going too," said Olivia, rising. "Great party, Liz. Next time, we'll do it at my place."

"But you already had a big party this summer," said Liz.

"Your wedding doesn't count. That was a special occasion. I'm talking about getting the Thirsty Thursdays gang together before it gets cold."

Amy Hsu gave Lucy a hug. She hadn't said much that evening, but that was her way—to watch and assess and avoid controversy. She made a perfect foil to Olivia's dominant, all-eyes-on-me personality.

Maggie came out from the kitchen. "I did my best to put things away," she said with a sigh.

Liz's eyes glittered with annoyance. An embarrassing confrontation after such a pleasant evening would leave everyone in a sour mood. Lucy quickly interposed herself. "Maggie, thanks so much for your help and all your delicious contributions to the meal."

Maggie scrutinized Lucy, perceiving that she was running interference, but she slipped into actress mode and replied in a voice dripping with cordiality, "Thank *you* for your hospitality and for putting up with all of us. Sam and I will have to plan something at the pond this fall."

"That's a great idea," Lucy said. "We should get together more often. Now that life has mostly gotten back to normal, we've fallen out of the habit. We get so wrapped up in our lives. And I'm the biggest offender."

"You're busy flying around the world being an opera star," said Olivia. "At least, you have an excuse." She gave Lucy a half hug. "Don't forget to put in a good word for me with your wife." She tried to get Liz's attention, but she was stubbornly looking the other way.

Olivia marched to the front door, and the others followed. Finally, they were alone.

Lucy ran her hand lightly up Liz's arm. "Do you want to sit on the porch and do a postmortem on the party? Or go upstairs?"

Liz raised a brow. "What do you think?"

"I thought so. Why do I even ask?" Lucy reached up and gave her a quick kiss, not lingering or they would end up having wild sex on the living room sofa. Last time, Lucy pulled a muscle in her buttock. It had ached for days and kept her from her morning walks. Since then, she'd decided she'd rather make love in bed. Whether or not she wanted to admit it, she was closing in on sixty.

"I'll be right up. I just want to collect the dirty glasses," said Liz, glancing in the direction of the porch.

"Don't be long," said Lucy, trailing her fingers down from Liz's shoulder to her breast. She was exhausted from the party, but too wired to sleep. Making love would relax her and pull them back together after their testy exchange earlier.

After taking off her makeup, Lucy slipped on a lacy nightgown and got under the covers. By late August, the temperature fell quickly once the sun went down.

"Don't you look inviting?" said Liz, coming into the bedroom. She yanked down her underpants along with her shorts and tossed them on the chair. She accurately landed her T-shirt on top of them, followed by her bra. Although Lucy appreciated a well-orchestrated seduction, she'd given up trying to undress Liz, who shed her clothes like she was going for a swim in Jimson Pond. Yet, there was something charming about Liz's youthful enthusiasm for sex.

"Thanks for putting on that gorgeous nightgown," Liz said, flopping down beside her.

Lucy smiled at having her efforts noticed. "Sometimes, I wonder why I bother. It takes so little to turn you on."

"I get turned on just thinking about you." Liz took Lucy's hand and put it between her legs, where it was wet and silky. "See?"

"What were you doing downstairs?"

"Loading the dishwasher," said Liz innocently. "It's running now. We'll have to empty it in the morning." She came closer on the pillow. "While I was dealing with the glasses, I remembered the millions of freckles on your back. When you showed up in that pretty dress, I wanted to kiss every single one, but I couldn't with all those people around." Through the sheer silk of the nightgown, Liz lightly teased Lucy's nipple, pinching it gently, which sent a jolt of excitement straight to her crotch.

The pretty nightgown didn't stay on long. Once it joined the heap on the chair, Liz insinuated herself between Lucy's legs, letting her weight down gently. Lucy gave herself over to the sensations caused by the urgent press of Liz's body. When she opened her eyes, she saw Liz smiling back. "What's your pleasure tonight?" she asked, so close, her blue eyes merged into one.

"Just you. Slow and gentle."

"You've been asking for that a lot lately," Liz said, raising her head. "Am I too rough?"

"No, I love your passion. It's just that the world is so crazy right now... and loud. Sometimes I just need to feel safe and loved."

"You are so loved," said Liz, kissing her forehead. She kissed her eyelids and her lips and moved down her body, kissing all the sensitive spots along the way. Finally, with delicate strokes, she brought Lucy to the sweetest climax.

"Wow," said Lucy as the sensations faded. "Just wow." Liz raised her face and grinned, obviously proud of herself. Lucy reached out her arms. "Come here, you."

On the way, Liz pulled up the covers. With all the windows open, it was chilly. Lucy reached between her wife's legs and found her all slick and wet. After only a few moments of gentle teasing, Liz's back arched.

"That's not fair!" Lucy protested after the orgasm passed.

"Oh, stop," said Liz, catching her breath. "I'm satisfied. Just Relax. I want to talk about the party. Everyone seemed to be having a good time, don't you think?"

"Yes, but I wish Olivia would have saved her sales pitch for another time. Are you going to run for the select board?"

"No. I'd make a terrible politician. I don't know when to keep my mouth shut." Lucy was glad Liz realized her own shortcomings without needing to be told. "I saw you looking at your phone," said Liz. "Pastoral crisis?'

"No. Another low Goodreads rating."

Liz leaned up on her elbow. "Lucy! Why do you keep looking? Some people take sadistic pleasure in tearing other people down. If you want to write books, you need to grow thicker skin or stop reading the reviews."

"Says the woman whose breast book has been on the best-seller list for years and years. How many five-star reviews does it have?"

"At least five hundred," said Liz, matter-of-factly. "I'm sorry Maggie annoyed you today. This isn't her house anymore. How I organize the kitchen is none of her fucking business."

"She feels displaced. Being your wife gave her status and a role in the community."

"She was chairman of the board at the Webhanet Playhouse, the drama coach at the high school, professor at the community college. She didn't need me to have a place in Hobbs."

"Liz, it's her insecurity. I don't like her taking over our kitchen either. And I'm sorry what I said earlier. I know it's our house. I don't doubt you, not for a minute!" Lucy kissed Liz deeply to reassure her.

"Speaking of exes, why didn't Susan come to the party?" Liz asked.

"I don't know." Lucy had invited her. At first, she said she might come, but then she didn't show up. For a while, she'd seemed to be happier and engaged. Suddenly, she was out of sorts. "Something's going on with her." Lucy caressed Liz's breast to soften her up for the request she was about to make. "Sweetie, would you mind doing me a huge favor?"

"Hmm, depends," said Liz. Savvy to the bribe, she grasped Lucy's hand to stop the motion. "What is it?"

"Will you go to Susan's service at the summer chapel tomorrow morning?"

"Why? It's bad enough you make me go to yours."

"Liz, I don't *make* you go. Don't exaggerate. Please, go to Susan's service. Afterward, invite her to brunch. I want to talk to her."

"Then why not call her in the morning and invite her yourself?"

"I don't want her thinking it's an intervention. "

"Which it is."

"Of course, it is, but with you inviting her, it won't look quite as obvious."

"Oh, the tangled webs we weave…" said Liz, letting her head fall back on the pillow.

***

Susan hung the green stole around her neck and carefully adjusted the ends to even them up. She'd skip the chasuble today because the brisk wind off the ocean could turn the colorful silk into a sail. She tied back her hair to keep it from flying all over her face.

As she stepped outside, she heard a pleasant female voice. "Good morning, Mother Susan." Susan turned around to see Abbie, the senior warden, a heavy-set, middle-aged woman with blond hair fading to white. She was a retired corporate executive and compulsively organized. Lucy counted on her to keep the parish humming. "Beautiful day for an outdoor service," Abbie said, gazing at the cloudless sky.

"It certainly is," Susan agreed.

Another vestry member passed and waved. Susan waved back. She'd often wondered how much these people knew about the scandal in South Dakota. Abbie was exceptionally thorough and had probably done a background check. Although the bishop in Pierre had managed to get all the charges dropped, the local papers had run stories on the hit-and-run accident, and the DUIs had been in the police blotter. While judicial records could be expunged, press coverage on the internet seemed to have eternal life. By now, someone must have found the stories, but so far, no one had said a word. Episcopalians were notoriously polite.

A glance at her watch told her it was time to head down to the stone altar. There was no procession at this service. The summer chapel was meant to be informal. Many of the attendees came in shorts or sundresses. The headline of the ad Lucy ran in the local paper read: "Come as you are. Our founder wore sandals."

Susan waited for the crowd to settle down. She smiled at the elderly couple in the front row. The man had his arm around the woman, perhaps to warm her in the cool morning air. Susan's eyes, scanning the congregation, landed on a tall woman standing at the back. *Why is Liz Stolz here instead of at Lucy's service in town?* Then Susan's gaze found a more surprising face. Anxiously watching the people around her, Bobbie sat in the third row.

Susan resolved to avoid eye contact with Bobbie and took some deep breaths to center herself. Liz was harder to ignore because she was so tall and obviously bored. Susan had always suspected the only reason she came to church was out of loyalty to Lucy. She stood in the back with her arms folded and didn't come up for Communion. To Susan's relief, neither did Bobbie.

Both lingered after the service, hanging back, apparently waiting for the greeting line to thin. When Bobbie's turn came, Susan forced a smile and accepted her handshake. "I thought you were allergic to religion."

The weak attempt at humor momentarily dispelled the worry in Bobbie's eyes. "I am, but you weren't returning my calls, so I...." Her voice dropped off. Then she began to speak rapidly. "I need to explain. Please give me a chance. Not here, of course."

Susan squeezed Bobbie's hand. "I need time to think about what happened. That's what I said in my text. Didn't you get it?"

"Yes, I saw it, but there is so much to say. Please come to our coffee date this week."

"I'm sorry, Bobbie, but I'm not ready for that." Susan glanced over Bobbie's shoulder and saw Liz frowning. She apparently took Susan's attention as an invitation to approach.

"Hey, Bobbie," she said, leaning on her shoulder, "what brings you today? I wouldn't take you for a churchgoer."

"Um. Usually, I'm not. I came to see Susan."

"Me too! My wife sent me to invite her to brunch. You're welcome too. We have a ton of leftovers from the party."

Susan panicked at the thought that Bobbie might accept. Nothing could be more awkward.

"Thanks, Liz, but I have to get home," Bobbie said. "My tenant has a school event today." Bobbie turned around and affectionately touched Liz's arm. "Nice to see you. Say hi to Lucy for me."

"I will," Liz agreed heartily. "See you soon." Her eyes followed Bobbie as she walked down the path to the parking lot.

Liz bent slightly so her gaze was level with Susan's. "Please don't say you're going to turn me down too. I'd hate to report to Lucy that my mission has failed. I'm sure you've seen her in a temper. It's not a pretty sight." Her persistent smile forced Susan to return it. She glanced over Liz's shoulder. The private conversation had discouraged some of the people waiting to greet the priest, and they'd drifted away.

Liz followed the direction of Susan's gaze. "Let me get out of the way so you can deal with other customers. You are coming, aren't you?" Her voice was firm. She wasn't about to take 'no' for an answer.

"Yes, let me change. I'll meet you at your house in a little while."

"Okay, but don't stand me up, or I'll have hell to pay." Liz grinned conspiratorially before heading down the path.

The people behind her were obviously vacationers and carried on about the beauty of the location. They wanted to know about the history of the chapel although its details were listed in every guidebook. They seemed genuinely interested, and Susan didn't want to hurry them away. Finally, they left, and the only person remaining in line was Abbie.

"I'll walk you back to the sacristy," she said and fell into step beside Susan. "Great sermon today. Lucy said that was your strong suit."

"I enjoy explaining how scripture applies to our lives in the here and now."

"It shows, and I could see you were really connecting with people. Mother Susan, I haven't said so, but I'm glad you joined the parish. With Tom leaving for half the year, it's going to be tough on Lucy. He did a lot around here. She's going to need more help."

"Thank you. I'm glad to be of help in any way I can."

They arrived at the fork in the path. "I just wanted you to know your presence in the parish is appreciated," said Abbie. "Enjoy the rest of your day."

Susan grinned as she took off her vestments. Finally, she was beginning to feel like she had a place in Hobbs. The senior warden saying she was pleased was practically confirmation that her temporary hire would be extended. Of course, Lucy had the last word, but she'd gone out of her way lately to include her. The invitation to brunch was the latest example. Either that or Lucy had something serious to discuss. Susan fought a sense of dread as she locked up the sacristy.

It was so easy for her to sabotage herself. One moment she was buoyant, the next she sank like a stone. Her sponsor had explained that she'd have to learn to ride out the highs and lows without a crutch. She'd used alcohol to numb both good feelings and bad. With God's help, she was never going back there again.

When Susan pulled up to the house in the woods, Lucy was returning from her service at the main church. Her red hair was unbound, and the clerical blouse she wore was sleeveless. She could get away with it because her slender arms were toned by regular exercise. Since moving in with Liz, she'd put on a few pounds, but they had settled in all the right places.

"Good morning!" she sang out, reaching up to give Susan a hug and a kiss on the cheek. "Thanks for coming."

"Oh, you're not fooling me, Lucy," said Susan, accepting the embrace. "You think I'd refuse a summons from my boss?"

Lucy made a petulant face. "That obvious?"

"Instead of calling me, you sent Liz to deliver the message. Why, I don't know. She looked bored the entire time."

"It used to be worse," said Lucy with a sigh. "She's really trying."

"I bet she is," Susan quipped.

Lucy got the joke and pursed her lips, but then she smiled. She hooked her arm in Susan's. "I don't know what Liz planned for brunch, but I'm sure it will be good. We have a lot of food left over from the party. Too bad you missed it."

A sign inside the front door proclaimed, "This is a barefoot home." Lucy slipped off her ballerina pumps. Susan did the same. They found Liz in the kitchen, already changed out of the smart suit she'd worn to church. She was wearing shorts and a worn polo shirt, but no shoes.

"Hello, ladies. I just put the frittata in the oven. Great way to use up the grilled veggies. It will be a few minutes until we can eat. Get yourselves some coffee or taste the spritzers I put out on the porch."

Susan glanced anxiously at Lucy. "Don't worry," Lucy assured her, "I'm sure there's no alcohol in it."

"Not a drop," Liz confirmed, "but, Susan, I also make a mean Virgin Mary."

"Thanks, Liz. I'll try your spritzers."

They went out to the porch where the table was set with colorful placemats and matching napkins. A globe-shaped vase held day lilies in a variety of shades.

"Your table is so pretty. Like eating in a restaurant," said Susan, pulling out the chair Lucy had indicated.

"We could have gone out. I just thought you'd feel more comfortable with privacy."

"And I do, Lucy. I just meant it's so convivial, the table with cloth napkins. The perfect centerpiece. Lovely." Susan settled herself anxiously. "Before Liz gets here, maybe you can give me a hint about what's on your mind."

Lucy shrugged. "Nothing specific. You were doing so well. Lately, you seemed a little down, so I wanted to check in with you."

"As my boss or as a therapist?"

"Neither. As your friend."

Liz came in, which put an end to the private conversation. She put a stack of plates on a trivet and went back into the kitchen. She returned with a cast iron skillet.

"I must really need redemption to be eating with two women in collars," she said, cutting perfectly equal wedges of frittata.

"Jesus frequently broke bread with the wicked," Lucy replied without missing a beat. "Take it as a sign that God loves you."

Liz sat down and tasted the frittata. "Hmm. Didn't think I'd like the chorizo in it, but that is damn good. Just the right amount of heat. I'll have to make this again."

"Liz is always reinventing her recipes," Lucy explained, gazing adoringly at her wife. "She's so creative." Watching, Susan wondered how she could ever think of coming between these two. They were so obviously in love.

"I would have made something more substantial," said Liz apologetically, "but after that big party last night, I'm—for want of a better word—cooked."

"We really missed you," said Lucy, which was obviously an opening.

Susan scrambled to think of an excuse. "I'm sorry, but I've been having headaches lately." When Liz looked up from her plate and scanned her face, Susan realized her mistake. "It's nothing serious," she hurried to add. "Summer allergies. I've always had them."

"See what it's like living with a doctor?" said Lucy with a side-eye toward Liz. "You have to watch every word you say."

Liz finished before everyone else. "I hope you don't mind, but I have a project going in my shop. Excuse me." She jumped up from the table and took her plate. Susan wondered if her exit had been planned.

"She eats so fast," Lucy said, leisurely continuing her meal. "She says it's from working in a hospital and never knowing when she might be interrupted."

"Old habits are hard to break."

Lucy's green eyes studied her. "They are. That's why I'm so proud of you for staying sober."

"Thank you," Susan murmured.

Lucy offered her another piece of frittata. Susan declined. Anxiety had dampened her appetite, and she'd eaten enough to be polite.

"Lucy, when are you going to tell me why you asked me here?"

Lucy steepled her fingers and tapped them against her lips. "I saw you come in on Friday night. You looked very upset." Susan bristled, feeling like she was being surveilled. A small town was like a fishbowl. "Wasn't that the night you were having dinner with Bobbie Lantry?" Like every good pastor, Lucy remembered important details.

"Yes, as a matter of fact, it was."

"You looked like you were crying. Were you?" Lucy's tone was gentle, which rocked Susan's defenses. She stared at her plate, remembering the awful scene at Bobbie's.

"Let's just say, I now understand why you were so angry when you found out my secret."

"I was angry, but even more, I was hurt that you didn't trust me enough to tell me the truth."

"That too. I wish Bobbie had shared her secret. Instead, I heard it blurted out by a woman with dementia."

Lucy's auburn brows came together in a frown as she tried to put the pieces together. "She takes care of an elderly woman, doesn't she?"

"Yes, she does. Except the elderly woman is her partner."

"Oh!" said Lucy. "Why is that a secret?"

"I don't know, and it shouldn't even matter except..."

Lucy studied her carefully. "...except you were interested in her... romantically."

Susan looked away to avoid Lucy's intense gaze. "Yes, silly of me, I know. I was getting the idea she felt the same. Now..."

"I see," said Lucy, sitting back. She folded and refolded her napkin as she digested the information. "A lie of omission is still a lie. Are they married?"

"I honestly don't know. I don't know anything, really."

Lucy glanced at the door through which Liz had exited. "I bet Liz knows. Bobbie works for her."

"Will you ask her?"

"Yes, but that doesn't mean she'll tell me. Professional confidence, you know. She takes it very seriously."

"Lucy, I don't know what to do."

"I understand. But don't judge until you know the whole story."

"I'm not sure I even want to know. It was a terrible scene, shocking! The woman started screaming, 'your new bitch.' I'm pretty sure she was referring to me."

"Yikes!" Lucy inhaled a long breath.

"What should I do?"

"You need to talk to Bobbie. She owes you an explanation."

"I'm not even sure I want to see her again."

"Give yourself time to get over the shock. You may change your mind."

Susan shook her head. "I may, but I doubt it."

8

The token was as big around as a poker chip and heavy for its size, made of some base metal tinted to look bronze. Groups bought them in bulk for pennies, but its monetary value was irrelevant. Susan had earned this coin by staying sober for a year.

With her finger, she traced the raised Roman numeral one. In the triangle around it was the motto "to thine own self be true." She thought back to that day in the restaurant when Lucy had given her an ultimatum: find an AA meeting or move out of the rectory. Under pressure, Susan had confessed how much trouble her drinking had caused—her priest's license revoked, her job at the school lost, becoming a fugitive from the state she'd once called home.

When Susan had first come to Hobbs, she was living in her car. Fortunately, Tom Simmons bought her story about coming East to look for a new church. During the busiest week of the tourist season, he believed her when she said she couldn't find a room. And it was true that she'd gone to seminary with Lucy. The kind man gave her the key to a cozy studio, where there was an abundance of hot water, even web access. She'd almost gotten away with the deception, until she was stopped for a minor traffic infraction.

When Susan told Lucy the truth, she was unyielding. The woman, who'd once melted in her arms, was coldly resolute, no longer the helpless victim of a rape, of gaslighting, of being dragged from her diva's perch. She was the rector of a parish and a seasoned therapist now. While it didn't feel like it at first, Lucy had thrown her a lifeline.

The waitress came, and Susan ordered another cup of coffee. Caffeine was the drug of choice for many recovering alcoholics. Susan tried to space out the coffee and tea, or she couldn't sleep.

Sally was late, but she would come. Since Susan had joined the Portland AA group, she'd never let her down. She was lucky to have a lesbian sponsor, an older woman, who understood what life was like before the current acceptance of LGBT. Young women didn't know what their older sisters had endured—the guilt, the rejection by friends and family...and especially the Church. Hiding was the only way to survive, but a double life could take a toll on sanity. Maybe that's why so many lesbians of Susan's generation had looked for solace in a bottle.

She put away the coin in the change purse in her wallet. After studying the plastic menu in the table holder, she decided to order some pie. It wasn't as good as in the diner, but Sally never met her in a place that served alcohol.

While Susan was waiting for the waitress to return, Sally came into the coffee shop. She looked rushed and tired, but she stopped to say hello to the owner, another member she sponsored. Finally, she slid into the opposite chair.

"I'm sorry. I had a client who wouldn't stop talking. I was so interested in what she was saying, I cut her hair too short. She wasn't too happy about that." Sally made big eyes to emphasize her point. She wore too much makeup. The heavy black liner wasn't flattering. Her crow's feet ran from her temples into her eye shadow. Sally was only a few years older than Susan, but her skin was leathery from too many sessions in a tanning bed. Her figure was wrecked from bulimia followed by malnutrition. When she got her life together in her forties, she finally began to eat normally. By then, it was too late.

In Sally, Susan saw how her life could have been if she hadn't gone into the convent and gotten an education.

Sally flipped her bleach-blond hair over her shoulders. "Well, honey, that's my story. How are you doing? Hanging in there?"

"Like I said. It's been a rough week."

"I'm glad you called me. Not a good idea to let these things fester." Sally signaled to the waitress to bring her coffee. "I'm thinking of having some blueberry pie."

"Me too."

Sally gave the waitress their order and leaned on her arms. "Oh, Susan. What happened? You sounded so upset when you called me the other night."

"I was. I went into the supermarket and stared at the wine shelf. But with inflation, everything costs so much. Even the cheap wine is expensive."

"Please don't tell me that's the only reason you didn't buy it."

"No, but I'm used to pinching pennies, and the cost was a deterrent." After Sally had told her she'd dropped out of school, Susan had avoided using big words. She'd since come to learn that Sally was smart in ways Susan couldn't even imagine.

"Sometimes we need to be grateful for anything that stops us. Even the price of booze. I used to skimp on groceries to afford it."

"Me too," Susan admitted glumly.

"But you didn't buy the wine, and I'm proud of you." Sally raised her hand for a high-five. Susan stared at it for a moment before realizing she was supposed to do something. She awkwardly smacked Sally's palm.

The waitress came with their pie. She brought a coffee cup for Sally and refilled Susan's.

"Tell me more about the situation that made you want a drink," said Sally, peeling open a creamer.

"Bobbie, the woman I've been seeing, invited me to dinner." Susan stopped to consider her words. This was the first time she'd admitted to anyone, even to herself, that she was "seeing" Bobbie.

"Yes, I remember. You were so excited."

"I thought the invitation meant this friendship might be heading somewhere."

"And it's not?"

"It's complicated. She takes care of an older woman with dementia. What I didn't know is, they were involved."

"What? I don't understand."

"I asked to meet the woman she cares for, not realizing the connection. Turns out she's not that far gone that she didn't see what was going on. She asked if I was Bobbie's 'new bitch,' which told me everything."

"That's certainly a big clue," said Sally. "But are you sure?"

"No, I didn't hang around for an explanation. I was too shocked by the nastiness. All I wanted to do was get out of there as fast as I could."

"So, you went to buy wine."

"Not at first. I went to the beach, near where I used to live, and I cried. Fortunately, it was low tide and hardly anyone was there. After crying my eyes out, I felt better, almost peaceful. I sat for a while, looking at the ocean. On the way back to the rectory—I don't know why— but I took a detour to the supermarket and ended up in the wine aisle. You have no idea how hard it was not to pick up a bottle."

"Oh, sweetie, I do know. I've been right there, exactly where you are. But you didn't buy the wine, you stayed sober one more day and another, and then a bunch more."

"Lucy saw me crying in my car."

"Lucy, your old girlfriend?"

"Yesterday, she sent her wife to invite me for brunch. She was worried about me."

"It's good to know that people care, isn't it. You're lucky to have connections. You have anchors outside the meetings. Many people don't. They've pissed off all their friends and family. No one will bother with them anymore. You're lucky to have Lucy."

"Yes, and I'm grateful. I've been lucky my whole life. I got a teaching job right out of the convent. I got a scholarship to Union. My bishop got the charges against me dismissed."

Sally put down her coffee cup and folded her hands in front of her. "People care about you because you have value. You're a teacher and a priest. According to some, that makes you worth saving."

"But what if I wasn't those things?"

"Then you'd have to find value in yourself. Like I did. You're lucky to have degrees and connections, but they don't mean anything if you don't believe in yourself. Your friends can keep trying to save you, but only you can save yourself."

Susan couldn't face Sally's intense gaze and looked away. "I know."

"Honey, I don't think you do. You hear the words, but you don't believe them."

"I'm trying," whispered Susan.

Sally sighed and sat back, probably weighing whether to push harder. "Everyone gets it in their own time. You will too. Don't stress it, Susan. Remember, one day at a time."

"What should I do about Bobbie?"

"You really care about her, don't you?"

"I do. As a friend and hopefully more."

"You've passed the one-year mark, but the advice on avoiding romantic relationships doesn't fit everyone. It depends on the person. And you're right, this one's complicated."

"What should I do?"

"Jesus. I have no idea."

"Bobbie wants to explain."

"I think she owes you that, don't you? And you should let her, out of simple fairness."

Susan stared at the oil slick the cream had left on her coffee. "Yes, I should."

"Plus, it will drive you crazy not knowing."

That prompted a chuckle. "Yes, it will."

❋❋❋

The white-haired woman breathed in and out at Bobbie's command. One good thing about practicing geriatrics was that older patients were mostly cooperative. A few of the men, especially those living alone, had lost social skills. The men who went to the diner for their morning coffee or hung out at the VFW hall were less cantankerous. They also had better prospects for long-term survival. Women, who tended to keep up their family relationships and connections in the community, usually outlived their male counterparts, no matter their other health conditions.

Mrs. Thibault was a perfect example. Ninety-three, she still lived independently in the little Cape where she had raised five children. She regularly drove herself to the senior center to play bridge and to church every Sunday. She'd lost both breasts to cancer. She'd had uterine cancer, colon cancer, and early-stage skin cancer. Her thin body was literally riddled with scars—"seams" she called them, although she'd given up sewing because of her eyesight. Despite all the cancer, she was healthier than many young people.

"Your weight is steady. That's good," said Bobbie. "Are you still cooking for yourself?"

"I do, but sometimes my granddaughter brings me care packages."

"Keep up whatever you're doing," said Bobbie, putting away her stethoscope. "You're in great shape."

"I made a date with my daughter to celebrate my hundredth birthday. She'll be seventy-five. I'll invite you too."

"Thanks. Looking forward to it."

"I'm serious," Mrs. Thibault said firmly.

"Me too."

Bobbie escorted her patient to the business desk to arrange her next appointment. She glanced into the waiting room and saw that it was finally empty. They never shooed patients out when the office closed at noon for lunch, and with Liz away, today had been busier than usual. The practice manager and the assistants had already gone on their break, but Connie, who handled payments and follow-up appointments, had stayed behind.

At the door, Mrs. Thibault reached up and gave Bobbie a little hug. "Take care of yourself, Bobbie. You're looking a little frayed at the edges."

"Thanks, Mrs. Thibault. I will," Bobbie said, but the well-intentioned remark had unnerved her. She didn't like hearing that her personal concerns were becoming obvious to patients. Since Joyce had been diagnosed, work had been a refuge. In the office, Bobbie had always been able to maintain her professional composure, no matter how difficult things became at home, not even when Joyce was in denial and there were daily arguments.

In the hall, Bobbie ran into Cherie, who was also late taking her lunch break.

"Whooeee!" the PA exclaimed. "Bobbie, you as swamped as I am?"

"It's been a madhouse with Liz gone."

Cherie nodded her head in exaggerated agreement. "Regular patients know to schedule follow-ups after the summer people leave. I just wish they wouldn't come in all at once!" Cherie's smile lit up her face. Bobbie envied her warm coloring, including a "tan" that wouldn't fade with the summer sun. Thanks to her biracial heritage, it lasted all year. "You going to lunch now?" Cherie asked. "Mind if I join you?"

"I'd love it." Bobbie looked for opportunities to spend time with Cherie, whose optimism and calm always made her feel better, even on the craziest day. By the time Bobbie had arrived, the long-time staff had already created regular lunch groups. The doctors tended to eat at their desks or go out for lunch. As a PA, Cherie occupied a position in the practice equivalent to Bobbie's, making them natural lunch partners.

"Get your lunch, girl, and I'll meet you outside. It's a beautiful day. We need to enjoy the nice weather while we have it. In a couple of months, there will be snow out there." Bobbie glanced out the window at the bright sunshine. It was hard to believe, but it was true. Summer in Maine was too short.

When they brought their lunch out to the little garden on the side of the building, the first crew was leaving.

"I hate to go back inside," said Ginny with a sigh. "It's so beautiful out here." There was a chorus of sad agreement from the others. Bobbie and Cherie settled at the table they'd vacated.

"I don't know why no one sits over there," said Cherie, pointing to the picnic table near the beach roses. "It's just as good as this one."

"Maybe it's the view. You can't see the salt marsh from there."

Cherie bit into her sandwich. "Mm...my Brenda makes the best tuna fish sandwiches. Even the kids like them, and they can be real fussy sometimes."

"Real mayonnaise. That's the secret ingredient. I learned that from Joyce. When I was growing up, we used Miracle Whip. Now, I can't stand the taste."

Cherie made a disgusted face and shook her head.

"I was never much of a cook before I met Joyce, but I'm getting better. Not my choice. We do what we have to do."

Cherie regarded Bobbie with a little frown. "What's going on with you, Bobbie? I count on your happy face to pick me up on gloomy days, but lately, your smile isn't quite as shiny. You're not yourself."

Bobbie took a bite out of her ham and Swiss sandwich and chewed thoughtfully. She didn't want to inflict her burdens on someone else. God knows, Cherie had enough of her own, trying to raise two children orphaned by gun violence. Talk was, the oldest had been getting into mischief at school.

"It's nothing I can't handle," said Bobbie.

Cherie studied her with the cool objectivity of a therapist. "That sounds brave, Bobbie, but is it honest?"

"Being a caregiver is never easy," she said in a soft voice, staring at the salt marsh in the distance.

"No, it's not. That's why you need a respite on a regular basis."

"The students who live with us are good about that."

"I don't mean watching Joyce when you come to work or go to the supermarket. I mean real time off. A whole day to yourself to do what you want. Go shopping. See a movie. Sit on the beach."

"I try to avoid the beach. With my coloring I burn like a piece of bacon."

"But wouldn't it be nice to know you could go if you wanted to?"

"Yes," Bobbie agreed wistfully. "It certainly would. When we have the freedom to come and go as we please, we take it for granted."

Cherie gave her a firm look. "You can get help, you know."

"I know, but it's hard to find good people. There's such a shortage of care workers. And I'm trying to save money in case I can't manage anymore, and we need a nursing home."

"If you wear yourself out, that will be sooner than you think. You need to keep yourself healthy and sane, or you'll both land in a nursing home."

"My mother had a stroke in her sixties." Bobbie remembered her mother struggling to relearn how to speak and walk. The same mother, who held her hand when she'd taken her first stumbling steps and taught her how to form words. A major stroke finally ended her life.

Cherie gave her a long hard look. "How's your BP?"

"It runs high. Amy added a diuretic to bring it down after the new guidelines came out. She's keeping an eye on it."

"Good idea." Cherie looked thoughtful as she ate her sandwich. She delicately wiped her fingers on a paper napkin. "My Aunt Simone just came up from Louisiana. She took care of her mama when she was on in years, so she has some experience. I bet she'd be willing to stay with Joyce for a few hours."

"I thought she was watching your kids."

"She is, but not when they're in school or activities. Keith's in every sport. Megan's taking dance lessons, and they go to choir practice after school at the church. That leaves Aunt Simone free most days. Want me to ask her?"

The idea of someone watching Joyce while Bobbie did something for fun was so tempting. "Let me think about it. Joyce is only comfortable with people she knows. It took her a long time to adjust to our house guests."

"You mean the students who live with you?"

"Yes. They're very good with her."

"But they're young women. I'm sure they have plenty of things to do besides hanging around the house. It might be good for them to have backup."

"I can pay your aunt."

"She doesn't really need the money, although it might make her feel good to have a little job on the side. I'll tell her about our conversation and see what she thinks."

"Thanks, Cherie. I usually don't ask for help."

"I know but pretending you're a superhero isn't going to make things better. And people like to help. It makes them feel good. In fact, you just made my day by accepting my suggestion."

"People are different here."

"They are. In Hobbs, we look out for each other." Cherie unwrapped some aluminum foil. "Want to try my new brownie recipe? It's made with almond flour. Very healthy."

"Anything looking that good can't be healthy."

"I promise. Try it."

"I shouldn't."

"Oh, yes you should. What's that they say? 'Life is short. Eat the cake.'" Cherie's beautiful blue-green eyes smiled warmly. "Go ahead."

***

Way too bright, Lucy decided. She furiously rubbed off the scarlet lipstick and picked through her makeup kit for a more subtle shade. The colors on the end of the tubes ran the gamut from vibrant red to inconspicuous nude. She chose something in between and skillfully slicked it on. Her daily makeup routine took minutes, but she was out of practice getting ready for a performance. At Union, she wouldn't be on the stage, or even under a spotlight, but she would be the focus of attention. Given all the controversy about the book, she wanted to look like a serious theologian.

She went into the powder room to look at herself in the full-length mirror. At Liz's suggestion, she'd worn a classic violet suit rather than all black. "It's a lecture, not a service," she'd said. "Purple is a good color on you." In the beginning, Lucy was surprised when Liz offered style advice because she seemed so indifferent about her own clothes. Living with her, Lucy had come to realize that Liz had a sharp eye for fashion. Her wardrobe was expensive and impeccably maintained. Her apparent lack of concern about her appearance was nothing but an act.

When Lucy opened the door, the sweet voices of choir boys greeted her. Liz was sitting on the bed, watching TV.

"Let me guess. Something to do with the queen's death," said Lucy.

"The prayer service at St. Paul's Cathedral is being streamed live. It's almost over, I think," said Liz, her eyes glued to the screen.

"I wish you'd pay as much attention to my services," said Lucy. "I'm surprised you're so interested. She's not your queen."

"No, but she's been queen as long as I remember. She's always been there."

"Her presence meant continuity."

"Yes, exactly. And, as you might guess from how much I love opera, I love pomp and circumstance."

"No, I'd never guess," said Lucy sarcastically.

"And no one does it better than the Brits, but where did they find this female bishop? She doesn't speak well at all."

"I'm guessing you mean Sarah Mullally. She's the first woman elected bishop of London. She used to head the entire British nursing service."

"That's a big job." Liz frowned as she adjusted her thinking. She could be stubborn but she always considered new information. "She may be accomplished, but she's a lousy speaker."

"Maybe she's nervous. This service is being broadcast all over the world. I bet you'd be nervous too." Lucy gently pulled Liz's arm. "Come on. We need to collect everyone and get going soon. The lecture starts at four."

Liz got up carefully to avoid messing her skirt. "That's a stupid time. Who do they expect to show up? You can tell academics planned it."

"They timed it so they could have a cocktail reception afterwards."

"Episcopalians. It's all about the wine. How long do we have to stick around? I hate academic cocktail parties."

"Liz, I'm the speaker. I think I need to stay, don't you? I bet you had to go to lots of receptions after giving papers."

"Don't remind me." Liz stepped into heeled pumps. Her shapely legs instantly got Lucy's attention. Liz might complain about being in drag in a skirt and high heels, but when she wore them, she was incredibly sexy. She slipped on her suit jacket and knocked on the door to the adjoining room. Reshma, wearing her collar, opened it.

"Good. You're dressed. What about the others?"

"Emily is sitting here waiting. Denise is still putting on her makeup."

"Tell her to get her ass in gear. Lucy can't be late." Liz closed the door. "Three women using one bathroom. Why did we think it was a good idea to let them share a room?"

"Reshma wanted to come, but she couldn't afford a room of her own."

Liz came within whispering distance. "What the fuck is going on with them? Are they a threesome?"

"None of your business or mine," Lucy snapped, instantly regretting it, but this was not a subject she wanted to discuss now or ever.

"Sure, it is," Liz insisted. "One of them is your daughter. The other two work for you." She eyed Lucy with a raised brow. "Lucy, you know something. What is it?"

Apart from the conversation she'd had with Reshma while the Lambeth Conference was going on, Lucy could honestly say she knew nothing. She shrugged. "They're all adults. Not our concern."

The door that connected their suite to the room next door opened. Reshma and Emily came into the room. "Denise will be right here," said Emily.

"Tell her to hurry up." Liz grabbed her bag from the desk. "I'll get the car. Meet me outside, and Lucy, don't forget your notes."

Lucy checked her tablet to make sure that they were accessible. She'd committed her lecture to memory, but she always liked to have prompts, in case of a momentary lapse.

"Sorry," said Denise, coming into the room. "I hope you weren't waiting long."

"No, but we need to be going," said Lucy, trying not to sound as impatient as she felt. She was anxious about the lecture, her first since the book had been published. The negative reviews had taken a toll on her confidence. "Uptown traffic is heavy on matinee day. A lot of shows will be letting out."

"You always can tell a New Yorker," said Denise.

"I lived here, but I was a transplant, like most people who live in Manhattan."

"Mom went to Juilliard," Emily said proudly as if everyone didn't already know.

When they emerged from the hotel lobby, they found Liz's car parked in the circular drive. She was drumming her fingers on the steering wheel of the Toyota SUV, her first and long-debated departure from German auto brands. Price, practicality, and the need for more seating had finally triumphed over ethnic loyalty. Lucy had been an unwilling sounding board during the debate. She knew next to nothing about cars, but she understood that her wife had an emotional bond with her vehicles. She still hadn't gotten rid of her Audi, which continued to sit on the auxiliary parking pad until she figured out what to do with it.

Silly with laughter, the young women piled into the rear seat, sticking Denise, who was the tallest, in the middle. She didn't seem to mind. Maybe it gave her a sense of solidarity with the other women.

Despite the heavy traffic, Lucy had no worries about arriving on time. Liz knew the way and navigated the New York streets like the cabby she'd been in college. Lucy spent the ride uptown rehearsing her lecture in her mind.

"I've never been in a seminary before," said Denise, admiring the campus towers as they approached. "I was invited several times when I was studying sacred music at Yale, but I always shied away. Too many collars, I think."

"You'll see plenty of them today," Liz grumbled from the front seat.

"I don't mind as long as their wearers aren't hostile."

Lucy sighed, feeling the same.

Emily took her mother's arm as they walked from the parking lot. "I hope you get a good turnout, Mom."

"Me too, sweetie. My editor will be here. They sent him to scout allies to write positive reviews in the journals."

"What's that old saying?" Denise said, catching Lucy's gaze. "There's no such thing as bad publicity?"

"I'm not too sure about that," said Liz, scowling. "When that movie star sued me for malpractice, I got plenty of bad publicity. I won in the end, but defending myself cost a lot of money, and by the time the decision came down, it got barely a paragraph. The only thing people remembered was my name on the front page of the tabloids." Liz almost never talked about that episode anymore. Lucy had hoped she'd forgotten it and the anger that had soured her on staying at Yale. Apparently not.

The lecture hall was crowded when they arrived. Lucy's editor, Kevin Douglas, found her right away and pumped her hand. "What a great turnout, so much better than I expected." Looking around, Lucy acknowledged familiar faces among the faculty and students with a nod or a wave. "I've got a camera set up," Kevin said pointing to a tripod. "We're filming it for YouTube. Maybe when people can see your face and hear your voice, they'll get a different perspective."

Lucy was about to say that could also backfire, but Professor Spangler, who'd been her dissertation advisor, pulled her aside. "I'm glad you have a good showing, Lucy, but don't get dragged into an argument. Pretend this is your dissertation defense and just answer the questions. There are a lot of people here I don't know."

Lucy found it hard to believe that her critics would go out of their way to hear an afternoon lecture in a seminary. Spangler was wearing a neutral, academic expression, so it was hard to judge the seriousness of his concerns. "You don't really expect trouble, do you? Not here, in a progressive seminary?"

"The reviews are much nastier than I expected. Social media makes some people think they can say whatever they want." Spangler engaged Lucy's eyes. "Just stay cool. I'm sure it will be fine." His deliberate and slightly forced smile didn't inspire confidence.

The academic dean was trying to get Lucy's attention. Liz, with a firm hand on her shoulder, bent to speak into her ear. "Good luck. We're going to spread out, so you'll have friendly faces in the audience."

"You'll be great, Mom," said Emily with an awkward hug, followed by embraces from Denise and Reshma.

On the way to the podium, Lucy said a silent prayer. Once she began speaking, it seemed no different from giving a Sunday sermon. She held on to that familiar feeling and soaked up the good will from the friendly crowd. Emily distracted her by raising her thumb in approval at key points. Liz smiled her encouragement, and Lucy began to relax. She even got a few laughs at intentionally humorous remarks.

After the polite applause usual at academic events faded, the dean opened the floor to questions. The first few were requests for technical clarification of her statements and easy to answer. Then an older man got up. Unhealthily thin, he was dressed all in black, although he wore no collar. That didn't mean he wasn't clergy. The technician rushed up the aisle to bring him the microphone.

"Dr. Bartlett, how can you say sex between unmarried people is allowed? It's clear that fornication is and has always been a sin." He ran through a litany of scriptural verses justifying his position.

"Thank you. I am aware of those passages," Lucy said.

"Then how can you make such outrageous claims?" the man insisted.

"I'm not claiming anything but my own views. You're welcome to disagree." In the front row, Spangler nodded his approval.

With an audible snort, the man sat down. On the other side of the room, a tall woman raised her hand and stood. The technician with the microphone raced in her direction.

"What do you mean by your statement that the theology of gender is unsettled? Is that a swipe at the trans community?"

The blunt accusation stunned Lucy. The half minute she took to formulate a response felt like an eternity. Finally, she said, "No, it's a statement of fact. The theology of gender is unsettled. I think everyone here would agree." During the murmur in the crowd, Lucy studied the woman, who was clearly trans. Unlike Denise who, despite her height, had shapely curves, this woman had maintained the square, solid figure of her former gender. Her dark eyes were hard and glittered with contempt.

"The Anglican Communion doesn't allow trans people to marry. What do you think about that policy?" she asked.

"I don't agree with it, but I'm not here to speak for the Church."

"You're wearing a collar," said the woman, stating an obvious fact.

"Yes, because I'm ordained, and it's customary at this seminary," Lucy said cautiously. "I'm here as a theologian, not as a priest."

"Your book doesn't say much about transgendered people. Was that deliberate?"

"No."

"Are you a transphobe?"

"I—"

"Maybe a TERF?" demanded the woman before Lucy could answer.

"A what…?"

"A trans-exclusionary, radical feminist. Never heard of that before? You're supposed to be an expert on sexuality, I'm surprised."

Denise stood up and faced Lucy's accuser. "I'm sorry, but you're out of line. Mother Lucy is a trans ally. I know. I'm her music director, and I'm trans. The vestry didn't want to hire me, but she convinced them. I'm also a professional singer, and she volunteered to coach me so I could restart my career as a woman. Mother Lucy is a kind, decent person. Leave her alone." Denise gave the questioner a menacing stare before she sat down. Lucy silently thanked her for coming to her defense, but she wasn't sure it had helped.

"I want to hear her views on trans," the questioner insisted, batting aside Denise's defense.

Fortunately, Lucy had a position on this subject. "Legally, I believe that trans people should have the same rights as anyone else. After life itself, bodily autonomy is our most fundamental right."

"And theologically?"

"God loves everyone, no exceptions. Trans people should be welcomed as full members of the Church."

"You don't sound like you *really* believe that."

She didn't *sound* like she believed it? Lucy stifled her anger as she tried to think of a response. Then Liz stood.

"That's enough," she said in a clear voice full of quiet authority. Everyone turned around to look at her. "You're badgering the speaker. How do you know what she *really* believes? Do you have an actual question?" Liz's hand was in her pocket. Lucy desperately hoped she wasn't carrying her gun. After being rescued from a Boston jail, hadn't she learned not to bring it where it wasn't legal? Then Liz relaxed her hand, and Lucy could breathe again. It wasn't a gun, just her clenched fist.

The academic dean interposed herself between Lucy and the audience. "We encourage discussion and debate, but we expect it to be *respectful*. Anyone who can't agree to that rule can leave *right now*."

The woman glared at the dean, then at Lucy, but she sat down. The tense exchange had put a chill on the discussion. There was some murmuring in the audience, but no more questions.

Relieved, Lucy collected her papers. Her armpits felt damp. When she blotted her forehead with the back of her hand, she found it was slick with perspiration.

9

Out of the corner of her eye, Liz caught her partner Cathy Pelletier passing in the hall. "Hey, Cath," she called, motioning to her to come back. "How's she doing?"

Despite her resolution to stay out of Lucy's medical care, Liz had been wondering what was going on in the exam room next door. She could peek at Lucy's files anytime and often did. It had been the same when she was married to Maggie, but then she'd had the worry of breast cancer to justify checking her medical records. Since the recurrence last year, Liz had been keeping track of Maggie's tumor markers and scans again. She wondered if she knew or even cared.

Cathy returned to Liz's door and backed her into her office. "She says I can tell you everything, so I will. She's not sleeping well, which I'm sure you know, and her pressure is a little high."

"Everyone's pressure is high with the new guidelines."

"Yes, yours too. You should lay off the single malt. Save it for special occasions."

"Hell, Cathy, you're no fun."

"Liz, you're in your sixties now. Things are different. You need to take better care of yourself."

"You know doctors aren't especially good at that. But Lucy's okay?"

"Very healthy for a woman her age."

Liz made a face at the "for her age." Lucy was nine years younger than Liz, but Cathy was only in her forties and coming from a different perspective.

"She told me you gave her alprazolam to calm her down after the lecture. I offered her a script, but she declined it."

"Lucy doesn't believe in psychotropics. Besides, she knows she can get them from me." Cathy frowned. Liz didn't approve of sharing scripts either.

"She never asks unless she's crawling the walls. Instead, she'll do yoga or try to Zen her way out of anxiety."

"Good for her, but that confrontation after her lecture sounded ugly."

"She was ambushed. Obviously, she didn't expect to be attacked on her home turf. A seminary is supposed to be a civilized place."

"Maybe that wedding this weekend will help take her mind off it."

"I hope so. She promised Tom she would sing. She's been rehearsing every morning. Music always makes her feel better."

Lucy appeared at the door. "I knew she'd jump on you the minute you left the room."

"Because she cares," said Cathy.

"I know," said Lucy, turning her green eyes on Liz. "I'm fine."

"I'll be taking your pressure every morning to see if today's reading was just white coat disease."

"You will if I allow it. Don't be so bossy, Liz." She gently stroked Liz's arm to mollify her.

"See what I have to contend with?" Liz turned to Cathy for sympathy.

"You think I'm getting in the middle of that one? Later, you two."

"Liz, are you done for the day?" asked Lucy, after accepting a kiss. "I thought we might go to the harbor for a drink."

"Cathy just told me I need to cut back on the scotch because I'm old, but we all know beers don't count." Liz grinned. "Let's get out of here before someone decides they need me."

On the way to the harbor, they passed some fishermen along Beach Road. Liz had no idea what they were trying to catch. She'd never heard of anyone having luck fishing from the bridge, but what did the tourists know?

She sent Lucy to the deck to find a table while she waited for their bar order. "We'll bring out your snacks, when they're ready, Doc," said the bartender, handing over a glass of pinot grigio and an overflowing IPA. Liz searched for her wife on the crowded deck. Finally, she spotted her at the far end, sitting next to Bobbie Lantry.

"Look who I found," Lucy said as Liz approached. "I asked if we could share her table."

"Day drinking? So, this is how you spend your days off." Liz distributed the glasses and sat down next to Lucy.

"I was out shopping, and I thought I'd treat myself to a Margarita. I haven't had one all summer, and it's already over!"

"Not quite, although it's flown by, as usual. Feels like it just got here." Liz adjusted her chair so she could have a view of the harbor. "Stick around, Bobbie. I ordered some calamari and fried zucchini. Lucy just had her physical, so of course, we're celebrating with fried appetizers."

"Everyone needs to have fun...even me. I've had the whole day to myself. Cherie's aunt is staying with Joyce. Cherie badgered me into taking a respite. Otherwise, you wouldn't find me here lazing around like this."

"When you're a caregiver, you have to pace yourself," said Lucy. "It's a marathon, not a sprint. Simone is a wonderful woman. So kind. I bet she'll be great with your patient."

"Honestly, I'm a little worried about what I'll find when I get home. Joyce isn't always the best with new people. That's one reason I haven't looked into a service. I'm lucky to have those two girls...women, I should say." Bobbie responded to the quizzical look on Lucy's face by explaining that her tenants were students with a special interest in elder care. "They look after Joyce in exchange for free rent. The house is huge. Why not use the space?"

While Bobbie had been speaking, Liz had been watching Lucy, who was completely focused on every word Bobbie said. Lucy had a gift for listening.

"That's so smart," she said. "Many elderly people live in homes with extra bedrooms and could use help. How did you get the idea?"

"One of the girls approached me after a lecture on geriatric care I gave at the Osteopathic medical school. We went out for coffee afterwards, and she told me she'd been shut out of the dorms and was desperately searching for a place to live. I told her to stop by and check out one of our spare bedrooms. It got around and a social work student got in touch. We share the kitchen. It works," said Bobbie with a shrug.

"I bet if we ask around the parish, we could find other people like Simone who'd be interested in helping, or—" Lucy started to say.

"I'm not a member of your church," said Bobbie, interrupting. "And I'm not looking for charity."

Liz did a double take, surprised to see her usually friendly and out-going NP pushing back so vehemently against Lucy's suggestion. "Bobbie, humor her," Liz said lightly. "She likes to make trouble. Good trouble, as they say. And her church ladies are very generous. Simone is just one of them."

Bobbie was calmer when she said, "With all due respect, Lucy, thank you for the offer, but I'm not religious."

"It's fine, Bobbie, and being religious isn't a requirement. People just want to help. It's as simple as that."

Bobbie glanced at her phone. "Oh, my God! I had no idea it was so late. See what happens when I get time off?" She grabbed her bag from the neighboring chair. "Great seeing you both." She certainly seemed like she was in a hurry to get away. Liz watched her thread through the crowd on her way to the door.

"I'm sorry she was so abrupt with you," said Liz, stroking Lucy's arm.

"Liz, you don't have to apologize for her."

"But she works for me, and…"

"And nothing. She was clear. She doesn't want my help. I have to re-spect that. But YOU," said Lucy, turning her eyes on Liz. "*You* need to tell me what's going on. What do you know about the woman she takes care of?"

The wire bistro chair wasn't comfortable to begin with, but Lucy's un-yielding scrutiny made Liz squirm. "I can't talk about her medical con-dition. You know that's privileged."

"But you can speak in general about what's going on. She has dementia. How bad?"

"She can still speak, has some mobility, and recognizes people. She's in and out, which is typical at this stage. Some days are better than others."

"What's her relationship to Bobbie?"

"They're not married."

"Liz, I'm not asking their legal status. Are they in a committed relationship?"

"Lucy, I didn't ask what the terms are. That's not one of the questions on a medical exam," said Liz impatiently. "Why is this so important?"

"You know why."

"Susan."

"Yes. I don't want her to get hurt." Lucy's firm look made that clear.

"Me neither. That's why I haven't encouraged the friendship. Susan has enough issues, and Bobbie doesn't need another burden."

Lucy leaned on her hand and thought for a moment. "Susan needs friends, and it sounds like Bobbie does too. That doesn't mean they're headed for a relationship."

"What if they are?" asked Liz. "Don't tell me you approve."

"It's not for me to say. And no matter how much you want to interfere, whether it's with Bobbie and Susan or Olivia and Amy or Maggie and Sam or any of our friends, it's not your place. And not mine either." Lucy sighed. "Shit. Why is everything so damned complicated?"

Encouraged by Lucy's use of expletives, Liz replied, "Fuck if I know. You're the one with the connections." She gazed skyward.

❀❀❀

The Margaritas had left Bobbie pleasantly buzzed. She wasn't about to admit to her boss and the Episcopal pastor that she'd imbibed more than one. When she'd started out that morning, she'd had so many plans for the day. After browsing the shops in Webhanet, she'd wasted a few hours in the consignment stores. By then it was lunchtime, and Dockside's twin lobster special had lured her to the harbor. After she ate, she decided to stay and watch the tide come in. Not having to rush off was a nearly forgotten pleasure, one that she never wanted to end. But even if Liz and Lucy hadn't shown up, she would have needed to leave. Natalie had class tonight, and Chloe was on duty at the hospital.

Natalie's Prius was backing up in the driveway when Bobbie arrived. She pulled onto the dying lawn to make room for her tenant to get by. Natalie opened her window. "Bobbie, thanks for bringing in that woman. I could finally get some work done for a change. She's wonderful. Did you find her through an agency?"

"No, from someone at work."

"Private referrals are always best," said Natalie. "Sorry, but I'm running late. See you later." She rolled up the window and waved as she drove away.

Bobbie wondered if Natalie found looking after Joyce a burden. She hadn't said so, but then neither had Bobbie, as if saying it aloud would make the weight of the load unbearable. Natalie would be graduating at the end of the term and would probably move on. Bobbie would miss her, especially because she was good company, and Joyce really liked her.

In the hallway outside the TV room, Bobbie heard the murmur of female voices. She was surprised to hear soft laughter bubble up. Before the disease had stolen Joyce's sense of humor, her intelligent wit had made her a regular on their friends' guest lists. When they met, Joyce had been part of a gold-earring club, a group of well-heeled lesbians, wealthy professional and businesswomen, nearly every one of them still in the closet.

As her brain began to change, Joyce became silly, and finally juvenile, amused only by slapstick comedy or potty jokes. At social events, she would reveal embarrassing personal details about Bobbie and then become giddy with shrill laughter. Their friends would gaze at Bobbie with worried concern. Some tried to be kind and continued to invite them, but finally, Bobbie felt she could no longer inflict her burden on others. Now, jokes and riddles went over Joyce's head. Bobbie wondered what Simone had done to make her laugh.

"Sounds like someone's having a good time," Bobbie said, coming into the room. "What's so funny?"

Simone turned with a smile. "I've been telling Joyce about the pranks I played on my sister when we were young."

"Pushed her in the water…in her Sunday dress!" supplied Joyce.

"I find that hard to believe," Bobbie said, turning to the elegant black woman, who was the epitome of Southern charm and grace.

"Oh, I was no angel as a child. My big sister, Cherie's mama, was a beauty. Grandma sewed her the prettiest dresses. I got her hand-me-downs, so I suppose I shouldn't complain, but she would prance around all proud of herself, preening for the boys like she was the queen of Sheba. When we passed the creek on the way home from church, I pretended to stumble and pushed her in. She stood there, looking all indignant in her wet dress and wilted straw hat, duck weed hanging out of her hair."

Joyce laughed hilariously, snorting at the end. The scene was humorous but not that funny. It didn't matter. Bobbie was pleased to see her so happy.

"I bet your parents didn't appreciate that little stunt," said Bobbie.

"Not a bit. My mama yanked up my dress and whupped my behind with the back of her hand. Oh my, did that smart! Her hand was all red afterward, so I think she hurt herself more than me."

"I bet she did," said Bobbie. "What did you ladies do today besides tell stories?"

"We danced!" Joyce said joyously, shimmying in her seat.

Bobbie glanced at Simone for an explanation. "Joyce and I are the same generation. I found a sixties channel on your TV, and we boogied." More animated than she'd been in months, Joyce swayed in her chair and began to sing, "Can't Hurry Love." She'd always had a good voice and remembered song lyrics.

"I got a good workout in the process," said Simone, wiggling her rear in time to Joyce's singing. "Joyce, you sing so nice!"

Joyce pointed to her throat. "Good voice."

"Yes, a wonderful voice," Simone agreed. "My mama did too. She liked hymns. We used to sing them together, but I never had her fine voice. She sang first soprano in the church choir. My niece, Cherie, sings almost as well as she did."

With the focus away from her, Joyce lost interest in the conversation and began to fidget. "Should I put on the weather channel?" Bobbie asked to distract her. "Excuse me."

Simone waved to dismiss the concern. "Joyce, thanks for dancing with me." Once the TV went on, Joyce was glued to the screen and didn't pay attention. Simone exchanged a look with Bobbie. "I left my bag in your kitchen. Let me go get it."

The movement caught Joyce's eye. "New maid. Can we keep her?"

"She's not the maid," said Bobbie in horror, realizing that Simone could hear them. "She used to be a school principal."

"Makes good sandwiches," said Joyce, smacking her lips to show her appreciation. In fact, Bobbie had made the egg salad sandwiches for their lunch. Joyce hadn't recognized her own recipe, with gherkin relish added for sweetness.

With a sigh, Bobbie patted Joyce's shoulder. "Let me say goodbye to Simone before she leaves."

"I'm so sorry," Bobbie hurried to say, after closing the pocket doors to the kitchen. "Her family had money when she was growing up, and they had a black maid. Joyce loved her."

Simone smiled. "Don't worry, Bobbie. Joyce has no idea what she's saying. When my mother's mind went, she would say the most hurtful things. At first, I was crushed. Then I realized her brain didn't know the difference between saying she loved me and telling me I was a no-good bitch."

"But being called a maid is so insulting. You're an educated woman. Trust me when I say, Joyce was never racist."

"Oh, honey, we're all racist. I make plenty of assumptions about white people. Joyce probably grew up thinking she wasn't prejudiced because her family was always good to the help."

"I'm so sorry," Bobbie repeated.

Simone studied her face. "Bobbie, you look about ready to cry." Bobbie pressed her lips together to stop them from trembling. "Breathe," whispered Simone, grasping her shoulders. "One breath at a time. Just breathe."

A tear broke away and ran down along Bobbie's nose. She furiously wiped it away with her fist.

"Come here." Simone gathered her in her arms and soothingly stroked her back. Bobbie gripped her with all her might. She allowed the tears to flow, but she fought the impulse to sob. She couldn't break down in front of someone who hardly knew her. If she did, everything would fall apart. Finally, the tears stopped, and Bobbie felt calmer.

"I could use a cup of tea," said Simone, sensing the storm had passed. "Do you mind if I make myself one?"

"Not at all." Bobbie said, yanking off a paper towel to wipe her face. "I'll make it."

"No need. I can do it. I even figured out where the cups are. Sit down. If you're interested, I'll make you a cup too."

Bobbie nodded and sank down in a kitchen chair. "Thank you for your kindness."

Simone filled the electric kettle and set it to heat. "Unfortunately, I know what you're going through. It's not easy."

"Why does it have to end like this?" Bobbie said, staring at the tabletop.

"I don't know, but it often does. Why don't you tell me about the beginning? That's a happier subject. Tell me how you met." The question told Bobbie that Simone knew or surmised about her relationship to Joyce. Maybe Cherie had told her.

"I was working on my credential as a nurse practitioner. I was moonlighting as a visiting nurse to earn extra money for my tuition. Joyce's mother had early Alzheimer's. The agency sent me to evaluate her for support."

"Ironic…and fateful," said Simone, pouring the boiling water into two mugs. "How do you like your tea?"

"Milk and one sugar."

Bobbie watched Simone prepare the tea and felt guilty being served in her own kitchen, especially after Joyce had called Simone the maid.

"Tell me about the day you met." Simone said placing Bobbie's cup in front of her.

"Joyce met me at the door, and I was stunned. She was so beautiful I could barely explain who I was and why I was there. Joyce was so different then. Her parents owned a multimillion-dollar plumbing fixture company. Her brother was supposed to take over, but when he died, Joyce was next in line. That was the era when women were encouraged to dress for success, and Joyce did it better than anyone. She always wore Brooks Brothers suits. Her button-down shirts were pressed just so. She was so sophisticated and beautiful..."

"She's still a beautiful woman," said Simone, leaning on her hand.

"Physically, yes, but in those days, her eyes sparkled with intelligence. She was always the smartest person in the room. She didn't miss a trick, part of why she was so successful in business. When the family sold the company, the new owners kept her on because she was so good at running it. She stayed for a while, but she didn't like how the new owners were managing it, so she cashed out and left. That's when things started to go downhill. Retirement made her depressed."

"It makes a lot of people depressed. For the first couple of years, I dreaded September because I knew the teachers would be going back to school, fixing up their classrooms, meeting their new pupils. Meanwhile, I was stuck at home, doing nothing."

"That's the reason I keep working. Sometimes, I think I should work until I drop dead."

Simone looked grave. "Honey, don't say things like that, or you'll make it happen."

"You don't look like the superstitious type."

"About death, I am," said Simone in a somber tone. "Not that I'm afraid to die, but let it be in God's good time. Not a moment sooner."

There were times when Bobbie wished death would take Joyce. On the current trajectory of her illness, she would continue to decline until she couldn't speak or walk or even eat. Hoping Joyce would die before that happened made Bobbie feel so guilty she beat herself up for days.

Simone obviously sensed Bobbie had gone into her own thoughts. "I enjoyed dancing with Joyce. She has a great sense of rhythm."

"It was smart to use music to connect with her. I bet singing and dancing made her happy."

"When a person's mind goes like that, giving them even a little joy is important."

"And you were so kind to give it to her. I hate to ask after what Joyce said, but will you come again?"

"How's next week?" asked Simone with a big smile. "I can come on Wednesday."

10

"Your wife is undeniably the most beautiful woman in the room," said Tom. "She knows it, but it doesn't seem to matter to her."

Liz looked at Lucy standing against the wall of windows facing Long Island Sound. Around her was a knot of mostly middle-aged, impeccably dressed gay men, rabid opera fans like Tom and Liz. Everyone was eagerly anticipating Lucy's performance, which had been billed as the high point of the wedding festivities.

"No one can deny she's beautiful," said Liz, trying to see her wife objectively. Lucy's flowing red gown, perfect makeup, and dazzling jewelry evoked the glamor of a famous opera star. She'd worn her hair loose over her shoulders, suggesting a character in an opera, perhaps the mad Lucia di Lammermoor or the desperate Maria Stuarda. "But, Tom, we're of a certain age. Someone younger might not see her the way we do."

"Nonsense, Lucy is a classic and ageless. You're such a lucky woman."

Liz completely agreed, but she knew Lucy would hate so much attention focused on her looks, which she saw as an accident of genetics. Her mother, also a singer, had been a model. Lucy didn't mind people praising her singing voice, her sermons, or her wisdom as a therapist. She actively solicited opinions about her theological writings. But Tom was right. Lucy seemed to take her beauty for granted. Feeling so comfortable in your own skin must be wonderful.

"This is a perfect venue for a wedding reception," Liz said, deliberately changing the subject.

"Thank you for persuading Jenny and Laura to host it."

"Oh, it didn't take much. The sum Jeff offered them for cleaning the house also got the exterior power washed. Even successful doctors have a hard time keeping up a big house like this. Never mind paying the taxes."

"Oh, don't spoil it, Liz. They were generous to agree. And you were bold to ask. Do you ever miss living here?"

Liz looked out at the sound, glittering in the late afternoon sun. The water was calm today. Not a single cloud interrupted the cerulean expanse overhead. "Sometimes, I miss having the water at my doorstep, but with climate change, that's not always an asset. Elevation above sea-level was an important factor when I bought in Hobbs. I may not end up with ocean-front property in my lifetime, but it's coming."

"You have a gorgeous view nevertheless."

"On cold or stormy days, it's Lucy's favorite place to meditate. She would probably say pray. Since she got her degree, she's not as obviously religious. Maybe she knows I'm a lost cause."

"Maybe she's using other ways to reach you instead of preaching to deaf ears." Tom raised his glass in Lucy's direction. "I never expected it, especially given all her other talents, but she's a very good theologian." He turned and looked directly into Liz's eyes. "Lucy is going to need an anchor, especially now that she's being pulled in so many directions. Fortunately, she has you, and you seem to be good for her. Erika was too, but you seem to have more influence. She really listens to you."

"After this disastrous book launch, Lucy is especially vulnerable. I'm doing everything I can to protect her."

Tom mocked a shiver. "So butch! I adore it." His meticulously trimmed beard almost hid his little smile. He and Jeff had chosen to wear classic summer formal wear—black tie with white dinner jackets. The light colors, along with multiple glasses of champagne, made Tom's cheeks look ruddier than usual. He frowned and shifted uncomfortably. "There's something I need to tell Lucy, but I've been holding off."

Liz mimed anguish. "Oh, Tom, don't do this to me again! Don't make me your messenger."

"No, this is between you and me for now. Last time, I had to fall on my sword for the triangulation. I'll tell her later when I can get her alone."

"All right. Tell me," said Liz, stepping closer. "I promise to keep it to myself."

"I've decided to retire. I mean, completely. Jeff wants to travel, and so do I. Being tied down to a parish, even for the summer, will make it difficult. It took me so long to come out. Now, I want to openly live my life with the man I love. I'm sure you understand."

"Of course, I understand. Why do you think I went along with the divorce? I probably would have stayed with Maggie if she hadn't left me. But, Tom, Lucy relies on you. When you said you planned to live in Florida all winter, she was devastated."

Tom looked contrite. "I know, but we'll be back in Maine in the spring. I'm happy to help in the summer chapel."

"She has Susan and Reshma for that. What she needs is your help navigating the politics. That vestry is a snake pit!"

Tom laughed heartily. "Liz, sometimes your gift for hyperbole rivals Erika's."

The flattery and the comparison to her late friend made Liz smile. "There was a reason we were close."

"I always knew it went beyond philosophy and the single-malt scotch. You were like two sides of the same coin. Imperfect twins. Dear Lord, I miss her!" Tom took a swallow of whiskey for solace.

"Erika would have enjoyed this party. It's the sort of urbane, sophisticated event she loved."

"And to think we wasted so much time without seeing one another. But I am grateful to have reconnected with her…and you…before she died."

"But now, you're disappearing again."

"I'll be back soon. Jeff and I agree that Florida is too hot in the summer. And there's always the telephone…and Zoom or Facetime or whatever miracle of technology can connect us. Jeff is good at tech."

Liz followed the direction of Tom's glance. His new husband, a former TV executive, was not only good at tech but also at orchestrating big events. He had positioned himself at the front, evidently trying to get people's attention. Finally, he used a microphone. "Ladies and gentlemen, I'm sure you've been anxiously awaiting the moment when our famous guest will perform. Please find a seat, and we'll get started."

Unfortunately, the nearest empty seat happened to be next to Jenny, Liz's ex.

"How exciting to have a famous opera singer perform in our house," she said near Liz's ear to be heard over the raucous applause. Liz noted the possessive pronoun Jenny had applied to the house. Of course, Jenny was referring to her wife, who'd finally bought out Liz's share of the mortgage.

"Thanks for letting them use the place, but you might have to put up with revelers into the wee hours."

"Laura and I booked a room in the B&B in town. We're leaving you and Lucy to deal with any revelers."

Liz let out an exasperated sigh and turned her attention to Lucy, who was getting ready to announce her first selection: "Ebben" from *La Wally*, a perfect vehicle for her mature voice. Liz had listened to her practice it in their media room every morning for the last week. When Lucy hit the high notes, Liz clutched her chest in sympathy. Around her, dozens of gay men did the same.

The next aria was from Puccini's opera, *Suor Angelica*. So far, the anemic string quartet Jeff had hired to provide background music during cocktail hour, was holding its own against Lucy's powerful soprano, but Tom and Lucy had chosen arias that didn't need big orchestral support.

Given the audience's predilection for the dramatic, the next selection was another famous tear-jerker. "Addio del passato" from *La Traviata*. For her final number, Lucy chose an aria guaranteed to make every gay man in the audience swoon, "Un bel di" from *Madama Butterfly*, a special request from Jeff.

The audience went wild. Some people were standing on the rented seats to cheer and whistle their appreciation. Lucy curtsied graciously. Jeff ran up to present her with a voluptuous bouquet of red roses.

"Wow, that was incredible," said Jenny into Liz's ear. "How can you stop yourself from carrying her to bed every time she sings?"

Liz laughed. "Sometimes, I do. But I listen to her practice every morning, and she doesn't look like that at five am."

"Liz, knowing you, that wouldn't matter."

Jeff returned to the front. "Thank you so much, Lucy," he said, throwing her kisses with both hands. "Don't forget that Lucy will be performing with the New York Philharmonic next month. Are there still tickets left?" he called to her.

"A few."

"Get them while you can!" Jeff urged the audience. "Don't miss the triumphant return of Lucille Bartlett to the New York stage! Now, give it up for Madame Bartlett!"

After the applause died, the quartet began to play again, looking relieved to return to chamber music. Tom had said there would be dancing later, but they had hired a DJ instead of a band.

A waiter passed with glasses of wine. Liz nabbed one to bring to Lucy, who was once again hemmed in by adoring men. Liz nudged her way into the huddle to hand her the wine.

"Thank you, sweetie. Water would have been better after singing."

"I know, but it was the best I could do." Liz craned above the heads of Lucy's admirers to find a place to get water.

"Gentlemen, I'm glad you enjoyed the little recital, but I think my wife needs attention," said Lucy, taking Liz's arm and leading her away. There were titters as the men drifted towards the bar.

"I don't need attention," Liz protested indignantly when they were alone.

"I know, but I need a break, and you made a good excuse. Come on. Let's find a place to sit down. My shoes are killing me."

Liz navigated through the crowd, gently fending off well-wishers until she found two vacant seats against the wall.

"Does it ever bother you that there are always people around me?" asked Lucy, sitting down.

"No, it makes me proud to be loved by such a beautiful and talented woman."

"You're so damn sure of yourself, Liz Stolz. I like that about you."

"I want you to get the applause you deserve, especially since you've been taking it on the chin with your book." When Lucy made a little face, Liz wanted to pinch herself for bringing up the sore subject.

Lucy slipped off a shoe and rubbed her foot. "Now that I've done my part, I'm going to enjoy this wedding." She drained her wine glass in a few gulps. Liz started to get up to look for a waiter to ask for water, but Lucy held her down by the arm. "Just sit for a minute and let me catch my breath. Then I have to find the bathroom." She gazed into Liz's eyes. "So, I sang well?"

"You were sublime. You gave them exactly what they wanted—a true diva."

"Good. Mission accomplished." Lucy leaned her head back against the wall. "I saw you talking to Tom. Is everything all right?"

Liz deadpanned so she wouldn't look guilty over knowing his secret. "Yes, we were just gossiping about our friends."

"I hope he's pleased with the performance."

Realizing Lucy didn't suspect a thing, Liz let out a sigh of relief. "After that response, why wouldn't he be?"

❉❉❉

Susan stared at the text message on her phone. *Please stop by my office if you can. I'm free from 4:30-5:30. Thanx.* She'd known Lucy was back from Connecticut because the requests for pastoral care had suddenly stopped. As the only priest at St. Margaret's, Susan had been backing up Reshma while Lucy was away. Otherwise, the deacon had efficiently managed the calls, important because Susan could only respond outside of school hours.

The dismissal bell finally rang. Susan was on bus duty that afternoon. With one eye on the students, she texted Lucy to let her know she would be there at four-thirty.

After the buses left, Susan had time to kill before her meeting with Lucy. The quiz she'd given that morning needed grading. She'd always prided herself in staying on top of the paperwork that drowned other teachers.

On her way to the teacher's room, Susan passed the new principal.

The school board had promoted Courtney Barnes after her predecessor had finally announced her retirement. Susan was glad she'd won the position over the outside candidates. As a former teacher, Courtney understood how fraught the profession had become since the staff shortages and the political debates over curriculum. She'd been supportive of Susan in a subtle way that didn't show favoritism. In a new school district, having an administrator on your side could make all the difference.

Susan offered the principal a friendly wave as she passed, but she'd barely gotten a few steps down the hall before Courtney called after her: "Susan, do you have a minute?" She pointed in the direction of her office.

After Susan took a seat, the principal closed the door—not a good sign. Susan scanned her memory for any recent missteps but came up with nothing. Earlier that week, Courtney had observed her in the classroom. Afterward, she'd been complimentary.

Courtney smiled, which put Susan more at ease. "I just wanted to tell you how much I enjoyed being in your classroom. Observing teachers can be a painful task for an administrator. Sometimes, I struggle to give constructive criticism, but your rapport with the students and your classroom management are excellent. It was a pleasure to watch you in action."

Susan's eyelashes fluttered with surprise. "Thank you," she murmured, wondering what had prompted the sudden praise.

"As you know, some of our new teachers finished their training during the pandemic. They're probably way ahead of us in remote learning, but completely lacking in good, old-fashioned classroom experience. So, I was wondering…would you consider mentoring them?"

"But I'm new here," Susan said cautiously.

"So are they. That's my excuse for making you a team. I don't want to make it obvious that they need help. With your tact, I think you could coach them without letting on. Am I right?"

"I can try."

"Have you done any mentoring before?" asked Courtney.

"When I was teaching in New York. City schools can be challenging. Without combat training, the new teachers dropped like flies."

"I bet. Can you meet this time next week to help me organize this project?"

"I'd be happy to." Susan pulled out her planner to make a note. She could feel Courtney watching her with amusement. "I know it's old-fashioned, but this is how I learned to stay organized."

"As long as it works for you, I don't care," said Courtney with a shrug. She waited for Susan to enter the details in her calendar. "How do you like it here? Are you settling in?"

"Yes, I really like Hobbs Elementary. The facilities are beautiful. The population has a nice mix."

"I can see the students really connect with you. That's the sign of an excellent teacher."

"Thank you," said Susan, feeling herself blush. "I do my best."

"Our first parent-teacher conferences are next week. How are you feeling about that?"

"I always enjoy meeting the parents. It helps me understand what my students are dealing with."

"Context is important," agreed Courtney with a nod. "We have a tradition at Hobbs Elementary. Before the first parent-teacher meetings, many of the teachers meet at La Scala for an early dinner. Would you like to join us?"

Susan was delighted by the invitation, but she didn't want to seem too eager. "What time?"

"Four-thirty. The owner lets us in before they officially open. That gives us plenty of time to eat before we need to get back. It's a nice break from a long day and fun to get together outside of school. Think about joining us."

"Thanks. I will," said Susan, entering the time and place in her planner.

"That's all I had to say. I'll let you get back to whatever you were doing."

Susan glanced at the clock over the door. "I was hoping to grade some quizzes, but I seem to have run out of time. I have a meeting with my other boss."

Courtney's eyes widened. "Sometimes I forget you work for Lucy Bartlett too. I won't keep you."

Susan was buoyant when she headed to her car. Then worry about her meeting with Lucy punctured her elation. Susan told herself to be positive. She'd been anxious when Courtney had invited her into her office, but the result had been a new assignment and an invitation to a social event.

"Hi, Mother Susan." Jodie, the parish admin, was packing up for the day. She shifted her eyes in the direction of Lucy's office. "She's waiting for you."

Susan was about to offer a nun's admonition for the disrespect: "*She* is the cat's mother," they used to say in Catholic schools, but Jodi was young and had probably never heard of that old-fashioned standard of respect.

When Susan knocked on Lucy's open door, she looked up and smiled. Susan wondered why she was wearing her fancy linen collar until she remembered that it was vestry day.

"Hi, Susan. Just coming from school?"

"Yes, I had a brief meeting with the principal." Susan sat down in one of the visitors' chairs.

"How'd that go?"

"Courtney asked me to help mentor the young teachers. She thinks their classroom management skills could use improvement."

"I'm sure you can give them some pointers. You're a great teacher."

Susan wondered how Lucy knew. She'd never observed her in the classroom. "Why do you say that?"

"When we were deacons, you did such a great job with that clergy intern." Susan had almost forgotten that episode because she was in the throes of her ordination dilemma. "I wouldn't have had a clue where to start," Lucy continued. "Sometimes, I don't know how to advise Reshma except to tell her to watch what I do."

"You're a great role model. We all have our talents, Lucy. You're much better at pastoral counseling than I am."

"That's the benefit of my extra training in social work. Too bad you didn't take advantage of it too."

"I didn't have the resources you had."

Lucy picked up on the bitter tone. "Susan, I offered to help you with the tuition."

"I know. My pride kept me from accepting."

The admission caused Lucy's expression to soften. "We both made mistakes."

"We did."

Lucy glanced out the window. "I'm sorry I haven't been more available to you. I've been busy and overwhelmed by my own problems."

"Your book?"

Lucy sighed and nodded.

"It didn't deserve such a harsh response. It's well-argued and well-written. You went out of your way to stay inside doctrinal norms. Maybe it's too conservative?" Lucy's eyes grew large. She probably never expected to hear such a thing from someone who'd once talked about joining the breakaway Anglican Church of America.

"That's what Liz says."

Liz. Susan didn't want to hear or talk about Liz. "You can explore a new direction in your next book."

"If there is a next book…"

"Oh, that's not the Lucy I remember. Look how you fought to keep your singing career going. How you overcame your depression after the rape. You even persisted with your Jiu Jitsu training until you got a brown belt. You're the most determined woman I know."

Lucy smiled sadly. "Thanks, Susan. You always believed in me. But I didn't ask you to come here to discuss my troubles. I have some news that will make you happy."

"More good news? I can hardly stand it," quipped Susan, which made Lucy smile.

"Tom has decided to retire. He and Jeff want to travel and don't want to be tied down. They'll summer here, but he only wants to serve as a supply priest."

"Which leaves an opening for an associate rector," said Susan, holding her breath that she might be considered.

"Yes, but we're not filling it."

"I see," said Susan, lowering her eyes to hide her disappointment.

"We're not filling it because we don't really need more administrators, especially with a strong senior warden like Abbie. But I can use help in liturgical planning and seasonal devotions. Advent is coming up, and I would like to offer some special services."

"And you were thinking of me?"

"Yes, if you're interested. The vestry voted today to end your probationary period. Abbie is a big fan of yours."

"You don't look completely sold on this idea," said Susan after studying Lucy's face.

"I'm not. I still have concerns. If I had my way, we'd keep you on as a temporary hire at least a year."

Susan shifted in her chair. "What are your concerns?" she asked, not sure she wanted to know. "Still don't trust me?"

"I'm getting there. It's not long ago that you lied to me about why you were in Hobbs. And you haven't been sober that long."

"But I've stayed sober, and I haven't done anything to make you doubt me."

"Liz said she caught you on the security camera."

Susan winced. She took a deep breath. "She said she wouldn't tell you."

"She sat on it for a long time, but eventually, she tells me everything."

"Communication is good," said Susan neutrally, but the words sounded sarcastic. "Did she also tell you I was there to check the watering system? I was trying to help Courtney, who was in a hurry to pick up her daughter."

"She told me, but it's out of your way. Would you have volunteered if it had been someone else's house?"

Susan thought for a moment.

"Tell the truth, Susan."

"I admit that seeing your yard was part of the appeal. I was curious."

Lucy's frown relaxed. "Well, that's honest."

"Lucy, I'd never do anything to hurt you or undermine your position here."

"That's good because I worked hard to build up St. Margaret's."

"Lucy, I..."

"And now you have this drama going on with Bobbie Lantry. I'm not going to tell you how to handle that situation, but you should let her explain."

"She befriended me under false pretenses. She didn't tell me the whole truth."

"Have you told her the whole truth? Does she know you're an alcoholic?"

Susan stared at the front of Lucy's desk and shook her head.

"I thought so."

"When I have the opportunity, I will tell her. I didn't want to frighten her away."

"I understand. We all have skeletons in our closets, but Susan, you have issues that go way back. I think you could benefit from therapy."

"Are you volunteering?" Susan forced herself to avoid sneering.

"You know I can't. That would be unethical. But I can recommend someone. You have health insurance now and can afford it. Even if you couldn't, she charges on a sliding scale." Lucy scribbled something on a piece of paper and ripped it off the pad. "Here's her number, if you're interested."

Susan reached for the paper and put it in her pocket. "Is that all you wanted to say?" With the tension in the room, she couldn't wait to leave, but Lucy shook her head. "No, I'd like you to take a more active role in mentoring Reshma, now that Tom is gone."

"You don't trust me, but you want me to work with young clergy?"

"She has doubts about her vocation, a problem you know something about. You may be able to help her." Lucy gave her a long evaluating look. "Congratulations on your approval by the vestry. You earned it."

"I'd rather have your approval...and your trust."

"That may come. But you always have my support." Lucy rose, indicating the meeting was over.

"Thanks for your time." Susan said, picking up her bags.

When she reached the second floor, Reshma and Denise were talking and laughing down the hall. They waved to her. Once Susan got the stubborn door open, she waved back.

She sank down into the old club chair in the sitting room. After she caught her breath, she realized that she'd been promoted. Before AA, she would have bought a bottle of wine to celebrate. She drank in good times and bad—any excuse for a drink. She'd have tea instead, but she wished she could share the good news with someone who cared. She thought of Bobbie and picked up her phone. After a long moment of hesitation, she texted: *I got a promotion.*

❀❀❀

The Waterpik they used for ear irrigations had died, so Bobbie was using a spray bottle—low tech, but it always worked. Mr. O'Malley had come in complaining of being deaf in one ear and constant ringing. The obvious solution was to remove any impacted ear wax. Bobbie stopped blasting his ear canal to judge her progress with an otoscope and heard a faint ping from her pocket. She'd forgotten that she'd enabled text notifications, hoping to hear from Susan.

"What's that damn noise?" Mr. O'Malley snarled.

"Just my phone. Sorry it's bothering you." Bobbie reached into her pocket to silence it.

"What's bothering me is that ice-cold water you're spraying into my ear. Are you trying to drown me?"

Bobbie showed him the pan filled with water and floating bits of brown debris. "That's how much old wax was in there. I'm sorry. Having your ear irrigated is no fun."

"You got that right," he replied with a grunt.

Bobbie continued to shoot water into his ear until an inspection showed the canal was clear. "Can you hear better now?" she asked directly into Mr. O'Malley's face.

"Yes, I can," he said, looking pleasantly surprised.

She handed him a paper towel to dry his jaw and neck. "Just head out to the front and let Ginny know we're done."

"Thank God!" His surly response made Bobbie want to smile, but she kept a straight face.

Although she was hopefully impatient, she finished cleaning up the exam room before checking her phone. Her heart took a joyful leap when the preview of the message showed it was from Susan. *I got a promotion.*

Bobbie smiled and typed back *Congratulations!!!!!* She looked at the string of exclamation points and compared it to Susan's completely unadorned message. You could tell she was a schoolteacher. She always punctuated her text messages correctly, including commas and periods.

The little cloud on the screen began to move. Susan was typing. *Sorry to interrupt. I know you're still at work.*

Almost done here. Just saw my last patient. It was a real blast. Bobbie chuckled at the pun. *Want to celebrate?*

Can you get away?

Let me check. I'll get back to you.

Bobbie texted Natalie, who was on duty at home. *Can you stay with her till 9?*

The reply came instantly. *No problem.*

Thanks. Stew in the fridge. The big pot of chicken stew could feed the two of them and Chloe too if she was interested. There was little worry Joyce would complain. It was one of her own recipes.

Great, Natalie replied. *Glad to help.* She'd also be glad for the "tip" she'd get for the extra time with Joyce. Using that word made everyone feel better about the money being exchanged.

In the privacy of the exam room, Bobbie did a little happy dance before texting Susan. *Let's go out for dinner.*

Are you sure you have time?

Got it covered. Pick you up in 20 mins.

Sounds great.

Bobbie hurried to change into street clothes. She always left a top and pants in her locker in case she'd need to go someplace where scrubs would be inappropriate. She made a mental note to bring replacements in the morning and groaned, thinking of all the things she had to keep in her mind. If it was overwhelming to her, how must it be for Joyce, who struggled to remember what happened five minutes ago? But maybe she was the lucky one. Others took care of remembering her doctors' appointments, paying the bills, when to take her meds. Joyce was as carefree as a child. But the idea of giving up so much control was terrifying. Bobbie had only really felt free after she'd become an adult and no longer had to depend on others to make decisions for her.

The minute Bobbie pulled into the church parking lot, Susan came out of the rectory. She wore a flowing, floral dress that made the hasty dinner arrangement seem more like a big date. Bobbie wondered if she'd dressed up for her.

"It's so good to see you," said Susan, getting into the car.

Bobbie didn't say anything because the words were stuck in her throat.

"I missed you so much," Susan said, even though it was she who'd kept them apart.

"I missed you too." The engine was running, but Bobbie gazed into Susan's eyes, hoping to find forgiveness for the awful scene with Joyce. She noticed the irises had a dark ring around them, as deep blue as the ocean on a bright summer morning.

The spell broke when Susan began searching for the seat belt clip. "We should go."

Bobbie backed out of the parking space. "I hope you like this place. It's become my favorite restaurant in Hobbs."

"Eating out is such a treat for me. I'm trying to save some money, so I never go out to dinner on my own."

As Bobbie waited at the light, she lowered her visor to block the sharp light of the setting sun. "Tell me about your promotion."

Susan smiled mysteriously. "Let's wait until we're at the restaurant. And don't get too excited. Neither are big promotions."

"Neither? You mean, more than one? Oh, come on, Susan. Don't keep me in suspense."

"Tell me about *you*," said Susan, turning in her seat. "How have *you* been?"

"Overwhelmed as usual, but now, a woman stays with Joyce once a week, so I finally get a day off. I almost forgot how good it feels to do nothing."

Bobbie could feel Susan's eyes scrutinizing the side of her face. "I'm happy for you," she finally said. "Everyone deserves a day off."

The light was red at the turn for the harbor. Trying not to be obvious, Bobbie admired her passenger out of the corner of her eye. "You look terrific."

"Thank you," demurred Susan, blushing a little. "I was hoping you'd like this dress."

So, Susan had dressed up for her.

"Is it new?"

"Relatively speaking. It's new to me. I needed to update my wardrobe for my new job. I found it in a thrift shop. "

"Oh, I love thrift shops. Maybe we can go shopping sometime."

"That would be fun…if you can find the time."

"I'll make the time," said Bobbie. Susan demonstrated her skepticism with silence, so Bobbie added, "I promise."

"I'll hold you to it."

Bobbie rejoiced because that meant more time with Susan.

The frazzled hostess tried to seat them in the middle of the crowded dining room even though Bobbie had reserved a window table. The woman compressed her lips and pointed to the bar. "Sorry your table's not ready yet. I'll page you when it is."

Bobbie turned to Susan. "You get a seat outside, and I'll bring the drinks. What are you having?"

"Tonic water with lime."

"It's a special occasion. Don't you want a *real* drink?"

"No, thanks. I don't drink." Susan leaned forward and whispered into her ear. "I'm an alcoholic."

Bobbie's eyes flew open. "Oh," she managed to say.

Susan stood straight and studied her face. "You're not the only one with secrets," she said with a little smile. "Go get the drinks. I'll find a table outside."

While Bobbie waited for the bartender, she wondered how a sweet-faced, saintly looking woman like Susan could be an alcoholic. She was a teacher *and* a priest! None of it fit. Of course, Bobbie was making assumptions based on stereotypes. Professionally, she knew that many middle-aged women were secret alcoholics. Faced with work stress, family obligations, relationship troubles, and God knows what else, they self-medicated. Facebook was full of sarcastic wine memes that fell flat when measured against the grim reality of closet alcoholism. After a rough day at the office or a frustrating episode with Joyce, Bobbie could easily put away a bottle of wine. She tried not to drink on work nights but then ended up having a drink to relax. She told herself she didn't have a drinking problem, but she sometimes wondered.

"Here's your virgin tonic," said the bartender, plunking a slice of lime into the glass. At least here, the lime wedges weren't brown at the edges. As in all bars, their cleanliness was questionable. Bobbie tried not to think about it as she carried away their drinks.

A young man held the door open for her with a silly grin and a mocking bow. Compared to the people in New York, everyone in Maine was so much kinder.

Susan jumped up to help Bobbie settle the drinks. "I'm sorry I ambushed you with that information."

"No, I should have listened to you the first time."

"Everyone assumes other people drink."

"But they shouldn't," said Bobbie, taking a seat on the same side of the table so she could look at the ocean. "Lots of people don't drink for health reasons or because of their religion. When someone says no, other people should take their word for it."

"People like me would appreciate it. No one likes to explain over and over."

"I don't blame you, and I'm sorry I wasn't more sensitive." Bobbie raised her glass. "To your promotion."

"Thank you for the congrats and for taking me out to celebrate. This is such a beautiful place."

"Thank you for accepting. I wasn't sure you'd ever talk to me again."

Susan looked away. "Sorry it took so long, but I was really shaken by what happened."

Bobbie cringed at the memory of Joyce's shrill accusations. "Joyce has temper tantrums, but she usually doesn't react that strongly in front of strangers. Something really set her off."

"She senses something...between us," ventured Susan.

Bobbie shifted uncomfortably in her seat. *Should they talk about it?* She waited for Susan to say more. When she didn't, Bobbie jumped in to fill the silence. "We're supposed to be celebrating. Why don't we hold off on the heavy conversation until another time?"

"That sounds like a good idea," said Susan, looking enormously relieved, "but we do need to talk about it."

"I agree, but tonight, let's just relax and enjoy our dinner. It's our first real date."

"It's a date?' asked Susan with amused surprise. "Yes, I guess it is."

Without talking about it, they had confirmed what they both already knew.

11

The mattress threatened to suck Susan down like the soft mud in the marsh. When she rolled over to find higher ground, it felt like hanging off a cliff. The brand name on the mattress tag was unrecognizable, probably overstock from Marden's. When Lucy had bought it, she was living on a rector's salary and needed to be frugal.

With her palm, Susan measured the breadth of the hollow. Tom, a big man with broad shoulders, had left that depression. It was much too wide and deep for tiny Lucy, but she had lain there too in one of her fancy nightgowns, the one extravagance she'd always allowed herself, no matter her resources. Ironic that such a naturally beautiful woman needed frilly things to feel pretty. The image of her full breasts straining against the lace of the bodice fluttered into Susan's mind.

Squeezing her eyelids tight, Susan tried to blind her mind's eye. *Lucy is married to Liz now,* she told herself, *and she isn't even here.*

They'd gone to New York for Lucy's Philharmonic concert. This time, Liz hadn't offered tickets, so Susan couldn't afford to go. Plus there was the expense of the hotel, and someone had to stay in Hobbs and fill in for Lucy and Tom. He'd gone with his new husband to Iceland to see the Northern Lights. Susan had read that they could sometimes be seen in Maine. Maybe someday, she'd find a traveling companion to make the road trip north.

She managed to banish the images of Lucy, but her regrets returned like hungry orphans in a charity commercial. Lately, her mother plagued her thoughts. Although she'd always encouraged her daughters to get an education, she was furious when Susan told her she wanted to enter the convent. Agnes Gedney was a pious Catholic, but her daughters were all she had, and she wanted to keep them close. Susan's sister had lived at home until she eloped in her fifties. Not long after, her husband ran off, leaving her bankrupt, a reprise of the family tragedy in another generation. What little money her sister earned at her job as a bookkeeper ran through her fingers. "Like water," her mother would say, but she kept giving her more. She cleaned herself out until there was nothing left to pay the taxes on the house.

When the old woman finally put aside her pride and asked Susan for help, she pretended she had nothing to spare. Her thousand-dollar stash was a fortune after years of putting her seminary tuition on credit cards. Giving her hard-earned money to her spendthrift sister went against everything she'd been taught. Later, she'd discovered that her mother had sold her gold jewelry to pay the taxes, even her wedding ring. She'd worn it long after her father died to prove she was an "honest woman." After hearing her grandfather constantly harp on her mother's out of wedlock pregnancy, Susan could understand why.

Susan's sister had wanted to end their mother's life with the morphine injections the hospice nurse had left behind. By that point, the congestive heart failure was a death sentence, but the Catholic Church taught that life must be preserved at all costs, and Susan still clung to those beliefs. Until the old woman drew her last tortured breath, her otherwise lifeless eyes were full of terror. If she'd been promised eternal life in exchange for her faith, why was she so afraid?

Those and other terrible memories tormented Susan once she turned off the light. If she gave them attention, her thoughts would go down a never-ending spiral like dark water circling a drain. Her therapist had explained that the twilight before sleep makes the brain chatter harder to resist. She suggested deep breathing. Susan listened politely, but she'd already tried everything—breathing exercises, focused thinking, meditation. She'd prayed the rosary, with and without the beads, counting the *Aves* on her fingers.

Dr. Hsu recommended melatonin. Susan knew it was technically a hormone, not a drug, and wouldn't compromise her sobriety. Even so, she reserved the sleep aid for nights when she was desperate, like tonight.

Her hand felt around the night stand and located the bottle of strawberry-flavored gummies. They stuck to her dental work, reminding her of the chewy candy sold in the movie theaters when she was a girl. The association with double-feature Walt Disney matinees usually made her cozy enough to fall asleep.

The melatonin gave her vivid dreams that she could remember, something she hadn't been able to do for years. The dreams were mostly pleasant. Sometimes she saw horrors like the flashing lights in her rear-view mirror when the police had stopped her for DUI, or her Catholic mother refusing her prayers on her deathbed. According to her, Susan couldn't be a *real* priest because she was a woman.

Around three, she awoke to use the bathroom, cursing her tiny bladder, although it was the tossing and turning in her thin sleep that had awakened her. She tried to stay drowsy by not turning on the light while she peed almost nothing. When she returned to bed, she instantly fell asleep.

The motel room was dark and smelled of mildew, but waiting there was someone she hadn't seen since high school. Sister Joan was her homeroom teacher in the seventh grade. Susan had been in love with her sixth-grade teacher, but when she was transferred to another school, she chose Sister Joan as the new object of her adoration. Gangly and newly tall, her skin erupting, her shape changing by the minute, Susan poured all the hormonal passion of her adolescent body into the crush. At recess, she would study the convent walls, wondering which window was Sister Joan's bedroom. She imagined her asleep or naked in the communal shower. She wondered if she touched herself in secret like Susan did.

When the nuns came out of the convent after their lunch, a gaggle of girls followed their favorites. Susan could blend in until her classmates discovered boys and lost interest in their teachers.

After Sister Joan was transferred, Susan wrote to her every week on expensive stationery purchased from the Hallmark store with her meager allowance. Her mother began to worry about her unhealthy interest in a woman. Defying her, Susan secretly took the train to Sister Joan's new convent to visit her. The nun never discouraged her interest. After Susan entered the convent, she understood why. Even surrounded by all those women, Susan felt isolated and lonely. Now, Susan would condemn a teacher for having such a close friendship with a young girl.

In the dream, Sister Joan was the same age she'd been when Susan was in high school. The motel room was seedy like the places where Susan had slept on her way back from South Dakota. The stained bedspread was sticky with the sweat of too-eager, unwashed bodies. Semen had a distinctive scent. But they were finally alone. Maybe this time it would really happen. She could finally kiss her idol and open her smooth thighs.

"I've been in love with you since I was twelve years old," Susan whispered fervently.

Sister Joan's brown eyes were kind like Bobbie's. Susan leaned forward to kiss her soft lips, desperately hoping for consummation.

She awoke with a start. It wasn't an actual memory, just another melatonin trick. Sister Joan had never touched her. She'd left the convent long before Susan entered. Over fifty years had passed since she'd last seen her. The woman she'd once worshiped would now be in her seventies, about the same age as Bobbie's partner. Maybe she had also lost her mind. Maybe she was already dead.

With a shudder, Susan pulled herself into a ball and tightly shut her eyes to stop the tears.

✻✻✻

Bobbie blinked when she turned on the overhead light in the supply closet. Coming in from the early morning darkness made every light in the office seem stunningly bright. The shelves needed replenishment, but the staff had been too busy giving COVID boosters and flu shots.

The patient Bobbie was going to see was in hospice care. Most of the things she might need should already be at the house, but many years as a visiting nurse had taught Bobbie to be prepared. She opened a canvas bag and tossed in incontinence pads, gauze of varying sizes, a couple of plastic emesis pans, as well as disposable syringes. She always kept spare instruments in her desk drawer. It was jammed with junk, and she had to poke through the clutter to find them. The stethoscope was all the way in the back.

She was relieved to see a vial of Lasix in the drug safe. The expiration date was on the edge, but it was still good. She skipped the morphine, knowing the hospice service would have left plenty.

The sodium lights in the parking lot cast long shadows. Once the time changed, it wouldn't be this dark in the morning, but the reprieve before real winter began would be brief. Late autumn in Maine seemed darker than in any place she'd lived. Joyce had once explained that the state was in the wrong time zone, which was why it got light and dark earlier.

On the way to Mrs. Hawley's house, Bobbie reviewed her case. The woman's heart condition had finally gotten the best of her. Although Hobbs Family Practice didn't have an official policy on house calls, Bobbie guessed that, if Liz weren't in New York, she would have come out on this one.

Mrs. Hawley proudly told anyone who would listen that she'd been Liz's first patient in Hobbs. Bobbie had heard the story several times—how the townspeople were suspicious of the high-profile surgeon from Yale who was buying the practice from the retiring osteopath. When they heard she was originally from New York, it was worse. Mainers had a thing about New Yorkers.

Mrs. Hawley was a prominent church lady, head of the altar guild, chair of the harvest fair committee, secretary of the vestry. While dressing the altar or rolling dough at the annual pie making, Mrs. Hawley spread the word about Dr. Stolz—how smart she was and kind. After that, the practice, which had gotten off to a slow start, began to flourish.

What if the venture had failed? Would Liz have returned to Connecticut and gone back to practicing surgery? Or retired to fish and build furniture? No one would ever know. Funny how something like Mrs. Hawley's church membership could determine the fate of so many.

When Liz heard the hospice service hadn't shown up for Mrs. Hawley, she'd be furious. Bobbie wouldn't want to be that hospice nurse after Liz got finished reaming her boss. Part of the reason Bobbie had come out this morning was the solidarity she felt with the nurse. Since big medical conglomerates had figured out that hospices made good profit-centers, they cut corners any way they could. The nurses were spread so thin they couldn't possibly make it to every call. When they did show up, it was often too late. Bobbie sometimes wondered if that was part of the plan. Death was hard to watch.

The GPS continued to bark instructions. When Bobbie had been coming to Hobbs as a summer visitor, she didn't even know this part of town existed. The backroads had no streetlights, and on a moonless night like this, they were pitch black. She drove down the street slowly, scrutinizing each driveway as she passed. The GPS was vague, but the house with all the lights blazing, inside and out, was probably her destination. In case an ambulance or police cruiser needed to pull in, Bobbie parked off the driveway on the lawn. The frozen grass crunched under her feet as she headed to the house.

After three rings, the door finally opened. "Thank God!" said the middle-aged, obviously gay man who answered the door. She recognized him from bringing his mother into the office.

"Hello, I'm Bobbie Lantry, Dr. Stolz's nurse practitioner."

"Yes, I remember you," he said, taking her outstretched hand. "You treated my mother for a UTI."

"You're Kevin, right?"

He looked pleased to be remembered. "Yes, please come in."

The house was surprisingly neat and clean, despite what must be an overwhelming task for a single man. A faint floral scent permeated the air. Bobbie guessed it was air freshener to cover the odor of stale urine and silently commended Kevin for good sickroom management.

"Where's the patient?" she asked, and he led the way to the living room, where a hospital bed had been set up.

Mrs. Hawley picked at her chest. Her mouth opened and closed like a newly landed fish. The poor woman was literally drowning in her own body fluids. Congestive heart failure was a terrible way to go. Bobbie scanned the hospice notes. The advance directives forbade any extraordinary measures. Bobbie debated whether she should administer the Lasix, but under these conditions, helping the patient breathe would count as palliative care.

"I can give Mom something to ease the lung congestion," she explained to Kevin. "It will prolong her life, but she'll be more comfortable."

"Please! I can't stand watching her go through this." Families always thought they were brave until they saw what death really looks like.

Bobbie was sanitizing her hands when the doorbell rang. "Did you call an ambulance?"

"Hospice said not to call 911," said Kevin. "It must be the priest. My mother said she wanted one with her at the end." No surprise to Bobbie. The old-timers always seemed to get religious at the end.

"I'll take care of Mom. You get the door." Bobbie snapped on sterile gloves and filled a syringe with Lasix. She pulled away the blanket to inspect the woman's thin arms for an injection site. "Hello, Mrs. Hawley. Remember me? I'm Bobbie from Dr. Stolz's office. I'm going to give you something to help you breathe. Is that okay?"

The old woman turned her eyes to Bobbie and nodded. She obviously understood what was happening, which made Bobbie doubt that today would be her last.

From the hall, she heard a familiar voice. Susan Gedney, wearing a black suit and a collar, stepped into the room. "Hello, Bobbie," Susan said with perfect calm and the slightest smile. "Will I be in your way?"

"One quick jab, and I'll be out of yours." The old woman flinched when Bobbie landed the syringe. "There, Mrs. Hawley. You should feel better soon." Bobbie tapped a bandage over the injection site. The labored breaths continued, but the woman's grateful gaze conveyed her relief.

Bobbie looked up to see a fleeting look of panic on Susan's face. Eye contact broke it, and Susan instantly became all-business. She opened a little bag and set out its contents: some vials, a cross, a small book, and a votive candle. She unfurled a strip of white satin embroidered with crosses on the ends and hung it around her neck.

"I'll get out of here, so you can get started," Bobbie said, capping the syringe for disposal in the office.

"You're welcome to stay," said Susan. "Maybe you could ask Kevin to come in too."

Bobbie didn't like the idea of being roped into a religious service but decided it was a kindness to Kevin. When she returned with him, she found Susan bending over Mrs. Hawley with her ear near the old woman's lips. To give them privacy, Bobbie waited in the doorway until Susan straightened and cut a cross in the air with her hand.

Bobbie had witnessed enough last rites to have a basic understanding of the ritual. She watched Susan lay her hand on Mrs. Hawley's pale forehead and make a little cross on it with oil. Bobbie paid close attention to make sure Mrs. Hawley didn't gag on the Communion host. Susan offered a white wafer to Kevin, but he shook his head. After that, Bobbie didn't feel bad when she declined it too.

As the prayers went on, Bobbie squirmed and glanced at the door. She'd come this far, which meant she couldn't respectfully escape. The patient began to look much calmer. Her color had returned, and her breathing was more regular. Bobbie knew it wasn't a miracle, just the Lasix kicking in.

Kevin's phone rang, and he left the room with it. "That was the hospice nurse. She's on the way," he reported on his return.

"That's good news," said Bobbie. "We'll wait with you until she arrives, won't we, Susan?"

Susan looked up from packing her kit. "Of course, we will."

Kevin tapped Bobbie's shoulder and nodded in the direction of the hall. When they were alone, he said, "I'm so sorry to have dragged you out so early. If I had known that woman was going to show up, I…"

"Don't apologize. Mom was scared, and so were you. You did the right thing." Bobbie leaned forward to speak confidentially. "She's still alert and strong. Today's not her day. But we can make her more comfortable until it is. With your permission, we'll encourage the hospice team to deal with the congestion more actively."

"Thank you. I know you're supposed to hand her off when hospice gets involved."

"But that doesn't mean we abandon her…or you."

His lower lip trembled, and he looked away, no doubt to hide his tears. She reached up and squeezed his shoulder.

"It's okay," she whispered. "I'm glad you called us."

"Us?" That caused a little glimmer of recognition. She'd meant the practice, but when he glanced toward the sickroom, she knew he'd meant Susan. "You know each other?" he asked, grinning.

"Everyone ends up at Hobbs Family Practice, but yes, we know each other socially."

"In a town filled with queer people, it's surprising how hard it is to find each other."

Bobbie wondered how he'd picked up on her, and she couldn't decide how she felt about being called queer. When she was growing up, it was a slur, a name hurled at you in the locker room to put you down. Kevin, who was of another generation, was obviously trying to bond with her, so she patted his arm and smiled.

"Let me get my things out of there before the other nurse shows up."

Bobbie found Susan sitting in a chair she'd pulled up to the bedside. Holding Mrs. Hawley's hand in hers, she was praying. The patient's lips moved in rhythm with the words, but no sound came out.

A loud bustle in the hallway rudely disturbed the peace Susan had created with her prayers. The hospice nurse's voice was loud, probably from dealing with too many half-deaf elders. "Sorry it took me so long. I didn't realize you'd call the doctor." She cast a suspicious eye on Bobbie but looked more favorably at Susan because of the collar. Susan continued to hold Mrs. Hawley's hand protectively.

"You're from Hobbs Family Practice?" the loud woman asked Bobbie. "I've heard they're *very* involved." That implied they meddled where they weren't supposed to. She emphasized her point with a threatening stare. Bobbie wondered why she'd ever felt sympathy for this bitch.

Ignoring the hospice nurse's hostile attitude, Bobbie explained in a professional tone that she'd administered Lasix to ease the congestion. "No need for her to suffer unnecessarily."

"We left an adequate supply of morphine. Ask the son." The nurse turned to Kevin for confirmation.

Bobbie wasn't tall, but she pulled herself up to her full height. "Helping someone breathe is palliative care too."

The hospice nurse looked Bobbie over and decided it wasn't worth an argument. "We always take physician recommendations into consideration," she said, suddenly polite. "I'll put it in my notes."

"Good. I'll ask Dr. Stolz to get in touch with your service."

Bobbie caught Susan's eye. She'd been watching the exchange with obvious trepidation, but Bobbie knew better than to get into a pissing contest in front of a patient's family. "Susan, are you ready to go?"

Kevin helped them into their coats. He stood in the driveway thanking them repeatedly until Bobbie ordered him to get out of the cold.

On her way to her car, Bobbie had an idea. "Hey, Susan. Why don't you come over and let me make you breakfast? We deserve it after that adventure."

Susan's face instantly brightened. "Are you sure?"

"Absolutely," said Bobbie. "Meet me at my house."

Except for the porch lights, the place was dark when they arrived. Sane people were still asleep.

Bobbie led Susan into the kitchen in the main house.

"Are you sure being in here is okay?" she asked, looking around cautiously.

"I know we have eggs in this kitchen. I have no idea what's in mine." Bobbie tossed her bags on the bench near the door. "Coffee?"

"Please."

Bobbie turned on the coffee maker and filled a pod. "Know how to use this thing?"

Susan nodded. "We have one at school."

"There's sugar on the counter and milk in the fridge. Please help yourself while I see what's going on here." Bobbie set a mug under the spout and started the coffee brewing. "Be right back."

Bobbie unlocked Joyce's door and peeked inside. She was sleeping like the dead from the sedative she'd given her before she'd left. Upstairs, she knocked on Natalie's door. "I'll take the monitor, so you can sleep," she said into the dark room. A hand came out and gave it to her.

Susan was drinking from the mug when Bobbie came back, so obviously she'd found whatever she'd needed. While Bobbie waited for her coffee to brew, she looked Susan over with a clinician's eyes. She was always a little pale, but the reddening of her sclera indicated persistent eye strain or a chronic sleep deficit. "You look tired, Susan. How are you sleeping?"

"Not well."

"I'm sorry. Something keeping you awake?"

Susan chuckled bitterly.

"I know. The craziness is keeping everyone awake. But you can always talk to me."

"You're so busy, and then there's the elephant in the room." Susan stared into her coffee.

"Fuck the elephant," The expletive appeared to shock Susan, so Bobbie softened her tone. "If we hadn't been out so early, I'd say spend the day with me and let's talk."

"I can't today. I'm busy while Lucy's in New York. I have both services tomorrow."

"So, let's set a date. How's next Saturday? The fall color is mostly gone, but we can drive up to Gray and visit the wildlife park. We'll see the moose and have a good, long talk."

"Okay," said Susan slowly. "But can you get away?"

"I'll make arrangements," said Bobbie confidently, taking out a skillet. "How do you like your eggs?"

"Doesn't matter. However you like yours."

Bobbie threw a plug of butter into the pan and cracked four eggs into the pan. One yolk broke. She'd take that one for herself. "Bacon? I know it's not good for us, but we were heroes this morning and deserve a treat."

Susan grinned. "I like how you think."

The adrenalin was wearing off. Bobbie was too tired to talk. Susan looked exhausted too. They ate their breakfast in silence, but Bobbie had kept one eye on the baby monitor. Joyce was beginning to stir.

"I need to dress Joyce and feed her breakfast. I'll just be a minute."

"Will she mind me being here?" Susan asked.

"I doubt she'll even remember your last visit."

Susan looked skeptical, but she nodded.

Despite her confident assurances, Bobbie worried as she got Joyce up and helped her change into a fresh diaper and comfy sweat suit. She hoped for the best when she brought her into the kitchen in a transit wheelchair.

"Joyce, this is Rev. Gedney," Bobbie said, parking her at the table. "We went on a sick call this morning."

Bobbie watched carefully while Joyce cautiously eyed Susan, relieved to see no recognition in her eyes. They fixated for a few seconds on the collar, but then the remaining piece of toast caught her attention. With a sigh of relief, Bobbie gave it to her.

***

Liz was texting congratulations to Bobbie for putting the hospice nurse in her place when Lucy came out of the bathroom. Her wet hair, wrapped in a towel turban-style, was piled on her head. Another enormous towel covered her torso. Five-star hotels always had the best towels.

"Liz, can you tear yourself away from your iPad long enough to get dressed?" Lucy's voice was testy, meaning she was anxious about the rehearsal.

When Liz didn't look up, Lucy dropped her towel, knowing that would instantly get her wife's attention. Liz closed the tablet but didn't budge from the bed. Instead, she sat back to watch Lucy vigorously brush out her hair. When she straightened, Liz admired her white thighs crowned by a bright red thatch. The hair on Lucy's head had darkened into a bronzy auburn, except for some strands of blond here and there. Liz had never thought about it before meeting Lucy, but she'd discovered that redheads don't gray like other people. Instead, their hair fades into a special golden shade unique to them.

Liz's eyes traveled down to Lucy's breasts, perfect hemispheres of pale, soft flesh, the areolae a delicate rose, the nipples pert. Lucy was approaching sixty but looked at least a decade younger. Not a sag anywhere. The only sign of her once secret pregnancy were the stretch marks like faint, silvery fish along her abdomen. Liz liked to trace them with her fingertips and kiss them. The fact that Lucy had borne a child touched her in a way she hadn't expected.

"Liz, either you get up or I'm going to leave you here. I can't be late." Despite the threat, Lucy looked surprised when Liz approached and knelt in front of her. With her thumbs, she parted the lips between her legs and began to kiss her. Lucy staggered a little, her fingers clutching Liz's shoulders, digging into the muscles as she tried to steady herself. The spasms came quickly, followed by a persistent pulsing that wouldn't stop, as if her clitoris refused to give up the pleasure. Her fingers gripped Liz's shoulders ever tighter until she finally relaxed.

"You're a beast!" she declared as Liz wiped her mouth with the back of her hand. Lucy's response had so invigorated her that she didn't struggle to get up from her knees, although she felt a twinge when she straightened.

"I'm a beast? You prance around naked, bounce your boobs in my face. What do you expect?"

"We don't have time now for me to return the favor."

"I can wait. Something to look forward to later."

"Then get dressed. Rehearsals are informal, but you can't show up in that ratty T-shirt." Lucy bent to plait her damp hair into a French braid.

"I'll take a quick shower while you put on your makeup." Liz didn't dawdle the way she would at home. Unlike Maggie, who could spend an hour putting on her face, Lucy was efficient. Liz was dressed and ready to go within fifteen minutes.

"You look nice," Lucy said, looking her over as they waited for the elevator. Liz was wearing black jeans and a black sweater under a wool blazer. She preferred a tailored look and had celebrated when jackets and suits came back into fashion by filling her closet with new ones.

"Thanks," said Liz, returning the inspection. "You look...tense."

"Actually, the orgasm helped me relax. How did you know?"

Liz hadn't planned it. Lucy naked was impossible to resist. Calming her anxiety had been a side benefit. "How can you be nervous? You're an international opera star."

"I *was* an international opera star. Now, I'm just a singer trying to make a comeback. Most people in the audience won't even remember me."

"Good. Then they won't compare you to the Lucille Bartlett of the past."

"Liz, this is *New York*, where there are more music critics per square mile than any place on earth. I can't take any more bad reviews. I'm already bruised from the book."

The elevator pinged and opened. Out of habit, Liz held back the door while Lucy entered. She took Liz's hand as the elevator descended. "Today, I need you to bless me." Their little elevator game always made Liz smile and remember the first time they'd made love. In the elevator to her third-floor bedroom, Liz had confessed she was afraid to be touched by Lucy's "priest's hands." In response, Lucy had blessed her.

"You're already more blessed than I'll ever be," said Liz, squeezing Lucy's hand.

Lucy looked up and studied her with cool green eyes. "Liz, you know that's not true."

To quash a potential theological debate, Liz quickly said: "Blessings on you and this rehearsal. May your concert be the first of many spectacular successes."

"Thank you." For the remainder of the elevator ride, Lucy leaned her head on Liz's shoulder.

They took a yellow cab to Lincoln Center. To Liz's relief, the driver chose to approach David Gellen Hall from the West Side, sparing Lucy the view of the Met across the plaza. Although the performance of *Lohengrin* was months away, Lucy had been mentioning it often. "What if I can't sustain an entire opera? Why did my return to the Met have to be Wagner?" she'd ask, sounding frantic.

She knew why, of course. Elsa of Brabant had been her debut role, one that she'd owned at the Met for years. The management had chosen it for its significance after Lucy had forced them to apologize for covering up her sexual assault. Lucy would sing three performances. A rising young star would sing the other two, a woman only a few years older than Lucy when she'd been the new sensation. Of course, they'd be compared.

"Davidsen is six foot two. You're barely five-four. Do they make separate costumes for each of you?" Liz wondered aloud. Lucy needed no context to know what Liz was asking.

"We each get our own costume. It has to fit right," Lucy explained. "Performers can't feel uncomfortable when they sing. There's already enough to think about."

The cabbie let them off at the stage door. Lucy, who knew the way, led Liz through the maze of underground tunnels.

"Madame Bartlett?" a young woman inquired, approaching from the side. "Welcome. I'm Brittany. I'm here to show you the way. They're running behind. Still rehearsing the companion piece. You can wait backstage, or I can show you to your dressing room." She looked at Liz. "Is this your agent?"

Lucy chuckled softly. "No, she'd make a terrible agent. This is Dr. Stolz, my wife."

"Ah," said the woman with obvious approval. "Welcome to Philharmonic Hall, Dr. Stolz, I can show you the way into the theater, where you can watch the rehearsal."

"I'll wait backstage," said Lucy. "Can my wife come?"

"Sorry. This conductor is very strict."

"Good luck," said Liz, landing a quick kiss on Lucy's cheek to avoid smudging her perfectly applied lipstick.

In the subterranean corridors, their footsteps echoed. Before the guide indicated where to turn to go upstairs, Liz looked back at Lucy. Her head was bowed. She was praying.

Liz hadn't been able to understand why Lucy was so nervous until she'd found a comparison. During Maggie's first bout with breast cancer, Liz's former protégée had goaded her into scrubbing in on the lumpectomy instead of observing from the gallery. Liz had left Yale years before, and it seemed like everyone was watching to see if the former chief of surgery still had the right stuff. She felt like a has-been whose time had passed, making an appearance where she no longer belonged. Liz wondered if Lucy felt something similar.

"You'll have to sit in the back," said Liz's guide apologetically. "The maestro doesn't encourage visitors and insists they be as inconspicuous as possible."

"He knows me," said Liz.

"Which is the only reason you're being allowed to observe. There's someone else here too. Please, please don't talk during the rehearsal, or you'll have to leave," Brittany said, pointing to someone sitting in the back.

Liz recognized Lucy's agent, Roger Weinstein, and walked to the row where he sat, also exiled from view.

"I see they put you in the cheap seats too," Roger quipped as Liz sat down beside him. "Thanks for coming. I think Lucy needs all the moral support she can get."

"How's it going?" asked Liz, trying to be sociable. Although Roger always negotiated top dollar for Lucy's fees, she didn't completely trust him. His aggressive style rubbed her the wrong way.

"The Wiener Staastsoper wants her for *Tannhäuser*. And there's interest from the Proms. Liz, you need to encourage her to do more high-profile performances. She needs the publicity."

Liz tried to temper her annoyance at the suggestion that she should influence Lucy's decisions. "Lucy picks her own gigs. How should I know what she should sing?"

"False modesty, Liz. You know more about classical music than a lot of agents, and she listens to you."

"Lucy has a full plate right now. Her book just came out. Her publisher wants her to promote it."

Roger shook his head. "I don't know why she's wasting her time on that crap. It doesn't do a damn thing for her career."

At that point, Liz could barely contain her anger. She forced herself to use her neutral 'doctor's' voice. "That's her job, Roger. She's a priest *and* an author. You need to accept that she might not be as invested in this comeback as you are. And you need to be talking to her, not me." Despite Liz's attempt to keep her voice firm, not angry, Roger's eyes narrowed.

"You know her best," he conceded. "But she's missing out on some big opportunities."

Lucy came out on the stage to the titter of bows bouncing off stringed instruments.

"I see that Madame Bartlett has many admirers here," said the conductor sarcastically. Lucy bowed to the orchestra. "Enough of that," snapped Morales. "We're late already. *Frühling*...from the top." He raised his arms, and the orchestra launched into the introduction to the first of Strauss' Four Last Songs. Lucy had just begun to sing when the conductor banged his baton on his music stand. "Madame Bartlett, would you like to conduct?"

"No, Maestro," replied Lucy in a tone that was respectful but certainly not meek.

"Good. Because I don't allow my soloists to set the tempo." He raised his arms again. "Once again...from the top."

The orchestra was still playing to Lucy's tempo, a little faster than the rhythm Morales was beating with his right hand. Again, the baton slammed down on the music stand. While Morales scolded the orchestra, he glared at Lucy.

"I don't know why he's being so cranky with her," Roger whispered. "He adores her."

Clearly, this was not Lucy's day. Liz saw that, as much as she wanted to protect the woman she loved, there were times when she simply couldn't.

12

Susan struggled with the key and grumbled at Lucy for ordering everyone who lived in the rectory to lock their doors. Only the residents ever came upstairs, but Lucy insisted on security because people were always coming in and out of the building.

"Mother Susan!" A tall, black woman loped through the hall like a young gazelle. "I hoped I would catch you." Reshma stopped short, nearly tripping over herself. "Are you just coming from school?"

"Yes, but let me get the door open. The darn key won't turn."

"It won't?" asked Reshma, bending to look. "I could squirt some graphite into the lock. All the hardware here sticks. This building is so old."

"Like me," said Susan glumly.

"You're not old!" Reshma protested.

"Oh yes, I am, and some days, like today, I really feel it. How old are you?"

"Twenty-five."

"Hah! My mother used to say, 'I have a headache older than that.'"

Reshma grinned, revealing her perfect teeth. "Funny. I'll have to remember that one."

"Oh, I'm full of old timey expressions that would entertain you. Believe it or not, there are places where people still talk like that."

"I enjoy old expressions. Discovering them is like linguistic archaeology."

"See? You admit I'm old." Susan continued to struggle with the lock.

"Let me get the graphite," Reshma offered. "You should have told me before. I would have fixed it long ago."

Reshma skipped back to her apartment. Moments later she returned with a small bottle. After a couple of squirts of the grimy liquid into the lock, she gingerly worked the key. The barrels finally turned, and the door opened easily.

"Voila!" exclaimed Reshma. "All fixed."

"That lock has been driving me crazy since the day I moved in. Thank you so much!"

Reshma bowed theatrically. "A deacon's role is to serve." She held up her hands, blackened with graphite. "Messy stuff."

"Come in. You can wash up inside," said Susan, pushing open the door with her shoulder. "I'll make you some tea. Do you drink tea?"

"I do. At my boarding school, we used to have formal afternoon teas. They were nothing but an excuse to teach us some manners. You'd be surprised how many girls from wealthy families had none."

"Wealth doesn't mean class. You went to boarding school?" asked Susan, realizing how little she knew about Reshma.

"When we came from Sudan, the Episcopal Diocese of Maine was very involved in helping new refugees. A few parishes got together and sponsored me and two other girls. I was lucky to get such a good education."

"I'll say." Susan led Reshma into the kitchen.

"So, this is the rector's apartment." Reshma looked around curiously.

"You've never been in here before?"

"Father Tom was very strict. He never allowed us inside and stood in the hall to have a conversation…even though we all knew he's gay."

"The way things are now, it's not a bad idea to take precautions."

Susan filled the kettle and stepped aside so Reshma could wash her hands. "Try that blue detergent by the sink. If it works for cleaning waterfowl after an oil spill, it might clean off that graphite."

"Technically, graphite is a non-oily lubricant. It's soft and slippery, which is why it's used for pencil leads."

Susan had learned something new, which made her smile. She put the kettle on the one stove burner that worked consistently. She'd meant to tell Lucy about the problem, but whenever they met, there were more pressing matters. "Reshma, how do you take your tea?"

"Cream and a little sugar."

"The proper way." Susan nodded in approval. "Did they teach you that in school?"

"Yes, of course, but I don't take sugar in my coffee, which makes no sense." Reshma frowned, apparently trying to reconcile the contradiction.

"You've been busy since Lucy's been in New York. Thanks for taking the pastoral calls while I'm at school."

"You're welcome." Reshma held up her clean hands like a proud child. "That stuff worked."

"I get it on sale at Reny's. Paper towels by the toaster." Susan opened a new tin of cookies and arranged them on a plate. She tied the tea bags to the handle of the pot. "Have you read the reviews of Lucy's concert? The *Times* called it a triumph. I so wish I could have been there."

Reshma interrupted her curious inspection of the kitchen. "Didn't you listen to the livestream?" she asked, surprised.

"No. I had no idea I could."

"I'm sorry. I should have told you. I just assumed you would know. Denise called from Dresden to remind me. She got up in the middle of the night to listen to it live."

"I wish I had known, but I'm an idiot when it comes to technology. I can barely figure out the Kindle Lucy gave me."

"If I find a recording of the concert, I'll send you the link. You can listen to lots of music online. I'll be glad to show you how. I heard Denise sing live the other night."

"Is she still in Europe?" Susan hadn't seen her lately, but she never paid much attention to the comings and goings of the young people down the hall.

"She's in Stuttgart rehearsing an opera. She'll be there another two weeks. I miss her." Reshma looked sad. "Being away so much is starting to worry her. She thinks she may have to talk to Mother Lucy soon about whether she can continue as music director." Reshma bit her lower lip, probably realizing she'd shared too much.

"Lucy won't give her any trouble. She's kind to a fault. Besides, what can she say? She's doing the same thing." Susan poured boiling water from the dented kettle into a teapot. She looked up to see Reshma frowning. "You probably think what I said about Lucy isn't fair, and it's not. Obviously, there's a big difference between Lucy singing a few performances and Denise trying to build a career."

"I just hope Mother Lucy doesn't leave St. Margaret's," said Reshma with a deep sigh.

"Me too, but I'm glad she's singing again." Susan poured half and half into a pitcher that matched the teapot. She hadn't been able to find the sugar bowl and assumed it had been lost to the hazards of time. "I wonder how old this set is. My mother used to have one just like it. I'll probably find it when I unpack my sister's things."

"So civilized to have tea brewed in a pot."

"Hardly anyone uses china these days. They just throw a tea bag and water into a mug and microwave it."

"This is much nicer," Reshma agreed.

Susan offered the plate of cookies. "The tea just needs another minute. While we wait, why don't you tell me why you wanted to see me?"

"I would ordinarily go to Mother Lucy with this, but she's so busy right now. I'm hoping you can help me."

Susan was flattered. As Reshma's dark eyes studied her face, Susan wondered what she saw—the cranky, difficult person she felt like this afternoon or a woman in the same profession whom she could ask for advice. When she smiled to put Reshma at ease, she smiled back, and Susan got her answer.

"It's a special project I'm working on...with Mother Lucy's permission, of course. I've gotten involved with a group that helps refugees."

"That's commendable," said Susan, pouring their tea. "A very Christian thing to do."

"Thank you, but it's not about religion. I just want to help people like me. When we left our camp to come to Maine, we had no idea what to expect. We had never seen snow. We had no idea it could get so cold. People gave us warm clothes and shelter. They welcomed us, the strangers. I want to give back for their kindness to me and my mother. I'm mentoring a woman and her daughter. The girl is about the same age I was when I came. They are from South Sudan, like me."

"I thought things were better there since independence."

"In some ways, yes, but political unrest has been the norm in that part of the world for generations. People starve. Children are recruited to be soldiers. Women are terrorized and raped. It's a nightmare."

"Isn't that conflict mostly over religion?"

"Religion is an excuse for many wars, but there are other causes—tribal rivalries, revenge for past wrongs, who controls the oil wealth...It's gone on so long, no one really remembers. The refugees I'm mentoring happen to be Christian, not that it makes any difference to me. I would help them anyway."

"Reshma, it sounds like you've been called to this ministry, but how can I help?"

"As you know, there's a terrible shortage of housing in Maine. Teresa and her daughter lost their apartment when their landlord raised the rent. For the last few weeks, they've been living in a shelter. It's overcrowded, and I'm not sure it's safe. I can't believe that people who have so little would steal from one another, but they do." Reshma's dark face paled with despair.

"Desperate people do desperate things," replied Susan in a reluctantly wise voice. "Tell me more about these refugees. Does the mother have a job?"

"She was a nurse in her own country, but she can't work in her profession until she trains and gets a license here. She's only had time to take one class a semester. At that rate, it will take her forever to be certified as a nurse. She had a low-level job in a hospital on the other side of town. Now that she's in a shelter, she can't get to work because there's no transportation."

"That's insane! How is she supposed to survive?"

"There's some government assistance. Refugee agencies help. With the housing shortage, there's rent assistance, but no apartments. Many people won't even consider renting to an immigrant family. There are language barriers and cultural issues. Landlords worry they can't get rid of their tenants if it doesn't work out."

"So where can they live?"

"We're trying to find private homes with extra space. Elderly people who wouldn't mind the company or extra help. Teresa, with her nursing background, would be ideal."

While Reshma had been speaking, the words "elderly" and "nurse" stuck in Susan's mind. "Actually, I know someone who has taken in some students to help care for her elderly partner. I don't know if she has room in her house for this woman and her child, but I can ask."

"Oh, Mother Susan, I knew you would help!" In her excitement, Reshma bounced up and down on the old kitchen chair. Watching her, Susan feared for its integrity.

"I'm not making any promises," cautioned Susan. "I've only been in the house twice. I don't really know what the living arrangements are there."

"All they need is a room where they can sleep and access to a bathroom where they can wash. Anything would be better than where they are now." Reshma reached for Susan's hand and pumped it. "Oh, thank you! Between your school and pastoral care, I'd hoped you'd know someone."

"I only said I'd ask, Reshma. Don't get ahead of yourself."

"But we must have hope, otherwise we won't even try to help." The young woman's voice was full of fervor. She would make such a good priest, and yet, she was hesitant.

"Reshma…Lucy shared that you've delayed your ordination. She said I might be able to help because I too had a difficult discernment."

Like a rabbit caught in a snare, the whites of Reshma's eyes were suddenly prominent. "What did she tell you?" she asked anxiously.

"Nothing really, only that you had doubts about your vocation."

Reshma bit into the cookie she'd been previously devouring and slowly chewed it. Her swallow was audible. "It's a big subject. I'm not sure I want to talk about it now."

"Understood. And you're under no obligation, but I'm here if you want to talk to me."

"I want to talk to you. Just not today." The light of inspiration suddenly shone in Reshma's eyes. "Come to dinner on Sunday. I'll make an African recipe. Something different for you, I bet."

Something different was not eating alone. Solitary dining made even the most well-prepared meal unpalatable.

"I'm looking forward to it," said Susan, offering the cookie plate again.

Reshma grinned slyly as she snatched one.

✳✳✳

From the front window, Bobbie saw Susan's antique Subaru pull into the drive. It was certainly a classic, but those older models were roomy, and you couldn't kill them, not even in a place where the salt from the ocean and the roads ate cars. When they'd moved to Hobbs permanently, Bobbie had reluctantly given up the old Forester she used to drive when they were in Maine for the weekend.

Susan led the charge up the front walk. Behind her was a lithe, black woman wearing a clerical collar under a colorful print sweater. The older black woman behind her held the hand of a young girl, slender as a stick.

To Bobbie's surprise and relief, they didn't look like refugees. She'd pictured them being like the pathetic people she'd seen in news stories about the unrest in Africa—men missing limbs, hobbling around on crutches, hollow-eyed mothers clutching babies whose fragile skin stretched against their skulls, their tiny caved-in chests showing every rib. Susan's friends looked so healthy. A good thing because Bobbie couldn't imagine facing walking skeletons every day.

"Hello, Bobbie," said Susan. "Thank you for letting us come on such short notice." She leaned forward as if she might kiss Bobbie's cheek but then twisted away. Bobbie wished she'd gone with her instinct, but maybe the collars meant this was an official church visit, and Susan wanted to avoid ambiguity.

"I started cleaning up last night," Bobbie said apologetically. "I'm afraid I didn't make much progress. I had to work today."

"Don't apologize. We barely gave you any notice." Susan turned to the young black woman in the collar. "This is Reshma John, our deacon."

Bobbie shook her hand, while Susan continued the introductions. "Rev. John is mentoring these ladies from South Sudan—Teresa Gai and her daughter, Grace."

"Thank you so much for your consideration," said the woman. Her English, laced with British and native intonations had a charming, musical lilt, but it was perfectly understandable, another relief. "My daughter, Grace, has been raised to be very helpful in the house. She is only ten, but she can cook, clean, wash clothes, and keep a garden. Whatever you need her to do." The enthusiasm in the woman's voice was poignant. No mother should ever have to sell her child's value to earn a roof over their heads.

The girl's eyes were fixed on the hummingbird feeder hanging from the porch roof. Its exaggerated red blossoms were almost obscene. "It's too late for the birds today", explained Bobbie, "but they may be back tomorrow. It's hard to say. They're already starting to leave for the winter." The girl smiled shyly. "Do you have hummingbirds where you came from?"

"We have sunbirds that drink nectar from flowers," the girl answered, her intelligent eyes focused on Bobbie, who felt an instant connection. Bobbie had always wanted a child, but Joyce wouldn't hear of it. She thought that career women, and especially lesbians, had no business having babies.

"Maybe you could show us the space," Susan suggested, gently reminding her of the purpose of the visit.

"Good idea," agreed Bobbie.

Susan stood aside and let the others go in first. "Thank you so much," she whispered into Bobbie's ear as she passed. Her warm breath was exciting. Bobbie shivered involuntarily. She smiled as she led her visitors through the long hallway to the other side of the house.

"There's also an outside entrance," she explained over her shoulder. The deadbolt on the apartment door was stiff from lack of use. "The previous owner had his accounting office in here. When we had a lot of summer visitors, we sometimes used this space for overflow guests. Now, it's just a storage area."

Bobbie was going to add that Joyce had planned to use the office for a consulting business when she retired, but she stopped herself just in time. Why would she give strangers so much unnecessary information? Part of her wanted them to know that Joyce wasn't just a senile, old woman. She'd once been a successful businesswoman, wealthy enough to afford this beautiful summer home on the ocean. If they were interested, she could explain all that later. For now, it was enough that she remembered the witty Joyce, the competent Joyce, the generous lover.

Bobbie blushed at the thought and glanced at Susan, who was studying the photographs of the ocean along the corridor. Joyce had taken them during her photography phase.

Transit file boxes, piled high, occupied the center of the main office. Bobbie had spent the previous evening cleaning out the file cabinets. Joyce had always played footloose with their taxes and worried about audits, so they'd kept business and tax records going back to the last millennium. When Bobbie had called their accountant to ask if the old files could be pitched, she'd laughed heartily.

"Please don't mind the mess," said Bobby. "Let me show you around." She explained that the previous owner had kept his business separate from the house, which was why the office had its own entrance. In a large alcove, the door of a half-sized refrigerator was propped open with a towel. Behind a pair of folding doors was a two-burner stove with an overhead oven. A tambour door hid a microwave, a toaster, and a coffee maker.

"All the appliances work, and I don't mind you cooking breakfast or a quick lunch. For serious cooking I'd prefer you use the main kitchen," Bobbie said. "Just don't burn down the house." She grinned to show she wasn't serious, but Teresa gave her a worried look.

"I assure you, madam, that we shall care for your home as if it were our own, even better."

"Don't worry. I was joking, but please use the main kitchen for big meals."

Bobbie showed them the former office of the accountant's secretary, where a full-sized bed and a chest of drawers now stood. There was a daybed and another bureau in the space that used to be the waiting area. The bathroom had a tiny stall shower, so snug that Bobbie could barely fit into it, but it counted on the real estate listing as a full bath.

"We used to put Joyce's cousins in here when they visited from California, but they're on in years now, so they don't come now." The real reason they no longer came was that Joyce didn't recognize them anymore. "I'm sorry the place is such a mess. On Saturday, my neighbor's son will take the papers to the dump for shredding and move the boxes into the garage. I'm hoping to have the place ready by next week."

The refugees and the deacon exchanged a surprised look. "They were hoping, if you found them acceptable, that they could stay the night," said the deacon. "Didn't Mother Gedney explain the urgency of the situation?"

Susan had described the crowded shelter and the danger it posed, but Bobbie had it in her mind that she could finish cleaning over the weekend. "Well, I don't know…" She liked to think she was flexible, but the idea that the place was still a mess bothered her. Susan looked at her expectantly, and the little girl's eyes were so full of hope.

"Please, Ms. Lantry, if there's any way…" the deacon begged.

Bobbie had already decided that she would give these people temporary shelter. There would be no lease, so she could easily end the arrangement if the relationship went sour. Now that she'd met Teresa and Grace, she doubted she could just throw them out. The little girl's imploring gaze clinched the decision.

"Oh, why not?" Bobbie said, throwing up her hands. "I wish I could have gotten the place ready, but I guess it's good enough for now."

"More than good enough," said Teresa eagerly. "If you have rags and detergent, we can clean the bathroom and the kitchen."

"Can I bring some of these boxes to the garage?" asked Reshma, taking off her sweater. She rolled up the sleeves of her clerical blouse, revealing muscular arms. Bobbie told her which boxes could go and showed her the path to the garage.

"Just pile them in the empty bay. The boys will put them in the attic later."

"What can I do?" asked Susan.

"I have sheets for the beds, but they haven't been laundered in years. We haven't had much company lately."

"Just point me in the right direction."

Bobbie took out a stack of sheets and towels from a cabinet and led Susan to the laundry room.

After the washer was running, Susan whispered into Bobbie's ear, "Thank you for your kindness. You have no idea how happy you've made these people…and me." Bobbie felt a soft kiss on her cheek. After the warm lips moved away, Bobbie reached up to touch the spot.

❊❊❊

Although Bobbie had promised to tell her everything, Susan didn't want to ruin a wonderful day with a heavy conversation. Since they'd arrived at the wildlife park, they had laughed at the antics of the raccoons, growled at the fierce fisher cat, and hooted at the owls. They'd hung on the wire fence enclosing the grazing moose, creatures neither of them had seen in the wild. Following the winding trail up and down hills and through the forest, Susan never wanted it to end, but it did—just in time for lunch.

They'd planned to buy sandwiches at the concession and eat at the picnic tables in the park, but as they'd walked the trail, the pale autumn sun had slipped behind the clouds. The November air chilled rapidly, and they both agreed it would be better to eat inside.

In a small town like Gray, the options were limited. Bobbie searched on her phone and came up with a Thai restaurant billed as authentic. Susan was understandably skeptical. "Who eats Thai food in the middle of nowhere?"

"But it has great reviews. Let's check it out," said Bobbie, daring her with a twitch of her blond brows.

When they arrived, they found a tiny storefront restaurant. The interior, with its old-fashioned post tables and tubular chairs, didn't look promising. Bobbie studied the menu taped to the door, while Susan peered inside. A photo of King Vajiralongkorn in an ornately decorated gold frame hung on the wall. Below it was a Buddhist shrine with an army of tiny, gilded statues. Susan couldn't be sure, not being an aficionado of Thai food, but this seemed like evidence of authenticity.

"The menu is pretty standard," said Bobbie. "What do we have to lose?"

Susan could think of multiple answers to that question. Food poisoning was definitely one of them, but she loved Bobbie's sense of adventure.

They were early for lunch, and the place was empty. A little bell over the door tinkled when they entered. The proprietor, wiping his hands on an apron, instantly appeared. While he set places for them at a table by the window, he recited the day's specials.

"Do you like squid?" asked Bobbie, making it obvious that she did.

Lucy had taken Susan to Little Italy in New York and convinced her to try calamari. "I had it once, but I wasn't keen on the texture. Kind of like fried rubber bands."

Bobbie laughed. "I'll order fresh spring rolls. I bet you'll love those."

They browsed their way through the appetizer menu, trying the coconut soup the proprietor recommended, pork dumplings, wrapped shrimp. They took their time, slowly and deliberately tasting dishes and drinking spiced tea. Finally, they ordered the squid special with basil leaves. The fiery sauce burned Susan's tongue and the texture still reminded her of rubber bands, but she enjoyed the dish. Bobbie declared that it was the best Thai food she'd eaten outside of New York.

Other diners came and went. It was off-season, so not many. The thin lunch crowd vanished, and they were alone again. Two women came out of the back with a wheeled cart full of metal bins and settled at a table near the kitchen door. While they chopped vegetables, they kept up a nonstop conversation in a musical language.

"Maybe we should go somewhere else," Susan suggested, watching them.

Bobbie shrugged. "They don't seem to mind. I like it here. Let's sit a while longer." To justify their presence, they ordered more tea and mango sticky rice with two spoons.

"Do you still want to talk?" Bobbie asked.

"I'm having so much fun. I don't want to spoil it," Susan honestly admitted.

"I know what you mean, but I'm sure you have so many questions."

"I don't even know where to start, so maybe I'll just ask the big one. What's your relationship with Joyce?"

Bobbie helped herself to another spoonful of the painfully sweet dessert. "I love mangoes." She licked her spoon and put it down. "As you've probably already guessed, we were once lovers."

"Were you in a committed relationship?"

"Sort of. We both made assumptions, but I wouldn't be surprised if Joyce had flings when she went away on business. She liked men too." Bobbie shrugged. "Different times," she said, as if that explained everything.

"How long have you been together?"

"A long time as lesbian relationships go. We met when I was taking care of her mother. I was attracted to Joyce right away, but I knew that getting involved with a patient's family member was unprofessional. I tried to ignore her advances at first. She'd leave me little gifts, say a friend couldn't make it to the theater, so she'd take me instead. Looking back, it was so transparent. The notes she left were suggestive, but never overt. She seduced me with her eyes. She wore a lot of makeup in those days to complete her dress-for-success look. When she fluttered those long lashes, I was putty in her hands."

"Sounds very romantic."

Bobbie shrugged. "She was a drop-dead gorgeous woman with a big house and a high-profile corporate job. I was a kid, impressed by her wealth and sophistication. Looking back, she took advantage of my youth and naivete."

"Do I hear some resentment?" asked Susan, cupping her ear.

"No, just the wisdom of age. I've known Joyce for over thirty years. I've had a lot of time to think about our relationship."

"But you're still together."

"We live in the same house. That's different."

"Are you still in love with her?"

"I love her, but I'm not in love. You understand the difference."

Susan nodded.

"Before the disease, we were good together. We traveled all over the world. She paid, of course. We had a wonderful time riding camels in Egypt, sailing down the Danube. She's fluent in French and German. She grew up with money and was used to the finer things like good food and excellent wine. My parents were ordinary people. They worked hard and didn't have time for museums and concerts. I absorbed all the experiences Joyce put in front of me, inhaling the culture I missed growing up. She'd dress me when we went out to a fancy place for dinner or a concert. Eventually, I became more like her, which pleased her, of course. She paid for both my master's degrees and encouraged me as I went up the ladder at my jobs."

"It sounds like she gave you a lot. What did you give her?"

"Devotion. I would do anything for her—drop off her clothes at the cleaners, deal with the tradespeople who came to the house, clean up the kitchen after she cooked. I listened to her when work stress overwhelmed her. I nursed her when she was sick. I was a good wife."

"Why didn't you marry?"

"Joyce didn't believe in it. She never came out to her family, even though we were carrying on right under her mother's nose. Joyce is, or maybe I should say was, a die-hard conservative. She never came out publicly, saying her industry was male-dominated, and it would destroy her career."

"That makes sense. Back then, things were nothing like they are now."

"She insisted our closet door remain, not just shut, but locked tight. She thought same-sex marriage was ridiculous. Instead, she used legal documents to ensure our security—wills, trusts, powers of attorney. I'm her conservator and the executor of her estate. When we sold the house in New York, we put all the money into a fund for her long-term care, but I get whatever is left when she dies. She quit-claimed the house in Maine to me, ensuring that a nursing home would never get it. We never married, but legally, our lives are completely enmeshed."

"Is that why you're still together?"

Bobbie shook her head. "No, I'm there because I still care about her. Leaving her now would be like abandoning a retarded child. She has no family, and all the legal documents in the world can't protect her interests now that she can't make her own decisions."

"You love her," Susan said, realizing the truth.

"Yes, I will always love her."

"Do you still sleep together?"

Bobbie looked surprised by the question. "She went into early menopause and lost interest in sex, but we slept in the same bed until she couldn't tell day from night. I finally moved out of her room for my own survival. I felt terrible about it, but I needed to sleep."

"I'm so sorry," Susan whispered. "It must be so hard."

"What's hardest is losing my companion. After the sex ended, our friendship remained. We had a real partnership. We could always rely on one another. We traveled well together. Now, she's like my child. That's the way I love her now, like a parent." Bobbie's brown eyes were full of unspeakable sadness. "Since we're not married, I can't even get divorced." She shook her head as if dismissing a thought.

"That's so sad," said Susan, reaching for her hand. "Is there anything I can do to help?"

"What you're doing. Be my friend. Listen to me. Don't run away." Bobbie looked grim. "I need a friend."

"So do I."

They sat for a long moment, just holding hands until the owner brought their check.

***

The quiet on the way back to Hobbs was unnerving. Bobbie knew that Susan, gazing at the bare trees along the highway, needed time to process what she'd learned. Bobbie tried to be patient, but finally, she couldn't stand the silence a moment longer.

"Did I say too much?"

Susan turned in her seat. "Not at all. You promised full disclosure, and you told me everything."

"Maybe not everything, but now you know the basic facts. Thank you for not judging me."

"Who says I'm not?" A little smile played around Susan's lips, which mostly relieved Bobbie's initial panic. "I am judging you. I'm impressed… by your loyalty…by your decency…by your caring. That's a judgment, a positive one. You could have left Joyce. She put aside money for her care. You could have put her in a nursing home and washed your hands of her, but you didn't."

"Sometimes, I think she'd get better care in a skilled nursing facility. Keeping her at home, I can't supervise her full-time."

"Your solution is creative. You have young women trained in social work and health care keeping an eye on her. Now, you have Teresa, a nurse, and Grace. How are they settling in?"

"They seem to love it there. The neighbor's son and his friends moved all the boxes and our personal stuff into the garage and brought down another dresser. Reshma found a bistro table and chairs, some bookcases, and a little desk for Grace. There was even an old TV, and it works. When you move out of one house into another that's completely furnished, you end up with lots of extra furniture."

"Reshma helped?"

"She worked side-by-side with the neighbor's kid and his friends."

"Good for her."

Bobbie stole a glance in Susan's direction. "So, you don't think I'm terrible for being interested in you?"

"You're interested?" Again, the little smile, but more in the eyes this time.

"Oh, come on, Susan! Don't pretend you haven't noticed."

"Of course, I've noticed, Bobbie," said Susan, rolling her eyes. "You're not always subtle."

Bobbie's cheeks flamed and she focused firmly on the road ahead. "At least, you're not offended."

"Why would I be offended? I'm flattered… I just don't know what to do with it."

"What do you mean?"

"I have my own problems. I'm a recovering alcoholic."

Susan always seemed so together that Bobbie had almost forgotten that part of her story.

"My sponsor reminded me that I'm supposed to wait a year before getting involved romantically. It's been more than a year, but that doesn't mean a relationship is a good idea."

That sounded like Susan hadn't completely written off the idea. "Over time…could you be open to a relationship? Maybe?" Bobbie hoped she didn't sound too eager.

"I'm not sure." When Bobbie glanced at Susan, she saw that the little smile had vanished. "I'm sorry, Bobbie, but since we're both being so honest, I feel I need to tell you the truth."

"Because of Joyce?"

"Partially, and because of my own issues. I'm not sure what you want from me. Friendship? Sex?"

"Much more than sex. I want a relationship. A whole relationship. You have no idea how it's been for me. Years ago, I would have given anything to have sex with Joyce. As the dementia got worse, she forgot that she wasn't interested. She'd make lewd gestures, like grabbing my crotch, or flicking her tongue suggestively, sometimes in front of other people. Once, I was helping her dress and she thrust her tongue into my mouth. When I jumped back, she said. 'You used to like that,' which was true, but at that moment, I was repulsed."

Susan nodded sympathetically. "I would be too. But you know lack of sexual inhibition is common in dementia. Try to be compassionate."

"I do! But it's hard to be patient, especially with someone I used to look up to. I expect more from her. Sometimes, I just snap."

"Because you're human. As far as Joyce goes, I need to think and pray over it. You're not married, but you were obviously in a permanent relationship. Now, you want to change the terms without her consent."

Bobbie glared at the car in front of her. The driver wasn't doing anything wrong, but Bobbie needed a target for her anger. "This is exactly why I didn't want to tell you. I knew you'd go all moral on me because you're a priest."

"I am a priest, but that's not why I'm concerned. Joyce is still with it enough to pick up on our attraction."

"That's how it is with dementia. Emotionally loaded things stick around longer."

"But she was upset, *really* upset. You had an agreement, formal or not, about your relationship. I know she has cognitive deficits, but shouldn't she have something to say about it?"

"I doubt she'd approve of me getting involved with someone else."

"There you have it."

"But that's not fair. You're not seeing the whole picture."

"I'm trying, but I only know what you've told me. I do understand that you're in a very difficult situation."

"If you understand, why don't you cut me some slack?"

"Bobbie, I'm completely sympathetic. I can't even imagine doing what you're doing."

"No one can until they've done it. I used to count on her to do certain things. She took care of our taxes and investments, the property, the cars. She cooked our meals, entertained our guests. If I needed a ride because my car was in the shop, she was there. I trusted her to make decisions for me if I became sick or incapacitated. Now, I can't. I'm on my own. Worse, I'm on my own and responsible for a woman who can't take care of herself."

"Oh, Bobbie, I can't imagine. It must be so hard."

"Providing healthcare to the elderly is what I do for a living, but it's different when it's someone you've shared your life with. Joyce has almost no memories of our life together—how we met, our home in New York, the places we visited, our friends. Our common experiences don't mean anything to her anymore. Like a bridge vanishing into the mist, I can still see my side, but not the other. Our connections are fading away."

Bobbie tried to blink away the tears stinging her eyes, but Susan's gentle touch on her shoulder was like opening a faucet. Tears flooded Bobbie's cheeks. Desperately, she tried to wipe them away with her hand, but she couldn't keep up.

"Take it easy, Bobbie," whispered Susan. "You're driving, and we both want to get home in one piece."

"Yes, of course," agreed Bobbie, wiping her wet palm on the leg of her pants.

Susan laid a tissue in her lap. "It's clean," she assured her.

"Thank you," Bobbie mumbled, mopping her face.

"If you want me to drive, I can."

"No, I'm all right." After Bobbie stashed the spent tissue in the cup holder, Susan discreetly passed her another.

"I don't want to give you false hope," said Susan in a soft voice, "but I said I'd think about it, and I will."

"Thank you. That's all I ask."

Bobbie took a deep breath, which cleared the air. She decided to leave the conversation alone. For one thing, she didn't know what else to say, and most of all, she didn't want to antagonize Susan.

When they arrived at the rectory, Susan didn't get out right away. Instead, she sat studying Bobbie's face with a little frown. "Thank you for a lovely day…and for a delicious lunch. You may have converted me to Thai food. But you don't have to pay all the time. I'm making a decent salary now. Two salaries, in fact."

"I still make more money than you do, and I invited you. Just enjoy the treat."

When Susan leaned in her direction, Bobbie realized she wanted to kiss her. Even though Bobbie had imagined this moment many times before, the sweetness of her soft lips came as a surprise.

"Don't give up on me," Susan said, searching her eyes before sitting up straight. She got out and hurried up the stairs. When she reached the door, she waved before going inside.

"I won't give up on you," Bobbie whispered aloud in the empty car. "Don't give up on me either."

***

Susan arranged the brownies on a pretty plate glazed with a floral pattern. She'd found it in the cabinet along with the other odd dishes collected by previous residents. Reshma had told her not to bring anything, but Susan's upbringing wouldn't allow her to arrive empty handed. The brownies were from a mix, something she could easily whip together after her morning service.

She'd been looking forward to this dinner with her young colleague because she found her stimulating. She knew Reshma was exceptionally bright. The scholarships she'd won to college and divinity school only hinted at her impressive intelligence. But Reshma's vivacious spirit was her most appealing quality. She was so full of life. Except for calls requiring a priest, like giving absolution, she had completely taken over the hospital and home visits from Lucy, yet she never seemed to tire.

Reshma's boundless vitality sometimes left Susan feeling old and weary, but more often it reminded her of herself as a young nun. She'd sparked with so much energy that the novice mistress had assigned her to physical tasks like hoeing the garden to keep her grounded. Young Sister Susan had even mastered the industrial-sized floor polisher that would fling its operators against the wall if they weren't careful. Her fellow novices were jealous, but she wore her conquest of the mechanical beast as a badge of honor.

Susan wondered what Reshma would think of her floor polishing adventures or the fact that she had once been a nun. Maybe she'd tell her, but not tonight. She'd been invited to dinner to listen to Reshma, not the other way around.

Susan knew her neighbor was home because she'd heard her come in less than an hour ago. She knocked on the door and waited patiently for it to open.

Reshma managed her usual bright smile despite looking frantic. "Oh, Mother Susan, come in. I'm making dinner. Maybe I should have chosen something less ambitious."

"Can I help you?"

"No, no. Just come in," Reshma said, pulling her inside. She took the brownies with a little bow. "Thank you. I love chocolate. I made something for dessert, but brownies are always welcome."

"I hope you don't have an allergy to tree-nuts. Everyone seems allergic to everything these days."

"No, I love nuts." Reshma looked around for a place to set down the plate, but all the surfaces were covered. The tiny counter next to the stove was littered with cooking utensils and spice bottles with exotic names. After dancing around the kitchen, Reshma finally put the brownies on top of the refrigerator.

"You shouldn't have gone to so much trouble," said Susan, craning to see what Reshma was preparing. "I'd be happy with anything edible, but whatever you're cooking smells delicious."

"Sudanese Kofta." Reshma explained, raising the lid of a pot. "This is only the sauce. Please, please sit down. I'm sorry, but there's no room if you stand!"

As instructed, Susan pulled out one of the kitchen chairs and tried to stay out of the way. She wondered how she and Denise managed when the two of them were cooking. While Reshma was occupied, Susan gazed around the snug, little studio, the same one she had occupied when she'd come to Hobbs the first time. The place looked so different now. During her stay, Susan had done nothing to alter the space, not even hang up a wall calendar. Reshma had painted the walls a vibrant blue and hung bright posters with inspiring Christian messages. On the daybed were old-fashioned Afghans, which gave the room a coziness reminiscent of a college dorm.

"I take it those Afghans weren't crocheted by your grandmother."

"Hah, no. Some of my best thrift store finds. Some unknown woman put so much work into them. They shouldn't be tossed into the trash to be forgotten. Plus, they were cheap. Two dollars each."

Susan liked Reshma's respect for the past and the work of other women. "I bet they're warm."

"Oh, they are. I've been in New England for years, but I've never gotten used to the winters."

"I've lived here nearly all my life, and neither have I."

Susan sat up to see what Reshma was adding to a bowl of chopped meat. "I'm making the Kofta with beef because some people don't like lamb."

"I like lamb."

"Good to know for next time. Think of these as Sudanese meatballs, except they're not round. See?" With her hands, she formed the ground meat into an egg shape. "They call this a quenelle in French cuisine," she said, impressing Susan with her culinary knowledge. "Usually, the Kofta are skewered for the grill. I didn't bother because I'm browning them in a skillet."

Susan recognized the cast-iron frying pan from her previous stay. "The aroma is making me very hungry."

"Good! It will be ready soon. I promise. Oh! I almost forgot the appetizer." She scrubbed her hands in the small sink and put carrot sticks, arranged in a water glass, and a container of hummus on the table. She added a bowl of mixed olives. "To keep you from fainting while I finish cooking. If you want something to drink, there's some wine open in the fridge."

Susan debated whether to tell Reshma about her drinking problem, but if she did, the evening would become about her issues instead of Reshma's. She decided to save it for another time. "I hate to be fussy, but do you have something else to drink?"

"On the door of the fridge, there' a bottle of flavored seltzer. The cheap kind, I'm afraid."

"That sounds perfect." Susan went to the cabinet where glasses had been stored when she'd lived there. It gave her an odd pleasure to find them in the same location.

As the batches of Kofta browned, Reshma added them to the sauce. "Now, for the flatbread." The kitchen was minimally provisioned, so Reshma carefully wiped out the pan to prepare the next dish. "Denise loves Kisra, even though she says the texture reminds her of memory foam."

"She said that?" Susan scrunched up her face. "That's not very kind."

"It's not, but I can never make enough of it for her."

"Does she eat here often?"

"We used to cook together all the time…to save money, especially when food became so expensive, even hamburger! Fortunately, there are many meatless dishes in African cuisine. It helped stretch our budget."

"Are you cooking one of your mother's recipes?" asked Susan, watching Reshma, pour the batter into the sizzling pan.

"I remember *Omm* cooking these dishes when I was young, but I found these recipes on the internet. I was at boarding school and only learned to cook as an adult."

"I think it's wonderful that you're connecting with your heritage. Many would have tried to forget such a difficult beginning."

"I needed to rediscover my culture. At my school, there was only one other student who wasn't white. Her parents were doctors from India. Advika and I are nothing alike, but we bonded because we were the odd ones. We're still friends. She's a virologist now."

Reshma deftly flipped the rubbery flatbread out of the frying pan one by one and folded them into an envelope shape. "We're almost ready to eat." She pressed some buttons on the microwave. "The sweet potatoes," she explained. "I almost forgot."

"Such an interesting variety of foods."

"These are typical foods of South Sudan, except that meat is reserved for special occasions. Your visit to my home counts as a special occasion" She ladled the meatballs and sauce into bowls and put the sweet potato dish on a trivet. "Can I offer you some wine with your dinner?"

"No, thank you," said Susan with a little smile. "I'm fine with the seltzer."

"Alcohol is illegal where I came from, but I like a good glass of wine. Denise knows a lot about it. But I have early home visits tomorrow morning, so I'll have seltzer too." Reshma refilled Susan's glass and poured one for herself.

After she sat down, she clasped her hands and bowed her head. Susan wondered if the pious gesture was for her benefit, but she bowed her head too. "Let us thank the gracious God, who created us, for the blessing of the food we eat and the companionship we share at this table." Informal and to the point. Susan approved.

"So how does one approach this beautiful creation?" Susan asked, admiring the perfectly formed Kofta swimming in a beautiful mahogany sauce.

Reshma picked up a piece of bread. "This is the key to everything. Of course, you can use a fork or a spoon, but Kisra is for soaking up the sauce. It's very good." Her unabashed self-confidence was refreshing. At her age, Susan would have slyly fished for compliments and then not believed them. Women were raised so differently now.

The dish was perfectly spiced. The meatballs were tender and savory. Although Denise's description of the Kisra being like memory foam fit, it was an ideal way to sponge up the savory sauce.

"Thank you for sharing part of your heritage with me, Reshma. This food is incredibly delicious."

"It is my pleasure to cook for you, Mother Susan."

"Reshma, we work together. Please call me Susan."

"Mother Lucy always says the same, but I call her 'Mother' because that's how I think of her. My mother died young of cancer, so it sounds nice to say the word. In seminary, my ministry professor advised me to find a mentor, an older woman in the clergy to model myself after. I was so lucky to be sent here. Mother Lucy is so kind and loving. I want to be just like her."

Susan didn't let on that she thought her hero worship was excessive. Of course, Reshma didn't know Lucy the way she did. "I'm glad you've found a role model in Lucy, but it's important to find your own path."

"With her help…and yours." Reshma looked at Susan's bowl. "We've been talking too much. Eat."

Susan needed no encouragement. As she ate the delicious meal, she thought how her palate had been challenged in the past days. First, Thai food, now Sudanese. Her new friends in Hobbs were introducing her to completely different new worlds.

Reshma picked up the bowl of Kisra and offered it to Susan.

"Thank you. I can see why Denise finds it addictive." Susan mopped up the sauce in her bowl, not wanting to leave one precious bit.

"There's more Kofta," offered Reshma, pointing over her shoulder.

"Thanks, but I feel pleasantly full. It was delicious."

A brilliant smile flashed on Reshma's face. "Maybe we can cook together…when Denise isn't here, or when she is."

Susan wasn't sure she wanted to get that close to her young neighbors and tried to find a gentle way to temper Reshma's enthusiasm. "I'm afraid I'm a very basic cook. Meat and potatoes. Nothing fancy."

"That's good too. I ate institutional food for years. I'll eat anyone's home cooking any day."

"We can talk about it later," Susan said vaguely. She carefully folded her napkin and put it beside her plate. "Now that we've finished eating, tell me more about why you delayed your ordination." Reshma's eyes grew enormous. After inviting her to discuss this topic, she could hardly be surprised that Susan would bring it up. "Did Lucy say how I could help you?"

"She didn't say," said Reshma, shaking her head. "Are you an expert on vocations?"

"Hardly." Susan successfully fought the temptation to roll her eyes. "In fact, I dragged my feet every step of the way. It's a miracle that I was ever ordained."

Reshma sat forward in her seat. "You had doubts too? I would have thought a woman of your generation had to be exceptionally confident. Unlike me, you had to fight to be ordained."

"We did. It was a radical idea, especially in the Roman Church. When it became clear that the RCs weren't going to budge, I became an Episcopalian. There was only one problem. My upbringing as a Catholic, capital 'C,' never left me. People would say, 'but you're not a real priest' because of apostolic succession, or Jesus only chose men, or some other nonsensical reason.

Niggling doubts in the back of my mind made me question whether I, a woman, could be a valid priest."

"I never doubted that women could be priests."

"Because, in your lifetime, we have always had female clergy. But it wasn't always that way."

"But you got past your doubts and were ordained. How did you do it?"

"I studied…and prayed. Lucy tried to convince me that I was meant to be a priest, and I so wanted to believe her. In those days, Lucy wasn't much of a theologian, but she could be very persuasive." Thinking of the many ways Lucy had used to persuade her made it impossible to meet Reshma's unwavering gaze. The young woman had already mastered the art of being fully present when listening to someone.

"Mother Lucy's been working on me too, and I think she's upped her game since your time. It's impossible to resist arguments made by a theologian of her caliber. But she's mostly rested her case. She told me to pray for discernment. She said that others can listen and make suggestions, but only I can decide."

"And if you go forward to please someone else, whether it be Lucy or the bishop, the doubts will still be there. Take it from me. I've been there. But what are these doubts, Reshma? What's standing in your way?"

Reshma picked up a piece of Kisra and vigorously scoured her bowl. "I'm ashamed to tell you."

"Then don't, but I can't help you unless you do."

"I acted badly and really hurt a friend."

"Have you apologized to your friend and asked forgiveness?"

"Yes, and she has forgiven me."

"So?"

"There's more." Reshma studied Susan with her dark eyes. "Denise and I became close. I admire her. What an amazing voice she has, and she's so worldly compared to me. She's traveled all over Europe. She lived in Italy and speaks the language fluently. I find her very impressive."

"I understand," said Susan, thinking of Lucy, and how her talent and sophistication had impressed her. "Forgive me for being dense, Reshma, but what's the issue?"

"One night, I slept with Denise. At the time, it seemed a natural extension of our friendship. Afterward, I was horrified."

Susan was beginning to get the picture. "Do you feel what you did with Denise is wrong?"

"In the African branch of the Anglican Church, homosexuality is a sin. The bishops of Global South want to keep it that way. Look at the tricks they played at Lambeth."

"But in our province, we accept all people into the church and the clergy. We allow same-sex marriage."

"I know, and it's not a matter of theology. It was my own reaction. I used to think I was so liberal and accepted everyone...until I slept with a trans woman. As a Christian, I'm supposed to love her as she is, not judge her, but I still have so many questions."

"Reshma, just because you went to divinity school doesn't mean you have all the answers. None of us do. Not even Lucy, and she has a doctorate in theology."

Reshma sighed. "After we slept together, I ignored Denise for weeks, except to say hello when we met in the hall. I'm sure she was really hurt by it."

"But I see you together all the time. Obviously, she forgave you and still wants to be your friend."

"I'm not sure I deserve it. I even asked Mother Lucy for absolution, but that didn't help."

"Because you first have to forgive yourself."

"But I don't understand. I never even thought much about Denise being trans. I just knew I was for trans rights."

"But when you made love with her, suddenly it wasn't so abstract." Susan understood. Her attraction to women had only become real after she'd made love to Lucy.

"We are commanded to love everyone," Reshma continued. "If I can't accept a dear friend, someone I've given my body...If I can't love her for who she is, how can I be a priest?"

"Reshma, there are many things other people do that I don't understand or accept. I agree with everything you've said about Denise, her talent, her attractiveness, her many appealing characteristics, but do I completely embrace her sexuality? Like you, I try to love each person for who they are, not who I want them to be. That doesn't mean I always succeed, but I don't ever stop trying."

"Would you like to wait for dessert or have it now?"

Susan recognized the clumsy attempt at diversion. "I'm full now. Can we wait a few minutes?"

"Of course, let me just rinse the dishes and put away the extra. I can make a dish for you to take home. Would you like that?"

"Thank you. Very kind."

Susan watched Reshma carefully rinse and stack the dishes and apportion the leftovers into two plastic containers.

"Reshma, I'd like to share something that might shed some light on your dilemma," Susan couldn't believe she was even thinking such a thing, but she couldn't let this talented young woman, who really should be a priest, continue to torture herself. "While I was in seminary, I fell in love with a woman."

"Susan! I never would have guessed! You look so..."

"Normal?" Susan laughed. "Far from it. And normal is only what most people do most of the time. When I fell in love with this woman, I believed it was intrinsically wrong. Of course, that's what the church was teaching at the time. I kept hearing all the negative doctrines about people who loved their own sex. In my heart I knew it wasn't wrong, but no matter what I did, I couldn't make it right in my head. I kept delaying my ordination while I agonized over my sexuality. I truly loved this woman, but I ended up destroying our relationship because of my feelings of guilt."

"That's so sad."

"The Church has so many rules about sex and its expression which aren't always loving. Lucy was brave to take them on. Have you read her book?"

"Cover to cover three times. It helped…On some things, I wish she had gone further."

"Well, I've encouraged her to write volume two, and I hope she does. There is an enormous need for intelligent thinking to help heal the church. Questioning is good. If you have questions about Denise's sexuality, you should talk to her about her experience. Learn everything you can, read about it, research the science, but please, Reshma, don't destroy your vocation with doubts. We don't ordain perfect people. We ordain flawed human beings. You are a gifted minister, and you'll make a wonderful priest. The Church really needs people like you."

"Thank you, Susan. I needed to hear that." Reshma looked ready to cry. Susan affectionately rubbed her shoulder. "Reshma, Denise forgives you. God forgives you and loves you more than you can ever imagine."

"I know." Reshma awkwardly wiped away a tear. Susan gave her a moment to get herself together.

"Where do things stand?" she asked gently.

"When I told the bishop I thought I was ready to be ordained, he suggested a retreat. After Thanksgiving, I'm going to an Episcopal convent outside of Boston. Most of the sisters are trained in spiritual direction. Mother Lucy is paying for it out of her own money."

"She's generous that way," said Susan. "I'm glad she's helping you."

"Me too. *Now* are you ready for dessert? I made something special—a coconut cake called Baseema. Would you like to try it?"

Susan smiled at Reshma's eagerness. "You've really gone all out. Yes, thank you."

"No, Susan. *Thank you.*"

13

Lucy obviously wasn't there on official business. She wore a green sweater that snugged to her good figure, but no clerical collar. Her nails were painted bright red, a color she never wore on duty, but since her wedding, she'd been wearing subtle shades that didn't attract too much attention. Apparently, her wife liked nail polish.

Lucy's casual appearance suggested that she'd only stopped into the rectory to check the mail. Despite the strenuous concert, she looked rested. Having gone through the long, painful death of Lucy's first career, Susan knew how difficult Lucy found preparing for a big performance. Afterwards, she was so calm, as if the release she'd experienced on stage was like an orgasm.

Engrossed in something on her phone, Lucy frowned as she flipped through screens. Susan cleared her throat to get her attention.

"Susan! I didn't hear you come in!"

"Remember when I told you how we learned to walk silently in the convent? It drives the kids in school crazy when I sneak up on them."

"I hated when the nuns did that. It scared the hell out of me."

Susan laughed. "I doubt it. There's still plenty of hell left. When did you get home?"

"About an hour ago. Liz dropped me off. She's at the supermarket picking up a few things we need. Have a seat and tell me what's been going on here." Lucy pointed to a chair. "Abbie said the services went perfectly."

"You sound almost surprised."

"Not a bit. You and Reshma are very capable. By the way, she stopped in before she went upstairs. That was nice of her to invite you for dinner."

"I think she's lonely with Denise gone."

"Hmm. Maybe. She said she cooked African food for you. That must have been interesting."

"It was delicious. She's quite a good cook. I really enjoyed it."

"She also said you gave her good advice."

"I just listened really. I think she already knew what to do but just needed to give herself permission to do it. She'll make an excellent priest."

Lucy drew a deep breath and smiled. "Now we have an ordination to plan. That will be fun. The bishop loves big productions."

"It's the Episcopal way. And you should talk, singing Wagner at the Met. Now, *that's* a big production. I already reserved tickets. I'm not going to miss that one."

"Oh, I meant to tell you. The Philharmonic concert was recorded for a classical music streaming service. My agent talked them into giving us a copy. Liz wants to get everyone together who couldn't make it to New York for dinner and a screening."

"Oh, that sounds like fun. I hope I'm invited."

"Of course, you're invited," Lucy said with an admonishing frown. "Why wouldn't you be?"

Susan shrugged, knowing she was being unnecessarily difficult.

"Reshma also told me you helped her refugee family find a place to live." Lucy's green eyes held a hint of mischief. "I tell you. I leave town for a week, and you two reinvent everything…in a good way, of course. I like it when people make good trouble."

"The stars aligned. Bobbie had room for them. The woman is a trained nurse, and Bobbie can certainly use the help. I hope this works out for all of them. The only issue is transportation. You can't get around in Hobbs without a car."

Lucy quickly swept her gaze over Susan, who instantly recognized a therapist's discreet evaluation. "And how are *you* doing?"

"I'm okay. I went out for dinner with the teachers before the parent conferences." Susan only mentioned the teacher's dinner because she knew Lucy would like to hear that she was making friends.

"How's it going with you and Bobbie?"

"Better. We've had some honest conversations. Of course, I don't like that she hid the truth from me, but I understand better now why she did."

"So, it's as you suspected?"

"She's in an impossible situation. She really cares for Joyce and feels responsible for her."

"How did you leave it?"

Susan thought for a moment. "We enjoy spending time together. There's no reason we can't be friends."

"Liz always says no one can ever have enough friends. God knows she has a lot of them. Speaking of Liz," said Lucy, glancing at her watch. "Thanks for stopping by, Susan, and for holding down the fort while I was away." Obviously, she was trying to bring the conversation to a close.

Susan got to her feet. "See? I can be trusted." She instantly regretted the little dig, but she'd been unable to stop it.

Lucy studied her with a little frown. "Susan, if you succeed at St. Margaret's, no one will be happier than me. I'm rooting for you."

"I know, but sometimes, it doesn't feel like it."

Lucy turned her attention to her phone, clearly to avoid a response. Susan was tempted to say she was sorry for the stupid remark, but an apology would only make an awkward situation worse. Instead, she said, "Welcome home, Lucy. Have a good night."

❈❈❈

Liz listened to the reassuring clatter of dishes from the kitchen. Tired after the long drive from New York, she'd thrown together a simple meal of steak and grilled vegetables. While her wife was occupied with the dishes, Liz decided to catch up on the medical reading she'd neglected while they were away.

There had been too many distractions in the city—exhibitions to see, a Broadway play, and dinner parties with old friends. Jenny and Laura had come into the city for the performance as well as Melissa's sister, Rabbi Morgenstern and her wife, Judith. Crazy that they had to go into the city to see their friends from out of town.

After the disastrous first rehearsal, Morales had taken Liz and Lucy out for dinner to make amends. Apparently, he'd been on good behavior during the Boston Symphony concert. Roger had confided that Morales had a reputation for berating soloists during rehearsals. Lucy was in too deep with him now, otherwise Liz would have suggested that Lucy dump him. She'd agreed to do a recording and three more concerts under his baton, but if the verbal abuse persisted, Liz would certainly have a word with him.

Lucy finally came into the living room and stretched out on the sofa. She put her bare feet into Liz's lap. When Liz didn't instantly pick up on the cue, Lucy tickled her armpit with her toes.

"Lucy, sometimes, you can be so demanding!" Liz set her tablet aside and began to massage the ball of Lucy's foot.

"That's what you get for seducing me with foot rubs. Sometimes, I think I like them better than sex."

"Well, in that case." Liz dropped her foot like a hot stone.

Lucy's toes insinuated themselves into Liz's armpit again. Liz recoiled defensively because she was supposed to. "Back to work!" Lucy ordered, holding up her foot.

Liz loved massaging Lucy's feet because she so obviously enjoyed it. As if to prove Liz's thought, Lucy closed her eyes and settled back against the throw pillow.

"How were things over at the rectory?"

Lucy opened one eye. "Why do you always bring up difficult subjects when I'm trying to relax?"

"Sorry. Just making conversation."

Lucy opened the other eye. "Susan is still resentful because I put her on probation when she first came."

Liz relocated her efforts to Lucy's instep. The tension in the muscles proved how unhappy high heels made her feet. "You'd think she'd be grateful for hiring her. You didn't have to."

"Yes, I did."

Liz looked at Lucy's face, trying to decide what that meant. "I thought you said the bishop's not your boss."

"Not in the same way as in other denominations. But I had to take Susan on staff because of…you know, politics."

"I was never good at politics, so maybe I don't know," admitted Liz. "But you can practically read people's minds, so you have an advantage. And you have good instincts."

"Thank you." Lucy flinched. "Ow!"

"Too hard? Sorry. I'll go easy. I can tell the high heels were hurting you."

"And to think I used to wear them every day. Good thing I'm just singing part time. I've gotten used to flats."

"Is that all Susan had to say…that she resents you? Geeze. What else is new?"

"She also told me she's given up the idea of a relationship with Bobbie."

"Good. Bobbie doesn't need more drama."

"She's taken in two of Reshma's refugees, a mother, and her young daughter. The woman was trained as a nurse and is willing to help."

"That's good. It's a big house. Just hope it doesn't get too crowded over there."

Lucy looked thoughtful. "I'm not sure what I think about Susan ruling out a relationship. It would divert her from being fixated on me. That's a selfish reason, of course, but having love in her life would be good for her." Lucy sighed. "What an impossible situation. How can you have three people in a relationship?"

"Why not?" asked Liz, partially playing devil's advocate but also curious to hear what Lucy would say.

"Intimate relationships should be between two consenting adults."

"Why?"

"Well, jealousy for one thing. It can make people do horrible things. Look how you behaved when you found out Maggie used that poor young actor to get back at you. Going to the range and shooting everything in sight."

"Better than killing people," mumbled Liz.

"Admit it. It really bothers you to see her with Sam."

"Maggie is a special case. When she fucks men, it runs my old tapes from college. I'm mad because she took Sam away. I can't confide in her anymore because I'm afraid what I say will get back to Maggie."

"Oh, I doubt she'd tell Maggie. Sam's loyal to you, and she loves you. You're just jealous."

"Well, it doesn't have to be that way. Look at Erika. It never seemed to bother her that Jeannine was screwing every woman at Colby."

"Liz…" said Lucy, raising an auburn brow.

"Okay, but Jeannine made a sport of conquest. I guess I did too. It sometimes bothered me that Jenny slept around, but being a player myself, I couldn't really complain."

"Should I be worried?" asked Lucy, looking worried. "You're the one who insisted on getting married. I would have been okay with waiting a while."

"I wanted you to know I was serious, especially after teasing you so long."

"Liz, I knew you were serious right from the beginning. You were the only one who didn't know. Erika used to shake her head and wonder when you'd wake up."

"Erika told you to have sex with me to get it out of your system. We could have become a threesome. Erika and I slept together before."

"Liz, I'm not sure I'm ready for polyamory. That is a bridge too far."

"Are you kidding me? The Biblical marriage your friends are so fond of talking about is full of patriarchs with multiple wives, men taking a slave to bed on the side…"

"That was the culture at the time. And it was always men who had all the women. In our culture, marriage has traditionally been defined as being between two people."

"Two people of the *opposite sex*. In your book, you stood on your head to justify same-sex marriage. Then you went right back to the same old argument for confining it to a couple. You tried to be such a good little girl and stick to Church dogma. That left some of your arguments squishy and wide open for your critics. Maybe you should have pushed the envelope harder."

"I tried, but Jerry kept pulling me back. He said it would be different if I weren't a priest. Because I wear a collar, I speak for the church, whether I want to or not."

"More politics," said Liz in a disgusted tone, although she liked Jerry Spangler and thought he had a first-rate intellect.

"Yes, politics, and other things, like my own convictions. How would you like it if I became interested in another woman? I think Sam is cute. I even find Maggie attractive. That doesn't mean I should act on it."

"I'm not worried," said Liz.

"Elizabeth Anne Stolz!" Lucy punched her lightly on the shoulder. "You're so darn sure of yourself, aren't you?"

"No, I just know you. You wouldn't cheat on me unless I gave you permission."

"That will never happen, and you know it. And don't you get any ideas either."

"I wouldn't dare. I've seen your temper. But consider this. What if Erika hadn't died from that aneurysm? What if she were in a permanent vegetative state? Would you spend the rest of your life sitting at her bedside, holding her hand? You loved her, but you knew I loved you too. Why wouldn't you accept the love and companionship I wanted to give you? Erika would have wanted you to accept it. She wanted you to be happy."

"Well, for one thing. You were married to Maggie."

"Let's be real. Maggie left the marriage long before you and I ever kissed on the boat. Believe me, Lucy, I tried."

"I know. Maggie has her issues, and you do too. Sometimes, I have to pry information out of you." The probing toes returned, and Liz flinched. "Erika would have wanted me to be happy. That's all she ever wanted. But I was horrified when she told me to sleep with you. I thought it meant she didn't really love me." Lucy looked sad. "But just the opposite was true."

"Erika adored you, Lucy. And so, do I. So, think of Bobbie. It's the same situation as Erika being in a coma. There's no possibility that Joyce will ever recover. Her brain will continue to deteriorate until her body no longer functions."

"But she's still alive and functioning. She picked up on the attraction between Bobbie and Susan. Did you know Joyce before the Alzheimer's?"

"She came in once or twice when she was up here on vacation. Bright woman, sharp about business, the arts. Very opinionated about politics. It's tragic to see what she's become. Bobbie never complains, but it can't be easy for her."

Lucy took her foot back and sat up. "Okay, Liz. I get your point. I guess I have some thinking to do."

"That's what I like about you, Lucy. You always keep an open mind. I wish your church buddies thought the same."

"Liz, I'm not getting into another argument about the Church."

"We could kiss and make up in bed," suggested Liz with a raised brow.

"Do you need sex every night?"

"Every night. I don't want you to forget me."

Lucy looked grave. "Liz, that's not funny. Not even a little bit."

"No, it's not."

***

Eagerly, Susan took the book out of her bag and laid it in her lap. When she'd first come to Hobbs, she was delighted to discover the town library. The collection was extensive, but she'd had to wait her turn for this novel by the Irish writer, Emma Donoghue. She could have read it on the Kindle Fire Lucy had given her for her birthday, but for pleasure reading, Susan still preferred a real hardcover book.

Settling into the leather club chair, she wondered how many of St. Margaret's rectors had sat there before her. Of course, that made her think of Lucy. Clearly, she was trying to make things right between them. Baiting her had only given Susan another regret to add to the jar.

Sally had suggested Susan store her regrets in a tight-fitting jar like pickles. "Put on the lid and leave them in there to marinate. They'll still be there to look at another time. Understanding why you drink doesn't come all at once." The pickle jar analogy always made Susan smile because she liked pickles, and she enjoyed Sally's way with words.

If Lucy hadn't forced her to go to AA, Susan never would have met Sally. Some people might call that fate. An astrologer would point to the influence of heavenly bodies, which apparently had been the inspiration for the title of the book in Susan's lap: *The Pull of the Stars*. She wondered how the idea, illustrated on the cover by an open pocket watch and magical symbols, connected to the flu pandemic of 1918.

Susan read Donoghue's books for their impeccably researched historical detail, but early twentieth-century childbirth practices didn't really interest her. Eventually, she was drawn into the tale of the overworked, young maternity nurse and her young volunteer, a refugee from one of those awful Irish convents that turned women into indentured servants. While Susan had been in the convent, she'd tried to be one of the good nuns. She hated the idea of abusing children.

Deep into her book, Susan barely heard the soft knock. She listened intently and heard it again. Someone was at the door. When Susan opened it, Reshma was standing there in a sleek exercise ensemble. The pale pink contrasted beautifully with her ebony skin, but if Susan had worn that shade, she'd look like a washed-out dish rag.

"I didn't want to wake you if you were asleep. That's why I didn't call," Reshma explained. Susan wondered if she'd expected her to be in bed because to her, she was old.

"But it's not even nine."

"I know, but you get up early for school."

"I appreciate the consideration, but my usual bedtime is ten."

"Good to know," said Reshma, tapping her fingertips to her temple as if it would help her remember.

Susan opened the door wider. "Well, would you like to come in?"

Reshma stepped in cautiously. "I don't want to disturb you."

"Too late for that," said Susan. She smiled to let Reshma know it was an attempt at humor. "Would you like some tea? I have decaffeinated."

"No thanks. I won't keep you."

"Sit down at least." Susan gestured to the armchair across from where she'd been sitting. Reshma glanced at the open book.

"I see you've been reading."

"Emma Donoghue, one of my favorite authors."

"I don't know her work. Should I check her out?"

"If you like well-researched historical fiction and fine language."

"My TBR pile is already so big I can barely find anything."

"TBR?"

"To be read," Reshma explained. "Sorry."

"Don't apologize. You're teaching me how to talk to you." Susan closed the book and put it on the side table. "So, Reshma, what brings you that couldn't wait until morning?"

"I had a call from Teresa. She and Grace are planning a feast to celebrate their new home. You'll get to taste African food again, authentic this time, not my sorry imitation."

"Stop, Reshma. I thoroughly enjoyed your meal. The leftovers too. When is this feast?"

"On Sunday afternoon around three. I suggested the time so we can catch our breath after services. You are the honored guest because you connected them with Ms. Lantry."

"That's very kind. Yes, I'd love to go."

"I promised I'd call Teresa right back. Do you mind?" asked Reshma, taking her phone out of her pocket.

"Go ahead. Are you sure you don't want tea? I'm making myself a cup."

Listening to the phone ring on the other end, Reshma nodded. Since the answer was completely ambiguous, Susan decided for her. She went into the kitchen and put on the kettle. Although it was late, she'd use the teapot because Reshma seemed to like old-fashioned civility. She opened a tin of shortbread and arranged the cookies on a plate.

"They are so excited you're coming!" Reshma said, running into the kitchen. She smiled at the plate of cookies. "A tea party!"

"Albeit an impromptu one." Susan carefully poured the boiling water over a spoon to prevent the old porcelain from cracking, which brought back memories of sharing a pot of tea with Lucy while they were at seminary.

"We should celebrate," said Reshma proudly. "Our mission with the refugees is a success, and I got important news today,"

"You did? Can you tell me?"

Reshma's enormous grin showed her perfect teeth. "I have a date for my ordination. *Gaudete* Sunday, one of my favorite feasts because of the rose vestments."

"Mine too. Too bad we only use them twice a year. But isn't it unusual to have an ordination during Advent?"

"Yes. I wanted to wait until after Christmas, but Mother Lucy reminded me how bad the weather can be."

"She's right about that. Although in coastal Maine, you never know. Congratulations."

"I'm both relieved and happy."

Susan leaned on Reshma's shoulder as she set the teapot on the table. "Good for you. This has been a long time in coming. You should be happy." She sat down on the other side of the table. After pouring the tea, she nudged the plate of cookies toward Reshma.

"I love shortbread. They used to serve it at high tea in my school."

"I like it myself." Susan put two on her plate. "How far are the plans for your big day?"

"In the morning, I will assist at Mother Lucy's service for the last time as a deacon. The ordination begins at three, followed by a small reception in the church hall. Afterward, Olivia Enright is hosting a big party at her house for invited guests."

"Will Denise be home in time?"

"That was a requirement. I want her to plan the music and sing. This will be her last service as music director. She realized she can't travel for her singing career and still work for the church. She called Lucy from Stuttgart to tell her. After my ordination, Maggie Fitzgerald will be taking over full-time. I like her very much, but she's not Denise."

"Will Denise still be able to live here?"

"The vestry says she must look for another place, but Mother Lucy told her she can stay for a few months until she finds something. Denise said she will probably move closer to Boston, so she can get to the airport more easily."

"I'm sure you'll be sad when she leaves."

"Of course. I'll really miss her. She welcomed me when I first came and didn't know a soul. And…"

"And she's a dear friend."

"But it's easy to stay in touch on social media," Reshma said bravely. "I already added international calling to my phone plan, and we can video chat online."

"But it's not the same," said Susan, patting her hand sympathetically. "You'll have to work harder to keep up your friendship."

"And I will." Reshma finished preparing her tea and took a sip. "Ah, good. Thank you."

"The party at Bobbie's sounds like fun. How are Teresa and Grace settling in?"

"Grace is enrolled in Hobbs Middle School. Dr. Stolz gave Teresa a job in her practice on a flexible schedule so she can take nursing classes at the community college. But she needs transportation. For now, Simone is driving her to classes, but we're looking for a car."

"I would love to replace my old Subaru, but it would be hard to get a loan. I've only been working at the elementary school a few months. That means I'd have to ask my old rector and my principal in South Dakota to sign off on my financial statement. Ugh!"

"Maybe you can find a used car."

"Used cars are harder to get than new ones and almost as expensive. My old Subaru doesn't owe me a thing. It still runs great, but it would be nice to have a more gas-efficient model."

"Forgive me for making a pig of myself." Reshma grinned as she pilfered another cookie. "Thank you for the tea party. I love celebrations, don't you? Denise is coming home tomorrow night. Would you like to come over for a drink?"

Susan wouldn't think of being an interloper in that bittersweet reunion. "It's a school night," she said. "Another time, perhaps."

"Okay," said Reshma reluctantly, "but promise we'll do it before she moves out."

Susan smiled, but she didn't promise.

***

Liz was reading the morning news on her tablet when Lucy came into the kitchen. On her way to the coffee maker, she nibbled Liz's ear.

"We already had sex this morning," Liz growled, raising her shoulder in defense. "Lucy, how many orgasms do you need?"

"I'm satisfied and ready to start the day, but your ear looked so inviting." Lucy blew a warm breath into it, making Liz shiver. "Let me make you another cup of coffee," she whispered, whisking away Liz's empty cup.

Liz wondered why her wife was being so attentive. Sometimes, Lucy refilled her cup when she wanted company or had something important on her mind. Liz tried to figure out which was on the agenda this morning. It was Liz's day off, when she usually spent more time with Lucy at breakfast, so she prepared herself for a discussion.

Lucy leaned on the counter while she waited for their coffee to brew, giving Liz a perfect view of her shapely rear. Now that the cold weather had arrived, Lucy had started wearing pants again. The clingy fabric snugly defined the perfect inverted heart.

"Thanks for making a fire this morning. When I looked out the bathroom window, I saw the lawn was covered with frost." Lucy turned and caught Liz staring at her rear. "Bad girl," she scolded, but after she sat down, she gave Liz one of those brilliant smiles that could make her do anything.

"Okay, Lucy. I know that look," said Liz, folding her arms on her chest. "What do you want?"

"Don't you think we have too many cars?" asked Lucy, pouring cream into her coffee.

Liz frowned. "What do you mean?"

"Well, you have your big new SUV and your truck. I have my car. Do we *really* need your old Audi cluttering up the yard?"

Liz uncrossed her arms to accept the cream pitcher. "It's for visitors who fly in or take the train. Why? Is it bothering you?"

"Now that your niece's children are older, they don't visit as much. And when Emily is here, we have even more cars in the yard. Think about it." Lucy stroked Liz's arm enticingly, raising the hair.

"Lucy, you're being especially seductive this morning. Obviously, you want something. What is it?"

"I'm sorry. It's shameless to use sex to make you more receptive."

"You use it because you know it works every time."

"Yes, but it's not fair. You're such an easy mark. All I have to do is smile at you and you cave." Lucy reached for one of the blueberry muffins in the basket on the table. Liz watched her leisurely butter it.

"Lucy, why are you suddenly so interested in the old Audi? It's been sitting in the yard since April."

"Emily has the old car you sold to Erika. Maybe we could sell it, and you could give her the newer model. With gas prices so high, she could probably use an upgrade."

"Emily's car runs fine because I maintain it. And I sold it to Erika for a fair price, which makes it yours. Sell it if you want to."

"Everything is OURS since our marriage. You insisted. Remember?"

"Okay, if you want Emily to have the newer model, give it to her, and we'll sell the old one."

"I have a buyer in mind," said Lucy and bit into the muffin, leaving Liz in suspense.

"Who?" asked Liz suspiciously.

"Susan."

Liz rolled her eyes.

"Liz, hear me out. She needs a better car than that beat up Subaru she brought back from South Dakota."

"But Emily's car is still worth good money!" Liz opened her tablet and looked up the Blue Book value. "See?"

Lucy drew back so she could focus on the screen Liz had shoved into her face. "That's a lot. I was thinking of asking two thousand."

"Lucy, that's crazy! It's *a tenth* of its value. You're giving it away!"

"Liz, it's what she can afford," Lucy said in a deliberately patient voice. "Susan has no credit, so she can't get a loan." Liz glared at Lucy until she looked at her. "All right, Liz. Three thousand. I'll lend her the money, and she can pay me back fifty dollars a month."

Liz mentally calculated the amortization. "That will take forever!"

"That's the idea. In a couple of years, it will have depreciated, and we'll forgive the loan, right?" Lucy stroked Liz's arm again to mollify her.

"Why don't you just give her the fucking car?" said Liz in disgust. She got up to take a yogurt out of the refrigerator.

"Because giving it to her would undermine her recovery."

Liz still didn't like the idea, but she tried to see it from Lucy's point of view. It was simple. Someone needed a car. They had an extra, so give it to them. "Honey, why didn't you just ask me to give Emily my car? It would have been quicker."

"This was more fun, don't you think? And if I just asked, you'd try to talk me out of it with all kinds of practical reasons and perfect logic, which I bet you're going to do now."

She was right, of course, but with Lucy thinking she could outsmart her, Liz had to do her one better. "I can have Harriet draw up a note to make the loan official. We can switch cars when Emily comes up for Thanksgiving. Meanwhile, Susan can drive my Audi."

"Thank you. Hadn't thought about formalizing the arrangement, but that's a good idea. After breakfast, I'll call Susan and ask her to come for dinner. We'll tell her the plan together."

Liz pictured the big sirloin she'd planned for dinner and wondered if it would be enough for three, but she always bought extra for Lucy's lunch. Besides, Susan ate sparingly.

"Okay," said Liz. "Invite her. But what are you going to do with Susan's car? Donate it?"

"Yes, to Reshma's refugee family. The woman needs a car to get to her classes. The Uber fees are killing them. Susan's car is so old that it will cost next to nothing to insure and register. The only thing they'll have to worry about is gas."

"Lucy, you've thought of everything. Maybe there's hope for you."

"Thanks, Liz. I love you too."

Liz ignored the sarcasm. She knew that beneath it, Lucy was telling the truth.

✾✾✾

Savoring the unusual flavor, Bobbie thoughtfully chewed the sandwich that Teresa had packed for her lunch. The spicy curry was a perfect complement to the rich mayonnaise. Seasoning aside, Bobby wondered why food prepared by someone else always tasted better. Occasionally, her student-boarders made a meal, but more often they waited for Bobbie to cook. How wonderful to have another woman to share her kitchen again.

"Hey," said a honey-toned voice behind her. Bobbie turned around and saw Cherie bending to get her lunch out of the refrigerator. "Mind if I sit with you?" She was already pulling out the chair opposite Bobbie, so the question was moot.

"What's for lunch?" she asked, eyeing Bobbie's sandwich.

"Chicken salad. I would have never thought of adding curry, but it's good."

"Mm. Yes, it is. I never think of it either. I should add it next time, but Brenda's been making lunch 'cause I'm running around so much." She tipped her bowl of salad with cut-up steak on top. "Basic, but tasty."

"Teresa made my sandwich. I never would have thought of curry as an African spice, but she reminded me that Sudan is a former British colony. She even knows how to bake scones. Joyce loves them."

"Sounds like you're enjoying your new guests."

"I'm enjoying the help even more. The nursing education in Teresa's country is every bit as good as ours, maybe better."

"I can see. Now that she's doing the blood draws, they get done faster. Good thing too. When people come in before work, they don't want to be late."

"No, when we get backed up, they get pissy," said Bobbie. "I'm glad Liz could give her a job that uses her training, even if it will be months, maybe years, before she's certified as a nurse. Meanwhile, we can certainly use the help here, and she's made such a difference at home. Sometimes, I feel a little guilty. Joyce is getting first-class nursing care without us paying a dime."

Cherie gave her a firm look. "You gave them a place to live. They're repaying you for your kindness by giving you a break."

"Before your aunt came to give me a day off, I didn't even realize how much I needed one."

"As we both know, caregiver's fatigue is real. When my father was still alive, I rushed to work, rushed home to make supper. I was rushing all the time." Cherie got up to rinse out the salad container in the sink. "I hear you're having a big party at your house."

Bobbie gave Cherie a sheepish look. Was she fishing for an invitation? "I'd ask you to come, but there's a limit to how many people can fit at our dining room table."

"I couldn't come anyway," said Cherie. "Keith has basketball on Sunday afternoons. Usually, we all go as a family to support him, but Aunt Simone is going to your party. She's been driving Teresa to her classes to cut down on the Uber expense. I think they've really bonded."

"Your aunt is a godsend."

"Yes, but she's going to be busy now. She's taking over the children's choir. I'll be sad when Denise goes. I love Maggie, but Denise really pushed us to sing more difficult music. Wait till you see Reshma's ordination. It will be quite the show."

"So, I hear. And I don't blame Denise for following her dreams. She is one talented lady. I loved hearing her sing at that concert in the cathedral."

"Denise is way too talented to hang around here. I'm glad her career is taking off. Mother Lucy really worked to retrain her voice. You can't even tell she used to be a countertenor."

"Lucy is talented too. Do you think she'd go back to singing full-time?"

"Mother Lucy loves to perform, but I don't see her leaving St. Margaret's. She built the parish up from nothing, and she has roots in Hobbs. Liz won't give up her practice until she's good and ready, no matter how much she adores Lucy. That's what I think, but who knows? Tom left. Denise is going on the road. I don't want to lose Mother Lucy too." Cherie pinched the skin of the orange she was peeling between her fingertips, releasing a geyser of citrus oil. She sniffed the air appreciatively. "Smells like Christmas, don't you think?" She offered half of the peeled orange to Bobbie, but she shook her head. "Bobbie, you should think about joining our parish. It's a good group, friendly people. You missed the pie making for the harvest fair. That's always fun."

"That sounds so sweet and old-fashioned," said Bobbie with a sigh, "but I'm not religious."

"Doesn't matter. I think a lot of people just go to church for the community. They grew up at St. Margaret's. It's part of their tradition, like making pies for the harvest fair. It's fun to work side by side with the church ladies rolling out dough for Christmas tourtières."

"Christmas what?"

"Tourtières, French-Canadian meat pies made with ground pork. They're delicious. My daddy's people came to Maine from Quebec. He met my mama when he was sent to Louisiana by the navy. She had to learn how to bake a tourtière as a condition of their marriage."

"Must be something special."

"I have a small one in the freezer. I'll bake it up tonight and bring it tomorrow for our lunch. You can tell me what you think."

"Ooh. That sounds like fun."

Cherie gave Bobbie a long inspection with her blue-green eyes. "Bobbie, I'm glad to see how much calmer you are."

"Finally, things seem to be settling down." Bobbie crossed her fingers. "My mother used to say, 'Enjoy the peace while you have it.'"

Cherie crossed her fingers on both hands. "Ain't that the truth!"

❋❋❋

244   *The Vanishing Bridge*

"You're wearing a collar?" Reshma stared with dismay at Susan's throat. The deacon was dressed for a party in a long brightly colored sweater, leggings, and high boots.

"I think we should, don't you? You reached out to the refugees as part of your ministry."

"But I thought today is supposed to be a celebration."

"It is. So is what we do in church every Sunday."

"You're right." Reshma's buoyant mood deflated like a punctured party balloon. "I'll go put on mine too."

After Reshma left, Susan wondered if she was overdressed. Maybe Reshma was right. Susan leaned closer to the mirror to check her makeup. Her shoulder-length hair had been carefully styled to look smooth and sleek. She was wearing a patterned black and white sweater over her clerical blouse to make the gray hairs that fell less obvious.

Reshma returned, wearing a clerical shirt with a plastic tab collar. "I didn't have a chance to do my laundry yet."

"It doesn't matter. You look lovely no matter what you wear." It was the truth. Like Lucy, Reshma was a natural beauty with a great figure. Everything looked wonderful on her.

"I hate being in uniform for social events," she grumbled as they walked down the stairs.

Susan reminded herself that, despite Reshma's intellect and apparent maturity, she was still young. "On another occasion, you can wear something informal. Tonight, you have a role to play. You created this connection, and if there's a request for a blessing before the meal, you give it."

"But you're a priest and senior to me."

"In age maybe." Susan affectionately rubbed Reshma's shoulder. "Do it. The practice will be good for you."

"I'll drive," said Reshma, "but I'd like you to be the designated driver. Not that I plan to drink too much." Susan realized that Reshma had no idea she was talking to an alcoholic.

"That's fine."

Susan enjoyed being a passenger because she could take in sights that went unnoticed when she drove—the dented barrier on the bridge, the rainbow flag flying over the mussel hut, a soccer ball lost in the marsh grass. It was still green, but the long shadows of impending winter were everywhere. A perfect V of geese flew overhead. "We are blessed to live in such a beautiful place," Susan mused.

"We are. I often wonder why I was brought here, half a world away from where I was born. I won't have any family at my ordination. My mother always encouraged me to get an education, even when it meant we would be separated. She would have been so proud."

"We'll all be proud for her."

"I'm grateful for all my Hobbs friends. Olivia Enright is bragging that the reception will be fancier than the one she threw for Mother Lucy's wedding. She is so impressed the bishop will be coming."

"Will you invite your new friends?"

"Of course. They will be representing the people I left behind, my African family. They don't know it yet. I'm telling them today."

They arrived at the large house near the beach. The yard looked so different in winter. Hard, red rose hips had replaced the delicate blossoms in the hedge. The arbor vitae that provided privacy from the neighboring house wore burlap coats to protect their tender branches from the ocean winds.

They pulled into the parking area where Susan's battered Subaru stood. Reshma squinted. "Susan, isn't that your car?"

"It was. Lucy sold me her daughter's car, so I could give mine to Teresa."

"I noticed that fancy Audi in the parking lot. I wondered where it came from. No one in our rectory could afford an expensive car like that."

"It's only temporary. Lucy's daughter is bringing an older model when she comes home. At Thanksgiving, we'll make the swap."

"Oh, Mother Susan, you are so cool, driving your hot performance car," said Reshma, boogying in her seat. "They'll wonder if you won the lottery."

"How did you know I always buy a ticket? I never win, but it goes to a good cause and maybe, just maybe, I'll get lucky."

"What would you do if you won?"

"Good question." Susan thought for a moment. "I've never had any money, so I have no idea. Probably give most of it away."

Bobbie met them at the door, explaining, "I've been banished from the kitchen and told to entertain my guests, but I'm not complaining. Come in." Her smile became noticeably warmer when she turned to Susan. "Thanks so much for coming."

"Oh, I wouldn't miss it, especially since Reshma introduced me to African food."

Susan handed her a potted miniature chrysanthemum she'd picked up in the supermarket, not expensive, but the calico flowers were such an unusual color. "Beautiful. Thank you," Bobbie said, leaning forward to give her a kiss on the cheek. Startled, Susan turned her head, and the kiss landed on her lips. "I'm so sorry." Bobbie's face flushed bright pink. She began to babble. "Simone is here, but it's a small gathering because Chloe's on duty today and couldn't make it. She really wanted to come. That poor girl is so busy. I don't know when she sleeps or…"

"Where is everyone?" Susan asked to stop the nervous chatter.

"They're in the common room." Bobbie led the way.

Simone was having a one-sided conversation with Joyce, who was sitting in a wheelchair by an electric fireplace. She gazed vacantly into the ornamental flames. Compared to the rectory, the room was overheated, an extravagance, given the high price of fuel. Susan told herself not to judge. Maybe Joyce was sensitive to the cold.

Bobbie left and reappeared at Susan's side with a glass of flavored seltzer. "That's such a pretty sweater, but I was surprised to see the collar."

"Reshma has a leadership role in this arrangement," confided Susan in a whisper. "I'm trying to set an example."

Bobbie nodded knowingly. "You make a good one," she whispered back.

"Thank you."

"Sorry about the kiss. I didn't mean to…"

"Let's talk about it later," Susan said, smiling at Simone, who had gotten up to greet the newcomers.

"Mother Susan," she said in a warm voice, reaching out her hand. "How nice to see you. Thank you for providing our friends with transportation. I'm going to be busy with the children's choir, and we can't leave Teresa stranded at school."

"Glad to help. It was actually Mother Lucy's idea."

"But you're the one who made it happen," said Simone, looking directly into her eyes. Susan hadn't thought of it that way. In her mind, she'd been giving Lucy all the credit. She'd only mentioned the refugee's need for transportation, and Susan had volunteered to give them her old car. But Lucy had made all the behind-the-scenes arrangements.

Susan leaned on her knees to be at eye level with the silent woman staring into the fireplace. "Hello, Joyce. How are you?" There was no response.

"Not a good day," explained Simone directly into Susan's ear. "But I'm so glad to see you. Keith always talks about how much he likes Ms. Gedney's class. You know how boys are. If they talk about their teachers, they either hate 'em or love 'em."

"You used to teach too," said Susan, remembering.

"Yes, before I became a principal. I miss it. I had to retire early when my husband got sick. Bobbie's lucky she can keep working. It's not all about the money, you know."

"No, it's not."

"I can hardly wait to be back in a classroom. Denise was teaching the children's choir how to read music, plus some basic theory and music appreciation. That's so good for children, especially since the schools have had to cut back on the arts."

"If you miss teaching, we're always looking for volunteers at the elementary school. Retired educators are especially welcome."

"Hmm. If I find I have too much time on my hands, you may see me."

Reshma came in to call everyone to dinner. An amazing variety of exotic dishes were arranged on the long dining table.

"Dear guests, please find a seat," Teresa said in her delightfully musical accent. "Welcome to our Sudanese feast. Let me explain what you'll be eating today." She went around the table, naming each dish, detailing its ingredients, and explaining how it had been prepared. "But before we eat, we must have a blessing." Her eyes met Susan's.

"Reshma will give the blessing," said Susan, nodding in her direction. She half expected her young colleague to offer her usual abrupt benediction, but Reshma spoke eloquently about gratitude for friendship and the Biblical imperative to welcome strangers. Susan was proud to add her "Amen" to those of the others.

She found herself sitting beside Bobbie. As if there was a conspiracy to make sure she sat there, everyone had avoided that seat.

When Bobbie thought no one was watching, she caught Susan's eye and smiled warmly. Otherwise, she kept up with the lively conversation at the table. Joyce on the other end of the table showed no interest in the conversation or the food. Natalie tried to encourage her to eat, but Joyce made a face and turned away from the spoon like a fussy baby. Finally, Natalie went to the kitchen to get her a protein shake.

Reshma's Sudanese meal had been delicious, but Teresa's food had a richer, more complex taste. Reshma had learned to cook from recipes on the internet. Teresa had been cooking these dishes her entire life.

"Some ingredients were hard to find," she explained. "We had to go to Portland. Natalie brought us, but now we can drive ourselves!" She crossed her hands over her heart and made a little bow in Susan's direction. "Mother Susan, we love our car. Thank you so much!"

"They're so excited about your car," said Bobbie, turning to Susan. "It means Teresa can take more classes next semester."

"And she can get her nursing license earlier."

"Exactly." Bobbie's smile was especially affectionate. "I'm *so* happy you could come."

"Of course, I would come. I'm here to support Reshma and her friends. And I wanted to see you." Susan gently patted Bobbie's arm.

"Don't touch her!" Joyce ordered in a shrill voice. "Don't touch her!"

Susan snatched back her hand like she'd touched fire. "Don't you...dare... touch her!" Everyone stared at the contorted face of the woman who, only a moment ago, had been silently staring into space. Now, her eyes blazed with fury. "Get away from her!" She furiously swiped the air with her hand. "Get away! Now!"

"Excuse me," said Bobbie, hurrying to other side of the table. She glanced at Susan for sympathy as she wheeled Joyce out of the room.

"Maybe we should leave," suggested Reshma under her breath.

"No," said Susan firmly. "We need to stay and see how we can help." Across the table, Simone's eyes met hers, and she nodded.

***

Bobbie was so furious she needed to take a few deep breaths before she could even speak. "Joyce, why did you say that? We have guests here." She spoke softly but knew their voices would carry into the next room.

"That bitch!" screamed Joyce. "Bitch!" She gestured with her pointed finger to her throat. Bobbie interpreted the sign language to mean Susan's collar.

"She's a priest. She's trying to help you. She brought Teresa to us. You like Teresa and Grace, don't you?" Bobbie wondered why she was trying to reason with someone incapable of abstract thinking.

"Bitch! Whore! Bitch! Whore!" Joyce beat her fists on the arms of her wheelchair in time with the words. "Bitch! Whore! Bitch!" she continued in a singsong like a chant at a sports game.

"Joyce, please stop shouting. Please!" Bobbie sighed.

"Collars everywhere! Even the black one!" Joyce spat in disgust.

"Joyce! Those people are here to help you...to help me. Simone has been coming every week. You said you liked her."

"Good maid. Keep her."

"Then you need to be kind to her and the others."

Joyce's face was red. A vein bulged on her neck. She needed to be sedated or she'd have a stroke or worse. Bobbie checked the strap that secured Joyce to the wheelchair before heading back to the dining room. When she opened the door, every stunned face turned in her direction.

"Can I do something, Bobbie?" asked Teresa, getting up. It was a generous offer, especially after the racist comments, but Bobbie knew seeing Teresa now would only upset Joyce more. "Thanks, Teresa, but she needs to be sedated first."

"I'll get it." Natalie jumped up from the table, looking glad to have something to do. Fortunately, she was an old hand at managing Joyce's tantrums and knew the drill.

Teresa motioned to her daughter. "Come, Grace. Let's clear the table." Some of the guests still had food on their plates, but everyone had stopped eating. Obviously, the feast was over.

"I'll help," said Simone, picking up dishes. Reshma went around the table, collecting the silverware.

Susan, awkwardly sitting at the table alone, got up and went to the door. "I'm so sorry," she whispered. "I meant nothing by it."

"I know you didn't, but that's how it is now," said Bobbie. "She seems perfectly calm. Then bang! Something triggers her and she starts screaming." Bobbie glanced over her shoulder. Joyce was quiet, but fidgety. "I'm sorry you had to witness this…again. I thought after we had breakfast together, she'd be all right."

Susan was pale and had that deer-in-the headlights look. "Can I do something?"

At first, Bobbie could only stare at her. "Thanks, Susan, but I think it's better she doesn't see you now."

"Don't send me away!" Joyce wailed from inside the room followed by a feral moan like a wounded dog.

"Joyce, stop it. I'm not sending you away," Bobbie called back.

"Don't send me away!"

Bobbie rolled her eyes. "For Chrissake. Natalie! Where are you?"

The young woman finally arrived with a bottle and syringe. "I didn't think she would take a pill."

"Smart thinking. This will work faster. Thanks." Bobbie hated to close the door on Susan, but she had to deal with this. "I'm sorry, Susan, but

Elena Graf 251

I have to go." The last thing she saw was Susan's pale, confused face imploring her.

"Don't throw me away!" screamed Joyce. "Please don't throw me away!" Her face was wet with tears, and she began to sob. "Please, Bobbie. Please! Don't...throw me away!"

Joyce's pleas were like knives stabbing her. There had been many days when Bobbie had felt desperate enough to put Joyce in memory care. Then something would happen to make the situation bearable. Chloe and then Natalie came to live with them. Simone provided a regular respite. Teresa and Grace helped share the household chores. Those little changes had made a big difference, and Bobbie could go on one more day.

Her hands were shaking. She struggled to puncture the diaphragm of the vial with the syringe. "Don't throw me away," Joyce moaned, rocking back and forth. Her eyes staring into Bobbie's face were like black holes of despair. Pure emotion without thought, pain as innocent as an infant's.

"Joyce, no one's throwing you away," said Bobbie, fumbling with the prep wipe. "You're staying right here with me."

"Our house."

"Yes, our house. You're staying here in our house."

"That woman," said Joyce, gesturing wildly. Finally, she got the direction right.

"Susan is my friend. She's not hurting you. She's helping us."

"Please...don't throw me away," Joyce begged in a harsh whisper. Bobbie tried to ignore her. She needed to focus to land the syringe. Joyce rarely bled but Bobbie taped the injection site with a cartoon band-aid left over from the kids' vaccination drive. Fortunately, this sedative was fast acting. Bobbie held Joyce's hand. "You're okay, Joyce. You're going to be okay."

Someone quietly knocked on the door. Now that Joyce was finally calming down, Bobbie hoped it wasn't Susan. "We're okay," she called in response. The door opened a crack.

"Why don't you let me talk to her?" asked Natalie. *What a good idea. A trained social worker can probably calm Joyce faster than I can.* Bobbie nodded and Natalie stepped into the room. "Your guests are leaving. Maybe you want to say goodbye?" Leave it to Natalie to suggest a way to rescue the social disaster.

Bobbie patted Natalie's arm and mouthed, 'thank you' on her way out. She heard voices from the entry foyer and found Reshma and Susan putting on their coats.

"I'm so sorry you had to witness this."

"In our line of work, we see everything," said Reshma, but she looked shaken. "Don't worry about us."

But Bobbie did worry because Susan looked like a ghost. "It's not personal."

"Oh, I think it's very personal," said Susan. "I should have known better than to come tonight."

"Let me." Reshma laid a kind hand on Susan's arm. "Bobbie, we know your situation is difficult. Thank you for your hospitality. It was a lovely evening. I thanked Teresa for the wonderful meal. Simone is staying to help with the dishes. I would stay to help too, but I want to get Susan home."

"I hope you'll come back another time when things aren't so…" Bobbie's thinking was so scrambled she just couldn't find the right word.

"Exciting?" supplied Reshma with a grin, nudging a sad chuckle from Bobbie's throat.

"Yes…exciting. Unfortunately, that's how it is around here."

On the way to the car, Susan turned back to look at Bobbie. Her expression was unreadable. Regret? Fear? Anger? After Bobbie closed the door, she could finally feel the full horror of the experience.

All she wanted to do was cry.

✳✳✳

The car was eerily quiet while Reshma drove back to the rectory. Susan almost wished she would ask the questions that were undoubtedly on her mind. Telling the truth would be a relief, but the young woman was too tactful and basically kind to pry.

After they parted in the hall, Susan was still shaking. She forced herself to undress and hang up her clothes. The formal collar had only been worn a few hours. She could wear it again on Sunday for services. She carefully brushed off the sweater. She put on a polar fleece top and warm slacks because the thermostat in the rectory had been lowered to conserve fuel.

She urgently needed to soothe her jangled nerves. She remembered the tea blend with calming herbs that she'd found in the health food store. While she waited for the water to heat, she thumbed through a prayer book Lucy had given her called *One Thousand Gifts*. Susan used to have a copy, but it had been lost somewhere between South Dakota and Maine. The copy Lucy had given her was her own. Here and there, passages were underlined or highlighted. On another occasion Susan might have picked through them, greedy to divine insights into Lucy's emotional state. Tonight, she didn't care, and the print swam before her eyes.

The kettle began to shriek. Susan whipped it off the burner, hoping the piercing whistle hadn't disturbed Reshma. Fortunately, the walls of the old rectory were thick. She'd never heard so much as a peep from the young people living down the hall.

While the tea brewed, she tried to focus on the book, but she still couldn't. When she closed it, the terrible scene replayed in her mind. Poor Bobbie must be so embarrassed. Maybe the people at the table would write off the outburst to the old woman's dementia, or some animus against Bobbie, a resentment deflected into an unwarranted suspicion. Susan had no idea how much Bobbie's boarders knew about their landlord's sexual preference, but they were all intelligent and perceptive. What they didn't know, they could now surmise based on what they'd seen and heard. Susan extended her fingers. The tremor was almost as bad as her first week in rehab.

The tea was finally ready. Susan always tried to tell herself these virtuous beverages were satisfying, but they weren't. They tasted like dishwater compared to wine, even a cheap one. After a sip of tea, she stuck out her tongue like a cartoon character. The blend contained valerian which smelled disgusting and tasted worse. Even honey couldn't improve it.

She watched the foul liquid go down the drain and thought of the all-night convenience store on the corner. It had a surprisingly extensive wine collection, probably for the tourists getting off the highway, who needed some refreshment after the long drive. She told herself to think of something else, but that only brought more flashbacks of the evening—the terrified faces around the table, the woman ranting in the other room.

The thought of the wine in the convenience store kept returning until she fixated on it. The place was within walking distance. She'd gone there one night to get cream for her morning coffee. On her way, a raised crack in the sidewalk had nearly tripped her. Luckily, she'd recovered her balance and escaped without injury. At her age, fractures were likely, despite the calcium pills she gobbled every morning. Instead of braving the broken concrete, she could take her car, but Reshma's studio faced the parking lot. The minute Susan turned on her headlights, Reshma would know she was going out.

Susan raised the blinds and saw the giant full moon rising over the ocean, the Snow Moon, they called it. The trees were bare, ghostly in the pale light, ice crystals glittering on their branches. The landscape was as bright as if lit by a spotlight. It was a perfect night for a walk.

The November air was chilly when Susan emerged from the rectory. Her clenched jaw vibrated in time to her determined steps. The idea that she should call her sponsor nagged her, but the phone in her pocket felt cold and useless.

The glass of the convenience store door was misted with vapor. Susan opened a window in the fog with her gloved fist. She could see the lottery jackpots flashing over the register and the young attendant playing on his phone. He didn't look up when the door chimed, or when Susan passed him on her way to the wine aisle. The prices were much higher than what she was used to paying, certainly higher than she would have paid in the supermarket. She fingered the twenty in her pocket as she looked for a recognizable cabernet priced under ten dollars.

The under-age attendant had to call an older woman out of the back to ring up the sale. She smelled of cigarettes and coffee and didn't look happy at being disturbed. Digging into the coin compartment of her wallet for exact change, Susan's fingers felt her AA anniversary token. She pushed it aside and dug deeper for another penny. The boy looked at the exact change like he didn't know what it was. Maybe they no longer taught children how to count money.

Susan hugged the package close to her body to make it less obvious that she was carrying a bottle. The moon over the ocean was playing hide and seek with the clouds when she passed the cemetery. She was tempted to stop and admire it, but the thought of the dead lurking at the gates made her hurry past. She came from superstitious people. No amount of education could rid her of the old beliefs her Irish grandmother had taught her.

She was glad that her rubber-soled shoes kept her climb up the stairs silent. She quietly opened the lock, which had performed perfectly since Reshma's attention.

After Susan took off her coat, she inspected the label on the bottle. It was an expensive wine for a convenience store, much better than the rot gut she used to buy in South Dakota. But now she had to find a cork puller. She'd never needed one before, so she had no idea where to find it. Rummaging in the kitchen drawers, she felt desperate.

The phone dancing on the table interrupted her search. She could guess the caller's identity by the hour. No one except Bobbie ever called her at night. Susan wasn't sure she wanted to talk to her, but she knew the poor woman would be embarrassed and sad after that horrible scene. Finally, compassion won out over caution.

"I'm so sorry!" Bobbie said, sounding as miserable as Susan expected. "I should have known better."

"Don't apologize. It's not your fault. Obviously, my touching you set her off. I probably shouldn't have come." There was an extended silence in response. "Have things settled down?" asked Susan.

"Yes, I hate to sedate her during the day, but when she's this bad, I have no choice. I don't want her to hurt herself or other people."

"I feel sorry for Teresa that her feast ended that way."

"Everyone who lives here knows what we're dealing with."

"Unfortunately, now they know more."

"I never tried to hide anything, but I hadn't made any announcements either. They'll just have to deal with it. Are you all right?"

Susan didn't know how to answer that question. "I'm upset."

"Understandable. I'm so sorry." There was another long pause. "Will I see you for our coffee date?"

Susan sighed. "Not this week. I have a teacher's meeting after school." It was the truth, but she probably would have declined anyway. She needed time to think.

"Oh," said the disappointed voice on the other end. "Can we meet soon?"

Susan looked at the bottle sitting on the table, clear evidence she needed a break from this drama. "I'll let you know," she said vaguely. She'd explain later. Bobbie was too fragile to talk about it tonight.

"Okay, I'll let you go," said Bobbie before Susan could answer. "Get some rest. I took a tranquilizer, and I'm going to bed."

"Good idea."

They wished each other good night, but the words sounded hollow, an empty formula, something they were supposed to say. After such a disaster, how could either of them have a good night?

Susan tossed the phone on top of the book she'd been reading and covered her face with her hands. Between her fingers, she looked at the bottle of wine. She'd almost taken a drink after more than a year of sobriety. She was tempted to blame Bobbie, but she knew it wasn't her fault. *Call your sponsor*, said the little voice in her head. Finally, Susan picked up the phone and tapped Sally's number.

"I bought wine," Susan admitted bluntly when Sally's sleepy voice answered.

"Okay," said Sally, instantly alert. "Tell me what happened."

"I went to dinner at my friend's house, and when I touched her arm, just a friendly pat, her partner started screaming."

"The woman has dementia, right? She probably didn't know what she was doing."

"Oh, I think she did."

"Well, you didn't do anything wrong, so don't punish yourself. You need to get rid of the wine. Right now. Pour it down the sink. Throw it away outside your apartment, where you can't get to it. Give it to someone."

After paying for decent wine, the last suggestion made the most sense. She thought of Reshma.

"I will."

"Now, Susan. Then call me right back."

Susan agreed and grabbed her keys from her coat pocket. With the wine under her arm, she headed down the hall. Reshma came to the door in a colorful nightshirt and fuzzy slippers.

"Susan! Are you all right?" she asked, anxiously searching her face.

"I want to give you something," Susan said, handing over the bottle.

Reshma glanced at the label. "This is nice wine. Why are you giving it to me?"

"I can't have it near me."

"Really? Why?"

"Because I'm an alcoholic."

Reshma blinked twice, letting the information sink in. "Oh," she said. "Would you like to come in and talk about it?"

"Not tonight. I promised my sponsor I'd call her back."

"Okay," said Reshma looking worried. "You can talk to me later if you want."

"Not tonight."

"When you're ready. Thanks for the wine."

"Thanks for taking it off my hands."

Reshma nodded and closed the door. Relieved, Susan walked back to her apartment to call Sally.

14

Lucy covertly checked the clock on her desk. Susan should have arrived by now. It wasn't like her to be late. Lucy glanced at Liz and Olivia, but they were too wrapped up in their argument to notice her picking up her phone. Susan had sent a message ten minutes earlier to explain why she was late: *Emergency meeting with a parent. Be there as soon as I can.*

"Liz, we had almost a hundred people at your wedding, and we managed," said Olivia, still complaining that Lucy had nixed her menu as too ambitious.

"For the wedding, you had help—Maggie cooking side by side with you, Cherie, that kid from the new pâtisserie."

"You mean Tiffany? She volunteered to do all the baking and help on the day of the reception."

"But Maggie's teaching again, and she has a big part to play in this ordination. She won't have the time to help you before the crowd gets there."

"She said she'd do as much as she can, and some of the church ladies volunteered to help me cook."

Olivia was being as intractable as ever. Lucy was happy to leave arguing with her to Liz. If Lucy pushed back too hard on Olivia, who was on the vestry and one of St. Margaret's biggest contributors, things could get sticky.

Finally, Susan stood in the doorway, looking rushed and harried. Lucy motioned to her to come in.

"Sorry to be late," she murmured, taking the vacant visitors' chair.

"You haven't missed much," said Liz. "Olivia and I have been arguing about the food."

"Hello, Susan." Olivia cast a filthy look in Liz's direction. "There's no argument. I have it all planned, and I'm paying for it, so I don't care what they say."

"Don't forget that Reshma's friends want to contribute some African dishes," interjected Lucy. "It will be nice for Reshma, and Bishop Greene is hyping that he's ordaining a refugee."

"Anything for the publicity," said Liz with disgust. "Olivia, better plan on feeding the press too."

"It sounds like Olivia has the food covered," said Lucy, realizing she was surrendering, but Olivia was a gourmet cook, who loved grand events. She would ensure that the bishop was not only well-fed but impressed. "All right. Now that Susan's here, let's get started. Where are we with the parking and transportation?" She turned to Liz for a report.

"I've already talked to the town about using the parking area on Gull Island Beach. Off-season, hardly anyone parks there. People can walk to Olivia's, but a winter trolley will be available to pick up guests. Also, from the church."

"And Susan, you've been in contact with the bishop's office. Are we settled on the order of the service?"

"Lucy, I've been copying you on all the emails," Susan replied, sounding irritated.

"I saw them. Anything we need to discuss?"

Susan shook her head.

"Well, that was a short meeting," said Lucy, closing her folder. "You're all so efficient. I love it!"

"I move that we adjourn the meeting to Dockside for dinner," said Liz, waving her hand. "Do I hear a second…?"

"I'd love to, Liz," said Olivia, "but I have company coming for dinner." She smiled coyly, forcing everyone to speculate on the identity of her guests. "Another time."

"But you'll join us, won't you, Susan?" asked Liz, shrugging on her parka.

Susan looked up, surprised. "Thank you, I will," she said, but without the expected smile.

"Luce, see you down there," Liz said and left.

Susan remained seated, looking expectant.

"Do you want a ride?" asked Lucy. "I can drop you back here on the way home."

"Lucy, I really wish you would read my emails with the bishop's office," said Susan in an extremely annoyed tone. "I copy you to make sure you know what's going on."

"Just because I don't comment doesn't mean I don't read them." The insinuation irritated Lucy because she read every one. She stopped putting her papers in her bag and sat down again. "Susan, I don't chime in because it looks like you're handling the situation perfectly. You need to tell me if you want my feedback or have a question. If I had something to say, you'd certainly know it."

Susan shrank back from the scolding. "I'm sorry. I guess I expected you to be more involved."

"Why? I put you in charge. It's obvious, you've got it covered. Susan, I thought you'd be happy that I'm not looking over your shoulder. I'm trying to show that I trust you."

Susan frowned. Obviously, that was not what she'd expected to hear.

"You're only part time at St. Margaret's, and you're teaching too. I'm sorry. Am I giving you too much? Do you feel we're taking advantage of you?"

"No, I can handle it. I apologize. I've been out of sorts lately. It makes me read things into whatever people say and do."

"What's going on?" asked Lucy with a solicitous look.

Susan stared at the front of Lucy's desk. "I witnessed a terrible scene at Bobbie's house."

"I know. Reshma told me about it."

"What did she say?"

"That she felt bad for Bobbie...and you. Her friends were disappointed after they put so much effort into the party, but they understood."

"Did she tell you I almost took a drink?"

"No," said Lucy, honestly surprised. "Was it that bad?"

"It was awful. I haven't spoken to Bobbie in a week. My sponsor said if the relationship makes me want to drink, it's probably not good for me."

Lucy got up from her desk chair and sat beside Susan. "That may be true, but your sponsor's not in the relationship. You are. And she's not a professional. What happened to the therapy idea?" Susan was still staring at the front of the desk. Lucy leaned down so she could engage her eyes. "Did you ever see the therapist I recommended?"

"I did…a couple of times. We didn't click."

"There are other therapists. I can give you a referral."

"Lucy, please. Just talk to me as a friend!" snapped Susan.

The accusation stung, but there was probably some truth in it. After years of playing so many roles, Lucy found they merged and often became hopelessly entangled. "Susan, I just want to help you. I can see you're struggling."

"I feel bad for abandoning Bobbie. She's the one who's struggling. What an impossible situation she's in."

"She's chosen it. She could have put Joyce in memory care."

"Those places are terrible. They're understaffed. They numb patients with drugs to keep them docile and cooperative. People have no dignity."

"They're not all like that. But even with Bobbie's training in gerontology, it's not easy to care for a dementia patient at home. When it's your own, you lose objectivity." Lucy rubbed Susan's shoulder affectionately. "Come on. Let's have a nice dinner and try to relax. I hate to rush you, but we need to get moving. My wife gets cranky when she's kept waiting." Lucy got up and took her jacket from the coat tree. "Do you want another therapy referral?"

"No, the one you gave me is fine. It's just me being resistant, like when I first went to AA." Susan got up. "Thank you for trusting me to deal with the bishop."

"You're welcome. I trust you because I know you're an exceptionally competent woman."

"But you said you didn't trust me."

"Because you lied to me about why you came to Maine. That was personal, and it really hurt. Your resentment hasn't helped."

Susan hung her head. "I'm sorry. It's juvenile isn't it?"

"No, we were once very close. The hurts by those we love go deep. It took a long time, but I forgave you for abandoning me after you were ordained. I was willing to start fresh, but then you tried to get between me and Liz."

"I never gave up hope that we'd get back together."

"Do you now accept that it will never happen?"

Susan nodded sadly.

"I love you, Susan, but not in that way. I've moved on." Lucy put her hand on Susan's arm. "I want you to succeed here because I care for you."

Susan looked skeptical.

Lucy sighed. "Please, Susan, take the love people give you at face value. You are loved by more people than you know. Reshma adores you. Even my wife, who has every reason to resent you, cares about you. And speaking of Liz, we need to get down to that restaurant, or she'll be really crabby. Believe me. That will be no fun."

For the first time since she'd arrived, Susan smiled.

❋❋❋

The bright sunlight shone on Joyce's face, defining her fine bone structure. When she smiled, her cheeks formed perfect hemispheres, what Bobbie's mother used to call "apples." With the new medication, Joyce's sense of humor had returned. Bobbie had thought it was gone for good, but today, a hint of private amusement played on her lips. The out-of-control rages were less frequent. Instead of a sedative, Bobbie had been giving Joyce melatonin to help her sleep, which so far seemed to be working.

Joyce had always loved to sit in the sun porch, even in cool weather. The three-season room, along with the in-law apartment and the private office, had sold them on the house. The November afternoon was chilly, but an electric heater with faux flames kept the space toasty. Bundled in a thick polar-fleece jacket, a blanket over her legs, Joyce looked content.

"Beautiful day," she said, startling Bobbie. Lately, words seemed to come more easily. Her conversations were rudimentary, but at least she was talking again. "Let's stay…here."

"Of course, we'll stay here," Bobbie assured her. "We live here."

"Not going to New York?" So, she remembered this had once been a summer house.

"No, we live here now. We sold our house in New York."

Joyce looked puzzled, trying to process the information. Then she nodded as if she remembered. "I'm glad…we live here. Beautiful."

Bobbie gazed out at the marsh, admiring the myriad colors and textures. There was still some green after the late autumn rains. It was high tide. A pair of wood ducks floated blissfully on the glistening water. "Yes, it certainly is," she agreed.

"Makes me happy."

"Me too."

"I want you…to be happy," said Joyce, looking distressed, which confused Bobbie. Why wouldn't she want her to be happy?

Bobbie tried to think of something to say. "Thank you," she finally said. "I want you to be happy too."

"I am…when I'm here. In this house." Joyce's attention was diverted by a chipmunk skittering around the deck. It climbed on the arm of the Adirondack chair and began to chirp loudly. "Silly thing," said Joyce, trying to imitate its high-pitched squeak. Assuming that meant the conversation was over, Bobbie went back to her book.

"I want to stay *here*," Joyce said again with clear emphasis.

"That was our plan," Bobbie reminded her. "That's why we sold the house in New York…to have enough money to take care of you at home. That's why you turned the house over to me, so no one can take it away."

"I want you to be safe."

"I know. I want the same for you."

"I want you to be happy." Joyce frowned, which contradicted her message, but Bobbie realized it was her way of saying she'd meant what she'd said. "Love…you," added Joyce.

"I love you too."

"Sorry not the same."

"Different but the same," said Bobbie to show she understood what Joyce was trying to say. "It's all right to be different."

"And be happy."

"Yes, Bobbie…be happy." Joyce gave Bobbie a real smile that showed those shiny apples. For a moment she looked like her old self, so beautiful and elegant. Then, like a child, she began to hum a tuneless melody.

❋❋❋

Susan wasn't a hugger like Lucy. She stood there awkwardly until Bobbie pulled her into her arms and squeezed her with all her might. Her soft body melded with Susan's, filling the voids like the perfect puzzle piece. Susan never wanted to let her go. "Oh, I missed you so much!"

After Bobbie finally released her, she shyly rested her hands on Susan's cheeks. When there was no protest, she drew their faces closer. What began as a friendly kiss quickly grew into something more profound. Susan's eyes flew open when Bobbie's gentle tongue came into her mouth, but she finally relaxed and enjoyed the sweetness and warmth.

"Well," Susan said, when they parted for air. "That was unexpected."

"And long overdue." Bobbie trailed her fingertips down Susan's cheek. "It's so good to see you." The yellow flecks in Bobbie's eyes seemed to twinkle. She pulled Susan's face close again, and this time, the kiss was deeper and more sensual. Susan dared to probe Bobbie's mouth. She almost lost her balance, but she could feel Bobbie holding her steady.

"We have to stop," said Susan between kisses. "We need to talk."

"You're right," Bobbie reluctantly agreed. "Thank you for inviting me to your place. As much as I love blueberry pie, this conversation needs privacy."

"No more secrets," said Susan.

"No more secrets," Bobbie agreed.

"Come into the kitchen, I'll make some coffee."

"Please make that tea you like. I've developed a taste for it," Bobbie said, which made Susan smile. "And you made lemon bars! My favorite!"

"I'll give you some to take home."

"Like I need the extra calories, but I won't turn them down. Joyce likes them too. I don't know why I don't make them more often."

"Maybe because you don't have time?" said Susan, putting the kettle on the burner.

"Having Teresa there is making a big difference. She cooks most nights. It feels more crowded with her using the kitchen, but I wouldn't turn down her cooking. It's always tasty, and I like that little African twist on English cuisine."

"Me too. Reshma invited me for dinner, but this time, I insisted she cook here because my kitchen is larger. Denise came too. It was a very pleasant evening. I only wish I had gotten to know Denise better before she started traveling so much."

"The young ones need to have their adventures, just like we did," said Bobbie with a sigh. "I'll miss Natalie. After she graduates in January, she's moving out, but she's already lined up another student who's interested in her room, maybe two students. It's a big room. She suggested I put in twin beds. I'm beginning to feel like I'm running a boarding house!"

"Well, you are," said Susan with a chuckle, "but it's an ingenious solution to a real problem. How's Grace?"

"She loves birds, so I put her in charge of keeping the bird feeders full. She can identify most of our winter visitors—chickadees, cardinals, waxwings, blue jays. She collects the feathers they shed during their territorial skirmishes. She was so excited when she found the tail feather of a hawk. I helped her mount them on poster board to hang in her room. Chloe takes her along on her hikes. I gave them my field glasses and field manuals to help identify the birds."

"That was kind. With Grace's interest in wildlife, she could grow up to be a biologist or maybe even a conservation officer. Sounds like you've bonded with her."

"I love children, and Grace is as smart as a whip. I help her with her homework sometimes. Teresa too."

"And Chloe, you said. With all those customers, you could start a tutoring service."

"Why not? We have so much else going on. The house is as busy as a hive. I'm just glad I can sneak away to my own place for privacy." Bobbie's fingers walked toward the plate of lemon bars.

Susan pushed it closer. "Go ahead. I made them for you."

"I'll have one now, and one with my tea." Bobbie sighed after tasting the sweet treat. "Reminds me of the lemon meringue pies my grandmother used to make. I really only liked the lemon part. I'd brush off the fluffy topping, and Grandma would scold me for the waste. I loved sweets as a girl. No wonder I struggle with my weight."

"I've lost weight since I quit drinking. Alcohol is full of useless calories," said Susan, pouring the hot water into the pot.

"Well, I needed a few stiff drinks after that nightmare of a party!" Susan thought of the bottle of wine she'd given to Reshma and wondered if she'd enjoyed it.

"Has anyone mentioned the incident since it happened?"

"No, not a word. Everything just went back to normal. I'm glad I didn't have to explain. Let them figure it out."

"They're all professionals used to dealing with difficult situations." Susan poured two cups of tea and slid one Bobbie's way. "I think for everyone's sake, I should stay away from Joyce. Obviously, she senses the attraction between us, and it sets her off."

Bobbie helped herself to another lemon bar. "I don't really understand. Before this, Joyce was never possessive. She had her friends and I had mine. She never asked me where I was going or what I did. Not that I ever gave her any reason for suspicion, but we just had an understanding. This sudden jealousy is so out of character."

"Maybe it's not jealousy," said Susan, stirring sugar into her tea. "Maybe it's something else."

"Like what?"

"From what I heard that night, I think she's worried you'll put her in an institution."

Bobbie shook her head. "I don't know why that's so shocking.

We agreed I should if she got too much for me to handle. Thank God, we're not there yet. So far, I'm managing." Bobbie rapped her knuckles on the wooden tabletop.

"You're managing with hiccups," said Susan.

"Yes, but I want to keep her at home as long as I can."

"For financial reasons?"

"No, there's plenty of money for her care. In addition to the trust, Joyce bought long-term care insurance when it was still cheap."

"Because you love her," ventured Susan.

"Yes. Just because she's changed and can't remember our life together doesn't mean I don't love her. I'm just her caregiver now, but I suppose I'm lucky she still recognizes me."

Susan covered Bobbie's hand with hers.

"I know the day will come when she doesn't know who I am," said Bobbie in a sad voice. "Many dementia patients forget the people they love. The frontal lobes aren't firing, and all their inhibition goes out the window. Nursing home patients forget their wives and husbands and suddenly become as horny as teenagers. The attendants have a tough job keeping them from humping each other. Awful, don't you think?"

"Really?" said Susan, raising her brows. "A few minutes ago, I thought you were going to suck my lips off."

Bobbie threw back her head and roared with laughter, a welcome sound in the middle of such a sad conversation. After a few mirthful sputters, her laughter finally stopped. "All right, I admit I want you like a horny teenager. As far as I know, my brain is still intact…mostly. And I think you want me too."

Susan frowned and stared into her teacup. "I do, but that doesn't make it right."

"Stop with the priest talk. Who knows what's right or wrong? All I know is I really like you and I enjoy being with you. I'd like to have sex again before I die. Is that wrong?"

"So, you want a casual affair."

"No!" protested Bobbie. "You're too good for that, and so am I." She emitted a long sigh. "It's been so long I hope I can remember what to do!"

"I'm sure you'll figure it out if the opportunity presents itself," Susan said with a little smile.

Bobbie helped herself to a third lemon bar. "Maybe we're too old for this. Most old people our age are thinking of retirement. Joyce left me well off, and I've saved a nice piece of change on my own. I could retire. I work because it keeps me sane."

"And it keeps you engaged in the community, which is healthy. You're lucky. I can't retire. Even with my many little pensions from different school systems and my social security, I wouldn't be able to survive. I'm still paying off my student loans from seminary."

Bobbie looked thoughtful as she nibbled the lemon bar. "Didn't that guy leave your church? Maybe your boss will hire you full time."

"That's possible, but Reshma is being ordained next month. The vestry already offered her a job. Plus, the benefits as a teacher are better." Susan tasted one of the lemon bars. They were good, even if they were from a mix. Between bites, she asked, "So where do we go from here?"

"If I didn't think you'd be shocked, I'd ask you to show me your bedroom."

"Bobbie, be serious."

"I am being serious. I'm not ashamed to say I want you. I'm doing my best to take care of Joyce, out of loyalty and friendship, but I'm not a martyr."

"Wouldn't you feel guilty going behind Joyce's back?"

"I do feel a little guilty. But I also know I have plenty of life left in me. What should I do? Wait until she doesn't know me at all? Wait until she dies? I need conversation. I need love. I need *you*."

The desperation in Bobbie's voice pulled at Susan's heartstrings. "I need you too, but we can't carry on right under her nose."

"We won't. You have your apartment. I have mine. We both need to be discreet, or the town will be talking. Between my job and yours, everyone in Hobbs knows us."

"Let me think about it," said Susan. Under the table, she felt Bobbie's hand rest lightly on her thigh. Susan's face flamed, but she couldn't deny the delicious sensations Bobbie's touch was arousing.

"Promise?"

"Yes. I promise."

15

"Thank you, Elizabeth," said Stefan as Liz put a plate of fried eggs and ham in front of him. "I always know where to go for the best cooked breakfast."

"And we're glad you're here, *Papi*," said Lucy, rubbing his shoulder. She still thought of Stefan Bultmann as her father-in-law and addressed him by the affectionate German diminutive for father. Emily called him *Opa*, except when they were discussing her theorem with her dissertation advisor. Then she respectfully called him Professor Bultmann.

Emily had finished her breakfast and sat on the other side of the table with her arms folded. She was sulking because Liz had made it clear that she didn't want Denise moving into the apartment over the garage.

Stefan nudged Emily gently with his elbow. "My dear, if you smile, I shall challenge you to chess after breakfast."

Emily compressed her lips to conceal a little smile. "You know I always beat you."

"Not always," said Stefan, wagging his finger. "And today, I can already taste victory." He kissed his fingertips. "And it will be sweet."

"Why can't Denise use the place?" Emily asked again. "When I'm at school, no one's there. What difference will it make?" Emily glared at Liz's back. "Mom, can you talk to her?"

"Sweetie, it costs money to heat the apartment and run the electricity."

"Now that I'm getting a stipend, I can pay for it," Emily insisted.

Liz served Lucy her breakfast and sat down with hers. "Emily, it's not a legal apartment. It's one thing for family to live there."

"Mom and Erika weren't family when they lived there during the lockdown."

"That's where you're wrong. Erika is family. Stefan is family. And you're family. Denise, as much as I like her, isn't."

"You let Courtney and Melissa live there. They're not family."

"If I didn't let them move in, Courtney would have been homeless." Liz was controlling her temper well, but Lucy could tell she was running out of patience.

"Denise is making good money now," Lucy said. "She's perfectly able to support an apartment, and she needs to be close to an airport. Now that her singing career is taking off, she'll be traveling all the time."

"If you didn't rent out the beach house I could still live there," Emily said with a pout. Fortunately, she hadn't brought up the beach apartment, which Lucy and Liz hardly used in the winter.

"Your mother hasn't thrown Denise out of the rectory yet," Liz finally said. "What are you so worried about?"

"But eventually, she'll have to leave," said Lucy calmly. "The vestry is sure to bring it up again at the next meeting. I'll hold them off as long as I can."

"But they wouldn't throw her out on the street," said Liz, mopping up her eggs with her toast.

"No, of course not," said Lucy. "But there are limits."

"Emily, I don't care if Denise visits while you're here," said Liz, "but she's not moving in over there. Do you understand?"

"Why can't I sublet the apartment?" asked Emily.

"How can you sublet it? There's no lease, and you're not paying rent!" Liz threw up her hands. "Lucy, say something."

Lucy waited until Emily gave her eye contact. "Sweetie, did Denise ask to move in with you?"

"No," Emily admitted, slouching in her chair. "It was my idea."

"I know you're trying to help your friend," Lucy said, "but you need to let Denise find her own way, just like you do. If the relationship means something to her, she'll come back, and we'll welcome her."

Emily got up in a huff and left the table. Stefan's eyes followed her out of the room. "Such a smart girl but not wise. Be patient, Lucy. She'll learn."

"I hope so," said Lucy with a sigh. Intellectually, her daughter was so advanced. Emotionally, she was younger than her chronological age. Lucy smiled at Stefan. "It's nice to have you here. I'm glad you're coming for Thanksgiving."

"If not, I would be eating tasteless gruel with the mummies." Lucy wanted to roll her eyes at Stefan's favorite name for the residents at the senior apartments. His other nickname, "the inmates," was somewhat more benign.

With all Stefan's grumbling about Ocean Terrace Senior Living, they'd assumed he hated the place and had invited him to move into the downstairs bedroom. He'd resisted their repeated offers, finally admitting that he enjoyed playing bridge and chess with the "inmates" and talking with the vets about twentieth-century wars. At ninety-five, he had witnessed more history than most of them.

"If you lived here, you'd get decent breakfasts every day," said Liz. "Good dinners too."

"I know, but the food there is not bad as institutional meals go. There's no salt in it, but I can always add some. I'm only complaining because that's what old men are supposed to do."

Lucy smiled. "Stefan, I've never known you to do something because you're supposed to."

He looked indignant. "I'm German. I always obey the rules."

Liz laughed. "Yeah, right."

"Besides, you are newlyweds and need your privacy." He wiggled his brows suggestively. "You don't need an old man hanging around. Someday, I may take you up on your offer, but not today." He glanced at the stove. "Is there more ham?"

Liz jumped up. "I'll heat some for you."

Stefan reached for Lucy's hand. "Lovely Lucy, you are doing the right thing setting limits for Emily. When Erika was young, she was always pushing for more privileges, which is natural for someone so bright. They are curious about the world and want to explore. Their high intelligence makes us think they are more mature than they truly are. As a professor, I taught many geniuses. They are no better at navigating life than most people. Often, worse." He glanced at Liz's back and raised his eyebrows. Lucy stifled a chuckle.

"I try to do the right thing," said Lucy, "but I have to go along with what Liz decides. It's her house."

"It's our house," said Liz emphatically. "But I won't have someone flopping here between singing engagements. If Denise were destitute, it would be another matter. I don't mind Emily living there. She's our daughter."

Hearing Liz use that word, Lucy felt a surge of warm feelings for her wife. They were a family now.

"Stefan, I'm not being too harsh, am I?" asked Liz.

"Elizabeth, I was tempted to take in many a student who'd fallen on hard times. They always found their way without me coddling them. Facing adversity is how we learn. Emily will get over this disappointment."

"I think she's worried Denise will find someone on her travels and move on," said Lucy.

"Then that is how it's supposed to happen," Stefan said. "Besides, Emily will be busy. I heard from an old colleague that after her thesis is accepted, Yale intends to put her on tenure-track."

"Wow! Good for her," said Liz, transferring ham from the skillet onto Stefan's plate.

"But she told me she's thinking of enrolling in the music school," said Lucy, then quickly examined her conscience to see if she had broken a confidence.

Stefan looked surprised, but he nodded. "She is a smart girl and she's young. She should explore all her talents. She could do both if she chooses. Look at you. You're a singer *and* a priest."

"More toast, Stefan?" Liz asked.

He patted his belly and smiled. "No, I think that's quite enough."

✻✻✻

Bobbie made quick work of tidying the exam room. The other practitioners usually left it for the medical assistants, even though it only took a minute.

The established hierarchy needed to be maintained, and people tried not to get in each other's way. Liz, passing by, stuck her head in. "Hey, thanks for doing that."

"You're welcome." Bobbie was surprised that Liz noticed, but the best doctors were highly observant. Liz stepped into the exam room and closed the door. Bobbie's eyes instantly went to the wall clock. She was supposed to meet Susan at the diner in exactly fifteen minutes. She hoped Liz didn't plan to stay long.

"Hey. Thanks for inviting Denise for Thanksgiving. Saved me from pissing off my stepdaughter even more." Bobbie didn't know what Liz was talking about, but in a small town, where people went for Thanksgiving had implications.

"Why is Emily upset?" Bobbie knew that she was prying, but Liz had left herself open to the question.

"She's trying to keep Denise in town, so she wants me to let her move into the apartment over the garage. Denise is making good money now. She should be on her own."

"Liz, none of my business, but does this have anything to do with Denise being trans?"

"No!" Liz gave her an extremely annoyed look. "Look, I don't pretend to understand this gender thing, but I never think about Denise as being trans, except in a medical situation, when I have to. I just don't like being blackmailed into being generous. Unlike Lucy, I'm not a professional Christian."

"I get it."

"You do?" asked Liz, looking surprised.

"Sure, I do. Generosity needs to be voluntary, or everyone involved ends up resentful. Even with the best intentions, there can be resentment."

"But you took in those refugees," said Liz, crossing her arms and leaning back on the counter like she intended to stay a while.

"That was a win-win. I help them. They help me. They're wonderful with Joyce, helpful around the house, and Teresa is a great cook."

"So, it's transactional."

"Not exactly. I also like them." Bobbie glanced at the clock again. "Sorry to rush you, Liz, but I have an appointment this afternoon."

Liz gave her shoulder a playful smack. "Okay, Bobbie. I won't keep you. Have a good night."

When Bobbie arrived at the diner, Susan was seated at their usual table. There was a wedge of blueberry pie at each place, untouched. Susan got up and gave Bobbie a full-body hug, hanging on like they hadn't seen each other in a month. It felt so good to feel her soft breasts against her and their cheeks touch. Susan's face was as warm and smooth as a child's.

"Don't you dare apologize for being late," said Susan before Bobbie could get out the words. "You have important work to do."

"So do you."

"You can explain, if you want," Susan said, finally letting Bobbie go, "but no apologies."

"It's my own fault. I hate to leave cleanup to the assistants. We're short-handed, and they're busy too. Liz caught me and wanted to talk."

"Let's sit down." Susan gestured into the booth. The vinyl covering of the seats had been patched multiple times with cloth tape that didn't match. It also tended to roll over and stick to people's pants. Bobbie slid in to avoid that spot. "I ordered your pie," said Susan. "I hope that's okay."

"I appreciate it, but you didn't need to wait for me."

"I almost didn't," admitted Susan with a grin. "But I waited...to share the pleasure." Her little smile was suggestive. Bobbie got the message. Pie orgasm was better than none. "So, why did Liz keep you after school?" asked Susan, picking up her fork.

"It had nothing to do with work. She wanted to talk about the arrangements for Thanksgiving."

Susan stared at her plate. "I'm sorry, but I accepted Lucy's invitation before you asked. And I'm going to exchange cars with her daughter. I hate to give up that fancy Audi, but that was the deal."

"It's okay. I realize where you go for Thanksgiving is political. We need to keep our bosses happy. I was surprised that Reshma is coming to us. Teresa asked if she could invite her. I guess she got to Reshma before Lucy could." Bobbie's pinky finger crept toward Susan's like an inchworm. They shared a smile when the tips of their fingers touched.

"I wish I could be with you," Susan said fervently.

"Maybe you could come for dessert." Bobbie didn't want to sound too hopeful.

"Maybe I could." Susan frowned and withdrew her hand. "Are you sure Joyce won't mind?"

"No, but she's a lot calmer and happier on this new medication. I hope it lasts. I didn't tell you, but we had this strange conversation. I think you were right. Her main worry is that I'll abandon her, which I would never do."

"I don't want to upset her again. I certainly don't want to risk another scene, especially not on a holiday. I can see you another time."

"Okay," said Bobbie and took a big forkful of pie to assuage her disappointment. "Maybe Friday? I took the day off. If it's a nice day, we could go for a walk on the beach."

"I'd love to but I'm going to be busy this week with Reshma away on retreat. After she's ordained, things will be easier for me. The bishop only needs to approve her joining St. Margaret's as a full-time priest, but he will. He adores Reshma."

"Does that mean they won't need you anymore?"

Susan looked like she hadn't considered the possibility. "I hope not. I like it here."

"Because of your job?"

"No, because of you."

Bobbie's pinky reached out again, and this time, their fingers intertwined.

16

Liz was reading medical journals on the living room sofa when she heard Lucy come in from the garage. The sound of her bags dropping on the kitchen stool was followed by a long sigh.

"Hey," said Liz as Lucy came into the room.

"Hey, you have a hole in your sock."

"I know," said Liz, raising her face for a kiss. "Hard day?"

Lucy raised her eyes to heaven. "God give me strength!"

Liz sat up, so Lucy could sit down. She put her arm around her and pulled her close. "Busy holding Reshma's hand?"

"No, she's surprisingly centered after that retreat. Those Episcopal nuns did a great job, but I wish some of Reshma's calm would rub off on me."

"You can't still be worried. You've got this event planned down to the tiniest detail."

"This is the first ordination at St. Margaret's in over thirty years! I want it to be perfect, and not just because it's my church. Reshma deserves a beautiful ordination. It was one of the happiest days of my life, and I want the same for her."

"Did Maggie and Denise settle up on who's running the show?"

"This will be Denise's last liturgy as music director. I'm glad she finally admitted she can't do both. Her singing calendar is full for the next eighteen months, and Roger has even more appearances lined up. By the way, she found a studio outside of Boston. It's near the airport, but close enough to catch the train into town, or come up here."

"That's perfect."

"She'll be traveling all the time. Roger is a good agent. He's going all out to launch her."

"Maybe that will get him off your ass for a while."

"I doubt it. I still have more box-office draw."

Liz was afraid of that. "How do you think Emily will take Denise moving to Boston?"

"If Emily wants to be in a relationship with a singer, she needs to learn what it means. If I'd kept her instead of putting her up for adoption, she never would have seen her mother, but I still feel guilty."

"Emily's fine, and you did the best you could at the time. Sit down. Let me get you some wine. You look like you can use it."

"What's for dinner?" Lucy called after her.

"Leftovers. Tomorrow night after the rehearsal, I'm taking everyone out for dinner." Liz smiled to herself. "Kind of like a wedding, isn't it?" She went into the kitchen and returned with two glasses of wine, crackers, and a block of cheese. "So, if Reshma's calm, and the battle between Denise and Maggie ended in détente, why was your day so busy?"

"I went shopping."

"But Lucy, you love shopping!"

"This wasn't for me. Usually, members of the ordinand's family present them. You know, like the father of the bride brings her up to the altar. But Reshma doesn't have any family, so she asked Teresa and Grace to stand in for them."

"What a nice idea!"

"Yes, but Teresa wanted to look appropriate, especially with the bishop and half the town coming. She's representing more than Reshma's family. She and Grace are the black and brown immigrants everyone's talking about—the people overrunning our borders, supposedly taking food out of the mouths of veterans, taking people's jobs." Lucy rolled her eyes before taking a sip of wine.

"I get that they want to make a good impression, but how did you get involved?"

"Reshma asked me to help, so we went to the thrift shops. Good thing I invited Simone to come along. In black churches, especially in the South, women wear a lot of color. African women love even more color. I mean eye-popping color—lime greens, neon orange, royal blues so intense they'd make your eyes burn. We also got them some winter clothes, which they desperately need."

Liz made a mental note to expect an especially large credit card bill. "Shelter the homeless…clothe the naked. Checking them right off, aren't you? I'm surprised Reshma didn't ask you to represent her family instead of Teresa and Grace. It's always 'Mother Lucy this' and 'Mother Lucy that.'"

"I have a different role this time."

"Ah, yes. The hostess with the mostest and the rector in charge."

"Which is both exciting and scary."

Liz noticed that Lucy had already drained her glass. "More wine?"

"No, just a cuddle, please." She put down her glass and took Liz's away too. She lifted Liz's arm over her head.

"Stop worrying," said Liz, kissing the top of her head. Her hair smelled faintly of the special shampoo that was supposed to keep the red from fading. So far, it hadn't worked, but the herbal scent was pleasant. "You've got Tom coming up from Florida. I bet he's hosted lots of ordinations. You have two experienced music directors, a great choir…Susan."

"You, I hope."

"Of course, you have me. I can be the bouncer." Liz braced herself for a pinch or some other tease, but Lucy only snuggled more deeply into her body. Liz gave her a squeeze. "Don't worry, Luce. I've got you."

❊❊❊

During a lull in the rehearsal, Susan saw Liz in the last pew, looking completely bored. Maggie's daughter, the senior news producer at the local TV channel, had put Liz in charge of the overhead camera. After testing the view from the organ loft, she had nothing to do.

Alina's station was filming the ordination as part of a series she'd been producing on the plight of African immigrants in the state. The Episcopal Church's numbers were dwindling in Maine as elsewhere, but Reshma's refugee background made an otherwise arcane religious event newsworthy. Apparently, the bishop was more than delighted to have the publicity.

He'd said he'd come down for a quick run-through of the ceremony, but so far, he hadn't shown up. Lucy had sent home the small orchestra Denise's Boston Symphony friend had recruited and dismissed the choir too. Wondering how long she intended to keep the others, Susan glanced at her watch.

She walked to the back of the church to commiserate with Liz. "Feeling useless too?"

"What a complete waste of time. Why are you hanging around?"

"Reshma asked me to preach tomorrow, and I have a minor role in the ceremony. But I'm really here for the same reason you are...to support Lucy." Liz's eyes narrowed for a moment, but then her expression softened.

"I can't understand why Lucy's so nervous. She's sung in the world's biggest opera houses."

"But when she sings opera, the only one she needs to manage is herself. Other people direct the production, take care of all the details—the costumes, the lighting, where everyone stands. Tomorrow, she's in charge of everything. She loves Reshma and wants her to have fond memories of her ordination."

"Well, I hope that fucking bishop shows up tomorrow," said Liz, not even trying to hide her contempt. "That bastard stiffed us for our wedding."

Susan knew the remark was disingenuous. Liz had always wanted Tom to marry them. She'd been delighted the bishop couldn't officiate.

"The man had COVID, Liz."

"What's his excuse this time?"

"I don't know, but Lucy looks out of patience."

Lucy was on the phone, pacing the front of the church. She finally ended the call and clapped her hands. "I'm sorry, everyone. The bishop can't make it today. We'll just have to rehearse without him. Tom, I'm going to promote you. You can play the bishop."

"But I never aspired to the episcopate," protested Tom, using the pew back in front of him to pull himself to his feet.

"Too bad," Lucy said in a humorless tone. "You would have made a good one."

"Too late now. I'm retired."

"Grab a couple of prayer books. We'll need them as props."

Jeff handed Tom his walking stick. "Your crozier, Bishop Tom."

"Lucy, we're not going through the whole rite, are we?" asked Tom incredulously.

"You bet we are."

"Too bad he can't do it for real," Liz whispered to Susan.

"You know it doesn't work that way," Susan replied. "Only a bishop can ordain a priest."

Liz shrugged. "It's just words."

Susan thought back to her own ordination. "Much more than just words, Liz. One day, you're just a deacon. The next day, you're a priest. Wasn't it like that when you recited the Hippocratic Oath and became a doctor?"

"Maybe." Liz tilted her head toward each shoulder, trying to decide. "For all practical purposes, I was already a doctor. I was treating patients, even doing surgery. My degree gave me more autonomy and responsibility, so yes, it was important to put on the academic robes and finally hold the parchment in my hands."

Susan realized that for the first time, Liz was talking to her as a peer. The undercurrent of suspicion that usually made Susan watch every word was absent. Maybe there was hope for a friendship with her archrival.

"We should probably stop talking," Susan suggested. "They can't really hear us back here, but I'm sure it's a distraction."

"Okay, but you're coming to dinner with us, right?"

People had been talking about a dinner party at Dockside since Susan had arrived. Until now, no one had spoken to her about it directly, and she didn't dare assume. "Sure. I'd love to come. Thanks."

Susan saw Lucy waving to her. "Liz, you'll have to excuse me. I'm being summoned," She got up and joined the others in the procession.

In a red-and-black buffalo-plaid shirt and jeans, Tom made an unlikely bishop, but when he stilled his hearty laughter, he created a completely convincing magisterial presence. Susan took her place in the line. Tomorrow, they would be joined by over a dozen priests and deacons coming from all over New England. In clergy circles, this was an event not to be missed.

Lucy suggested they skip the ritual prostration because it was just a rehearsal, but Reshma insisted on getting down on the floor to get a feel for it. Susan closed her eyes, remembering what it was like to lie face down, her arms outstretched, her heart swelling as the bishop invoked the Spirit. Yes, it was so much more than words.

After they'd run through the entire rite, Lucy applauded. "Thank you for your patience and staying past time. Reshma and I appreciate it. The entire congregation appreciates it."

Liz came to the front to collect her dinner guests. Alina secured her video equipment. Tom checked the church doors. Denise invited Susan to ride with them to the restaurant. In the salt marsh, the multiple shades of salmon and purple in the evening sky reflected in the tidal pools.

"I can't believe this is really happening," said Reshma, her voice higher than usual from the anxiety.

"Believe it," said Susan, leaning forward to pat her shoulders. "Tomorrow, you'll be a priest."

"Were you nervous before your ordination?" asked Reshma.

"Terrified," Susan admitted, squeezing the smooth, young hand that had reached between the seats searching for hers. "Yet somehow, God and Lucy got me through it."

"Thank God for Mother Lucy…and you," whispered Reshma fervently before releasing Susan's hand.

Watching so much wine and beer consumed at the table made Susan extremely thirsty, but she massaged the AA coin in her pocket and prayed for strength. Reshma, the guest of honor, was sitting at the far end, opposite Liz, who presided over the feast like someone who enjoyed hosting a party. If Susan listened carefully, snippets of conversations drifted to her ears. Liz was on her third beer and sounded somewhat more opinionated than usual.

"And now we can get married and divorced like straights and be equally miserable. How is that progress?"

Although Maggie was sitting at the opposite end, she heard Liz's comment. "I should have believed you when you said you weren't the marrying kind," she called down the table, sounding testy.

Lucy glared at Liz for the provocation. Maggie looked like she had more to say, and so did Liz. Susan tensed.

"Oh, look," interjected Tom in a genial tone, lifting his hand to show his wedding ring. "Even I got married. Where would we be without hope for the future? That's why people keep getting married and having babies." He gestured toward Reshma. "And that's why we keep ordaining priests to perform weddings and baptisms."

"Nice sermon, Tom," said Liz, raising her glass. "To Reshma and hope for the future."

Susan raised her glass of tonic water with the others. The slice of bright green lime on the bottom worked its way through the ice cubes and popped merrily to the top.

***

Descending the circular stairs from the organ loft, Liz was glad that she'd nixed Lucy's suggestion to wear high heels. Her dressy high-traction pumps were a better choice to deal with the loft stairs and last night's dusting of snow. Even if the pavement were dry, she wouldn't have worn high heels. The bishop was a short man. In flats, Liz dwarfed him, and she wasn't about to get into a pissing contest with the little prick on Reshma's big day.

She headed to the transept, where Alina had set up a video production station. Peering over the young woman's shoulder, she tried to identify the camera feed from the loft. "Is that shot wide enough?" she asked.

"Perfect, but listen for my cue. If we need to pull in, I'll let you know. Otherwise, use your judgment. You have a good eye for camera work."

Liz flushed with pleasure at the compliment.

"Where's Mom?" Alina asked, craning her neck to scan the church.

"She's in the lower church hall, rehearsing the soloists. Need her for something?"

"No, just wondering where my children are."

"Brenda is reading to all the kids in the nursery."

"My kids might be a little old for that."

"People are never too old to listen to stories. When I couldn't sleep, your mother would tell me stories she'd learned for children's theater."

"When things were still good between you," said Alina, looking sad.

Liz gave her shoulder a little squeeze. "Things change. I still love your mother…and you and your sister, and your kids. You've moved on too. I see that handsome guy hanging out in the back."

"He's here because he's the news director," said Alina defensively, glancing toward the man. He smiled in her direction.

Liz bent to whisper into her ear. "Your mother and I still talk, you know."

Alina giggled and blushed. "What did she say?"

"That he's pretty much moved in with you. That's good news, isn't it?"

"Yes," Alina agreed with a sly smile. "Very good."

Liz's smile mirrored Alina's. "I'm happy for you."

"Maybe you and Lucy could come up for dinner one night. I'd like you to get to know him."

"I'd like that too," said Liz.

Out of the corner of her eye, she saw Lucy shoot out of the sacristy and race up the center aisle. Her determined look meant she was on a mission. "Liz," she said, pulling her aside. "The bishop is stranded on the highway. They were on the way, running a little late, so they were rushing. The car began to rumble, and they realized something was wrong with the tire. By the time they pulled over to the shoulder, it was completely flat."

"Maybe Brenda can send one of her officers," Liz said before remembering the local police had no jurisdiction on the interstate. Eventually, the troopers would arrive, but only the contract service could respond to turnpike breakdowns. It could be hours before they showed up. Liz looked at her watch.

"Please, Liz," Lucy begged.

"All right. I'll go."

"Thank you! I love you!" When Lucy stood on tiptoes and kissed her, Liz found herself thinking that chivalry had its rewards.

Liz decided to take the backroads through Kennebunk to get on the turnpike because the bishop had pulled off above their exit. Driving slowly in the right lane, she easily spotted the two men staring forlornly at their disabled SUV.

"Dr. Stolz, thank you for *saving* us," said the bishop dramatically when Liz stepped out of her car. She took in the situation at a glance. The bishop's red vestments hung in the back seat. The tire was too flat for the aerosol repair kit she kept in her car. Fortunately, they'd stopped driving before they ripped out the sidewall.

"I noticed it looked a little soft before we left," explained a tall man, approaching.

"Dr. Stolz, this is my husband, Reverend Bradford Collins," said the bishop. Liz recognized the man from the newspaper story.

"Brad," said the man offering his hand.

"Liz," she replied, taking it firmly. "Do you have a spare?"

"Yes. I paid extra for a full spare," the man said proudly.

"Keys," said Liz, reaching out. Brad opened the driver's door and got them for her.

"You're going to change the tire?" exclaimed the bishop, as Liz headed to the trunk. "I thought you could just drive us into town."

"I can, but you need your vestments, and you don't want to abandon your car on the interstate. The troopers will give you a ticket. Don't worry. It will only take a minute."

The two men stared at one another. Brad said, "Can I help?"

"Look for the manual so we can find the tool kit." Brad opened the door and rifled through the glove box. Meanwhile, Liz opened the trunk. She figured out how to open the spare compartment and loosened the tire bracket. "Never mind," she called. "Found the jack." She bounced the tire on the pavement and rolled it around the car.

"I can't believe you're going to do this," said the bishop.

"What? You can't believe a woman can change a tire?"

"I can't believe a doctor would do it instead of calling for help."

"Believe me, this will be much faster," said Liz, loosening the lug nuts. She had to stand on the tire iron to get them to budge.

"Don't you have to jack it up first?" asked the bishop.

Liz managed to avoid rolling her eyes. She calmly explained how the weight of the car prevented it from rolling while loosening overtightened lug nuts.

"We missed you yesterday," she said casually, assembling the jack.

"One of our rectors quit unexpectedly. Clergy burnout. His exit was rather dramatic, so the vestry called me to go up there and keep the peace. I hope Lucy's not angry with me."

"She kept everyone as long as she could. You could have called."

"I'm sorry. It was a real crisis. I'm sure Lucy managed on her own."

"You bet she did." Liz inserted the handle in the jack and began pumping it.

"You're really good at that," Brad observed.

"One of the first things my dad taught me when I was learning to drive…that and how to change the oil."

The two men crowded in while Liz inspected the tire and found a rusty wood screw stuck between the treads. "Doesn't look serious. Good thing you stopped when you did. You'll make it home on your spare, but get the flat repaired as soon as you can, and have them put it back on. Otherwise, you'll need a whole new set of tires. That's the trouble with all-wheel drive. Sounds great until you need a tire."

"I didn't know that," said Brad. "You really know a lot about cars."

"My father was an engineer. He taught me." Liz imagined her father smiling like he did when she'd changed her first tire. In those days, they used to put on snow tires in the winter, so she'd gotten lots of practice.

Liz's knees protested when she squatted to position the spare. She couldn't stop the groan.

"I could do that," offered Brad.

"Thank you. You're a little younger." Liz stepped aside and let Brad mount the tire. She handed him the nuts one by one. "Just hand tighten them. Opposite nuts to balance the pressure."

"I think I remember that part," said Brad.

"Have you ever changed a tire before?"

"No, but I watched someone do it…a long time ago."

"And you remembered. That's good," said Liz. "Want to do the rest?"

"Yes," said Brad, grinning eagerly. Liz congratulated herself on smoothly pulling off the old Tom Sawyer trick. She talked Brad through lowering the jack and tightening the nuts. "Good job," she said, patting him on the shoulder. "Now, throw the flat in the trunk. No need to secure it because you'll be taking it for repair, right?"

"Tomorrow. I promise."

"Good." Liz liked people who learned quickly.

From the glove box of her car, Liz took out some napkins from Awakened Brews and a bottle of hand sanitizer. After squirting some into her palm, she offered the bottle and some napkins to Brad. She smiled at the idea that they were bonding over hand sanitizer.

"Dr. Stolz, I don't know how to thank you," the bishop said, approaching. "That was certainly above and beyond the call of duty."

Liz shrugged. "I did it because I love my wife, and she really wants this ordination to go right. So, get down to that church and make it so."

The bishop laughed. "Lucy is lucky to have you."

"Make sure to tell her," Liz called over her shoulder.

***

"Miss Bobbie, what do you think?" Dancing into the sunroom, Grace made a pirouette to show off her new thrift-store outfit. She wore a headdress made of brightly colored cloth that complemented her dress. "It's so pretty, don't you think?"

"Beautiful," Bobbie agreed.

Teresa poked her head in looking for her daughter. Her dress was equally vibrant, and she too wore a headdress of intricately wrapped fabric. Together, they looked like a pair of exotic birds. "Come, child, or we'll be late." Her eyes took in Bobbie's outfit. Without saying a word, she expressed her opinion of the conservative charcoal pantsuit. Bobbie understood her disapproval. Next to her vibrantly dressed companions, she felt muted and plain.

"We are leaving now, Bobbie. If you like, you may drive with us," said Teresa proudly. Susan's old wreck had instantly become their most treasured possession. Teresa, who was an excellent driver, had qualified for her license on her first try.

"I'd love to, but you want to go to the reception, and I have to come back right after the service to relieve Natalie." Bobbie was disappointed she'd miss the opportunity to see the inside of Olivia Enright's house. She couldn't decide how she felt about the enormous neo-Victorian on Gull Island, which she often passed on her way to the beach. If the exterior of the house was that ostentatious, what would the interior be like?

"Such a shame you can't come to the celebration," said Teresa, "but we shall save you a seat in the church when we get there."

"Please come with us, Miss Bobbie," Grace begged.

"I'm sorry, honey, but I have to come back early."

Disappointed, the girl stared at the floor.

"Come, child. We cannot be late for the ceremony. We are representing Reshma's family," Teresa said, puffing up with pride.

"I'm right behind you," Bobbie called after them.

Bobbie turned to Joyce, who had been mostly listless today. The new medication had shown promise, but like all of them, it had only helped for a short time.

"I'll be back soon," said Bobbie, kissing her forehead. She snatched a tissue from a nearby box to blot some spittle on her chin.

"Going? Where?" asked Joyce.

"Church. Teresa's friend is being ordained today."

Joyce pointed to Bobbie's suit and shook her head. "Dark." She clutched her throat and gestured in the direction of Teresa and Grace heading down the hall. Bobbie was puzzled by the sign language until she realized Joyce was trying to say her outfit needed more color. Even now, Joyce was giving her fashion advice.

"Good idea," said Bobbie. "I'll put on a scarf."

Joyce grimaced but the brightness in her eyes conveyed how happy she was to be understood. When Natalie returned, Bobbie went back to her apartment for something colorful to wear around her neck.

Although it was early, the church parking lot was nearly full. Bobbie had to walk a distance in her dress shoes, which pinched a little because she hardly ever wore them.

The bright outfits Teresa and Grace wore instantly drew Bobbie's eye. Seated in the third pew, they were chatting with Reshma. She wore a long white gown, cinched with a cord at the waist, looking like a Christmas-pageant angel. An incandescent smile lit up her face, and she scooped Bobbie into her long arms. "Thank you so much for coming!" Even though this was not her church, Bobbie felt completely welcomed. She'd associated people in collars with angry, disapproving old men, but Reshma, Lucy, and Susan certainly didn't fit her pictures.

"Good luck today," said Bobbie, not knowing if that was the right thing to say.

"Thank you. I'm *so* nervous." She held out her hand to show that it was trembling.

"It's a big day."

"And not easy getting here, but God and Mother Susan helped me limp to the finish line." Bobbie smiled at hearing Susan acknowledged. She might be quiet and self-effacing, but her subtle influence seemed to touch many. Reshma hugged her again. "I'm so happy you are here," she whispered into Bobbie's ear before turning to greet another well-wisher.

"Won't she make a wonderful priest?" Teresa asked, beaming in the direction of her young mentor.

"Yes, she will," agreed Bobbie with a sigh. "And a beautiful one too."

"Hey!" Bobbie looked up to see her boss standing in the aisle, grinning like a kid full of mischief. Liz had a dark smudge running from her cheekbone to her chin. Bobbie, who always carried wet wipes for Joyce, found one in her bag and handed it to Liz. In answer to her quizzical look, Bobbie pointed to her cheek.

Liz laughed and tore open the packet. "That's probably from providing roadside assistance. Thanks for noticing." Liz wiped away most of the dirt, but missed a little, so Bobbie came out of the pew to finish the job.

"Where are you sitting?" asked Bobbie.

Liz pointed to the organ loft. "I'm minding the overhead camera. Want to keep me company?"

"I'm afraid of heights."

"Me too, but the view is worth it. Come with me." Liz urged her on with a wave. Bobbie debated abandoning her brightly dressed pew-mates, but Teresa had been shrewdly listening to the exchange.

"Go with Dr. Stolz. You'll have a good view, and she can explain the ceremony."

Liz led Bobbie to the back of the church. "I'm no expert, but I was here for the rehearsal, and my wife has explained more than I ever wanted to know about ordinations."

Climbing the narrow stairs was harrowing, but as Liz had promised, the view justified the adventure. They sat in folding chairs placed behind the camera tripod.

"I have the mic turned off. We can talk up here if we keep our voices down."

Bobbie watched a group of musicians carrying stringed instruments file into the church and settle into chairs behind the altar. "Is there going to be a concert?"

"Not exactly. Denise's friend from the Boston Symphony arranged for this baroque group to play. Denise is going to sing a meditation before the service begins. They planned this prelude, but the bishop was running late, so it will buy time for him to get his act together." Bobbie studied Liz, wondering if the inside information had anything to do with the dirt on her face.

"'Nisi Dominus' is a famous countertenor piece," Liz explained. "Denise recorded it before she transitioned. This is the first time she'll be singing it publicly as a woman. Vivaldi is big on this program because he was a priest. You see the connection."

"You really know a lot about music."

The compliment seemed to please Liz, but she modestly admitted, "Denise explained why she chose the selections. She studied sacred music at Yale. Everything they're performing today has special significance for Reshma's ordination."

"That's so cool." Bobbie ventured closer to the railing. If she avoided looking down, the height wouldn't bother her.

When Denise began to sing, people came out of a back room to listen, including a man wearing a bright red cloak. "That's the bishop," Liz whispered. "The others are priests and deacons." Bobbie zeroed in on Susan, standing near Lucy.

"Why do some of them wear their scarves over one shoulder?"

"That's called a stole. Deacons wear it over one shoulder, priests over both. Red signifies the Holy Spirit, who is invoked during an ordination."

The prelude ended to enthusiastic applause from the congregation. Bobbie noticed people scurrying to the back to get into position. Some brass players joined the little orchestra. The choir, which seemed larger than for a regular church service, launched into "Zadok the Priest." "It was written for a coronation, but they adapted the lyrics for today's service," Liz explained, subtly conducting. "Don't mind me. I'm just an amateur." She winked. Bobbie had never seen this side of her boss before, but she loved it.

After the bishop opened the ceremony, Reshma stepped forward with Teresa and Grace at her side. Susan, Lucy, and other people Bobbie recognized from town gathered around them. In unison, they recited a formula, presenting Reshma to the bishop. He posed questions, which they answered, certifying Reshma's fitness for priesthood. She was given a document to sign along with the witnesses. Next, Lucy ascended the pulpit to sing a responsive prayer.

"I'm glad I came," Bobbie whispered to Liz. "This is fascinating."

"Just wait. It gets better."

After Tom read the Gospel, Susan took the pulpit. She said a short prayer before turning to Reshma. "God has called a beautiful and talented young woman here today. When she was brought to our country as a refugee from war-torn Africa, she probably had no idea she would one day become a priest. When three Maine parishes joined together to send her to an Episcopal boarding school, they probably never expected to launch her on this path. Yet here she is, presenting herself for ordination to the sacred order of priests. I know from speaking and praying with Reshma that it has been a long, winding path. There were times when she felt unworthy...as we all do. I've tried from my ancient perspective, being a few years older..." Susan paused to let the titters in the crowd subside. "...I've tried to explain that God doesn't call perfect people. There is not a single member of the clergy who has not had doubts, who has not been tested, who has not failed again and again..."

Bobbie recognized that Susan was talking about herself and her own battles. Only a few listening to this sermon would make the connections, but its themes could apply to anyone who had struggled to find the path forward. As Susan continued, Bobbie was moved by her eloquence and the personal experiences she shared.

"Doubt is not the absence of faith. It is faith asking questions. If we ask them honestly, the answers have the power to transform and teach us things we could never learn through blind faith alone. Questioning is good."

When Susan came down from the pulpit, she wiped away a tear from her cheek. Bobbie realized that her sermon had been a confession.

The prayers continued. The bishop addressed Reshma directly, asking her to affirm a series of statements. "She's taking her vows as a priest," Liz whispered.

Then Reshma got down on the ground and extended her arms. "What is this?" Bobbie asked, alarmed.

"Prostration signifies death. Reshma is being reborn to her new life as a priest." Liz played with the camera to get a better shot of the white form lying face down in the center aisle.

Following the bishop's invocation, the choir sang a meditative round, "Veni Sancte Spiritus." Liz smiled while her ex-wife sang the soprano solo.

When the singing ended, Reshma got up and knelt before the bishop. White gowned people gathered around while the bishop laid his hands on Reshma's head and prayed. Lucy put a red stole around Reshma's neck and carefully retied the white cord at her waist. Together, Lucy and Teresa put a large scarlet garment embroidered with a cross over her head. "That's a chasuble. They're dressing her as a priest for the first time," Liz explained. After more prayers and presenting Reshma with a Bible, the bishop rose and helped her to her feet. His mic picked up his whispered cue. "Go ahead, Reshma. Offer the peace."

"The peace of the Lord be always with you," said Reshma, beaming.

"Ladies and gentlemen, please welcome our new Episcopal priest!" proclaimed the bishop and began to clap. Next to her, Liz's enthusiastic clapping threatened to hurt Bobbie's ears.

"Is it over now?" she asked over the applause.

Liz made a face and sat down. "Hell, no. Now they do a whole Communion service like on Sundays, but it's a big deal for Reshma because it's her first time."

Bobbie recognized some of the ritual from the day she'd come to the summer chapel to see Susan. While people lined up for Communion, Denise sang the meditative aria "Ombra mai fu." Bobbie watched Liz to see what she would do. First, she played with the camera. Then, she took out her phone to check her messages. Bobbie was relieved to see that being married to a priest hadn't turned her boss into a holy roller. Good to know, thought Bobbie.

When Liz didn't come down from the organ loft, her wife, holding a Communion cup, raised her eyes to where they sat. Liz replied with a tiny, mocking wave. Lucy shook her head and followed the others back to the altar. Liz sat respectfully for the rest of the service, but Bobbie could see she was getting fidgety.

Finally, the bishop motioned to Reshma to come forward and give the final blessing. The orchestra launched into triumphal music. As Reshma went down the aisle, she shook hands with people in the congregation.

"They'll be lining up to see her, because it's supposed to be good luck to be blessed by a new priest," said Liz, fiddling with the camera. "Bobbie, you don't have to hang around up here with me. I think someone's waiting for you." She glanced down.

Bobbie was going to stay with Liz out of loyalty, but she followed the direction of her gaze and saw Susan looking up to the organ loft.

"Thanks for explaining everything, Liz. See you later."

Despite her hurry, Bobbie watched her step on the spiral staircase. When she emerged through the door at the bottom, Susan was waiting for her.

"Were you up there the whole time?" she asked with a wry smile. Bobbie wanted to explain that Liz had invited her, and how the ceremony had fascinated her, but suddenly her tongue wouldn't work. Confused, she could only stare at Susan, pleading for understanding.

Susan enfolded her in her arms. "I saw you up there during my sermon," she whispered into her ear. "I'm so happy you came." To Bobbie's disappointment, Susan's warm body moved away. "What did you think of the service?" she asked, studying Bobbie's face.

"Liz tried to explain it to me."

Susan laughed merrily. "I bet that was interesting."

"It was," said Bobbie loyally. "I asked her a lot of questions, and she could answer most of them."

"I'm actually not surprised." Susan's blue eyes, intently peering into Bobbie's, were mesmerizing. "I'm glad you were interested enough to ask questions." She reached for Bobbie's hand. "Can you come to the reception?"

"I can't. Natalie is writing her last term paper."

"I'm sorry. I would have liked to spend more time with you."

"Come over afterward. I'll make you a cup of tea."

"I'd like that," Susan said, taking a step closer.

"Maybe you can spend the night." The words had jumped out of Bobbie's mouth before she could stop them.

Susan's gentle gaze never wavered. She squeezed Bobbie's hand a little tighter. "Maybe I can."

A lump formed in Bobbie's throat. She blinked away the tear that threatened to fall. "I can stay until the orchestra finishes playing. I like this music."

"So do I. Vivaldi's "Gloria." It's magnificent."

They moved into the nearest pew. Thighs touching, hand in hand, they listened to Lucy and Denise blend their superb voices in sublime harmony.

Also by Elena Graf

SUMMER PEOPLE

Melissa Morgenstern, a high-profile lawyer from Boston, is spending the summer with her widowed mother. She's doing some trust work for Liz who introduces her to the attractive Courtney Barnes, Hobbs Elementary's new assistant principal. The arrival of Susan, Lucy's ex, complicates her deepening relationship with Liz.

STRANDS

Cherie hears her biological clock ticking and would like to start a family. When a shocking tragedy creates an opportunity for her and Brenda to become parents, their friends need to step up to make it happen.

THE RECTOR'S WEDDING

The sudden opportunity for Lucy to return to her singing career throws everything in her life into doubt—her vocation as a priest, her settled life in Hobbs, even her upcoming marriage to the woman she loves.

PASSING RITES SERIES

THE IMPERATIVE OF DESIRE

A coming-of-age story that takes a brilliant aristocratic woman from La Belle Époque through a world war, a revolution that outlawed the German nobility, and the roaring twenties to the decadent demimonde of Weimar Berlin.

OCCASIONS OF SIN

For seven centuries, the German convent of Obberoth has been hiding the nuns' secrets—forbidden passions, scandalous manuscripts locked away, a ruined medical career, and perhaps even a murder.

LIES OF OMISSION

In 1938, the Nazis are imposing their doctrine of "racial hygiene" on hospitals and universities. Margarethe von Stahle has always avoided politics, but now she must decide whether to remain on the sidelines or act on her convictions.

ACTS OF CONTRITION

After the fall of Berlin, Margarethe is brutally assaulted by occupying Russian soldiers. Her former protégée, Sarah Weber, returns to Berlin with the American Army and tries to heal her mentor's physical and psychological wounds.

About the Author

Elena Graf has published four historical novels set in twentieth-century Europe. Two of the titles in the Passing Rites series have won Golden Crown Literary Society and Rainbow awards for best historical fiction. In addition to her historical series, the author has written a series of contemporary novels set in Maine. She pursued a Ph.D. in philosophy but ended up in the "accidental profession" of publishing, where she worked for almost four decades. She lives in coastal Maine.

Find out about events and new books at her website, elenagraf.com. You can write to Elena at elena.m.graf@gmail.com. Or find her on Facebook.

Elena is a member of iReadIndies, a collective of self-published independent authors of Sapphic literature. Please visit our website at iReadIndies.com for more information and to find links to the books published by our authors.

CPSIA information can be obtained
at www.ICGtesting.com
Printed in the USA
BVHW050756030523
663499BV00012B/201